THE BRIDE
FONSECA NEEDS

BY
ABBY GREEN

MILLS
BOON

Published in Great Britain 2015
by Mills & Boon, an imprint of Harlequin (UK) Limited,
Eton House, 18-24 Paradise Road, Richmond, Surrey, TW9 1SR

© 2015 Abby Green

ISBN: 978-0-263-25064-0

Printed and bound in Spain
by CPI, Barcelona

Irish author **Abby Green** threw in a very glamorous career in film & TV—which really consisted of a lot of standing in the rain outside actors' trailers—to pursue her love of romance. After she'd bombarded Mills & Boon® with manuscripts they kindly accepted one, and an author was born. She lives in Dublin, Ireland, and loves any excuse for distraction. Visit abby-green.com or e-mail abbygreenauthor@gmail.com

Books by Abby Green

Mills & Boon® Modern™ Romance

Forgiven but Not Forgotten?
Exquisite Revenge
One Night with the Enemy
The Legend of De Marco
The Call of the Desert
The Sultan's Choice
Secrets of the Oasis
In Christofides' Keeping
The Virgin's Secret

The Chatsfield

Delucca's Marriage Contract

Billionaire Brothers

Fonseca's Fury

Blood Brothers

When Falcone's World Stops Turning
When Christakos Meets His Match
When Da Silva Breaks the Rules

**Visit the author profile page at
millsandboon.co.uk for more titles**

CHAPTER ONE

'WELL, WELL, WELL. This *is* interesting. Little Darcy Lennox, in my office, looking for work.'

Darcy curbed the flash of irritation at the not entirely inaccurate reference to her being *little* and fought against the onslaught on her senses from being mere feet away from Maximiliano Fonseca Roselli, separated from him only by an impressive desk. But it was hard. Because he was quite simply as devastatingly gorgeous as he'd always been. More so now, because he was a man. Not the seventeen-year-old boy she remembered. Sex appeal flowed from him like an invisible but heady scent. It made Darcy absurdly aware that underneath all the layers of civility they were just animals.

He was half-Brazilian, half-Italian. Dark blond hair was still unruly and messy—long enough to proclaim that he didn't really give a damn about anything, much less conforming. Although clearly along the way he'd given enough of a damn to become one of Europe's youngest 'billionaire entrepreneurs to watch', according to a leading financial magazine.

Darcy could imagine how any number of women would be only too happy to watch his every sexy move. She did notice one new addition to his almost perfect features, though, and blurted out before she could stop herself, 'You have a scar.'

It snaked from his left temple to his jaw in a jagged line and had the effect of making him even more mysterious and brooding.

The man under her close scrutiny arched one dark blond brow and drawled, 'Your powers of observation are clearly in working order.'

Darcy flushed at being so caught out. Since when had she been gauche enough to refer to someone's physical appearance? He had stood to greet her when she'd walked into his palatial office, situated in the centre of Rome, and she was still standing too, beginning to feel hot in her trouser suit, hot under the tawny green gaze that had captivated her the first time she'd ever seen him.

He folded his arms across his chest and her eye was drawn helplessly to where impressive muscles bunched against the fine material of his open-necked white shirt, sleeves rolled up. And even though he wore smart dark trousers he looked anything but civilised. That gaze was too knowing, too cynical, for *politesse*.

'So, what's a fellow alumna from Boissy le Château doing looking for work as a PA?' Before she could answer he was adding, with the faintest of sneers to his tone, 'I would have thought you'd be married into European aristrocracy by now, and producing a gaggle of heirs like every other girl in that anachronistic medieval institution.'

Pinned under that golden gaze, she regretted the moment she'd ever thought it might be a good idea to apply for the job advertised on a very select applications board. And she hated to think that a part of her had been curious to see Max Fonseca Roselli Fonseca again.

She replied, 'I was only at Boissy for another year after

you left...' She faltered then, thinking of a lurid memory of Max beating another boy outside in the snow, and the bright stain of blood against the pristine white. She pushed it down. 'My father was badly affected by the recession so I went back to England to finish my schooling.'

She didn't think it worth mentioning that that schooling had taken place in a comprehensive school, which she would have chosen any day over the oppressive atmosphere of Boissy.

Max made a sound of faux commiseration. 'So Darcy *didn't* get to be the belle of the ball in Paris with all the other debutantes?'

She gritted her jaw at his reference to the exclusive annual Bal des Débutantes; she was no belle of any ball. She knew Max hadn't had a good time at Boissy, but she hadn't been one of his antagonists. Anything but. She cringed inwardly now when she recalled another vivid memory, from not long after he'd first arrived. Darcy had come upon two guys holding Max back, with another about to punch him in the belly. Without even thinking, she'd rushed into the fray, screaming, *'Stop!'*

Heat climbed inside her at the thought that he might remember that too.

'No,' she responded tightly. 'I didn't go to the ball in Paris. I sat my A levels and then got a degree in languages and business from London University, as you'll see from my CV.'

Which was laid out on his desk.

This had been a huge mistake.

'Look, I saw your name come up on the applications board—that you're looking for a PA. I probably shouldn't have come.' Darcy reached down to where she'd put her briefcase by her feet and picked it up.

Max was frowning at her. 'Do you want a job or not?'

Darcy felt tetchy with herself for having been so impetuous, and irritated with Max for being so bloody gorgeous and distracting. *Still.* So she said, more snippily than she'd intended, 'Of course I want a job. I *need* a job.'

Max's frown deepened. 'Did your parents lose everything?'

She bristled at the implication that she was looking for work because her family wasn't funding her any more. 'No, thankfully my father was able to recover.' And then she said tartly, 'Believe it or not, I like to make my own living.'

Max made some kind of a dismissive sound, as if he didn't quite believe her, and Darcy bit her lip in order to stay quiet. She couldn't exactly blame him for his assumption, but unlike the other alumnae of their school she *didn't* expect everything in life to be handed to her.

Those mesmerising eyes were looking at her far too closely now and Darcy became excruciatingly conscious of her dark hair, pulled back into a ponytail, her diminutive stature and the unfashionably full figure she'd long ago given up any hope of minimising, choosing instead to work with what she had.

Max rapped out in Italian, 'You're fluent in Italian?'

Darcy blinked, but quickly replied in the same language. 'Yes. My mother is from just outside Rome. I've been bilingual since I learnt how to talk and I'm also fluent in Spanish, German and French. And I have passable Chinese.'

He flicked a look at her CV and then looked back, switching to English again. 'It says here that you've been in Brussels for the past five years—is that where you're based?'

Darcy's insides tightened at his direct question, as if warding off a blow. The truth was that she hadn't really had a base since her parents had split up when she was eight and they'd sold off the family home. They'd shuttled her between schools and wherever they'd been living which had changed constantly, due to her father's work and her mother's subsequent relationships.

She'd learnt that the only constant she could depend on was herself and her ability to forge a successful career, cocooning her from the pillar-to-post feeling she hated so much and the vagaries of volatile relationships.

She answered Max. 'I don't have a base at the moment, so I'm free to go where the work is.'

Once again that incisive gaze was on her. Darcy hated the insecurity that crept up on her at the thought that he might be assessing how she'd turned out, judging her against the svelte supermodel types he was always photographed with. Beside them, at five foot two, Darcy would look like a baby elephant! In weak moments over the years she'd seen Max on the covers of gossip magazines and had picked them up to read the salacious content. And it had always been salacious.

When she'd read about his three-in-a-bed romp with two Russian models she'd flung the magazine into a trash can, disgusted with herself.

He suddenly stuck out his hand. 'I'll give you a two-week trial, starting tomorrow. Do you have accommodation sorted?'

Darcy blanched. *He was offering her the job?* Her head was still filled with lurid images of pouting blonde glamazons, crawling all over Max's louche form. Reacting reflexively, she put out her hand to meet his and suddenly was engulfed in heat as his long fingers curled around hers.

He took his hand away abruptly and glanced at a

fearsome-looking watch, then back to her, a little impatiently.

Darcy woke up. 'Um…yes, I have somewhere to stay for a few days.' She repressed a small grimace when she thought of the very basic hostel in one of Rome's busier tourist districts.

Max nodded. 'Good. If I keep you on then we'll get you something more permanent.'

They looked at each other as Darcy's mind boggled at the thought of working with him.

Then he said pointedly, 'I have a meeting now, I'll see you tomorrow at nine a.m. We'll go through everything then.'

Darcy quickly picked up her briefcase and backed away. 'Okay, then, tomorrow.' She walked to the door and then turned around again. 'You're not just doing this because we know each other…?'

Max had his hands on his hips. He was beginning to look slightly impatient. 'No, Darcy. That's coincidental. You're the most qualified person I've seen for the job, your references are impeccable, and after dealing with a slew of PAs—gay and straight—who all seem to think that seducing the boss is an unwritten requirement of the job it'll be a relief to deal with someone who knows the boundaries.'

Darcy didn't like the fact that it stung her somewhere very deep and secret to think that Max would dismiss her ability to seduce him so summarily, but before she could acknowledge how inappropriate that was she muttered something incoherent and left before she could make a complete ass of herself.

Max watched the space where the door had just closed, rendered uncharacteristically still for a moment. Darcy

Lennox. Her name on his list of potential PAs had been a jolt out of the blue, as had the way her face had sprung back into his mind with vivid recollection as soon as he'd seen her name. He doubted he could pick many of his ex-classmates out of a police line-up, and Darcy hadn't even been in his year.

But, as small and unassuming as she had been, and some four years behind him, she seemed to have made some kind of lingering impact. It wasn't an altogether comfortable realisation for a man who regularly excised people from his life with little regret, whether they were lovers or business associates he was done with.

Her eyes were still seared into his mind—huge and blue, a startling contrast to that pale olive complexion, obviously inherited from her Italian mother.

Max cursed himself. *Startling?* He ran a hand through his hair, leaving it even messier. He was running on fumes of exhaustion since returning from a trip to Brazil a couple of days ago, and quite frankly it would be a relief to have someone working for him who *wouldn't* feel the need to see him as a challenge akin to scaling a sexual Everest.

Darcy Lennox exuded common sense and practicality. Dependability. The fact that she had also been in Boissy, even if her time had been cut short, meant that she knew her place and would never overstep the mark. Not like his last assistant, who had been waiting for him one morning, sitting in his chair, dressed only in one of his shirts.

He tried for a moment to conjure up a similar image featuring Darcy. but all he could see was her serious face and her smart, structured shirt and skirt, the tidy glossy hair. A sense of relief infused him. Finally an assistant who would not distract him from the deal of a lifetime.

A deal that would set him up as a serious player in the very competitive world of global finance.

Quite frankly, this was the best thing that had happened to him in weeks. Darcy would meld seamlessly into the background while performing her duties with skill and efficiency. Of that he had no doubt. Her CV was a glowing testament to her abilities.

He picked up the phone to speak to his temp and when she answered said curtly, 'Send all the other applicants away, Miss Lennox is starting tomorrow.'

He didn't even bother to reiterate the two-week trial caveat, so confident was he that he'd made the right decision.

Three months later

'Darcy, get in here—*now*!'

Darcy rolled her eyes at the bellowed order and got up from behind her desk, smoothing down her skirt as she did so. When she walked into Max's office and saw him pacing back and forth behind his desk she cursed the little jolt she always got in her solar plexus when she looked at him.

Virile, masculine energy crackled in the air around him. She put her uncomfortable reaction down to the fact that any being with a pulse would be incapable of *not* responding to his charisma.

He turned and locked that dark golden gaze onto her and snapped out, 'Well? Don't just stand there—come in.'

Darcy had learnt that the way to deal with Max Fonseca Roselli was to treat him like an arrogant thoroughbred stallion. With the utmost respect and caution and a healthy dollop of firm-handedness.

'There is no need to shout,' she said calmly. 'I'm right outside your door.'

She came in and perched on the chair on the other side of his desk and looked at him, awaiting instruction. She had to admit that, while his manners could do with finessing, working for Max was the most exhilarating experience of her life. It was a challenge just to keep up with his quicksilver intellect, and she'd already learnt more from him than she had in all of her previous jobs combined.

Shortly after starting to work for him he'd installed her in a luxurious flat near the office at a ridiculously low rent. He'd waved her protests away, saying, 'I don't need to be worrying about you living in a bad area, and I will require you to be available to work out of hours sometimes, so it's for my convenience as much as yours.'

That had shut Darcy up. He was putting her there so she was more accessible to him—not out of any sense of concern because she was on her own in a city she didn't know as well as she might, considering her mother's Italian background. Still, she couldn't complain, and had enjoyed the chance to have a central base from which to explore Rome.

Max had been true to his word. She'd found herself working late plenty of evenings and on some Saturdays for half the day. His work ethic was intimidating, to say the least.

He rapped out now, 'What was Montgomery's response?'

Darcy didn't have to consult her notes. 'He wants you to meet him for dinner when he's here with his wife next week.'

Max's face hardened. 'Damn him. I'd bet money that

the wily old man is enjoying every moment of drawing this out for as long as possible.'

Watching his hands, splayed on his slim hips, Darcy found it hard to focus for a second, but she forced her gaze back up and had to acknowledge that this *was* unusual. Most people Max dealt with knew better than to refuse him what he wanted.

His mouth was tight as he spoke almost to himself. 'Montgomery doesn't think I'm suitable to take control of his hedge fund. I'm an unknown, I don't come with a blue-blooded background, but worst of all, in his eyes, I'm not respectably married.'

No, you certainly are not, Darcy observed frigidly to herself, thinking of the recent weekend Max had spent in the Middle East, visiting his exotically beautiful lover, a high-profile supermodel. A little churlishly Darcy imagined them having lots of exotically beautiful babies together, with tawny eyes, dark hair and long legs.

'*Darcy.*'

She flushed, caught out. Surely working with someone every day should inure you to his presence? Not make it worse?

'It's just dinner, Max, not a test,' she pointed out calmly.

He paced back and forth, which threatened Darcy's focus *again*, but she kept her eyeline resolutely up.

'Of course it's a test,' he said now, irritably. 'Why do you think he wants me to meet his wife?'

'Maybe he just wants to get to know you better? After all, he's potentially asking you to manage one of the oldest and most illustrious fortunes in Europe and his family's legacy.'

Max snorted. 'Montgomery will have already deemed me suitable or unsuitable—a man like that has nothing left to do in life except amuse himself and play people off each other like pawns.'

He raked a hand through unruly hair, a familiar gesture by now, and Darcy felt slightly breathless for a moment. And then, angry at her reaction to him, she said with not a little exasperation, 'So take...' She stopped for a moment, wondering how best to describe his mistress and settled for the most diplomatic option. 'Take Noor to dinner and persuade Montgomery that you're in a settled relationship.'

Max's expression turned horrified. 'Take Noor al-Fasari to dinner with Montgomery? Are you *mad*?'

Darcy frowned, and didn't like the way something inside her jumped a little at seeing Max's reaction to her suggestion. 'Why not? She's your lover, and she's beautiful, accomplished—'

Max waved a hand, cutting Darcy off. 'She's spoilt, petulant, avaricious—and in any case she's no longer my lover.'

Darcy had to battle to keep her face expressionless as this little bombshell hit. Evidently the papers hadn't yet picked up on this nugget of information, and he certainly didn't confide his innermost secrets to her.

She looked at Max as guilelessly as she could. 'That's a pity. She sounds positively delightful.'

He made that dismissive snorting sound again and said, with a distinct edge to his voice, 'I choose my lovers for myriad reasons, Darcy, not one of which I've ever considered is because they're *delightful*.'

No, he chose them because they were the most beautiful women in the world, and because he could have whoever he wanted.

For a moment Darcy couldn't look away from Max's gaze, caught by something inexplicable, and she felt heat start to climb up her body. And then his phone rang. She broke the intense, unsettling eye contact and stretched across to answer it, then pressed the 'hold' button.

'It's the Sultan of Al-Omar.'

Max reached for the phone. 'I'll take it.'

Darcy stood up with not a little sense of relief and walked out, aware of Max's deep voice as he greeted his friend and one of his most important clients.

When she closed the door behind her she leaned back against it for a moment. What had that look been about? She'd caught Max staring at her a few times lately, with something unreadable in his expression, and each time it had made her silly pulse speed up.

She gritted her jaw as she sat down behind her desk and cursed herself for a fool if she thought for a second that Max ever looked at her with anything more than professional interest.

It wasn't as if she even *wanted* him to look at her with anything more than professional interest. She was not about to jeopardise the best job of her career by mooning about after him like she had at school, when she'd been in the throes of a very embarrassing pubescent crush.

Max finished his call with his friend and stood up to look out of his office window, feeling restless. The window framed an impressive view of Rome's ancient ruins—something that usually soothed him with its timelessness. But not right now.

Sultan Sadiq of Al-Omar was just one of Max's very small inner circle of friends who had given up the heady days of being a bachelor to settle down. He'd broken off their conversation just now when his wife had come into his office with their toddler son, whom Max had heard gabbling happily in the background. Sadiq had confided just before that they were expecting baby number two in a few months, and happiness had been evident in his friend's voice.

Max might have ribbed him before. But something about that almost tangible contentment and his absorption in his family had made him feel uncharacteristically hollow.

Memories of his brother's recent wedding in Rio de Janeiro came back to him. He and his brother weren't close. Not after a lifetime spent living apart—the legacy of warring parents who'd lived on different continents. But Max had gone to the wedding—more because of the shared business concerns he had with his brother than any great need to 'connect'.

If he had ever had anything in common with his brother apart from blood it had been a very ingrained sense of cynicism. But that cynicism had all but disappeared from his brother's eyes as he'd looked adoringly at his new wife.

Max sighed volubly, forcibly wiping the memory from his mind. Damn this introspection. Since when did he feel *hollow* and give his brother and his new wife a moment's consideration?

He frowned and brooded over the view. He was a loner, and he'd been a loner since he'd taken responsibility for his actions as a young boy and realised that he had no one to turn to but himself.

And yet he had to concede, with some amount of irritation, that watching his peers fall by the wayside into domesticity was beginning to make him stand out by comparison. The prospect of going to dinner with Montgomery and his wife was becoming more and more unappealing, and Max was certain that the old man was determined to use it as an opportunity to demonstrate his unsuitability.

At that moment Max thought of Darcy's suggestion that he take his ex-lover to dinner. For some reason he found himself thinking not so much of Noor but of Darcy's huge blue eyes. And the way colour had flared in her cheeks when he'd told her what he thought of that suggestion.

He found himself comparing the two women and surmised with some level of grim humour that they couldn't be more different.

Noor al-Fasari was without a doubt one of the most beautiful women in the world. And yet when Max tried to visualise her face now he found that it was amorphous—hard to recall.

And Darcy... Max frowned. He'd been about to assert that she *wasn't* beautiful, but it surprised him to realise that, while she certainly didn't share Noor's show-stopping, almost outlandish looks, Darcy was more than just pretty or attractive.

And, in fairness, her job was not to promote what beauty she did possess. Suddenly Max found himself wondering what she would be like dressed more enticingly, and with subtle make-up to enhance those huge eyes and soft rosebud lips.

Much to his growing sense of horror, he found that her voluptuous figure came to mind as easily as if she was still walking out of his office, as she'd done only minutes before. He might have fooled himself that he'd been engrossed in the conversation with his friend, but in reality his eyes had been glued to the provocative way Darcy's pencil skirt clung to her full hips, and how the shiny leather belt drew the eye to a waist so small he fancied he might span it with one hand.

His skin prickled. It was almost as if an awareness of her had been growing stealthily in his subconscious for the past few months. And as if to compound this unsettling revelation he found the blood in his body growing heated and flowing south, to a part of his anatomy that was behaving in a manner that was way out of his usual sense of control.

Almost in shock, Max sat down, afraid that Darcy might walk in and catch him in this moment of confusion and not a little irritation at his wayward responses.

It was the memory of his ex-lover that had precipitated this random lapse in control. It had to be. But when he tried to conjure up Noor's face again, with a sense of desperation, all he could recall were the shrill shrieks she'd hurled his way—along with an expensive vase or two—after he'd told her their affair was over.

A brief knock came to his door and Darcy didn't wait before opening it to step inside. 'I'm heading home now, in case you want anything else?'

And just like that Max's blood sizzled in earnest. A floodgate had been opened and now all he could see was her glossy dark brown hair, neatly tied back. Along with her provocative curves. Full breasts thrust against her silk shirt. The tiny waist. Womanly hips, firm thighs and shapely calves. Small ankles. And this was all in a package a couple of inches over five feet. When Max had never before found petite women particularly attractive.

She wasn't even dressed to seduce. She was the epitome of classic style.

He couldn't fault her—not for one thing. Yet all he could think about doing right now was walking over to her and hauling her up against his hot and aching body. And, for a man who wasn't used to denying his urges when it came to women, he found himself floundering.

What the hell…? Was he going crazy?

Darcy frowned. 'Is there something wrong, Max?'

'Wrong?' he barked, feeling slightly desperate. 'Nothing is wrong.'

'Oh,' said Darcy. 'Well, then, why are you scowling at me?'

Max thought of the upcoming dinner date with Montgomery and his wife and imagined sitting between them like a reluctant gooseberry. He made a split-second decision. 'I was just thinking about the dinner with Montgomery…'

Darcy raised a brow. 'Yes?'

Feeling grim, Max said, 'You're coming with me.'

She straightened up at the door. 'Oh.' She looked nonplussed for a moment, and then said, 'Is that really appropriate?'

Max finally felt as if he had his recalcitrant body under some kind of control and stood up, putting his hands in his pockets. 'Yes, it's highly appropriate. You've been working on this deal with me and I'll need you there to keep track of the conversation and make nice with Montgomery's wife.'

Darcy was clearly reluctant. 'Don't you think that perhaps someone else might be more—?'

Max took one hand out of his pocket and held it up. 'I don't want any further discussion about this matter. You're coming with me—that's it.'

Darcy looked at him with those huge blue eyes and for a dizzying moment Max felt as if she could see all the way down into the depths of his being. And then the moment broke when she shrugged lightly and said, 'Okay, fine. Anything else you need this evening?'

He had a sudden vivid image of ripping her shirt open,

to see her lush breasts encased in silk and satin, and got out a strangled-sounding, 'No, you can go.'

To his blessed relief, she did go. He ran both hands through his hair with frustration. Ordinarily Max would have taken this rogue reaction as a clear sign that he should go out and seek a new lover, but he knew that the last thing he needed right now in the run-up to the final negotiations with Montgomery was for him to be at the centre of headlines speculating about his colourful love-life.

So for now he was stuck in the throes of lusting after his very capable PA—an impossible situation that Max felt some god somewhere had engineered just for his own amusement.

CHAPTER TWO

A WEEK LATER Darcy was still mulling over the prospect of going to the Montgomery dinner the following evening with Max. She assured herself again that she was being ridiculous to feel so reluctant. Lots of PAs accompanied their bosses on social occasions that blurred into work.

So why was it that her pulse seemed to step up a gear when she thought about being out in public with Max, in a social environment?

Because she was an idiot. She scowled at herself and almost jumped out of her skin when Max yelled her name from inside his office. If anything, his curtness over the last week should have eased her concerns. He certainly wasn't giving her the remotest indication that there was anything but business on his mind.

She got up and hurried into his office, schooling her face into a neutral expression. As always, though, as soon as she laid eyes on him her insides clenched in reaction.

He was pacing back and forth, angry energy sparking. She sighed inwardly. This protracted deal was starting to wear on *her* nerves too.

She sat down and waited patiently, and then Max rounded on her and glared at her so fiercely her eyes widened with reproach. 'What did I do?'

He snapped his gaze away and bit out, 'Nothing. It's not you. It's—'

'Montgomery,' Darcy said flatly.

He looked at her again and his silence told her succinctly that that was exactly what it was.

'I'll need you to work late this evening. I want to make sure that when we meet him tomorrow I'm not giving him one single reason to doubt my ability.'

Darcy shrugged. 'Sure thing.'

Max put his hands on his hips, a look of determination stamped on his gorgeous features. 'Okay, clear the schedule of anything else today and let's take out everything to do with this deal. I want to go through it all with a fine-tooth comb.'

Darcy got up and mentally braced herself for a gruelling day ahead.

Much later that evening Darcy sat back on her heels in Max's office and arched her spine, with her hands on the small of her back. Her shoes had come off hours ago and they'd eaten take-out.

It had to be close to midnight when Max finally said wearily, 'That's it, isn't it? We've been through every file, memo and e-mail. Checked into the man's entire history and all his business endeavours.'

Darcy smiled wryly and reached up to tuck some escaping hair back into her chignon. 'I think it's safe to say that we could write an authorised biography on Cecil Montgomery now.'

The dark night outside made Max's office feel like a cocoon. They were surrounded by the soft glow of numerous lights. He didn't respond and she looked up at him where he stood behind his desk, shirt open at the throat and sleeves rolled up. In spite of that he barely looked rumpled—whereas she felt as if she'd been dragged through a hedge backwards and was in dire need of a long, relaxing bath.

He was looking at her with a strange expression, as if caught for a moment, and it made Darcy's pulse skip. She felt self-conscious, aware of how she'd just been stretching like a cat. But then the moment passed and he moved and went over to the bar, his loose-limbed grace evident even after the day's hard slog. Darcy envied him. As *she* stood up her bones and joints protested. She told herself she was being ridiculous to imagine that Max was looking at her any kind of which way.

He came back and handed her a tumbler of dark golden liquid. Her first thought was that it was like his eyes, and then he said with a wry smile, 'Scottish whisky—I feel it's appropriate.' He was referring to Montgomery's nationality.

Darcy smiled too and clinked her glass off Max's. 'Sláinte.'

Their eyes held as they took a sip of their drinks and it was like liquid fire going down her throat. Aware that they were most likely alone in the vast building, and feeling self-consciousness again, Darcy broke the contact and moved away to sit on the edge of a couch near Max's desk.

She watched as he came and stood at the window near her, saw the scar on the his face snaking down from his temple to his jaw.

She found herself asking impulsively, 'The scar—how did you get it?'

Max tensed, and there was an almost imperceptible tightening of his fingers around his glass. His mouth thinned and he didn't look at her. 'Amazing how a scar fascinates so many people—especially women.'

Immediately Darcy tensed, feeling acutely exposed. She said stiffly, 'Sorry, it's none of my business.'

He looked at her. 'No, it's not.'

Max took in Darcy's wide eyes and a memory rushed back at him with such force that it almost felled him: a much younger Darcy, but with the same pale heart-shaped face. Concerned. Pushing between him and the boys who had been punching the breath out of him with brute force.

He'd been gasping like a grounded fish, eyes streaming, familiar humiliation and impotent anger burning in his belly, and she'd stood there like a tiny fierce virago. When they'd left and he'd got his breath back she'd turned to him, worried.

Without even thinking about what he was doing, still dizzy, Max had straightened and reached out to touch her jaw. He'd said, almost to himself, '"Though she be but little, she is fierce."'

She'd blushed and whirled around and left. He'd still been reeling from the attack—reeling from whatever impulse had led him to quote Shakespeare.

Darcy was reaching across to put her glass on the table now, standing up, clearly intending to leave. And why wouldn't she after he'd just shut her down?

An impulse rose up within Max and he heard himself say gruffly, 'It happened on the streets. Here in Rome, when I was homeless.'

Darcy stopped. She lifted her hand from the glass and looked at him warily. 'Homeless?'

Max leaned his shoulder against the solid glass window, careful to keep his face expressionless. Curiously, he didn't feel any sense of regret for letting that slip out. He nodded. 'I was homeless for a couple of years after I was kicked out of Boissy.'

Darcy said, 'I remember the blood on the snow.'

Max felt slightly sick. *He* still remembered the vivid stain of blood on the snow, and woke sometimes at night sweating. He'd vowed ever since then not to allow anyone to make him lose control again. He would beat them at their own game, in their own rarefied world.

'A boy went to hospital unconscious because of me.'

She shook her head faintly. 'Why did they torment you so much?'

Max's mouth twisted. 'Because one of their fathers was my mother's current lover and he was paying my fees. They didn't take kindly to that.'

Darcy had one very vague memory of an incredibly beautiful and glamorous woman arriving at the school one year with Max, in a chauffeur-driven car.

She found herself resting against the edge of the desk, not leaving as she'd intended to moments ago. 'Why were you homeless?'

Max's face was harsh in the low light. 'My mother failed to inform me that she'd decided to move to the States with a new lover and left no forwarding details. Let's just say she wasn't exactly at the nurturing end on the scale of motherhood.'

Darcy frowned. 'You must have had other family... Your father?'

Max's face was so expressionless that Darcy had to repress a shiver.

'I have a brother, but my father died some years ago. I couldn't go to them, in any case. My father had made it clear I was my mother's responsibillty when they divorced and he wanted nothing to do with me. They lived in Brazil.'

Darcy tried not to look too shocked. 'But you must have been just—'

'Seventeen,' Max offered grimly.

'And the scar…?' It seemed to stand out even more lividly now, and Darcy had to curb the urge to reach out and touch it.

Max looked down at his drink, swirling it in his glass. 'I saw a man being robbed and chased after the guy.' He looked up again. 'I didn't realise he was a junkie with a knife until he turned around and lunged at me, cutting my face. I managed to take the briefcase from him. I won't lie—there was a moment when I almost ran with it myself… But I didn't.'

Max shrugged, as if chasing junkies and staying on the right side of his conscience was nothing.

'The owner was so grateful when I returned it that he insisted on taking me to the hospital. He talked to me, figured out a little of my story. It turned out that he was CEO of a private equity finance firm, and as a gesture of goodwill for returning his property he offered me a position as an intern. I knew this was a chance and I vowed not to mess it up…'

Darcy said, a little wryly, 'I think it's safe to say you didn't waste the opportunity. He must have been a special man to do that.'

'He was,' Max said with uncharacteristic softness. 'One of the few people I trusted completely. He died a couple of years ago.'

There was only the faintest low hum of traffic coming from the streets far below. Isolated siren calls that faded into the distance. Everything around them was dark and golden. Darcy felt as if she were suspended in a dream. She'd never in a million years thought she might have a conversation like this with Max, who was unreadable on the best of days and never spoke of his personal life.

'You don't trust easily, then?'

Max grimaced slightly. 'I learnt early to take care of myself. Trust someone and you make yourself weak.'

'That's so cynical,' Darcy said, but it came out flat, not with the mocking edge she'd aimed for.

Max straightened up from the window and was suddenly much closer to Darcy. She could smell him—a light tangy musk, with undertones of something much more earthy and masculine.

He looked at her assessingly. 'What about you, Darcy? Are you telling me *you're not* cynical after your parents' divorce?'

She immediately avoided that incisive gaze and looked out at the glittering cityscape beyond Max. A part of her had broken when her world had been upended and she'd been split between her parents. But as a rule it wasn't something she liked to dwell on. She was reluctant to explore the fact that it had a lot to do with her subsequent avoidance of relationships.

She finally looked back to Max, forcing her voice to sound light. 'I prefer to say realistic. Not cynical.'

The corner of Max's mouth twitched. Had he moved even closer? He felt very close to Darcy.

He drawled now, 'Let's agree to call it realistic cynicism, then. So—no dreams of a picturesque house and a white picket fence with two point two kids to repair the damage your parents did to you?'

Darcy sucked in a breath at Max's unwitting perspicacity. Damn him for once again effortlessly honing in on her weak spot: her desire to have a base. A home of her own. Not the cynical picture he painted, but her own oasis in a life that she knew well could be upended without any warning, leaving her reeling with no sense of a safe centre.

Her career had become her centre, but Darcy knew she needed something more tangibly rooted.

She tried to sound as if he hadn't hit a raw nerve. 'Do I *really* strike you as someone who is yearning for the domestic idyll?'

He shook his head and took a step closer, reaching past Darcy to put his glass on the table behind her. She knew this should feel a little weird—after all they'd never been so physically close before, beyond their handshake when she'd taken the job. But after the intensity of their day spent cocooned in this office, with the darkness outside now, and after Max had revealed the origin of his scar, a dangerous sense of familiarity suppressed Darcy's normal impulse to observe the proper boundaries.

She told herself it was their shared experience in Boissy that made things a little different than the usual normal boss/PA relationship. But really the truth was that she didn't *want* to move as Max's arm lightly brushed against hers when he straightened again. The sip of whisky she'd taken seemed to be spreading throughout her body, oozing warmth and a sense of delicious lethargy.

Max looked at her. He was so close now that she could see how his eyelashes were dark gold, lighter at the tips.

'No,' he said. 'I don't think you are looking for the domestic idyll. You strike me as someone who is very focused on her career. A bit of a loner, perh

That stung. Darcy had friends, b
away so much that she only saw
the UK. He was right, though.
The revelation that she might
as romantic relationships v

She cursed herself. Sh
whisky and some unex
seriously impair her ju
here. They were both

She straightened

even closer to Max. She looked anywhere but at him. 'It's late. I should get going if you want me to be awake enough to pay attention at dinner tomorrow evening.'

'Yes,' Max said. 'That's probably wise.'

Her feet seemed to be welded to the floor, but Darcy forced herself to move and turned to walk away—bumping straight into the corner of the desk, jarring her hip bone. She gave a pained gasp.

Max's hand came to her arm. 'Are you okay?'

Darcy could feel the imprint of Max's fingers, strong and firm, and just like that she was breathless. He turned her towards him and she couldn't evade his gaze.

'I... Thanks. It was nothing.' Any pain was fast being eclipsed by the look in Max's eyes. Darcy's insides swooped and flipped. The air between them was suddenly charged in a way that made her think of running in the opposite direction. Curiously, though, she didn't want to obey this impulse.

And then something resolute crossed his face and he pulled her towards him.

Darcy was vaguely aware that Max's grip on her arm wasn't so tight that she couldn't pull free. But a sense of shock mixed with intense excitement gripped her.

'What are you doing?' she half whispered.

His gaze moved from her mouth up to her eyes and time stood still. Max's other hand moved around to the back of her neck, tugging her inexorably towards him. voice was low and seductive. 'I haven't been able to ng about what this would be like.'

would be like?'

ould catch up with the speed at x's mouth came down and

covered hers, fitting to her softer contours like a jigsaw piece slotting into place.

He was hard and firm, masterful as he moved his mouth against hers, enticing her to open up to him—which she found herself doing unhesitatingly. The kiss instantly became something else...something much deeper and darker.

Max was bold, his tongue exploring the depths of her mouth, stroking sensuously, making her lower body clench in helpless reaction. His body was whipcord-hard against hers, calling to her innermost feminine instincts that relished such evidence of his masculinity.

The edge of the desk was digging into Darcy's buttocks, but she barely noticed as Max urged her back so that she was sitting on it, moving his body between her legs so she had to widen them.

It was as if he'd simply inserted himself like a sharp blade under her skin and she'd been rendered powerless to think coherently or do anything except respond to the feverish call of her blood to taste this man, drink him in. It was intoxicating, heady, and completely out of character for her to behave like this.

Max's hands were moving now, sliding down the back of her silk shirt, resting on her waist over the belt of her trousers. And then he moved even closer between her legs and Darcy felt the thrust of his erection against her belly.

It was that very stark evidence of just how far over the edge they were tipping that blasted some cold air through the heat haze clouding her brain.

Darcy pulled back to find two slumberous pools of tawny gold staring at her. Their breathing was laboured and she was aware of thinking with sudden clarity: *Max Fonseca Roselli can't possibly want me. I'm not remotely his type. He's playing with me.*

She jerked back out of his arms and off the desk so abruptly that she surprised him into letting her go. Her heart was racing as if she'd just run half a marathon.

Some space and air between them brought Darcy back to full shaming reality. One minute they'd been knee-deep in the minutiae of Montgomery's life and business strategies, and the next she'd been sipping fine whisky and Max had been telling her stuff she'd never expected to hear.

And then she'd been climbing him like a monkey.

She'd never behaved so unprofessionally in her life. She lambasted herself, and ignored the screeching of every nerve-end that begged her to throw herself back into his arms.

Max looked every inch the disreputable playboy at that moment, with frustration stamped onto hard features as he observed his prey standing at several feet's distance. His cheeks were slashed with colour, his hair messy. *Oh, God.* She'd had her hands in his hair, clutching him to her like some kind of sex-starved groupie.

When she felt she could speak she said accusingly, '*That* should not have happened.'

Her hair was coming down from its chignon and she lifted her hands to do a repair job. The fact that Max's gaze dropped to her breasts made her feel even more humiliated. If they hadn't stopped when they had— She shut her mind down from contemplating where exactly she might be right now.

Allowing him to make love to her on his desk? Like some bad porn movie cliché: Darcy Does Her Boss.

She felt sick and took her hands down now her hair was secured.

Max looked at her and didn't seem to share half the turmoil she felt as he drawled, with irritating insouciance, '*That* did happen, and it was going to happen sooner or later.'

'Don't be ridiculous,' Darcy snapped on a panicked reflex at the thought that he had somehow seen something of her fascination with him. She was aghast to note that her legs were shaking slightly. 'You don't want me.'

Max folded his arms across his broad chest. 'I'm not in the habit of kissing women I don't want, Darcy.'

'Ha!' she commented acerbically as she started to hunt for her discarded shoes. She sent him a quick glare. 'You really expect me to believe you want *me*? That was nothing but a momentary glitch in our synapses, fuelled by fatigue and proximity.' She finally spotted her shoes and shoved her feet into them, saying curtly, 'This shouldn't have happened. It's completely inappropriate.'

'Fatigue and proximity?'

Max's scathing tone stopped Darcy in her tracks and she looked at him with the utmost reluctance. He was disgusted.

'That was chemistry—pure and simple. We wanted each other and, believe me, if we'd been wide awake and separated by a thick stone wall I'd still have wanted you.'

Darcy's heart pounded in the explosive silence left by his words. *He wanted her?* No way. She shook her head. Panic clutched her. 'I'll hand in my notice first thing—'

'You'll do no such thing!'

Darcy's heart was pounding out of control now. 'But we can't possibly work together after this.' She crossed her arms tightly. 'You have issues with PAs who don't know their place.'

He scowled. 'What just happened was entirely mutual. I have no issue with that—it was as much my responsibility as yours. More so, in fact, as I'm your boss.'

'Exactly,' Darcy pointed out, exasperated. 'All the

more reason why I can't keep working for you. We just crossed the line.'

Max knew on some rational level that everything Darcy was saying was true. He'd never lost control so spectacularly. He was no paragon of virtue, but he'd never mixed business with pleasure before, always keeping the two worlds very separate.

In all honesty he was still reeling a little from the fact that he'd so blithely allowed it to happen. And then his conscience mocked him. As if he'd had a choice. He'd been like a dog in heat—kissing Darcy had been a compulsion he'd been incapable of ignoring.

All day he'd been aware of her in a way that told him the feeling of desire that had sneaked up on him wasn't some mad aberration. As soon as she'd arrived for work he'd wanted to undo that glossy chignon and taste her lush mouth. All day he'd struggled with relegating her back to her appropriate position, telling himself he was being ridiculous.

Then they'd ordered takeout and she'd sat cross-legged on the floor, eating sushi out of a carton with chopsticks, and he'd found it more alluring than if they'd been in the glittering surroundings of a Michelin-starred restaurant. And when she'd taken her shoes off earlier and knelt down on the floor, to spread papers out and make it easier to sort them, he'd had to battle the urge to stride over and kneel down behind her, pulling her hips back—

Dio.

And now she was going to resign—because of *his* lack of control. Max's gut tightened.

'You're not walking away from this job, Darcy.'

She blinked, and a mutinous look came over her face. Her mouth was slightly swollen and Max was distracted by the memory of how soft it had felt under his. The sweet yet sharp stroke of her tongue against his… *Maledizione*. Just the thought of it was enough to fire him up all over again.

Darcy was cool. 'I don't think you have much choice in the matter.'

A familiar sense of ruthlessness coursed through Max and he reacted to her cool tone even when he felt nothing but heat. 'I do—if you care about your future job prospects.'

Darcy paled and a very unfamiliar stab of remorse caught at Max. He pushed it aside.

'I will not remain in a job where the lines of professionalism have been breached.'

Feeling slightly desperate, and not liking it, Max said again, 'It was just a kiss, Darcy.' He ran a hand impatiently through his hair. 'You're right, it shouldn't have happened, but it did.'

He thought of something else and realised with a jolt that he'd lost track of his priorities for a moment.

'I need you to help me close this deal with Montgomery. I can't afford the upheaval a new PA will bring at the moment.'

Max saw Darcy bite her lip, small white teeth sinking into soft pink flesh. For a wild second he almost changed his mind and blurted out that maybe she was right—they'd crossed a line and she should leave—but something stopped him. He told himself it was the importance of the deal.

She turned around and paced over to the window and looked out, her back to him. Max found his gaze travelling down over that tiny waist. Her shirt was untucked, dishevelled. *He'd* done that. He could remember how badly he'd wanted to touch her skin, see if it was as silky as he imagined it would be.

The knowledge hit him starkly: the most beautiful women in the world had treated him to personal erotic strip shows and yet Max was more turned on right now by an untucked piece of faux silk chainstore shirt.

And then Darcy turned around. Her voice was low. 'I know how important this deal is to you.'

The way she said it made Max feel exposed. She couldn't know the real extent of why it was so important— that it would bring him to a place of acceptance, both internally and externally, where he would finally be able to move on from the sense of exposure and humiliation that had dogged him his whole life. And, worse, the sense of being abandoned.

Yet he couldn't deny it. 'Yes. It's important to me.'

She fixed her wide blue gaze on him but he could see how pinched her face was. Reluctance oozed from her every pore.

'I'll stay on—but only until the deal is done and only if what happened tonight doesn't happen again.'

She looked at him, waiting for a response. The truth was that if Max wanted something he got it. And he wanted Darcy. But for the first time in his life he had to recognise that perhaps he couldn't always get what he wanted. That some things were more important than others. And this deal with Montgomery was more important than having Darcy in his bed, sating his clawing sense of frustration.

Also, he didn't want her to see that it was a struggle for him to back off. That would be far too exposing.

So he said, with an easiness that belied every bone in his body that wanted to throw her onto the nearest flat surface, 'It won't happen again, Darcy. Go home. We've got another long day and evening ahead of us tomorrow.

Don't forget to bring a change of clothes for dinner to-morrow night. We'll be going straight from the office.'

Darcy didn't say anything. She just turned and walked out of the room and the door closed with incongruous softness behind her.

Max walked over to the window. After a few minutes' delay he saw her emerge from the building in her coat, walking briskly away from the building, merging with Rome's late-night pedestrian traffic.

Something in his body eased slightly now that she was no longer in front of him, with those wide blue eyes looking so directly at him that he felt as if he were under a spotlight.

No woman was worth messing up this deal and cer-tainly not little Darcy Lennox, with her provocative curves. Max finally turned around again and sighed deeply when he saw the slew of papers strewn across his desk and floor.

Instead of leaving himself, he went back to the bar, re-filled his glass with whisky and then sat down and pulled the nearest sheaf of papers towards him. He put Darcy firmly out of his head.

Darcy tossed and turned in bed a little later, too wired to sleep. It was as if her body had been plugged into an electrical socket and she now had an excess of energy fizzing in her system.

She'd been plugged into Max.

Even though she was lying down, her limbs took on a jelly-like sensation when she recalled that moment of suspended tension just before he'd kissed her and every-thing had gone hazy and hot. She could still feel the im-print of his body against hers and between her legs she tingled. She clamped her thighs together.

They'd taken a quantum leap away from boss/PA, and it had happened so fast it still felt unreal. Had she really threatened to leave her job? And had he more or less threatened her future employment prospects if she did? She shivered slightly. She could well imagine Max doing just that—she'd witnessed his ruthlessness when it came to business associates first-hand.

The deal with Montgomery meant more to him than the potential awkwardness of having shared an intimate and highly inappropriate moment with his PA.

No matter what Max said, Darcy had no doubts that what had happened had been borne out of insanity brought on by fatigue and the moment of intimacy that had sprung up when he'd told her about his past.

She hadn't expected to hear him reveal that he'd been homeless. Any other student from Boissy wouldn't have lasted two days on the streets. But Max had lasted two years, and crawled his way out of it spectacularly.

He'd mentioned a brother, and his father. His parents' divorce. Questions resounded in Darcy's head as the enigmatic figure of Maximiliano Fonseca Roselli suddenly took on a much deeper aspect.

Unable to help herself, she leaned over and switched on the bedside light, picked up her tablet. She searched the internet for 'Max Fonseca Roselli family' and a clutch of pictures sprang up.

Darcy's breath was suspended as she scrolled through them. There was a picture of a very tall and darkly handsome man: Luca Fonseca, Brazilian industrialist and philanthropist. Max's brother. His name rang a bell. And then more pictures popped up of the same man with a stunningly beautiful blonde woman. They were wedding photos. Darcy recalled that she'd read about the wedding between Luca Fonseca and the infamous Italian socialite Serena DePiero recently.

Had Max gone to the wedding? Darcy was about to search for more information on his parents when she realised what she was doing and closed the cover of her tablet with force.

She flipped off the light and lay down, angry with herself for giving in to curiosity about a man with whom she'd shared a very brief and ill-advised moment of pure unprofessional madness. A man she should have no further interest in beyond helping him to get this deal so that she could get the hell out of his orbit and get on with her life.

CHAPTER THREE

DARCY LOOKED AT herself critically in the mirror of the ladies' toilet next to her office, but she didn't really see her own reflection. She was on edge after a long day in which Max had been overly polite and solicitous, with not so much as a sly look or hint that they'd almost made love on his desk the previous night.

At one stage she'd nearly snapped at him to please go back to normal and snarl at her the way he usually did.

The fact that she'd allowed a level of exposure and intimacy with Max she'd never allowed before was something she was resolutely ignoring. Her previous sexual experiences with men had come only after a lengthy dating period. And in each case once the final intimacy had been breached she'd backed off, because she'd realised she had no desire to deepen the commitment.

She snorted at herself now. As if she would have to worry about something like that with Max Fonseca Roselli. He was the kind of man who would leave so fast your head would be spinning for a week.

She forced her mind away from Max and took a deep breath. Her dress was black and had been bought for exactly this purpose—to go from work to a social event. And, as far as Darcy had been concerned when she'd bought it, it was modest.

Yet now it felt all wrong. It was a dress that suited her diminutive hourglass shape perfectly, but suddenly the scooped neckline was too low and the waist too cinched in. The clingy fabric was a little *too* clingy around her bottom and thighs, making her want to pluck it away from her body. The capped sleeves felt dressy, and when she moved the discreet slit up one side seemed to shout out, *I'm trying to be sexy!*

All at once she felt pressured and frazzled, aware of time ticking on. She'd already been in the bathroom for twenty minutes. She imagined Max pacing up and down outside, looking at his watch impatiently, waiting for her. Well, too late to change now. Darcy refreshed her make-up and spritzed on some perfume, and slid her feet into slightly higher heels than normal.

She'd left her hair down and at the last moment felt a lurch of panic when she looked at herself again. It looked way too undone. She twisted it up into a quick knot and secured it with a pin.

Her cheeks were hot and beads of sweat rolled down between her breasts. Cursing Max, and herself, she finally let herself out, her work clothes folded into a bag. It was with some relief that she noted that Max wasn't pacing up and down outside.

Stowing her bag in a cupboard, making a mental note to take it home after the weekend, Darcy took a deep breath and knocked once briefly on Max's office door before going in.

When she did, though, she nearly took a step back. Max was standing with a remote control in his hand, watching a financial news channel on the flat screen TV set into his wall. His hair was typically messy, but otherwise any resemblance to the Max she'd expected to see dissolved into a haze of heat.

His jaw was clean-shaven, drawing the eye to strong, masculine lines. He was wearing a classic three-piece suit in dark grey, with a snowy-white shirt and grey silk tie. Darcy swallowed as Max turned and his gaze fell on her. She couldn't breathe. Literally couldn't draw breath. She'd never seen anyone so arrestingly gorgeous in her life. And the memory of how that lean body had felt when it was pressed against hers, between her legs, was vivid enough to make her sway slightly.

There was a long, taut silence between them until Max clicked a button on the remote and the faint hum of chatter from the TV stopped.

He arched a brow. 'Ready?'

Darcy found her voice. 'Yes.'

He moved towards her and she backed out of his office, almost tripping over her own feet to pick up her evening bag and a light jacket matching the dress. As she struggled into it inelegantly she felt it being held out for her and muttered embarrassed thanks as Max settled it onto her shoulders.

She cursed the imagination that made her think his fingers had brushed suggestively against the back of her neck, and strode out of the office ahead of Max before she could start thinking anything else. Like how damn clingy her dress felt right then, and what rogue devil had prompted her not to wear stockings. The slide of her bare thighs against one another felt sensual in a way she'd never even noticed before. She'd never been given to erotic flights of fancy. Far too pragmatic.

Darcy didn't look at Max as they waited for his private lift, but once they were inside his scent dominated the small space.

He asked, 'You have the documents?'

'Yes.' Darcy lifted the slim attaché case she carried

alongside her bag. It held some documents they wanted to have on hand in case Montgomery asked for them.

The lift seemed to take an eternity to descend the ten or so floors to the bottom.

'You know, we *will* have to make eye contact at some point in the evening.' Max's voice was dry.

Reluctantly Darcy looked up at him, standing beside her, and it was as if a jolt of lightning zapped her right in the belly. She sucked in a breath and saw Max's eyes flare. The shift in energy was as immediate as an electric current springing up between them, as if it had been waiting until they got close enough to activate it.

No wonder they'd been skirting around each other all day. They'd both been avoiding *this*.

For the nano-second it took for this to sink in, and for Max to make an infinitesimally small move towards her—for her to realise how badly she wanted to touch him again—there was nothing outside of the small cocoon of the lift. Desire pulsated like a tangible thing.

But then a sharp *ping* sounded, the doors opened silently and they both stopped—centimetres from actually touching each other.

Max emitted a very rude Italian curse. He took her arm to guide her out of the lift, although it felt more as if he was marching her out of the building.

Once outside, walking to his chauffeur-driven car, he said tersely, 'I said eye contact, Darcy, not—'

'Not *what*, Max?' Darcy stopped and pulled her arm free, shaky from the rush of adrenalin and desire she'd just experienced, and self-conscious at the thought that she'd been all but drooling. 'I didn't do anything. *You're* the one who looked at me as if—'

He came close. 'As if *what*? As if I suddenly couldn't think of anything else except what happened last night?'

His mouth was a thin line. 'Well, I couldn't—and neither could you.'

Darcy had nothing to say. He was right. She'd been utterly naïve and clueless to think that she could experience a moment like that with Max Fonseca Roselli and put it down as a rash, crazy incident and never want him again. A hunger had been awoken inside her.

But she could deal with that.

What she couldn't deal with was the fact that Max—for some unfathomable reason—still wanted her too.

He glanced at his watch and said curtly, 'We'll be late. We can't talk about this now.'

And then he took her arm again and led her to the car, following her into the plush interior before she could protest or say another word.

The journey to the restaurant was made in a silence that crackled with electric tension. Darcy didn't look anywhere near Max, afraid of what she'd see if she did. She couldn't handle that blistering gaze right now.

One thing was clear, though. She would be handing in her notice *before* this deal was done. She couldn't continue to work for Max after this. But she didn't think he'd appreciate hearing her tender resignation right now.

The car came to a stop outside one of Rome's most exclusive restaurants. It took lesser mortals about six months to get a table, but Max had a table whenever he wanted.

He helped her out of the car, and even though Darcy wanted to avoid physical contact as much as possible she had to take his hand or risk sprawling in an ungainly heap at his feet.

She'd just stood up straight, and Max was still holding her hand, when a genial voice came from nearby.

'You didn't mention that you were bringing a date.'

Darcy tensed, and Max's hand tightened on hers reflexively. But almost in the same second she could tell he'd recovered and his hand moved smoothly to her arm as he brought her around to meet their nemesis.

Cecil Montgomery was considerably shorter than Max, and considerably older, with almost white hair. But he oozed charisma, and Darcy was surprised to find that on first impression she liked him.

His eyes were very blue, and twinkled benignly at her, but she could see the steeliness in their depths. A tall woman stood at his side, very elegant and graceful, with an open friendly face and dark grey eyes. Her hair was silver and swept up into a classic chignon.

'Please—let me introduce you to my wife, Jocasta Montgomery.'

'Pleasure...' Darcy let her hand be engulfed, first by Montgomery's and then by his wife's.

It was only when they were walking into the restaurant that Darcy realised Max hadn't actually introduced her as his PA—or had he and she just hadn't heard?

She hadn't had anything to do with Montgomery herself, as he and Max had a direct line of communication, so it was quite possible he still thought she was Max's date. The thought made Darcy feel annoyingly self-conscious.

They left their coats in the cloakroom and were escorted to their table, the ladies walking ahead of the men. The restaurant oozed timeless luxury and exclusivity. Darcy recognised Italian politicians and a movie star. The elaborate furnishings wouldn't have been out of place in Versailles, and even the low-pitched hum of conversation was elegant.

Jocasta Montgomery took Darcy's arm and said *sotto*

voce in a melodious Scottish accent, 'I don't know about you, my dear, but I always find that places like this give me an almost overwhelming urge to start flinging food around the place.'

It was so unexpected that Darcy let out a startled laugh and something inside her eased out of its tense grip. She replied, 'I know what you mean—it's an incitement to rebel.'

They arrived at a round table, the best in the room, and took their seats. To Darcy's surprise the conversation started and flowed smoothly. Max and Montgomery dominated it, with talk of current business trends and recent scandals. At one point between starters and the main course Jocasta rolled her eyes at Darcy and led her into a conversation about living in Rome and what she liked about it.

They skirted around the edges of the fact that this dinner was really about whether or not Montgomery was going to hand his precious life's blood to Max to manage until coffee had been served after dessert.

Darcy had almost forgotten why they were there, she'd enjoyed talking to Jocasta so much. But now there was a palpable buzz of tension in the air and Darcy saw the very evident steely gleam in Montgomery's eyes as he looked at Max, who was unmistakably tense.

It was slightly disconcerting to recognise how keenly she felt Max's tension as Montgomery looked at him over his coffee cup before putting it down slowly.

'The fact is, Max, quite simply there is no one I can imagine handling this fund and making it grow into the future better than you. As you're aware I'm very concerned about philanthropy, and your own brother's work has been inspirational to me.'

Max inclined his head towards the older man, but his face was expressionless.

'My one reservation, however, is this...'

Darcy tensed and avoided looking at Max.

'You have been leading a committedly single life-style for a long time.' He glanced at Darcy and said half apologetically, 'Present company notwithstanding. My fund and my life's work has been built upon and developed with family in mind. *My* family, primarily, of course, but also for the benefit of many others. This would never have happened if I hadn't had a very strong sense of family values running through previous generations. That's why the Montgomery fund has lasted as long as it has, and grown so strong...'

Darcy was barely aware of Montgomery's continued misunderstanding about who she was. He was going on...

'And you, Max—you come from a broken home... For years you were estranged from your father, you didn't speak to your own twin brother, and you are not close to your mother.'

Darcy's mind boggled. Max's brother was a *twin*?

She looked at him now and could see his face was still expressionless, but a vein popped slightly over one temple, near his scar, which stood out against that dark olive skin. The scar he'd got because his own mother had forgotten about him. Left him defenceless on the streets.

'You've done your research,' Max said easily, but Darcy recognised the edge of something dangerous.

Montgomery shrugged. 'No more than you yourself have done, no doubt.'

'My relationship with my brother, my mother, has no bearing on my ability to manage your fund, Cecil.'

A lesser man would have quailed at the distinct threat in Max's voice. Not Montgomery.

'No,' said the other man, looking at Max assessingly. 'I think for the most part you are right. But my concern would be the risks you'd be prepared to take on behalf of my fund—risks that you might not consider taking if you had a different perspective on life. My fear is that, based on your experiences, you might actually be biased against the very values I've built this fund upon, and that it would influence your decision-making process because you have only yourself to worry about.'

Darcy's insides had turned to stone. Cecil Montgomery, with a ruthless precision she'd never even witnessed in Max, had just laid Max's life bare and dissected it with clinical and damning detachment.

She felt a very disturbing surge of something like protectiveness. A need to defend.

Even Jocasta Montgomery had put her hand on her husband's arm and was saying something indistinct to him.

Darcy looked at Max, who had carefully put his own coffee cup down. The restaurant was largely empty by now.

'You are right about almost everything, Cecil.' He smiled, but it was a thin, harsh line. 'I do come from a broken home, and my brother and I did suffer at the hands of two parents who really couldn't have cared less about our welfare.'

Jocasta broke in. 'Please, Max, don't feel you have to say—'

But Max held up a hand, not taking his gaze off Montgomery. 'I said that your husband is right about *almost* everything. There's one thing his research hasn't shown up, however.'

Montgomery raised a brow. 'I'm intrigued. What is it that I've missed?'

Max's jaw clenched, and to Darcy's shock he reached over and took her hand in his, holding it tight.

'Darcy.'

Darcy looked at Max, but he hadn't said her name to call her attention and speak to her.

He was still looking at Montgomery and gripping her hand tight as he said, 'You can be the first to congratulate my fiancée and I on our engagement.'

Darcy might have enjoyed Montgomery's almost bug-eyed response if she hadn't been so afraid that her own eyes were bugging out of her head at the same moment.

'But... But...' Jocasta Montgomery said, 'Darcy told me she's your PA...'

Max looked at Darcy briefly and through waves of shock she could see something implacable in his expression that forbade her from saying anything.

He looked back to the couple on the other side of the damask-covered table. 'She is. That's how we met... again.'

'Again?' asked Montgomery sharply.

Max nodded. 'Darcy and I went to the same school— Boissy le Chateau in Switzerland. That's where we first met. She came to work for me three months ago...' Max shrugged, 'And the rest, as they say, is history.'

'Oh, Cecil.' Jocasta Montgomery put her hand over her husband's and looked at him with suspiciously bright eyes. 'That's how *we* met.'

Darcy felt it like a punch to the gut. She remembered that small detail now. Jocasta had been his secretary in the seventies, in Edinburgh.

Cecil Montgomery was looking at Max through narrowed eyes. Obviously suspicious. And then he turned his gaze on Darcy and she could feel her cheeks grow hot.

'Well, then, my dear, it would seem that congratulations are in order. When did this happy event occur?'

Max's hand tightened on hers as he inserted smoothly, 'Some weeks ago… I knew after just a few weeks that Darcy was unlike any other woman I've ever known. We had a bond at school…and it was rekindled.'

Darcy was still too shocked even to consider saying anything, but she tried to pull her hand out from under Max's—to no avail.

'My dear, are you quite all right? You look a little ill.' Jocasta Montgomery was leaning forward with concern.

Darcy sensed Max's tension beside her, reaching out to envelop her, inhibit her. She knew that she should pull away, stand up, throw her napkin down and say that it was all untrue. This was her chance. She should walk away from Max right now and not look back.

And put a nail in the coffin of his chance to get this deal with Cecil Montgomery.

If she wanted revenge for what he'd just done that was what she'd do.

But she couldn't get out of her head the way Montgomery had so brutally assessed Max's background, casting doubts on his ability. And she couldn't get out of her head the way she'd felt that instinctive need to defend him. And right now the instinct was still there, in spite of the rage bubbling down low at having been put in this untenable position.

She forced a smile and looked at Jocasta. 'I'm fine—really. It's just a bit of a shock to hear it made official. Up till now it's been our secret.'

She risked a glance at Max and her gaze was caught and snared by his. It was expressionless, but something flickered in the depths of those extraordinary eyes. *Relief?* His hand loosened on hers fractionally.

Jocasta was making a *tsk*ing noise. 'And my husband provoked Max into letting it slip? Well, I think the least we can do is celebrate now that your secret is out.'

Before Darcy could say anything else a waiter was summoned and a bottle of vintage champagne was being delivered to the table and expertly poured into slim flutes. It seemed to Darcy that everything was moving at warp speed, and her heart was beating too fast.

They were all holding up their glasses and Jocasta was beaming at them. Her husband was still looking less than convinced though and Max's jaw was tight. Darcy felt an urge to giggle, and quickly took a sip of the sparkling drink to make it go down.

'When are you getting married?'

Darcy looked at Montgomery, just as Max said, with all the natural-born charm of a ruthless man intent on his prize, 'Two weeks.'

His hand tightened on Darcy's again and when she turned to him he looked at her so intently that her insides combusted.

'I want to make her mine before she realises what I'm really like and leaves me for ever.'

For the first time since Max had made his outrageous statement Darcy felt her wits return. She pulled her hand free and said with some acerbity, while holding up her hand, 'Well, seeing as you haven't even bought me a ring yet, *darling*, I'm thinking that perhaps there's a flaw in the arrangements.'

Jocasta chuckled. 'Yes, Max, a lady in possession of a marriage proposal generally deserves a beautiful ring.'

Max smiled, and it was dangerous. He took Darcy's hand again and lifted it to his mouth, pressing a kiss over her ring finger, making any of the wits that had come back to her melt again.

'Which is why I've arranged to take my fiancée to Paris tomorrow, for a private appointment in Devilliers—it was meant to be a surprise.'

Darcy's eyes opened wide. Devilliers was possibly the oldest and most exclusive jewellers in the world.

Jocasta made a noise. 'And now we've ruined it. Cecil, stop goading Max. They're engaged. Look at them—they can't keep their eyes off each other.'

'Well, then,' said the older man. 'It seems that perhaps your perspective is indeed changing, Max. However, I've decided that the announcement of my decision as to whom I'm entrusting my fund will take place at our fortieth wedding anniversary celebrations in Scotland, surrounded by my family.'

The Montgomerys shared a fond look and Max let Darcy's hand go. Montgomery looked at him, and then to Darcy. 'You will both, of course, be extended an invitation. It takes place in three weeks. Perhaps you could include the trip to Inverness as a detour on your honeymoon?'

Honeymoon?

The full enormity of what was occurring hit Darcy, and as if sensing her dawning horror Max put a firm hand on her leg, under the table, just above her knee.

'We would like nothing more—would we, *cara*?'

Max was looking at her, his big hand heavy on her leg, and treacherous heat was spreading upwards to between her thighs. 'No...'

Max knew exactly what Darcy's very ineffectual 'no' meant. It didn't mean that she agreed—it meant *Stop this now.* But he took ruthless advantage of the ambiguity and angled his body towards hers, slipping his other hand around the back of her bare neck, pulling her towards him so that he could cover her mouth with his and stop her from saying anything else.

By the time he let her go again she was hot, breathless, addled and completely out-manoeuvred by a master. The Montgomerys were preparing to leave, saying their goodbyes, clearly believing that they were playing gooseberry now.

Darcy didn't know if she wanted to stamp her foot, slap Max, or scream for them all to *stop* so she could put them right. But, like the treacherous heat that had licked up her thighs and into her belly during Max's kiss, something was holding her back—and she was too much of a coward to investigate what it was.

They stood to bid goodbye to the older couple and Darcy was vaguely aware that the restaurant had emptied. When they were alone again Max sat down, a look of supreme satisfaction on his face.

This time Darcy *did* throw down her napkin, and he looked at her. Anger at herself for being so weak made her blurt out, 'What the *hell* do you think you're playing at, Max?'

Max cast a quick look around and took Darcy's wrist, pulling her down. She landed heavily on the seat.

Something occurred to her then—an awful suspicion. 'Please tell me you didn't have that planned all along?'

Max's jaw firmed. He was unapologetic. 'No, but I saw an opportunity and took it.'

Darcy let out a slightly horrified laugh. 'An *opportunity*? That's what you call fabricating a fake engagement to your PA?'

He turned to face her, stretching an arm across the back of her chair, placing his other hand on the table. Boxing her in.

'It won't be a fake engagement, Darcy. We're going to get married.'

Darcy's mouth opened but nothing came out. On some level she had known what she was doing, going along with Max's crazy pronouncement, but she'd also expected that as soon as they were alone again he'd reassure her that of course it wouldn't happen. It had been just to placate Montgomery and there would be some method of undoing what had been done.

She shook her head, as if that might restore sanity and order. But he was still looking at her.

She found her voice. 'Maybe it's the fatigue, Max, or the stress, but I think it's quite possible that you've gone entirely mad. This conversation is over and this *relationship* is over. Find someone else to be your convenient bride/PA, because I'm not going to be it just because I'm under your nose and you've decided that it's appropriate to kiss me when you feel like it. We both know I'm not your type of woman. No one will ever believe you've chosen to marry someone like me—Montgomery patently didn't believe a word of it—so in the end it'll achieve nothing.'

Darcy was breathless after the tumult of words and stood up on shaky legs. Before Max could stop her she turned to walk quickly through the restaurant, reality slamming back into her with each step. And humiliation. Max had seen an opportunity, all right—a cheap one, at Darcy's expense. To think that he would *use* her like this, just to further his own aims, shouldn't have come as a shock. But it did.

Max watched Darcy walk away, rendered uncharacteristically dumb. He could appreciate her very apparent sense of shock because he was still reeling himself, trying to recall what exactly had prompted him to make such an outrageous statement to Montgomery.

And then he remembered. *'You come from a broken home...estranged from your mother...brother...different perspective...'* He remembered the hot rush of rage when Montgomery had so coolly laid his life bare for inspection. Questioning his motives and ability based upon his experiences.

He'd wanted to do something to take that knowing smirk off Montgomery's face. And in a moment of mad clarity he'd known what he had to do to push the man off his sanctimonious perch. Fake a marriage. To Darcy.

And she'd gone along with it—even if she *had* looked as if someone had just punched her in the belly.

Darcy. Max's usual clear-headed focus came back and he went cold inside at the thought of Darcy leaving. She wasn't going anywhere—not now. Not when everything was at stake.

'Get in the car, Darcy. Please.'

Darcy was valiantly ignoring Max and the open car door nearby. She was about to stretch her arm out to hail a passing taxi when he took her arm in a firm grip and all but manhandled her into the back of the car.

She sputtered, 'This is kidnap.'

Max was terse. 'Hardly. Take us to my apartment, please, Enzo.' And then he hit a button so that a partition went up, enclosing them in silence.

Darcy folded her arms and looked at the man on the other side of the car. In a louche sprawl of big long limbs, he'd never looked more like a rebel.

'You've gone too far this time, Max. I don't care what you have to do but we're *not* getting married—I've changed my mind, I'm not waiting until the deal is done. I'm on the first plane out of Rome as soon as you let me go.'

Max gave her a withering look. 'There's no need for dramatics. We are just going to talk.'

He leaned back and looked out of the window, clearly done with the conversation for now. Darcy fumed, hating the ever-present hum of awareness in her blood at being in such close proximity to him. He was such an arrogant...*bastard*. Saying the word, even silently, made her feel marginally better.

Within minutes they were pulling up outside a sleek modern building. Max was out of the car and holding out a hand for Darcy before she could think what to do. Knowing she couldn't escape now, she scowled and put her hand into his, let him help her out, jerking her hand away as soon as she was on her own two feet.

Max led her into a massive steel-and-chrome foyer, where huge works of modern art were hung on the walls. It was hushed and exclusive, and in spite of herself she found herself wondering what Max's apartment would be like.

With an acknowledgement to the concierge, Max led Darcy to an open lift and stabbed at the 'P' button. Of course, Darcy thought snarkily. Of *course* he'd be living in the penthouse.

Once in the lift she moved to the far corner. Max leaned back against the wall and looked at her from under hooded lids. 'No need to look like a startled rabbit, Darcy. I'm not going to eat you.'

'No,' she said sharply. 'Just turn my world upside down.'

CHAPTER FOUR

DARCY FOLLOWED MAX into his apartment warily. From what she could see, as he flicked on low lights, it was as sleek and modern as the building that housed it. Floor-to-ceiling windows offered astounding views of Rome glittering at night.

Her feet were sore in the high-heeled shoes, but she would let them bleed before taking them off. She was still recalling her bare feet in the office the previous night—the cocoon of intimacy and where that had led.

'Drink?'

Darcy looked over to where Max was pulling his tie out of its knot and undoing the top buttons of his shirt. He'd already taken off his jacket and he looked sinfully sexy in the waistcoat of the three-piece suit.

She shook her head. 'No. I don't want a drink, Max, and I don't want to talk. I'd like to go to some corner of the earth far away from you.'

He just shrugged, ignoring her pronouncement, and proceeded to pour himself a measure of something. He gestured to a seat. 'Please—sit down.'

Darcy clutched her bag tighter. 'I told you...I don't want to—'

'Well, tough, because we're talking.'

Darcy made a rude sound and stalked over to an uncomfortable-looking chair and sat down.

Max started to pace, then stopped and said, 'Look, I didn't plan to announce an engagement to you this evening.'

'I'm not so sure you didn't, Max. It certainly seemed to trip off your tongue very easily—along with that very inventive plan to treat me to a Devilliers ring. Tell me, are we taking your private jet?'

Max cursed before downing his drink in one and setting the glass down with a clatter.

He glared at her. 'I didn't plan it. He just... *Dio*. You heard him.'

Darcy's insides tightened as she recalled the sense of protectiveness that had arisen when Montgomery had baldly dissected Max's life. The truth was that no one goaded Max. He'd remained impervious in the face of much worse provocation. *But this had been personal. About his family.*

Darcy stood up, feeling vulnerable. 'I heard him, Max. The man clearly has strong feelings about the importance of family, but do you think he really cares if you're married or not?'

'You heard him. He believes my perspective will be skewed unless I have someone to worry about other than myself.' Max sounded bitter.

'So you fed me to him?'

He looked at her. 'Yes.'

'I'm just a means to an end—so you can get your hands on that fund.'

Max looked at Darcy. Her hair had begun to get dishevelled, falling down in tendrils around her face and neck. *'I'm just a means to an end.'* Why did those words strike at him somewhere? Of *course* she was a means to an end—everything in his life was a means to an end. And that end was in sight.

'Yes.'

Her jaw tightened and she stepped back. Max did not like the flash of something like panic in his gut.

'Yes, you *are* a means to an end—I won't pretty it up and lie to you. But, Darcy, if you do this you won't walk away empty-handed. You can name your price.'

She let out a short curt laugh and it made Max wince inwardly. It sounded so unlike her.

'Believe me, no price could buy me as your wife, Max. I don't think I even *like* you all that much.'

Max felt that like a blow to his gut, but he gritted out, 'I'm not asking you to like me, and I'm not *buying* a wife, Darcy. I'm asking you to do this as part of your job. Admittedly it's a little above and beyond the call of duty... but you will be well compensated.'

Darcy tossed her head. 'Nothing could induce me to do this.'

'Nothing...?' Max asked silkily as he moved a little closer, his vision suddenly overwhelmed with the tantalising way Darcy filled out her dress.

She put out a hand. 'Stop right there.'

Max stopped, but his blood was still leaping. He'd yet to meet a woman he couldn't seduce. *Was he prepared to seduce Darcy into agreement?* His mind screamed caution, but his body screamed *yes*!

He erred on the side of caution.

Darcy's hand was still held out. 'Don't even *think* about it, Max. That kiss...whatever happened between us...was a mistake and it won't be happening again.'

He kept his mouth closed even as he wanted to negate what she'd said. He needed her acquiescence now.

'Everyone has a price, Darcy. You can name yours. We only need to be married for as long as it takes the deal to be done, then we'll divorce and you can get on with your life. No harm done. It's just an extension of your job, and I'll make sure that you get a job wherever you want in the world after this.'

She snorted, telling him succintly what she thought of *that*. She moved away from him now, stalking over to one of the big windows.

Max felt disorientated for a moment. It wasn't usual for him to bring a woman back to his apartment. He preferred to keep women out of his private space. Especially women he seduced. Because he never wanted them to get any notions.

But Darcy was here, and it felt bizarrely as if she'd been here before. He was too consumed with bending her to his will right now to look at *that* little nugget. Too consumed with ignoring the inferno raging in his blood as he took in her curvy silhouette against the backdrop of Rome outside.

And then she turned around, her hands still clutching her bag. 'Why is this so important to you?'

Max immediately went still, as if drawing his energy back inwards. Darcy had a moment to collect herself, to try and remove her see-sawing emotions and hormones from this situation.

As she'd looked out of the window she'd had to ask herself why the prospect of marrying Max was such a red-hot button for her. Apart from the fact that it was a ludicrous thing to ask of anyone.

After all, she came from a *very* broken home, so if anyone had the necessary cynicsm to embark on a marriage of convenience it was her. And she was ambitious enough to appreciate the aspect that Max wasn't exaggerating—she *would* have the pick of any job she wanted if she did this. It would be the least he owed her.

But she was not stupid enough to think that the way she'd felt when Max had kissed her could be ignored. He'd tapped into something untouched deep inside her— something that went beyond the physical to a secret place she'd never explored herself, never mind with anyone else.

And there was his astounding arrogance in thinking she would just go along with this decree. Like some king who expected his minions to obey his every word.

'Well, Max? If I'm to even consider this crazy idea for one second I want to know why you want this so badly.'

He seemed to glower at her for a long moment, and then he stuck his hands in the pockets of his trousers and came closer. Darcy couldn't move back because the window was behind her. He came and stood near her, looking out at the view, face tight.

'Montgomery mentioned my brother. We're twins. We were six when our parents split up and split *us* up. I only ever saw Luca again when he came to Rome for brief holidays or on trips to see our mother. I see him a little more frequently since we've been adults.'

Max sighed.

'He grew up being groomed to be my father's heir. There was never any question of me getting a share. That was my punishment for choosing to go with my mother... not that our father really cared which son he got as long as he had an heir to pass his corrupt legacy on to. But that's just part of it. Luca did offer me my half of his inheritance after our father died, but I didn't want it.'

He looked at Darcy then, almost accusingly.

'I didn't want his charity and I still don't. By then I'd

already made my first million. I wanted to succeed on my own merit—surpass anything my father had ever done. Do it on my own. It's the one thing that's kept me going through it all. The need to know that I've done it without anyone handing me anything.'

He looked away again and Darcy was silent. Mesmerised by the passion blazing out of Max. And the unmistakable pride.

'For years I felt tainted. Tainted by my mother's lack of care and her sordid affairs. That's how she made her living—little better than women who call themselves what they really are: prostitutes.'

Darcy winced.

'I was on the streets one night, foraging for food in a bin at the back of an exclusive restaurant, when some guests came outside to smoke. Boys from my class at Boissy.'

She sucked in a breath, imagining the scene all too well.

As if he'd guessed her suspicion his mouth quirked and he said, 'There was no blood. I walked away—but not before they recognised me and told me that they'd never expected anything more of someone like me. I'd been born into one of the wealthiest families in South America, but thanks to my fickle parents my brother and I were used almost like an experiment to see who would flourish better. One of us was given everything. The other one had everything stripped away.'

He turned to look at her, his face stark in the dim lights.

'That's why I want this. Because if Montgomery hands me his fund I'll have proved that even when you have your birthright stripped away it's still possible to regain your dignity and get respect.'

He didn't have to elaborate for Darcy to imagine how his litany of humiliations had bred the proud man in front of her. Montgomery held an almost mythical place in the world's finances. Akin to financial royalty. Darcy knew that what Max said was true. His endorsement would make Max untouchable, revered. The boys who had bullied him at school and witnessed him at his lowest moment on the streets would be forced to respect him.

'And it's not just for me,' he said now, interrupting her thoughts. 'I'm a partner in a philanthropic organisation with my brother. We're finally putting our father's corrupt legacy to good use, and I'll be damned if I can't contribute my own share.'

Max turned to face her more fully.

'*That's* why I want this, Darcy. Everyone has a price. I've just told you mine. You can name yours.'

Why did that sound like the worst kind of deal with the devil?

Because it is, whispered a small voice.

When Darcy woke up the next day she felt strangely calm. As if a storm had passed and she'd been washed up on land—alive and breathing, if a little battered.

Max had made no further attempt to stop her from leaving once she'd said, 'I need a night to think it over.'

It was as if he'd recognised how precarious his chance was. He'd escorted her down to his car and bade her goodnight, saying, 'Just think of your price, Darcy.'

And so she had.

After hours of tossing and turning she'd got up and looked at her tablet, at the properties she'd marked on a website. It was her secret, most favourite thing to do. Earmark the properties she'd buy if she had the money.

Her heart had thumped hard when she'd seen that her current favourite was still available. The price, in her eyes, was extortionate; London property gone mad. But she knew to Max it would be a pittance. Was *this* her price? A place of her own? The base she wanted so badly? The base it would take her years to afford under normal working circumstances?

Darcy could empathise with Max's determination to do it all on his own. She could ask her parents for the money to buy a house and have it tomorrow. But when she'd seen her father almost lose everything it had forged in her a deep desire to ensure her own financial stability, to be dependent on no one else.

She'd been eight when her parents had split up and she'd been tossed back and forth like a rag doll, across time zones and countries, with nice airline ladies holding her hand through airports. It had been in those moments that Darcy had wished most fervently that she still had a home—somewhere she could go back to that would always be there. *Something that wasn't in a constant state of flux.* Security. Stability.

When Max had revealed that he'd been only six when his parents had split up her silly heart had constricted. And he had a twin brother. She couldn't imagine what it must have been like to have been ripped apart from a sibling. Never mind taken to the other side of the world, never to connect with one of your parents again.

She got up and showered and made herself coffee. She hated that knowing about Max's tumultuous past made it harder for her to keep seeing him as ruthless and cynical. But he *was*, she assured herself. Nothing had changed. He was out for himself—unashamedly. And yet who could blame him? He'd been abandoned by his own mother, forgotten by his father. Estranged from his brother.

The thing was, did he deserve for her to help him?

Darcy's mobile phone pinged with a text message. From Max.

Well?

She almost smiled. Something about his obvious impatience at the fact that she wouldn't come to heel easily comforted her. Things had morphed from relatively normal to seriously weird in a very short space of time.

She texted back.

Do you think you could use that word in a sentence?

She pictured him scowling. A couple of minutes passed and then...

Dear Darcy,
Please will you marry me so that I can secure Montgomery's fund and live happily ever after?
Yours truly, Max.

Darcy barked out a laugh. The man was truly a bastard. Her phone pinged again.

Well?

Now *she* scowled.

I'm thinking.

Think faster.

Darcy threw her phone down for a moment. Pressure was building in her chest. And then the picture of the property she loved so much caught her eye. If she did this, she would get that.

We all have a price.

She picked up the phone, almost daring it to ping again with some terse message—because if it did she would tell Max where to go. But it didn't, almost as if he knew how close she was to saying no.

She took a deep breath and texted.

If—and that's a big if—if I agree to do this I want £345,000.

She let out a breath, feeling like a mercenary bitch. But it was the price of the flat she loved. And if she was being a mercenary bitch she was nothing in comparison to Max. His soul was black.

She continued.

Also, this farcical marriage will last only for as long as it takes Montgomery to announce his decision, and then you will give me a stunning reference which will open the door to whatever job I want.

Her heart thumped hard as she looked over the text, and then her finger pressed the 'Send' button. 'Delivered' appeared almost straight away.

It took longer than she'd expected, but finally Max's response came back.

Done and done. Whatever you want. I told you. Now, what's it to be?

Darcy's finger traced over the picture of the flat. In a few months she could be living there, with a new job. A new start. A settled existence for the first time since she'd been a child. And no Max messing with her hormones and her ability to think clearly.

She texted quickly before she lost her nerve: Yes.

Almost immediately a message came back.

Good. My car will pick you up in an hour. We're going to Paris.

The ring. For a moment Darcy almost texted Max back, saying she'd changed her mind, but her fingers hovered ineffectually over her phone. And then she got distracted.

What the hell did someone wear on a whirlwind trip to Paris to buy an engagement ring for a fake wedding?

In the end Darcy decided to wear one of her smarter work outfits: a dark navy wrap dress with matching high heels. She felt self-conscious now, in the small plane, and resisted the urge to check and see if her dress was gaping a little too much. The way Max had looked at her when she'd walked out of her apartment building had almost made her turn around and change into jeans and a T-shirt.

He was dressed similarly, smart/casual in a dark blue suit and white shirt. When she'd walked over to the car earlier he'd smirked slightly and said, 'We're matching— isn't that cute?'

Darcy had scowled and dived into the car. When he'd joined her she'd said, 'Can you put up the partition, please?'

She'd been more discomfited than she'd liked to admit by this more unreadable and yet curiously accessible Max. The boundary lines had become so blurred now they were non-existent, and she'd needed to lay down some rules.

When the window had gone up she'd crossed her arms over her chest. Max's eyeline had dropped to her cleavage.

'We need to discuss some formalities.'

Max's eyes had snapped up. 'Formalities?'

'All this marriage is, as far as I'm concerned, is a serious amount of overtime. You're basically paying me to be an executive PA par excellence. It's still just *work*. And if I hadn't agreed to this I would still be tendering my notice because of what happened the other night.'

Max sat back, looking dangerous and sexy, jaw dark with stubble. 'What happened, Darcy?'

Darcy shot a look at the partition and back again, her cheeks growing hot. 'You know very well what happened. We crossed the line.'

'We almost made love on my desk.'

Darcy felt hotter. 'But we didn't.' *Thank God.* 'We came to our senses.' She waved a hand. 'What I'm trying to say is that even now we are embarking on this ridiculous charade—'

'That I'll be paying you handsomely for...' Max pointed out, immediately making Darcy's irritation levels rise.

'And for which you'll be earning your place among the financial giants of the world,' she lashed back.

Max's jaw clenched. 'Touché.'

Darcy had leaned forward in her agitation but she pulled back now, forcing herself to stay calm. 'What I'm saying is that this marriage is going to be fake in every sense of the word. If you want anything physical then I'm sure you can get it from the legion of women in your little black book.'

Max folded his arms and regarded her. 'There's something incredibly ironic about the fact that I always swore I'd never enter into the state of matrimony and yet now I find myself on the brink of such a situation—'

'Caused by *you*,' Darcy flung at him.

That made him dip his head in acknowledgement before he continued, 'I find myself with a wife who won't sleep with me. I would never have anticipated that as a problem to be surmounted.'

'No,' Darcy said waspishly. 'I don't imagine you would have. Like I said—call someone else to provide you with any extra-curricular services you might require. I'm sure you can be discreet.' She looked at him, wondering just why this conversation was making her so angry. 'I would just avoid a three-in-a-bed romp—that won't endear you to Montgomery if it gets out like the last one did.'

Max made an irritated sound. 'For what it's worth that was a PR stunt for charity that ended up being leaked before we could explain it, so it never got used. You can't seriously think I'd be so crass?'

Darcy looked at him and cursed him. He looked positively angelic. Wrapped up in a demon. And of *course* he wouldn't be so crass. Max oozed sophistication. She should have known better. And now she'd revealed that she'd been keeping an eye on his exploits. *Damn him*.

She looked away. 'Whatever, Max—just don't make me look like a fool.'

'The same goes for you, you know,' came the softly delivered response.

Darcy looked at him and for a moment all she could see was the way Max had looked at her the other night, when she'd pulled back from his embrace, cheeks flushed, eyes glittering dangerously. 'Don't worry,' she said, as frigidly as she could, 'I won't have a problem curbing *my* urges.'

Max had muttered something she couldn't catch— something like *We'll see about that*—just as the car had pulled up outside the small plane.

Darcy's attention came back to the plane. Max was staring out of his window. Not goading her or looking at her with those mesmerising eyes. She remembered what he'd told her last night and how she'd wanted to leave his apartment—get away before he might see something on her face or in her expression. Empathy. A treacherous desire to help him achieve what he wanted.

'I didn't know your brother was a twin.'

Max turned his head slowly and looked at her. 'It's not really common knowledge.'

'I saw pictures of him...the wedding. You're not identical?'

Max shook his head and smiled, but it was hard. 'I'm prettier than my brother.' His self-mocking expression was anything *but* pretty. It was utterly masculine, making a mockery of 'pretty'. Especially with that scar running from his temple to his jaw.

Darcy felt breathless. 'You said you're closer now?'

Max raised a brow. 'Did I?'

'Last night...you said you were working with him.'

Max's mouth tightened. 'For a cause—not because we sit up at night drinking cocoa and reminiscing about our childhood experiences.'

Darcy rolled her eyes at his sarcastic response just as the plane banked. She took the opportunity to escape Max's gaze and looked out to see Paris laid out in all its glory, the distinctive Eiffel Tower glinting in the distance. Fine. Obviously Max wasn't about to launch into any more confessionals. He'd probably already told her far more than he wanted to.

And she wasn't curious. Not at all.

Max watched as Darcy inspected the trays of rings laid out for their perusal. He almost smiled at her overwhelmed expression. She had been pretty slack-jawed since they'd walked into the opulent Rococo interior of one of the oldest jewellery establishments in the world. A byword in luxury, wealth and romance. These jewellers had supplied jewels for all the major royal houses, iconic movie stars and heads of state.

But he was still curbing the irritation he'd felt ever since Darcy's very stark insistence that they observe professional boundaries—marriage or no. Was the woman completely blind? All he had to do was come within two inches of her and the electricity was practically visible.

Even now he couldn't take his gaze off the way her breasts pressed lushly against the edge of the glass case they were sitting in front of. He'd noticed the sales assistant's eyes drop too, and had glared at the man so fiercely he'd almost dropped a tray of priceless rings.

Darcy's reminder that she would have been long gone if not for this wedding arrangement caused another ripple of irritation. Max wasn't used to things morphing out of his control. It was a sense of control hard won and fought for—literally.

But when Darcy looked at him with those huge blue eyes all he wanted to do was throw control out of the window and give in to pure basic instinct. And yet she had the wherewithal to sit there and draw a little prim circle around herself saying, *Not over the line.*

She looked at him now, and Max couldn't imagine a woman looking *less* enthusiastic to be here.

He frowned. 'What is it?'

She glanced at the assistant, who moved away for a moment, discreetly polishing a ring.

'I don't know what to choose—they're all so ridiculously expensive... I mean, you're going to insure the ring, right? I'd hate for anything to happen to it—especially when this isn't even for real.'

Max saw the clear turmoil on Darcy's face and it was

like a punch to his gut to realise just how different she was from any other woman he might have brought to a place like this. They would have had absolutely no qualms about choosing the biggest and most sparkly bauble in the shop. And he would have indulged them without even thinking. It gave him a sense of distaste now.

He took her hand in his. It felt unbearably small and soft. 'Darcy, you're overthinking this. Just choose a ring. We'll get it insured. Okay?'

After a moment she nodded, and then said, 'Sorry, I'm probably making this boring for you.'

She looked back at the rings and some hair slipped over her shoulder, obscuring her face. Without thinking Max reached for it and tucked it behind her ear again. She looked at him and he couldn't resist. He leaned forward and pressed a kiss next to the corner of that surprisingly lush mouth.

Immediately her eyes went darker, but then they flashed. 'I told you—'

His hand gripped hers and he smiled as he said, 'We're buying a ring for our whirlwind engagement, *cara mia*, people are watching.'

She looked around quickly and then ducked her head, whispering fiercely, 'Fine...just in public.'

Max said nothing, but vowed right then to make sure they were in public as much as possible.

Darcy looked at the ring on her finger from different angles as Max discreetly paid the bill. Someone had delivered her a glass of champagne and she sipped it now. Grateful for the slightly numbing sensation. Numbing her from thinking about how choosing the ring had impacted on her so much.

It had brought up all sorts of unwelcome and tangled

emotions. As a small girl she'd used to love going into her mother's jewellery box and looking at the glittering earrings and bracelets. But the engagement ring had been her favourite, made of nine baguette diamonds surrounded by sapphires and set in white gold.

Darcy had used to put it on, holding it in place and imagining herself in it, marrying a handsome prince.

And then one day it had disappeared. Darcy had asked her mother where it was, only to be told curtly that she'd sold it. That had been the beginning of the end of the fairytales in Darcy's imagination, as her parents' marriage had fractured and split apart over an agonising year of arguments and bitter recrimination.

Today the ring Darcy had chosen in the end had been far too close to something she might choose for real, but she hadn't been able to resist—some rogue devil had urged her on. A rectangular-shaped diamond, surrounded by smaller baguette diamonds, set in platinum. It was positively discreet when compared with some of the other choices, but right now it felt like an unbearably heavy weight on her hand.

'Ready?'

Darcy looked up to see Max waiting. She grew warm, thinking of him watching her as she'd been inspecting the ring, and almost sprang out of the chair.

'Ready.'

Max guided her solicitously out of the shop and Darcy couldn't help noticing a young couple as they passed, obviously head over heels in love. The pretty woman was crying as her boyfriend presented her with a ring.

Darcy caught Max's look and raised brows and scowled as he tutted, 'Now, *that's* not going to convince anyone.'

Just inside the clear revolving doors Max stopped her

and turned her towards him. 'What—?' was all she managed to get out before Max cupped her jaw in one big hand and angled her face up to his so that he could kiss her.

Immediately the hot insanity of the other night slammed back into Darcy with such force that she had to cling onto his shirt to stay standing. It was an explicit kiss, and Darcy was dimly aware that someone like Max probably couldn't deliver a chaste kiss if his life depended on it. He was like a marauding pirate, sweeping in and taking no prisoners. It was hot, decadent, and the slide of Max's tongue against hers made her want to press her breasts against his chest and ease their ache.

When he pulled back she went with him, as if loath to break the contact. She opened her eyes and Max said smugly, 'That's a bit better.'

Darcy's brain felt sluggish as Max pulled her out of the shop, but it snapped back to crystal clarity when they faced a veritable wall of flashing lights.

'Max! Over here! Max! Who is the lucky lady? What's her name?'

The barrage of questions was deafening and terrifying. Max had his arm around Darcy and her hand was still gripping his shirt. She could feel the tension in his body as he said, in a masterful voice that sliced through the cacaphony, 'We will be releasing a statement on Monday. Until then please afford my fiancée and I some privacy.'

'Show us the ring!'

But Max's car materialised then, as if out of nowhere, and he was guiding Darcy into the back of it, shutting the baying mob outside as it took off smoothly into the Paris traffic.

Darcy vaguely heard Max curse, and then a glass was

being pushed into her hands. She looked down, feeling a little blank and blinded.

'Take a sip, Darcy, you're in shock... *Maledizione*, I should have realised... You've never been papped before.'

When she didn't move he cursed again and lifted the glass to her lips, forcing liquid to trickle into her mouth and down her throat. She coughed as it smarted and burned and realised she was shaking from the adrenalin and shock of being in front of the paparazzi for the first time.

She looked at Max, who took the glass away and put it back in the car's mini-bar. 'How did they know?'

He had the grace to look slightly sheepish. 'I got my PR people to tip them off.'

Darcy thought of their kiss just inside the door, and all the lenses that must have been trained on them every moment, capturing her reaction. Not for one second did she want Max to know how angry it made her or how betrayed she felt. Stupid to think that a private moment had been invaded. It hadn't been a private moment—it had been manufactured.

'Well,' she said, as coolly as she could, 'I hope Montgomery sees it—or they'll have wasted an afternoon when they could have been chasing someone far more exciting.'

'I'm sorry. I should have warned you.'

Darcy feigned unconcern. 'Don't worry about it—at least it'll look authentic.'

'Good,' Max said briskly. 'Because we're going to a function in Rome this evening. It'll be our first official outing as a couple.'

Darcy looked at him and hated the way her voice squeaked as she said, 'Tonight?'

Max nodded. 'It's a charity gala.' His eyes flicked down over her chainstore dress and he glanced at his watch as he said, 'When we get back to Rome you'll be taken straight to meet with a stylist. She's going to put together a wardrobe for you. And a wedding dress.'

Darcy's hands curled into fists. She was barely aware that they were already on the outskirts of Paris again, heading back to the airport. 'I might have plans for tonight.'

Max looked at her, and there was something distinctly proprietorial in his gaze. 'Any plans you have from now on are *my* plans. And I've been thinking: it'll look better if you move in with me. You should pack a weekend bag for now—we can move the rest of your stuff next week…'

Darcy didn't even bother opening her mouth, knowing resistance was futile. That was it. In the space of twenty-four hours her life had been neatly pulled inside out, and the worst thing was she'd agreed to it all.

CHAPTER FIVE

MAX LOOKED AT his watch again. *Where was she?* He'd meant to go and meet her at the apartment, but he'd been delayed in the office by a conference call to New York, so he'd changed there.

He'd texted Darcy to explain and got back a terse, Fine. See you there.

Max almost smiled; he couldn't imagine many women he knew texting him back like that. His almost-smile faded, though, when he thought of that morning and choosing the ring in Paris, and afterwards when they'd run into that wall of paparazzi.

He could still recall Darcy's jerk of fright and the way she'd burrowed into him instinctively. He'd felt like a heel. He'd totally underestimated how frightening that might be for someone who hadn't experienced it before. He was used to women revelling in the attention, preening, lingering... Darcy had been pale and shaking in the aftermath—not that she'd let it show for too long.

Something in Max's chest tightened. And then she was there, in the doorway of the function room, looking for him. Hair pulled up. One shoulder bare in an assymetrical dress that clung to her breasts, torso, and hips, before falling to the ground in a swirl of black silk and chiffon.

The room fell away, and the ever-present thrum of awareness made his blood sizzle.

How had he ever thought she was unassuming? She was stunning.

He could see her engagement ring from here, the brilliant flash of ice-white, and he pushed down the tightness in his chest. That same sense of protectiveness and possessiveness he'd felt earlier outside the jewellers hit him again, and he pushed that down too. It was nothing. It was the thrill of anticipated triumph over the deal that would finally take him away from that moment on the streets in Rome, when his own peers had seen him shabby and feral. Reduced to nothing.

Her eyes met his and he went forward to meet her.

Darcy saw Max almost as soon as she stopped in the doorway. Of course she did. He stood head and shoulders above most of the crowd. He was wearing a classic black tuxedo and she felt as if someone had hit her right between the eyes.

He'd made some effort to tidy his hair and it was swept back from his face now, dark blond and luxurious, but still with that trademark unruly length. And she could see from here that his jaw was clean-shaven.

In truth, she'd been glad of a little space from Max for the rest of the day—especially now she knew she'd be heading back to his apartment with him that night. She wasn't ready for that at all.

He was cutting a swathe through the crowd, heading straight for her, and—damn it—her breath was short again.

When he got to her he just looked at her for a long moment before slipping a hand across her bare shoulder and around the back of her neck. Her skin sizzled as his head came closer and his mouth—that perfect sensual mouth that rarely smiled—closed over hers.

She wanted to protest—*Stop kissing me!*—even as she knew he was only doing it for the benefit of their audience. But the fact was that every time he kissed her another little piece of her defences around him fell away.

There was nothing but blinding white heat for a second, as the firm contours of Max's mouth moved enticingly over hers, and then a rush of heat swelled all the way up her body from the pulse between her legs.

When he took his mouth away and pulled back she was dizzy, hot. It had been mere seconds. A chaste kiss on the mouth.

Max still had a hand around her neck. He was so close she could smell him, feel his heat around her. It was as if he was cocooning her slightly from the crowd and Darcy was reminded of the shock and vulnerability she'd felt in front of those paparazzi.

She pulled away from him.

'You look...beautiful.'

'You don't have to say that.'

Darcy felt exceedingly self-conscious in the dress the stylist had picked out for her to wear tonight. She glanced up at him from her eyeline, which was roughly around the centre of his chest—she'd been avoiding his gaze till now and his jaw was tight.

'It's not a line, Darcy, I mean it. You look...stunning.'

'I...' She couldn't speak. No man had ever complimented her like this before. She'd never felt *beautiful* before. But for a second, now, she did.

Max took her hand and led her into the throng, stopping to take the glass of champagne offered by a waiter before handing it to Darcy. She took a gulp, glad of the sustenance, aware of the interested looks they were getting—or rather that *she* was getting.

She hated the prickling feeling of being under scrutiny. The crowd in the ballroom of the exclusive Rome hotel was seriously intimidating. This was A-list territory. Actually, this made the A-list look like the B-list. She'd just spotted a European royal and an ex-American president talking together in a corner.

In a bid not to appear nervous, Darcy asked, 'So, what charity is benefiting from this function?'

Max glanced down at her. 'Numerous charities—I've nominated one I run with my brother.'

Darcy looked at Max, wondering again about his relationship with his brother, but she found herself distracted by his clean-shaven jaw and the white line of his scar that gave her a small jolt every time she saw it.

Just then a gong sounded and the crowd started to move into another room.

Max explained, with a cynical tinge to his voice, 'They'll get the charity auction and the posturing out of the way now, so that they can get on with the *really* important stuff.'

Max let go of her hand so she could sit down, and Darcy smiled politely at the man next to her. When Max took the seat next to hers she said, 'You mean the wheeling and dealing? The real reason why people are here?'

He looked at her approvingly. 'I'll make a proper cynic of you yet.'

Darcy felt a little hollow. She didn't need Max to make her a cynic. Her parents' spectacular break-up had gone a long way to that end already. Not to mention this pseudo-engagement.

She thought of something then, and looked at Max.

'You said to Montgomery that we'd be getting married in two weeks?'

He looked at her. 'We will. I've arranged for a special licence.'

Darcy felt as if she was drowning a little. 'Is it really necessary to go that far?'

Max nodded. 'It's just a piece of paper, Darcy. Neither of us really believes in marriage, do we?'

For a moment Darcy wasn't sure *what* she believed. She'd always sworn she'd avoid such a commitment, but she knew deep inside that some small part of her still harboured a wish that it could be different. Buying the ring today had tapped into it. And she hated it that this weakness was becoming evident here, in front of Max, under that gold gaze.

She forced a brittle smile. 'No, of course not. With our histories we'd be mad to expect anything more.' And she needed to remember that—especially when Max's touch and kisses scrambled her brain.

To take her mind off that she looked around and took in the extreme opulence. Even though her parents had always been well off—apart from her father's recessionary blip—she'd never moved in circles like this. Except for her time at Boissy. She grimaced at that memory, wondering if any of her old Boissy classmates were here. It was quite likely. This was definitely their stomping ground. Some of the offspring of Europe's most prominent royal families had been at the school.

The auction started and it was mesmerising. The sheer amounts being bid escalated well into the millions.

After one bid she gasped. 'Did someone *really* just buy an island?' Max's mouth quirked and Darcy immediately felt gauche. 'Don't laugh at me. I haven't been to anything like this before.'

There was a lull after the last few bids and he reached for her hand and lifted it up, turning it so that he could press a kiss to her palm. Darcy's heart-rate accelerated and she tried to pull her hand back, but he wouldn't let go, those eyes unnervingly direct on hers.

Feeling more and more discomfited, she whispered tetchily, 'We need to set some rules for an acceptable amount of PDAs. I wouldn't have thought you were a fan.'

Inwardly, Max reacted to that. Normally he wasn't. *At all*. He hated it when lovers tried to stake some kind of a public claim on him. But every time he touched Darcy he felt her resistance even as she melted against him. It was a potent mix of push and pull, and right now he wanted to touch her.

'You're big on rules and boundaries, aren't you?' He kept her hand in his when she would have pulled away, fascinated by the way colour washed in and out of her face so easily.

Her mouth tightened. 'They're necessary—especially when one is trying to be professional.'

Max chuckled, surprised to find himself enjoying being here with her so much. It had been a long time since he'd seen anyone interested in a charity auction. 'I don't think I need to tell you our professional boundaries are well and truly breached.'

She hissed at him. 'As if I'm not aware of that. Do I need to remind *you* that if it wasn't for this crazy marriage farce I'd be long gone by now?'

Something inside Max went cold. She would be gone because of what had happened in his office that night. He didn't doubt it. But Max knew now that he would have felt compelled to try and persuade her to stay...or to seduce her properly. She'd set a fire alight that night, and a very unwelcome and insidious suspicion occurred to him. Had he on some level wanted to keep her at all costs? Precipitating his flashbulb idea of marrying her?

Panic washed through him and he handed her hand back. 'You're right. We don't want to overdo it—no one would believe it.'

The sudden hurt that lanced Darcy made her suck in a breath. Of course they wouldn't believe it. Because why on earth would someone like Max—a golden god—be with someone like *her*?

She got up jerkily and Max frowned.

'Darcy—wait. I didn't mean it like—'

But she cut him off with a tight smile and muttered something about the bathroom, making her escape.

Everyone was standing up now and moving, starting to go back out to the main ballroom, where a world-famous band were about to play a medley of their greatest hits. She found a blissfully empty bathroom off the main foyer and looked at herself in the mirror with horror.

In spite of Max's cruel words she was flushed, and her eyes looked wide and bright enough to be feverish. Just because he'd held her hand? *Pathetic*.

She ran the cold water and played it over her wrists, as if that could douse the fire in her blood. *Damn Max anyway*. He shouldn't have the power to hurt her.

Sounds came from outside—voices. She quickly dried her hands and left just as some women were coming in on a wave of expensive perfume. They were all chattering, and stopped abruptly as soon as they saw her.

Darcy pinned a smile on her face and tried not to let the fact that they'd obviously been discussing *her* intimidate her.

As she approached the ballroom again Darcy saw Max standing at the main door, hands in his pockets. He looked…magnificent. *Hateful*. Proud. But also apart. Like a lone wolf. *Good*. A man like him didn't deserve friends. And that just made Darcy feel horrible.

He turned around and saw her and she could almost feel the place where the cold water had run on her wrists sizzle.

He frowned as she came closer. 'Are you okay?'

Now she felt silly for rushing off. 'Fine. Needed to go to the bathroom.' She thought a little despondently that his usual lovers probably didn't suffer the mundane bodily functions of mortals—and certainly never mentioned them to him.

He took her arm. 'We're done now. Let's go.'

Suddenly the thought of going back to his apartment with him loomed like a spectre in the dark. Anger at him pierced her, and anger at herself—for letting him hurt her so easily.

A rogue voice made her dig her heels in and say, 'Actually, I'm not ready to go yet.'

He looked at her, not a little stunned. He was not used to people saying no to him.

She tipped up her chin and took a moment of inspiration from the music nearby. 'I like this band. I want to dance.'

Now Max looked horrified. 'Dance?' Clearly he never indulged in such pedestrian activities.

She arched a brow, enjoying needling Max a little. 'Dance, Max. You know—a recreational social activity designed to bring people together in a mutually satisfactory way.'

Clearly angry now, Max moved closer to Darcy and pulled her into his body. 'I can do a "mutually satisfactory" activity, *dolcezza*, if that's what you're looking for—but it's not called dancing.'

Darcy's breath hitched. She should have known better than to tease him. She was serious. 'A dance, Max. That's what I'm talking about.'

He lifted a hand and cupped her jaw, for all the world the besotted fiancé. She cursed. She was playing right into his hands.

'Fine, then. Let's dance.'

Max took her hand in a firm and slightly too tight grip that told her of his irritation and led her onto the dance floor just in time for a slow number. Darcy cursed herself again for opening her big mouth.

He turned and gathered her close and she had to put her arms around his neck. He looked down at her and said mockingly, 'Forgive me. I had no idea you were so eager to make our charade look even more authentic.'

Darcy snorted, and then went still when one of Max's hands moved lower, to just above her buttocks, pressing her even closer. She closed her eyes in frustration for a moment—as if she needed to be reminded that he resented this PDA as much as she did.

And then she felt his hand brush some hair back off her cheek and he said, in a different tone of voice that set off flutters in her belly, 'Darcy, look at me.'

Reluctantly she opened her eyes, far too aware of his lean, hard body pressed against hers.

'I think you misunderstood me before... I meant no one would believe it because I don't usually indulge in any kind of overt affection with lovers in public.'

Darcy hated it that he'd seen her hurt. She shrugged. 'It's cool, Max, you don't have to explain anything.'

Even so, the hurt dissipated like a traitorous little fog.

'The problem is,' he went on, as if she hadn't spoken, 'I can't seem to stop myself from touching you.'

She looked up at him, and they stopped moving on

the dance floor while everyone kept going around them. Max pressed against the small of her back, moving her closer to his body, where she could feel the distinctive thrust of his arousal.

Now he looked intense. 'This is not usual for me, Darcy.'

She was barely aware of where they were any more, and she whispered, 'You think it's usual for me?'

Max started to move again subtly, ratcheting up the tension between them. Panic flared at the thought of going back to his apartment. 'Max, this isn't… We can't do this. We need to keep this pro-professional.'

Great. She was stuttering now. All she knew was that if Max seduced her she wouldn't have anything left to hold him at bay with. He'd already swept through her life like a wrecking ball.

He arched a wicked brow. 'You know what I think of professionalism? It's overrated.'

And then he kissed her, deeply and explicitly, and Darcy knew she was right to fear him—*this*. Because she could feel her very cells dissolving, merging into his. She was losing herself.

She pulled back with effort. '*No*, Max.'

A faster, more upbeat song was playing now, and she and Max were motionless in the middle of the floor. He grabbed her hand and pulled her from the throng. Her legs were like jelly.

Once away from the dance floor Max stopped and turned to Darcy, running a hand through his hair, an intense look on his face.

'Look, Darcy—' He stopped suddenly as something caught his eye over Darcy's head. He cursed volubly and an infinitely hard expression came over his face.

Darcy frowned and looked behind her to see a stunningly beautiful woman in the far corner of the room.

Something pulled at a vague memory. She was wearing a skin-tight black dress that shimmered and clung to her spectacular figure. Dark hair was swept back and up from her high-cheekboned face, and jewels sparkled at her ears and throat.

Darcy's insides cramped a little as she wondered if it was an ex-lover of Max's she'd seen in a magazine.

He was propelling them across the room before she could say anything, and as they got closer she could see that the woman was older than she'd imagined—but incredibly well-preserved.

She was arguing with a tall, handsome man, holding a glass of champagne and gesticulating. The wine was slopping messily onto the ground.

The man looked at Max with visible relief and more than a little irritation. He said curtly, 'I've had enough— you're welcome to her, Roselli.'

The woman whirled around, and just as Darcy noticed with a jolt of shock that she had exactly the same colour eyes as Max he was saying, in a tone tinged with steel, 'Mamma.'

His mother issued a stream of vitriol. Her eyes were unfocused and there was a sheen of perspiration on her face. Her pupils were tiny pinpricks. It was shocking to come face-to-face with Max's mother like this, and it made Darcy's heart clench to think he'd probably only told her half of what she'd been like.

The other man had walked away. Max's mother made as if to go after him but Max let go of Darcy's arm to stop her, taking her glass away and handing it to Darcy. His mother screeched and Darcy could see people looking.

Max had his mother in a firm grip now, and he said to Darcy, 'I'll take her home. If you wait here I'll get my driver to come back for you.'

Darcy was about to agree, but then she said quickly, 'Shouldn't I go with you? It'll look a little odd if I don't.'

Max was clearly reluctant to have Darcy witness this scene—she had a keen sense that he wouldn't allow many, if *any* people to witness it—but he obviously realised she was right.

'Fine, let's go.'

Staff had ordered Max's car to come round and he got into the back with his mother, who was remonstrating volubly with Max now. Darcy got in the front, her nerves jumping. Max was apparently used to this, and was on his phone making a terse call.

When they pulled up outside an exclusive apartment block in a residential part of Rome a man in a suit was waiting. Max introduced him as Dr. Marconi and he came in with them. Once inside a palatial apartment Max and the doctor and his mother disappeared into one of the rooms, with the door firmly closed behind them.

Darcy waited in the foyer, feeling extremely out of place. Max's mother was shouting now, and crying. Darcy could hear Max's voice, low and firm.

The shouting stopped.

After a long while Max re-emerged and Darcy stood up from where she'd been sitting on a gilt-edged chair.

'How is she?'

Max's hair was dishevelled, as if he'd been running his hands through it, and his bow tie was undone. He looked grim. 'I'm sorry you had to witness that. I would have introduced you, but as you could probably tell her response was unlikely to be coherent.'

'You've dealt with this before…?'

Max smiled, but it didn't reach his eyes. 'You could say that. She's a drug addict. And an alcoholic. The man at the party was her latest enabler, but evidently he's had enough. So what'll happen now is she'll enter an exclusive rehab centre, that's got more in common with a five-star resort than a medical facility, and in about a month, when she's detoxed, she'll rise like a phoenix from the ashes and start all over again.'

The other man emerged now, and spoke in low tones to Max before taking his leave after bidding goodnight to Darcy. Max turned to her.

'You should go. My driver is outside. I'm going to wait for a nurse to come and then make sure my mother is settled before I go. I'll see you in the morning.'

Clearly he wanted her to go now. She backed away to the door.

'Goodnight, Max.' She turned back from the door to say impulsively, 'I'm sorry…about your mother. If there's anything I can do…' She trailed off, feeling helpless.

'Thank you,' Max said shortly. 'But it's not your problem. I'll deal with it.'

For a fleeting moment Darcy thought that if this was a real engagement then it would be her problem too. She wondered if a man like Max would ever lean on anyone but himself and felt an almost overwhelming urge to go to him and offer…what?

She left quickly, lest Max see anything of her emotions on her face.

In the car on the way home Darcy had a much keener and bleaker sense of what things must have been like for Max when he'd left Brazil with his mother. The fact that he'd ended up on the streets wasn't so hard to believe now, and the empathy she felt for him was like a heavy weight in her chest.

A few hours later Max sat back in the chair in his dark living room and relished the burn of the whisky as it slid down his throat. He finally felt the tension in his body easing. He'd left his mother sleeping, with a nurse watching over her.

When he'd seen Elisabetta Roselli across the function room earlier tension had gripped him, just as it always did. It was a reflex born of years of her inconsistant mothering. Never knowing what to expect. And even though he was an adult now, and she couldn't affect his life that way any more, his first reaction had been one of intense fear and anxiety. And he hated it.

Darcy… He could still see her face in his mind's eye when she'd turned back from the door, concerned. The fact that she'd handled seeing his mother in that state impacted on him in some deep place he had no wish to explore.

His brother had not had to suffer dealing with the full vagaries of their mother. Max was used to dealing with it on his own… But for a moment, with Darcy looking back at him, he'd actually wanted to reach out and pull her to him, feel her close, wrapping her arms around him…

A soft noise made Max's head jerk up. Darcy stood silhouetted in the doorway of the living room as if conjured right out of his imagination. She was wearing loose sleep pants and a singlet vest that did little to hide those lush heavy breasts, the tiny waist. Her hair was long and tumbled about her shoulders.

'Sorry, I heard a noise…you're back. Is she…your mother…is she okay?'

Max barely heard Darcy. He was so consumed with the sight of her breasts, recalling with a rush of blood to his groin how they'd felt pressed against him on that dance floor.

Damn it to hell. He didn't want to want her. Especially not when he felt so raw after the incident with his mother. But even from across the room her huge blue eyes seemed to see right through him—into him. Right down to the darkest part of him.

It made something twist inside him. A need to push her away, push her back. Avoid her scrutiny.

'Getting into character as my wife already, Darcy? Careful, now—I might believe you're starting to like me. I guess having an addict for a mother is bound to score *some* sympathy points...'

CHAPTER SIX

DARCY IMMEDIATELY PALED in the dim lighting, and Max didn't even have time to regret the words that had come out of his mouth before her eyes were flashing blue sparks.

'I know you're a ruthless bastard, Max, but I've never thought you were unnecessarily cruel. If that's the way this will play out then you can find yourself another convenient wife.'

She whirled around and was almost gone before Max acknowledged the bitter tang of instant remorse and shot up out of his chair, closed the distance between them and grabbed her arm in his hand, stopping her in her tracks.

He cursed and addressed the back of that glossy head. 'Darcy. I'm sorry.'

After a long moment she turned round. She was so tiny in her bare feet, and it reminded him of how she'd fitted against him earlier that day, making him aware of an alien need to protect, to cosset.

Her eyes were huge, wounded. He cursed himself silently. 'I'm sorry,' he said again, aware that he'd probably never uttered those words to anyone.

'You should be.'

Her voice was husky and it had an effect on every nerve-ending in Max's body.

'You didn't deserve that.'

'No, I didn't.'

And then, because it felt like the most natural thing in the world, as well as the most urgent, Max took her other arm and pulled her round to face him. The air crackled between them. He could see Darcy's breasts rise and fall faster with her breathing, and he was so hard he ached.

He dipped his head and pressed his mouth to Darcy's, drawing her up against him. She was as still as a statue for a long moment, as if determined to resist, and then on a small indrawn breath her mouth opened under Max's and the blood roared in his head.

His hands dropped and settled on her waist, over the flimsy fabric of her vest, relishing the contours of her tiny waist. She triggered something very primal in him in a way no other woman ever had.

His tongue stroked into her mouth, finding hers and tangling with it hotly. His erection jerked in his pants in response and he groaned softly.

Darcy tasted like the sweetest nectar on earth, but her small sharp tongue was a pointed reminder that she had an edge. That only fired up his blood even more. She was soft, sweet, malleable...and melting into him like his hottest fantasy.

Max took ruthless advantage, deepening the kiss, his hands gripping her waist, pulling her into him, feeling his aching hardness meet the soft resistance of her body. Her breasts were full, pressing against him, and his hand snaked under her vest, spreading out over her lower back. Her skin was silky and hot to the touch.

Lust such as he'd never experienced had him in a grip so strong he couldn't think beyond obeying this carnal need.

* * *

Darcy was dimly aware of a very distant voice in her head, screaming at her to stop and pull back. Moments ago she'd been blisteringly angry with Max. And hurt. But she didn't care any more. She was in his arms and her world was made up of heat and glorious pounding desire.

Every part of her exulted in his masculinity and his sheer size. Big hands were smoothing up her back, lifting her vest until it snagged under her breasts. He pulled away from her mouth and Darcy sucked in much needed oxygen—but it didn't go to her brain, it seemed only to fuel the hunger in her body.

Max's mouth feathered kisses along her jawbone and down to the sensitive part of her neck just under her ear.

The scent of sex was musky in the air and it was mixed with something very feminine. *Her desire.* Oh, God. She was so weak, but she didn't care any more.

When he pulled back to take her hand in his and lead her over to the sofa she went with him without hesitation. He sat down and guided her over him so that she ended up with her knees either side of his thighs, straddling his lap, his erection a hard ridge between her legs.

Some vital part of her brain had abdicated all responsibility for this situation. It felt dangerously liberating. He was looking at her with such dark intent that she felt dizzy even as her hands were already on his shirt, fumbling with the buttons, eager to explore the wide expanse of his chest.

He said thickly, '*Dio*, I want you so much.'

Darcy couldn't speak. So she bent her head and kissed him again. His hands gripped her waist for a moment before exploring upwards, pulling her vest up and over her breasts, baring them.

He broke the kiss and looked at her, eyes wide, feverish. *'Si bella...'*

He cupped one breast in his hand and squeezed the firm flesh. Darcy bit her lip at the exquisite sensation, and then cried out when he leaned forward and took the straining tip into his mouth, sucking it deep before letting it pop out and then ministering to her other breast with the same attention.

She wasn't even aware that her hips were making subtle circular motions on Max's lap, seeking to assuage the building tension at her core, where the slide of his erection between her legs was a wicked temptation. She only became aware when his hand moved down to her buttocks and held her there. His arousal was thrusting between them, touching her intimately through their clothes. She was pulsating, all over.

A wave of incredible tenderness moved over her as she saw his scar, gleaming white in the low lights. Without thinking Darcy reached out and traced it gently, running her finger down the raised and jagged length. Then she bent to kiss it.

And just as she did so the wave of tenderness finally triggered some faulty self-protection mechanism and she tensed all over, her mouth hovering just over Max's scar.

What the hell was she doing?

He'd just been a complete bastard and yet after a brief apology and a kiss hotter than Hades she was writhing in his lap, about to let emotion overwhelm her! A man who saw her as just a means to an end.

What was even worse was that she'd already seen some pictures online, of them in Paris, outside the jewellers. She looked like a rabbit caught in the headlights, small and chubby next to Max's tall, lean form, clutching at him. It was galling. Mortifying how ill-matched they were.

Darcy scrambled up and off Max's lap so fast she nearly fell backwards. She tugged her vest down over straining breasts.

Max sat forward, his shirt half open, deliciously dishevelled. 'Darcy...what the *hell*?'

Darcy's voice was shaky. 'This is a mistake.'

Every masculine bone in Max's body was crying out for completion, satisfaction. He could barely see straight. He'd been moments away from easing his erection free of confinement, ripping Darcy's clothes off and embedding himself so deeply inside her he'd see stars.

He hated it that she seemed to have more control than him—that she'd been the one to pull back. The rawness he'd felt earlier had returned. He felt exposed.

He stood up in a less than graceful movement, his body still clamouring for release, but he was damned if he was going to admit that to Darcy.

He bit out, 'I don't play games, Darcy, and I don't believe in mistakes. I believe in choices. And you need to be honest with yourself and make one.'

Darcy looked up at him for a long moment and the very thin edges of Max's control threatened to fray completely. But then she took a step back and said in a low voice, 'You're right. I'm sorry. It won't happen again.'

Frustration clawed at Max with talons of steel. That was *not* the answer he'd wanted to hear. As she moved to walk away he reached out and took her arm again, not liking the way she tensed.

'Damn it, Darcy. We both want this.'

She turned her head and looked at him. 'No, Max, we don't.'

She pulled free and walked quickly from the room.

Two weeks later

'I do hope that you haven't put me [...] father. Honestly, if he turns up with [...]

'*Mother*. Please stop.' Darcy tried [...] peration out of her voice. 'You're not [...] you're at opposite ends of the reception [...] *and* the registry office.'

Her mother, as petite as Darcy but über-slim sniffed. 'Well, that's good.'

Darcy sighed. She and Max had agreed that it would look better to have family there, and that they could serve as witnesses. Her parents were as bad each other in different ways: her passionate Italian mother was on a constant quest to find security with ever younger and richer men, and her hopelessly romantic father got his heart broken on a regular basis by a stream of never-ending gold-diggers who saw Tom Lennox coming from a mile away.

She forced a smile at her mother in the mirror, not wanting to invite questions about anything beyond the superficial.

To say that the last two weeks had been a strain was an understatement. Luckily work had kept Darcy busy, preparing for the final reckoning with Montgomery. But the personal tension between Max and her had almost reached breaking point. Even though they'd barely seen each other in his apartment. He worked late most nights, so she was in bed when he returned, and he was gone before her in the morning. And Darcy, of course, had refrained from any more dangerous nocturnal wanderings.

Even now she burned with humiliation when she thought of the concern she'd felt when she'd seen him that night, staring broodingly into his drink. Alone...

ble… *Ha!* The man was about as vulnerable as forced steel.

Darcy was sure that he'd only been in London to meet with Montgomery for the last two days to get away from her, and she hated how that stung.

Since that night in his apartment he'd been cool to the point of icy. And she only had herself to blame. She'd been the weak one. Blowing hot and then cold. Running away because she couldn't handle the thought of Max breaching the final intimacy, afraid of what would happen to her if he did.

No doubt he was used to women who knew what they wanted and went after it—and him. No qualms. No questions. Maybe he'd been seeing one of those women in London, discreetly?

Her mother tugged at the back of her dress now, tutting. 'Honestly, Darcy, why couldn't you have bought a nice *long* dress? This one's more suitable for a cocktail party. This *is* quite likely to be your only wedding day, you know.'

Darcy welcomed the distraction and said fervently, 'I'm counting on it. And it's a registry office wedding, Mother. This dress is perfectly suitable.'

Her mother sniffed and tweaked Darcy's chignon, where a mother of pearl comb held the short veil back from her face. 'Well, I suppose it *is* a nice dress, for all that,' she admitted grudgingly.

Darcy ran a critical eye over herself, feeling slightly disembodied at the thought that she was getting married that day. To Max Fonseca Roselli. The dress was off-white satin, coming to just over her knee. It was a simple sheath design, overlaid with exquisitely delicate lace. It covered her arms and up to her throat.

It's fine, she told herself, hating that the little girl in her still yearned for something long and swirling…romantic.

Wanting to avoid any further scrutiny, she said to her mother, '*You* look gorgeous.'

Her mother preened—predictably. She was indeed stunning, in a dusky pink dress and matching jacket. An exotic fascinator was arranged in her luxurious dark hair, which was piled high.

As she zipped up her dress at the back Darcy referred to her mother's comment about her father. 'It's not as if you haven't brought your own arsenal, Mother.'

Viola Bianci glared at her daughter. 'Javier and I are very much in love.'

Darcy just arched a brow. From what she'd seen of the permatanned Spanish Lothario, he was very much in love with *himself*, but he was obviously enjoying parading the very well preserved and beautiful older woman on his arm. For whatever reason—whether it was love or something less—he was lavishing attention and money on her mother, so Darcy desisted from making any more comments.

Her mother came in front of her now, to pull the veil over her face, but she stopped and looked at Darcy.

'*Carina*…are you sure you're doing the right thing?' Her mother looked slightly discomfited for a moment. 'I mean, after your father and I… Well, our break-up… I always got the impression that you weren't really into marrying *anyone*.'

A familiar impulse to deflect any concern about her rose up, and even though Darcy recognised that it was totally misplaced she put a hand on her mother's arm and said reassuringly, 'Don't worry. I know what I'm doing.'

And she did, she told herself.

Her mother wasn't finished, though. 'But are you in

love with him, Darcy? You might think I don't notice much, but one thing I've always known about you is that you'd never settle for anything less than a lifetime commitment—whether it's through marriage or not.'

Darcy all but gaped at her mother. Since when did Viola Bianci display any perspicacity in looking into her daughter's psyche? It slammed into her gut and made her want to recoil and protect herself. *Lifetime commitment.* Was that really what she wanted? As a result of her experiences? More than a sense of security and a successful career?

Her mouth was opening and closing ineffectually. Finally she croaked, 'I... Well, I do... I mean, I am—'

Just then a knock came on the door and one of the wedding planner's team popped her head round the door. 'It's time to go.'

Saved by the bell—almost literally. As Darcy's mother began to flap, gathering up her personal belongings and Darcy's bouquet, she'd never been so glad for her gnat-like attention span. Clearly she wasn't that concerned about whether Darcy was marrying for true love or not—and frankly that one insight, no matter how erroneous Darcy assured herself it was, was discombobulating enough.

The registry office felt tiny and stifling to Max, but as he was about to ask for the window to be opened he saw that it was already open. He'd been talking to Darcy's father, who was a pleasant affable man, completely preoccupied with his much younger glamorous girlfriend, whom Max had categorised as a gold-digger in seconds. She was busy making eyes at Max whenever Tom Lennox's back was turned.

Max had to curb the urge to scowl at her. She was tall, slim, blonde and undeniably beautiful, but his head was still filled with the way Darcy had felt straddling his lap that night, the size of her tiny waist spanned by his hands. The feel of that hard nipple against his tongue. The scent of her.

Hell. It had been two weeks ago. He was usually hard-pressed to recall any liaison more than twenty-four hours after it had happened. Making love with women was a very pleasurable but transitory thing in his life.

He didn't wake up at night sweating, with the sheets tangled around his aching body like a vise. *He did now.* Which was why he'd been in London for the last two days, putting himself through more unsatisfactorily in-conclusive meetings with Cecil Montgomery.

The man was still insisting that all would be revealed in a week's time. *Damn him.* The one thing easing his frustration was that Montgomery's attitude had definitely changed since Max had announced his marriage to Darcy. Gone was the slightly condescending and derisory tone. There was a new respect that Max couldn't deny.

So this would be worth it. The fact that Darcy was driving him slowly insane would all be worth it.

Max felt a prickling sensation across his skin and looked up just as the few people gathered in the room hushed.

She was here. And he couldn't breathe, seeing how beautiful she looked. It felt as if he hadn't seen her in weeks, not two paltry days.

She stood in the doorway with a woman he assumed to be her mother. But he only saw Darcy. The delicious curves of her body were outlined in a white lace dress. A short veil came to her chin, obscuring her face. But he could make out her huge blue eyes even through the gauzy material and he felt his belly tighten with some-thing like…emotion?

She was doing this for him. A monumental favour. *You're paying her*, pointed out a pragmatic voice. But still... This went above and beyond payment.

It was gratitude he felt. Gratitude that she was doing this for him. That was all.

Her mother moved ahead of her, smiling winsomely at Max, who forced a smile back. But he couldn't take his eyes off Darcy as she came the short distance between the chairs towards him. She held a bouquet of flowers in front of her—not that Max could have said what they were.

And then she was beside him, and he was turning to the front, acutely aware of her body heat and her scent. He felt an urge to reassure her but pushed it down. Darcy knew what this was. She was doing it for her own reasons and because he was paying her handsomely.

He frowned minutely. Why had she asked for that specific amount of money?

'Signor Roselli?'

Max blinked. *Damn.* The registrar repeated the words for Max, which he duly recited, and then he was facing Darcy. He felt slightly dizzy. Rings were exchanged. Darcy's hands were tiny, her fingers cool as they slid the ring onto his finger. Her voice was low, clear. No hesitation.

And then he was lifting her veil back from her face and all he could see was an ocean of blue. And those soft lips, trembling ever so slightly.

'You may kiss your bride.'

He heard the smile in the registrar's voice but he was oblivious as he cupped Darcy's small face between his hands, tipping it up towards him, and bent to kiss her.

Darcy's mouth was still tingling and she had to stop herself from putting her fingers to it, to feel if it was swollen. Her hand was in Max's firm grip, her bouquet in the other hand, as he led her through the foyer of the exclusive Rome hotel and into the dining room where an intimate lunch was being held.

Along with her parents, who had been their witnesses, Max had invited his brother and new sister-in-law, and some business associates from Max's company.

Darcy felt like an absolute fraud, and was not looking forward to being under the inspection of people she didn't know well. Max made her feel so *raw*—and even more so now, after two weeks of minimal contact.

Max turned at the door to the dining room, where their guests were waiting, stopping her. His grip on her hand tightened and compelled her to look up at him. She'd been too wound up to really take him in before now, but his dark grey morning suit along with a silk cravat made him look even more handsome and masculine. He could have stepped out of the nineteenth century. A rake if ever there was one. Even though he was clean-shaven and his unruly hair was tamed. Well, as tamed as it would ever be.

Darcy felt a rogue urge to reach up and run her fingers through it, to muss it up.

'Okay?'

She looked deep into those golden eyes and felt her heart skip a beat. She nodded minutely. Max cupped her face with his hand and rubbed a thumb across her lower lip. Her body clamoured, telling her how much she'd missed his touch.

And then he tensed. Darcy looked to the side to see a tall dark man with possibly the most beautiful woman she'd ever seen in her life. White-blonde hair and piercing ice-blue eyes. But they were warm, and the woman was smiling at Darcy.

Max took his hand away from her jaw and stood straight. She could feel the tension in his form. 'Darcy,

I'd like you to meet Luca Fonseca, my brother, and his wife Serena.'

Max's twin was as tall, and as powerfully built as he was, but much darker, with black hair and dark blue eyes.

Darcy shook hands with both of them and Serena came closer to say, 'Your dress is beautiful.'

Darcy made a small face, feeling completely inadequate in the presence of this goddess. 'I felt less might be more, considering it was a registry office wedding.'

Serena made a sound of commiseration and said, 'My husband and I had a beach wedding, just us and close family, and I can't tell you how relieved I was not to be paraded down some aisle like a wind-up doll.'

Darcy let out a little laugh, surprised that she was so warm and friendly. She felt a pang to realise that she probably wouldn't ever meet her again after this.

A staff member interrupted them to let them know that everyone was ready for Max and Darcy to make their entrance as a married couple. Luca and Serena went inside and Darcy took a deep breath, glad that it was only a handful of guests. Max took her hand and she pasted a bright smile on her face as they walked into a welcome of clapping and cheers.

They were soon separated and caught up in a round of congratulations and chatter. Darcy felt even more like a fraud, aware of Max's tall form on the other side of the room as he spoke to his brother. She felt as if she had '*fake bride*' emblazoned on her forehead.

When there was a lull Serena surprised her by coming over and handing her a glass of champagne.

Darcy took a grateful sip. 'Thanks, I needed that.'

Serena frowned minutely. 'Are you okay? You look a little pale.'

Darcy smiled weakly. 'It's just been a bit of a whirl-wind two weeks.'

Serena was about to say something when her husband Luca appeared at her side and wound his arm posses-sively around her waist. They shared a look so intimate that Darcy felt like a voyeur. And something worse: *envy*.

To Darcy's intense relief a gong sounded then, indi-cating that lunch would be served. She siezed on the ex-cuse to break away and find her seat, and pushed down the gnawing sense of emptiness that had no place here, at a fake wedding.

The tension that gripped Max whenever he saw his brother had eased somewhat by the time they were sip-ping fragrant coffee after lunch. He looked around at the guests at the long table. He and Darcy were at the head and she was leaning towards the man on her left, one of Max's accountants.

This wedding was putting him in pole position to achieve everything he'd ever wanted: the ultimate re-spect among his peers. So why wasn't he feeling a sense of triumph? Why on earth was he preoccupied with his very fake wife and how delectable she looked in her wed-ding dress? How he'd like to peel it bit by bit from that luscious body?

At that moment he spied his brother and his wife, sit-ting halfway down the table. They were side by side and looking at one another with utter absorption. It made something dark twist inside him.

He shouldn't have invited them. All anyone would have to do would be to look at Luca and Serena and re-alise how flimsy the façade of his marriage to Darcy was.

Once again his brother was effortlessly proving Max's lack. And worse was the evidence that whatever blows

Luca had been dealt in his life they hadn't touched some deep part of him, tainting him for ever. For the first time, Max felt more than envy—he felt hollow.

'What is it? You look as if you're about to murder someone.'

The low voice came close to his ear and Max turned his head to see Darcy's face, a small frown between her eyes. He felt exposed—and frustrated. There was a futile sense of rage in his gullet that was old and dark, harking back to that one cataclysmic day in his childhood. Still to be bound by that day was galling.

He acted instinctively—seeking something he couldn't put a name to. Perhaps an antidote to the darkness inside him. An escape from the demons nipping at his heels. He uncurled his hand and put it around Darcy's waist, tugging her into him before claiming her mouth in a kiss that burned like wildfire through his veins.

It didn't bring escape, though. It brought carnal hunger, and a need that only she seemed able to tap into. Incensed that she could do this to him so easily—and here, in front of witnesses—made Max deepen the embrace. He felt rather than heard Darcy's moan as both hands moved around her back.

Eventually some sliver of sanity seemed to pierce the heat haze in his brain and he pulled back. Darcy took a second to open her eyes. Her mouth was pink and swollen, her breasts moving rapidly against him.

And then he saw her come to her senses. Those blue eyes went from hot to cold in seconds and she tried to pull free, but Max didn't let her go, keeping her attention on him.

Darcy couldn't seem to suck enough oxygen into her heaving lungs. When she could, she hissed at Max, 'What the *hell* was that little caveman move?'

She knew damn well that his urge to indulge in that very public display of affection hadn't been entirely inspired by the need to fool their guests, because the look on his face just before he'd kissed her had been dark and haunted. It struck a raw nerve.

She pushed herself free of Max's embrace and stood up.

He stood up too, frowning. 'Where are you going?'

Darcy whispered angrily, 'I'm taking ten minutes' break from this charade—if that's all right with you?'

She forced a poilte smile at their guests, who had now started moving around after lunch, but didn't stop, heading straight for a secluded balcony through an open set of French doors. She needed air. *Now.*

She went and stood at the stone wall and looked out over Rome, basking benignly in the midafternoon sun. It was idyllic, and a million miles from the turmoil in her belly and her head.

Damn Max and his effortless ability to push her buttons. The galling thing was she didn't even know what button he was pushing. She just knew she was angry with him, and she hated feeling like a puppet on a string. This was a mistake. No amount of money was worth this. She'd happily live as a nomad for the rest of her life if she could just be as far away from Max as possible.

Liar.

'Darcy?'

She closed her eyes. No escape.

Darcy turned from the view. It was the thread of concern in his voice that made her glance at him, but his face was unreadable.

She looked at him accusingly. 'Why did you kiss me like that? It wasn't just to put on a show for people.'

'No,' he admitted reluctantly, 'it wasn't just for that.'

A pain that Darcy knew she shouldn't be feeling gripped her when she thought of the anger and frustration she'd sensed in the kiss.

'It's one thing to be wilfully and knowingly used for another's benefit, and to agree to that, but I won't let you take the fact that I'm not the lover you want out on me.'

Max's eyes widened. And then he came in front of her and put his hands on the wall either side of her, caging her in. In a low, fierce voice he said, 'That statement is so far from the truth it's not even funny. The only woman I am remotely interested in is right in front of me.'

Darcy swallowed and tried not to let Max's proximity render her stupid. 'But you were angry...I could feel it.'

Max pushed himself off the wall and ran a hand around his jaw. He stood beside Darcy and looked out at the view. Then he sighed and without looking at her said, 'You're right. I was angry.'

Darcy rested her hip against the wall, her own anger diffusing treacherously. 'Why?'

Max's mouth twitched, but it wasn't a smile. More a reflex. 'My brother, primarily. I saw them—him and his wife...'

Without elaborating Darcy knew exactly what he meant. She'd seen it too. Their almost unbearable intimacy.

Max shrugged and looked down for a moment. 'He gets to me like no one else can. Pushes my buttons. I always feel like I'm just catching up to him, two steps behind.'

Darcy could see it then: the intense hunger Max had to feel he wasn't in competition with his brother any more. Whatever had happened when their parents had split up had marked these two men indelibly.

Feeling tight inside, she said, 'Well, I don't like being used to score a point. Next time find someone else.'

She went to move away, to go back inside, but Max caught her before she could leave with his hands around her waist, holding her fast. His eyes were blazing down into hers.

'I kissed you because I want you, Darcy. If there was anger there at my brother it was forgotten the moment my mouth touched yours. I do not want you to be under any illusions. When I kiss you I know exactly who I'm kissing and why.'

Darcy stared up at him, transfixed by the intensity of his expression.

'*Maledizione.* I can't think when you look at me like that.'

He pulled her closer and Darcy fell against him, unsteady in her shoes. She braced her hands against his chest. He was warm. Hard.

'Max…' Darcy protested weakly—*too* weakly. 'There's no one here to see.'

'Good,' he said silkily. 'Because this is not motivated by any reason other than the fact that I want you.'

One hand cupped the back of Darcy's head and the other was tight around her waist, almost lifting her off her feet. When Max's mouth met hers she was aghast to realise how badly she wanted it, and she met him with a fervour that should have embarrassed her. But it didn't. She wound her arms around his neck, her breasts swelling against his chest.

He backed Darcy into the wall, so it supported her, and their kiss was bruising and desperate. Two weeks of pent-up frustration and denial. Max's hands were on her hips and he gripped her so tightly she wondered dimly if the marks of his fingers would be on her flesh.

Darcy became aware of a noise after a few long seconds of letting Max suck her into a vortex of mindlessness and realised it was someone clearing his throat in a very obvious manner when she pulled back and was mortified to see a staff member—also mortified—waiting for them to come up for air.

Max released her hips from his grip and stood back. His hair was mussed, his tie awry. Darcy felt as if she might float away from the ground, she was so light-headed.

Max turned to face the red-faced staff member, who was obviously eager to pass on his message so he could escape.

'Sorry to disturb you, Signor Roselli, your car is ready when you are.'

The young man left and Darcy looked at Max, feeling stupid. 'Car? Where are we going?'

'The villa—Lake Como—for a long weekend.'

She must have looked as stupid as she felt.

'Our honeymoon?' he said.

Max had informed her a week before that they'd go away for a long weekend after the wedding, just so that everything looked as authentic as possible. She'd completely forgotten. Until now.

And suddenly the thought of a few days alone in a villa with Max was terrifying.

'Surely we can just stay here in Rome? There's so much to prepare for Scotland—' she gabbled.

Max was shaking his head and taking her hand to lead her back inside. 'We're going to Como, Darcy. Non-negotiable.'

He let go of her hand inside the door to the dining room and, as if sensing her growing desire to escape said firmly, 'Say goodbye to your parents, Darcy. I'll meet you in the foyer in an hour.'

She watched, still a little numb, as he strode over to some of the guests to start saying goodbye and felt a looming sense of futility wash over her. A weekend alone in a villa with Max Fonseca Roselli...after that kiss... She didn't stand a chance.

CHAPTER SEVEN

THE JOURNEY TO his private jet passed mainly in silence. Max had been waiting for Darcy in the lobby, as promised, and she'd been aware of every move he'd made in the car. Now, in the jet, he took a seat with graceful athleticism.

As much as she didn't want to attract his attention, it was hard to drag her eyes off him. He'd changed into dark trousers and a dark grey lightweight long-sleeved top that did little to disguise the sheer breadth and power of his chest. The grey of his top seemed to make his eyes burn more intensely, and Darcy looked away quickly, in case she was caught, as the small plane left the ground.

She'd changed too, into a 'going-away' outfit—a soft flowing knee-length sleeveless dress of dark cream with a matching jacket. Her hair was down and her scalp still prickled from the pins that had been holding it up, along with the veil.

She gently massaged her skull and thought of the poignant moment that had caught her unawares when she'd packed the dress and veil away in their boxes. She'd been thinking what a pity it was that she'd never have a daughter to hand it down to.

The stylist had seen her expression and said, 'Don't worry, Signora Roselli, we'll take good care of them for you.'

Hearing *Signora Roselli* had been enough to break her out of that momentary weakness and bring her back to reality. She was only Signora Roselli because Max craved world domination, and she—the fool—was helping him achieve it.

'For a new bride you're surprisingly quiet. Nervous about our wedding night, darling?'

Darcy cursed Max. If there was one mood in which he was pretty much irresistible it was this more playful one that he so rarely displayed.

She glared at him and quirked a brow. 'I wouldn't know—not having much experience of being a new bride, and having even less inclination to be one ever again.'

Max tutted and smiled wolfishly. 'Don't worry, *dolcezza mia*, I'll be gentle with you.'

To Darcy's horror she felt herself getting hot, wondering what it would be like if this was *real* and Max was *really* promising to be gentle. She had an image of him with that intent look on his face as he thrust into her carefully, inch by inch... Between her legs she spasmed, her muscles reacting to her lurid imagination.

Horrified at her wayward body and, worse, at her desire to know what it would be like, she said curtly, 'Save it, Max. I'm not a virgin.'

She looked away when he said, 'So I don't need to be gentle, then? Good, because when we come together—'

Darcy snapped open her seatbelt and stood up, swaying a little as the plane hit some turbulence. She gripped the back of the seat to stay steady and said, 'I'm going to lie down. I'm tired.'

Max caught her wrist as she went past him and when she looked down he was frowning, all humour gone. 'What the hell, Darcy...? I'm just teasing you.'

She pulled her wrist free, already feeling like a prize

idiot to have risen to such easy bait. 'I'm fine. I told you—I'm just tired. It's been a long day.'

She made her way to the small bedroom and slammed the door shut behind her, pressing the backs of her hands to hot cheeks. She cursed herself roundly as she paced back and forth. Of all the stupid— Why had she let Max wind her up like that?

She sat down on the edge of the bed, suddenly weary. Because the truth was that this whole day had got to her much more than she'd ever imagined it would, and his teasing had just highlighted that.

When she'd agreed to this marriage with Max she'd somehow believed that she could do it and remain relatively intact. Unscathed by the man.

But that had all been shot to hell. It had been shot to hell after that night in his office, when the true depth of her attraction to him had become painfully apparent.

Why did he have to find her attractive? This wasn't how the world worked—men like Max did *not* find women like Darcy attractive. She had no doubt that it was an aberration—a freakish anomaly. A desire borne out of the fact that she was so different from his usual type of woman. Stress-induced. Something-induced. But not real.

Her circling thoughts brought her back to one question: why had she followed that crazy instinct to apply for a job working for the man in the first place?

With a heartfelt groan Darcy flopped back onto the bed and shut her eyes, willing sleep to come and make her mind blissfully blank.

A sleek car was waiting for them when they arrived at the small airport just outside Milan. When their bags had been stowed Max sat in the driver's seat and Darcy got into the passenger side. The car was luxurious, and obviously high-end. When Max drove out of the airport it felt as if it was barely skimming the road.

He must have seen something of her appreciation because he said, 'This is the new Falcone road car. I'm friends with Rafaele—he lends me cars to test-drive every now and then.'

Darcy's mouth quirked, even though she was still wary after her outburst earlier. But she couldn't let Max see that he could get to her so easily. 'The perks of being friends with one of the world's most famous car manufacturers?'

Max shrugged lightly, wearing his mantle of privilege easily. Darcy sighed. She couldn't even fault him for that, though. It wasn't as if he hadn't earned it.

'Darcy...' he said carefully. 'What happened earlier—'

She sat up and said quickly, 'It was nothing, really. It's just been a lot to take in.'

Max's hands clenched on the steering wheel and he said after a long moment, 'Do you know I've never really said thank you?'

She looked at him and his jaw was firm. He glanced at her, and then back to the road. 'Thank you, Darcy, for doing this. I don't underestimate how big a favour it is.'

Darcy felt herself weakening, any residual tendrils of anger fading. She knew Max well enough to know that he rarely said thank you unless it really meant something to him.

She was about to say something in response when an insidious suspicion occurred to her and her eyes narrowed on Max, taking in his oh, so benign expression in the half-light of the car. She folded her arms. 'I'm not sleeping with you, Max.'

He glanced at her again and that mocking look was back on his face. 'I wasn't aware I'd asked the question.'

'You don't have to. It's there between us… But I just can't.'

Because you'll hurt me.

Darcy sucked in a breath, the truth finally revealing itself to her. She was in way too deep with Max already. If they slept together his inevitable rejection would crush her. The thought was utterly galling, but it was a fact.

Max's jaw was firm again in the low light of the car. 'I said before that I don't play games, Darcy. It's your choice.' He slid her a darkly wicked look. 'But I won't promise not to try to change your mind.'

In a firm bid to ignore that disturbing promise, Darcy changed the subject. 'Who owns the villa we're going to?'

'A good friend of mine and his family—Dante D'Aquanni.'

'I've heard of him,' Darcy said. 'He's in construction?'

Max nodded, negotiating a hairpin turn by the lake with skill. 'He and his family are living temporarily in Spain while he works on a project.'

'How do you know him?'

Max's hands tightened momentarily on the wheel. 'We go back a long way… He was one of the first clients I had who trusted me to invest his money for him.'

Precluding any further conversation, Max turned into a clearing where huge ornate gates loomed in the dark, with stone walls on either side. When the gates swung open Max drove in and a stunningly beautiful villa was revealed, with stone steps leading up to an impressive porch and door.

Golden light spilled from the doorway when it opened and a housekeeper came bustling out. A younger man joined the old woman who met them and took their bags. Max greeted the housekeeper warmly and introduced Darcy to the woman, who was called Julieta.

The D'Aquannis' housekeeper led them inside, chatting to Max easily, and Darcy guessed he'd been there before. The interior was awe-inspiring, with high ceilings, an impressive staircase, and huge rooms visible off the stone-flagged reception area.

One room, when Darcy peeked into it, seemed to have a blue glass ceiling. Murano glass? she wondered.

Max turned to Darcy after Julieta had offered some refreshments and Darcy seized the opportunity to reply in front of a witness, saying in Italian that she was tired and would like to go to bed. She ignored Max's undoubtedly mocking look.

It was with a feeling of mounting dread, however, as they followed Julieta upstairs, that Darcy wondered if they were going to be shown to one bedroom...

To her abject relief Julieta opened a door, motioning to Max, and then led Darcy to the next door along the wide corridor, opening it to reveal a sumptuous bedroom with en suite bathroom and dressing room.

Julieta bustled off again, after pointing some things out to Darcy and telling her that breakfast would be ready at nine a.m.

Darcy's relief lasted precisely as long as it took for Max to appear in an adjoining doorway, with a wicked glint in his eye.

Arms folded across that broad chest, he leaned gracefully against the doorframe. 'I told Dante about the true nature of our marriage...needless to say I'm regretting that impulse now.'

Darcy put her hands on her hips. 'Well, I'm not. Goodnight, Max.'

Max said musingly, almost as if she hadn't spoken, 'You know, I've never really had to woo a woman before—I'm looking forward to it.'

Her belly exploded as if a hundred butterflies had been set free. Of *course* Max Fonseca Roselli Fonseca had never wooed a woman before, because they always fell into his lap like ripe plums.

She started walking towards the door, prepared to shut it in his face. 'I'll save you the trouble. I'm really not worth it.'

Max's gaze dropped down over her body with explicit directness. 'On the contrary...I think you'll be very worth it.' He stood away from the door then, and said, 'Goodnight, Darcy.'

And then the adjoining door closed in *her* face, before she could make a smart retort, and she looked at it feeling ridiculously deflated, curbing the urge to open it again and follow Max into his room.

What had she expected? That Max would ignore a challenge? She was very afraid that she'd handled this all wrong. Max would accept nothing less than total capitulation, and his tone of voice said that he didn't expect it to take all that long.

Darcy stomped around the thickly carpeted room, getting unpacked and ready for bed, and muttered to herself, 'Do your worst, Roselli. I'm stronger than you think.'

Apparently she wasn't as strong as she thought after all. When she emerged for breakfast the following morning and saw Max sitting at the table which had been set up on a terrace at the back of the villa she immediately felt weak.

She studiously ignored the spectacular view of the lake—she had a very old fear of any expanse of water, no matter how scenic it was.

Max was wearing worn jeans and a dark polo top, his hair dishevelled by the breeze. When he lifted his hand to take a sip from a small coffee cup his well-formed bicep bulged and Darcy went hot all over.

As if sensing her scrutiny, he looked up and smiled. 'Good morning...sleep well?'

She fixed a bright smile on her face and moved forward, avoiding direct eye contact. 'Yes, thank you—like a baby and all people with a clear conscience.'

Max made an *ouch* sound and said dryly, 'Then I hate to inform you that I must be on the side of the angels as I slept well too.'

Darcy snorted inelegantly, helping herself to some pastries and pungent coffee, closing her eyes for a moment to savour the smell. *Heaven.*

When she opened them again it was to find Max giving her a leisurely once-over. His gaze stopped at her breasts and Darcy looked down, aghast to see the hard points of her nipples pushing against the thin material of the light sundress she'd put on, in the absence of anything remotely businesslike.

She resisted the urge to fold her arms over her chest and took her time over eating the delicious pastries and some fruit, avoiding Max studiously. When she did glance at him he seemed fixated on the corner of her mouth, and then he leaned forward to reach out and touch it with his index finger.

When he sat back she saw some jam on it, and he proceeded to lick it off the top of his finger—which had a direct effect on the pulse between Darcy's legs and abruptly made her appetite fade to be replaced by a much earthier one.

Not willing to sit there like a mouse, while Max the predatory cat played with her, Darcy stood up and said briskly, 'I'll find out where the study is, shall I? And check e-mails and—'

Max stood up too and reached for Darcy easily, taking her hand. 'You're doing no such thing. I've got plans for today and they won't be taking place in a study.'

Darcy pulled free and stepped back, panic fluttering along her nerve-endings at the thought of Max devoting all his attention to her. 'I don't mind. We should really make sure that—'

Suddenly Max dipped out of sight and Darcy's world was upended. She found herself in his arms, clinging onto his neck in fright.

'What the hell—?' she got out in a choked voice.

But Max was saying something to Julieta over her head about being back later for dinner. The woman smiled at them benevolently, as if she saw this kind of thing all the time. It made Darcy wonder about the owners.

Max finally let her down once they were outside, in order to open the passenger door of the car. Darcy tried to make a dash for it, back to the villa, but he wound an arm around her waist, practically lifting her into the passenger seat.

Darcy fumed as she watched him come around the front of the car, his eyes on hers warning her not to defy him again. When he swung in and quickly locked the doors from the inside Darcy sputtered, 'This is tantamount to kidnap...and you're blatantly taking advantage of my size... You're a...a *sizeist*!'

Max was already driving smoothly out of the villa and he looked at her with dark amusement and said, 'I have to admit that your...portability makes you a little easier to control.'

Darcy made a strangled sound of outrage and crossed her arms over her chest, glaring out of the window as Max drove away from the villa. Damn him and his superior strength.

But while she hated the ease with which he was able to compel her to do his bidding all she could think about was how it had felt to be held so securely in his arms—how her instinct had been to burrow closer and seek a kind of refuge she'd never felt like seeking before. The fact that she could be as susceptible as the next woman to Max's caveman antics was not welcome.

Darcy only recognised where they were when she saw the signs for Milano. She turned to Max and said eagerly, 'You've come to your senses and we're going back to Rome to work?'

He quirked a half-smile. 'No. I'm taking you out.'

Out *where*, though? Darcy looked at him suspiciously but he gave nothing away.

And then he said, 'Apart from my very serious intention to get you into my bed, it'll be good for us to be seen together the weekend after our marriage. We *are* meant to be on honeymoon, after all.'

Darcy had no answer for that. He was right.

They parked in a private and exclusive car park with valet parking and emerged onto a busy Milan street that was bustling with weekend activity.

It was like a fashion parade, with beautiful women walking up and down—some with the requisite small dogs—and beautiful men... A little too metrosexual for Darcy, but then this was the fashion capital of Italy and arguably Europe. Predictably, Max stood out among these beautiful people and there were plenty of heads turning in recognition and appreciation.

After all, Darcy recalled, hadn't the Italians invented a word for walking around in order to be seen? *Passeggiata?*

Max took Darcy's hand in his and led her down the

street. She wanted to pull away, but as if reading her mind he held on tight. Veering off to a small side street, Max ducked into a boutique with a world-famous designer's name over the door.

He was greeted like a superstar—and as a regular, Darcy noted with a dart of something dark. But before she could emit so much as a squeak she was whisked away behind a curtain and Max was left out in the foyer. At one stage she caught a glimpse of him sipping coffee and reading a newspaper.

She was completely bemused as industrious assistants flitted around her like exotic butterflies. Finally fitted into a stunning bodycon cocktail dress—a bit *too* bodycon for Darcy's taste—she was all but pushed back out onto the main salon floor. She realised she was being paraded for Max's benefit when he lowered his paper and looked her over as if she were a brood mare.

Anger started down low and then rose through her body in a tidal wave of heat and humiliation. She hissed at him, 'What the *hell* is this?'

His eyes snapped to hers. 'I'm taking you shopping.'

'I don't need any more clothes.'

Max looked nonplussed for a moment, as if he literally could not compute Darcy's reaction. It would have been funny if she hadn't been so angry. And what was making her even angrier was the evidence that this was obviously a regular occurrence for him...bringing women shopping.

So angry that she couldn't see straight, and feeling seriously constricted in the dress, she went straight to the door and walked out, almost tripping in the ridiculous heels. She was halfway down the street, with steam coming out of her ears, before Max caught up with her, standing in front of her to block her way easily.

'What the hell was *that*?'

'Exactly. What the hell *was* that? I thought you said you weren't used to wooing women? Does taking them shopping not count as wooing? Because evidently you do it a lot, going by your familiarity with those assistants in that shop—and quite a few others, I'd imagine.'

Max threw his hands up in the air. 'What woman doesn't love shopping?'

Darcy pointed a finger at herself. 'This one.' Then she folded her arms, her eyes narrowed on him. 'Maybe you consider taking women shopping as foreplay?'

They glowered at each other for a long moment, and then Max sighed deeply and put his hands on his hips. Eventually he muttered something like, 'Should have known better...'

Darcy put a hand behind her ear. 'Sorry? What was that?'

Max looked at her and his mouth twitched ever so slightly. He said, with exaggerated precision, 'I'm sorry for assuming you would want to go shopping. I should have known better.'

Darcy's own mouth was tempted to twitch, but she curbed the urge. 'Yes, you should. And I can't breathe in this dress.'

Max's gold gaze dropped and took her in, and then he said roughly, 'I don't think *I* can breathe with you in that dress.'

Immediately Darcy's brain started to overheat and she was in danger of forgetting why she was angry.

Max put out his hand. 'Come on—let's take it back.'

With her hand in his, walking back down the street, Darcy felt a little foolish for storming out like a petulant child. That wasn't her. She winced. But it *was* her around Max. He just wound her up. After all, he'd only been doing what he'd thought would make her happy.

She squeezed his hand and he looked at her just before they got to the shop. 'I'm sorry. I just… I'm not that into shopping. It's not that I'm not grateful.'

Max gave her a wry grin. 'I didn't exactly go about it with any finesse. Come on.'

He pushed the door open and a very sheepish Darcy walked in behind him, mortified under the speculative gazes of the staff.

When she was dressed in her own clothes she breathed a sigh of relief, and when she was out in the main part of the shop again she spied a bright, colourful scarf and took it to the till.

Immediately Max was there to pay for it. Darcy glared at him, but he ignored her and she sighed. When they were outside she tucked the scarf into her bag and he looked at her expressively. Feeling defensive, she said, 'Well, I felt like I had to buy *something*!'

Max rolled his eyes and said dryly, 'Believe me, those saleswomen are like piranhas.'

Darcy sniffed. 'I just felt bad, that's all.'

Max took her hand and Darcy glanced up. He was looking at her with a funny expression on his face. 'You've got a good heart, Darcy Lennox.'

She snorted, but inwardly fluttered. 'Hardly.'

And then, just as they were passing another boutique— much smaller but no less exclusive—Darcy stopped in her tracks. The dress in the window was exquisite—off the shoulder, deep royal blue satin, with a scooped neck and a boned bodice that would accentuate an hourglass figure.

When Darcy realised what she was doing she grew hot with embarrassment and went to keep walking, but Max stopped her, an incredulous look on his face.

'And you call *me* mercurial?'

Darcy smiled weakly. 'I didn't say I *hate* shopping.

I'm like a heat-seeking missile—once I see what I want I go for it and then get out again.'

'*Do* you want it?' he asked.

Darcy squirmed. 'Well...I like it...' She looked at it wistfully.

Max pulled her into the shop and this time paced the small space while she tried the dress on, together with suitable underwear and shoes.

The assistant stood back and said appreciatively, *'Bella figura, signora.'*

Max appeared at the dressing room door, clearly a little bored. When his eyes widened Darcy's heart-rate zoomed skywards.

'Is it okay?' she asked shyly. And then she babbled, 'You know, I probably do need a dress for the Montgomerys' party, so...'

'We'll take it.' Max's voice sounded slightly constricted.

Once Max had arranged for the dress and sundries to be sent to his office in Rome they left again. Darcy had tried to pay for the dress but of course he hadn't let her.

Back out in the sunshine, he looked at her and said, almost warily, 'What now?'

Darcy looked around, enjoying seeing Max knocked slightly off his confident stride. 'Well, first I want some gelato...'

Max's eyes boggled. 'After you've just bought that dress?' And then he shook his head. *'Incredibile.'*

Smiling now, he took her hand and pressed a kiss to the palm. Darcy looked around surreptitiously for paparazzi, but couldn't see any obvious cameras pointed at them.

'And after the gelato?'

She screwed up her nose and thought. 'Well, I've never seen *The Last Supper* by Leonardo Da Vinci, so that'd be nice, and I'd like to walk on the roof of the Duomo and see if we can see the Alps.' Darcy looked at Max. 'What about you?'

Max blinked. What about *him*? No one had ever asked him before what *he'd* like to do. And the fact that he'd assumed for a second that he could just take Darcy shopping— He shook his head mentally now at his lack of forethought. But he hadn't been thinking—he'd just wanted to get them out of the villa before she could lock herself in the study.

Clearly, though, he'd underestimated her and would need to be far more inventive. For the first time in a long time Max felt the thrill of a challenge and something else—something almost...*light*.

'Do you know what I'd like?'

She shook her head.

'To go and see the AC Milan game.'

Darcy looked at her watch and then said impishly, 'Well, then, you're going to have your work cut out making sure we fit it all in, aren't you?'

'That last goal...' Darcy shook her head and trailed off.

Max glanced at her, sitting in the passenger seat. They were almost back at the villa and he couldn't remember a day he'd enjoyed as much.

They'd stood before one of the great artworks of the world and then climbed to the top of a magnificent cathedral to see the spectacular view. They hadn't seen the snowy Alps through the heat haze that hung over the city, much to Darcy's disappointment, and it had made Max feel an absurd urge to fix that for her. And they'd been to a football match. He *never* got to go to see his favourite team play. He was always too busy.

He teased Darcy. 'So you're a fan of AC Milan now?'

She looked at him and grinned. 'I could get used to it. I never realised football was so gladiatorial. My father's a rugby man, so I grew up being dragged to rugby matches. Whatever country we were in I found it was a way of orientating myself, because we moved around so much.'

Max found himself thinking of something that had nagged at him, and asked curiously, 'Does that have anything to do with the very specific amount of money you requested?'

Darcy went still, but then she wrinkled her nose and said lightly, 'Isn't it a little crass to talk about money with your fake wife?'

Max shook his head. 'You're not avoiding the question so easily. You should have asked for a different amount. Ever heard of rounding up?'

Darcy scowled, making Max even more determined to know what the money was for. He would have given it to her in bonuses anyway, but the fact that she'd asked for it...

She sighed, and then said, 'When my folks split up they sold the family home. They never really settled again. I went to boarding school, my dad was travelling all over the world, and my mother was wherever her newest lover was. When my father's business fell apart and I went back to the UK to a comprehensive school it was my most settled time—even if we were living out of a cheap hotel.'

She shrugged.

'I've just always wished that I had somewhere... somewhere that I knew would always be there.' She let some hair slip forward, covering her face, and muttered, 'It's silly, really. I mean, lots of people don't have a home at all—'

Max reached out and put his hand over hers. 'It's not silly.'

He couldn't say any more because he knew exactly what Darcy was talking about. He'd never had that safe centre either.

He took his hand away to change gears. 'So, the money—it's for a house?'

Darcy nodded and smiled, not looking at him. 'It's a small flat in London. I've been keeping my eye on it for a few months now.'

Max could see Darcy all too easily—stepping out of a cute little flat on a leafy street, getting on with her life, disappearing into the throng of people. And he wasn't sure he liked it at all. In fact, if he wasn't mistaken, the flare of dark heat in his gut felt suspiciously like jealousy.

When Darcy had freshened up and changed into comfortable loose trousers and a silk top she went downstairs to dinner. It was set up on the terrace, in the lingering twilight. Flickering candles lent everything a golden glow and the opulent rugs and furnishings made her wonder about the couple who were lucky enough to own this idyll. Did they have a happy marriage? Somehow, Darcy thought they must, because there was an air of quiet peace about the place.

And then she shook herself mentally. She wasn't usually prone to such flights of the imagination.

Max wasn't there yet and she breathed a sigh of relief, going to the stone wall and looking out over the dark expanse of the lake at the lights coming on on the other side.

Even here, far away from the water, she felt it like a malevolent presence and shuddered lightly.

'Cold?'

Darcy whirled around, her heart leaping into her throat, to see Max holding out a glass of wine. She took it quickly, ducking her head. 'No, I'm fine...just a ghost walking over my grave.'

She sneaked a look at him as he stood beside her. He'd changed too, into dark trousers and a white shirt which inevitably made his dark skin stand out even more. He oozed casual elegance, and yet with that undeniable masculine edge that made him all man.

The day they'd spent together had passed in an enjoyable blur of sights and sounds, but mostly Max had been a revelation. Darcy had never seen him so relaxed or easygoing. As if a weight had been lifted off his shoulders.

At the football match he'd been like a little boy—jumping up and down with the crowd, embracing her and the man next to him when his team scored. Also spouting language that had shocked her when things hadn't gone well.

Julieta and the young man who it had turned out was her grandson delivered their dinner: fragrant plates of pasta to start, and then a main course of tender pork in a traditional sundried tomato, prosciutto and sage sauce.

Darcy groaned appreciatively when she tasted the delicious pork and said wryly, 'I may have to be rolled out of here in a couple of days.'

Max looked at her, and his gaze running over her curves told her exactly what he thought of that. Unused to being appreciated for what she normally considered to be a drawback, she avoided his eye again. A part of her still couldn't really believe he wanted her, but all day he'd touched her with subtle intention, keeping her on a knife-edge of desire.

In a bid to try and pierce this bubble of intimacy that surrounded them on the terrace, with the sound of the lake lapping not far away, Darcy asked about the couple who owned the house. 'I just wondered what they're like. This seems to be a happy place.'

Max pushed his empty plate away and then stood up, saying, 'I'll show you a picture.'

He returned a couple of minutes later with a beaming Julieta, who was dusting a picture with her apron. She handed it to Darcy. It showed an insanely handsome dark man, smiling widely, with a very petite blonde woman whose hair was a mass of crazy curls. She was also grinning, and holding a young boy with dark hair by the hand, while the man held a toddler high in his arms—a little girl with dark curly hair, a thumb stuck firmly in her mouth, eyes huge.

Something lanced Darcy deep down. This was a picture of familial happiness that she only knew as a distant dream. And who was to say that they wouldn't split up, with those poor children destined to spend a lifetime torn between two parents?

Aghast that she was even thinking of this in the face of such evident joy, she handed the picture back quickly with a fixed smile. 'They're lovely.'

Julieta took the picture away, carefully cleaning it again. She obviously missed them. She must be more like a member of the family than a housekeeper to them, Darcy guessed.

Max said into the silence, 'Perhaps not everyone goes through what we experienced.'

Darcy looked at him, wondering why she was surprised he'd read her mind. It seemed to be a speciality of his. 'Do you really believe that?'

He smiled and shook his head. 'Personally? No. But I have to admit that Dante and Alicia seem very...happy.' And then he asked abruptly, 'Why did you step in that day? During the fight?'

Darcy knew immediately that Max was referring to what she'd witnessed at Boissy, when she'd intervened. The memory of how exposed she'd felt after doing it made her squirm now. 'I can't believe you remember that.'

Max's mouth tipped up at one corner. 'It was pretty memorable. You single-handedly scared off three guys who were all easily three times your size.'

Max took her hand in his and hers looked tiny. It made her too aware of their inherent differences.

She shrugged. 'I just…saw them…and I didn't really think, to be honest.' She bit her tongue to stop herself from revealing that she'd used to watch Max far too intently, far too aware of his presence. Aware of the insolence he'd worn like a shield.

Afraid that he might see it, she deflected the conversation back onto him.

'You and your brother…do you think you'll ever be close?'

Darcy thought he'd pull his hand away, but he left it there, holding hers.

Quietly, he said, 'We used to be close. Before we were separated. Closer than anyone.' He looked at Darcy and smiled. 'We had a special language. It used to drive our parents crazy.' And then the smile faded. 'Luca was stronger than me, though…older by a few minutes. When our parents told us they were taking one each he just stood there—not crying, not saying anything. I'll never forget it.' Max's mouth twisted. 'I was the one that fell apart.'

Darcy turned her hand in Max's and gripped it. A sense of rage at his parents filled her, shocking in its intensity. 'You were little more than a baby, Max…'

Just then Julieta appeared, with a coffee pot on a tray, and Darcy blinked up at her, broken out of the web of intimacy that had come down over her and Max without her even realising it. Suddenly she felt very raw, and absurdly emotional. The full impact of the day was hitting her. She was in danger of losing herself out here with Max.

Acting on impulse, she seized the opportunity like a coward, pulling her hand back from Max's, avoiding his eye. She stood up, smiled, and said, 'No coffee for me, thanks—it's been a long day.'

Unfortunately she couldn't quite manage to leave at the same time as Julieta because Max had caught her wrist. Darcy looked down and her heart skipped a beat. To her intense relief his expression indicated nothing of their recent conversation. He looked altogether far too sexy and dangerous. Far too reminiscent of that younger Max—cocky and confident, but still human underneath it all.

He smiled, and it was the smile of a shark. 'You're not willing to concede defeat yet?'

Darcy shook her head and struggled against the blood that pounded in her veins. 'No, Max, I still don't think it's a good idea.'

To her surprise he let her go and leaned forward to pour himself some coffee. '*Buonanotte*, then, Darcy...'

Feeling unsure, because she didn't trust Max an inch, Darcy sidled around him to get to the doorway.

And then she heard him say softly, 'It's better that you go to bed now because you'll need your sleep. I'll be waking you early in the morning. I've got more plans for tomorrow.'

She looked at him suspiciously. 'What are you talking about?'

He just smiled and said, 'You'll see.'

Darcy started to speak. 'Look, Max—'

He speared her a look that told her in no uncertain

terms that he was hanging on to his control by a thread and that if she stayed a moment longer he wouldn't be responsible for his actions.

'Goodnight, Darcy. Go to bed while you still can… or it won't be alone.'

She had the sense not to ask anything else and fled.

CHAPTER EIGHT

'LEMME ALONE. IT'S the middle of the night.' Darcy burrowed back into the bed as deep as she could, but big firm hands reached in determinedly and ripped the covers back.

She squealed, wide awake now, and looked at Max looming over her, in the *very* early morning gloom.

'*Buongiorno, mia moglie.*' My wife.

Darcy scowled, feeling thoroughly disgruntled and aware that she was in just skimpy pants and a vest top.

She scrabbled for a sheet but Max insisted on pulling it back again, saying briskly, 'Now, I can dress you, or you can dress yourself—it's up to you. I've laid some clothes out for you.'

There was enough light in the room for a squinting Darcy to see that Max was wide awake, dressed casually, and that those mesmerising eyes were making a very thorough and leisurely appraisal of her body.

Then he said throatily, '*If,* on the other hand, you'd prefer to stay in bed, I won't object.'

Her body jumped with anticipation but she ignored it and scrambled off the bed, reaching for a robe. 'I'm up.' She rounded on him, saying grumpily, 'And I can dress myself.'

Max made a considering noise. 'Not a morning person? I'll make a note to prepare myself for that in the future.'

'It'd be more accurate to say not a middle of the night person,' Darcy snapped.

Max was thankfully backing away, and he glanced at his watch, saying, 'Downstairs in fifteen minutes. We've time for a quick breakfast.'

Darcy grumbled about arrogant bossy men as she washed and got dressed in jeans and a pretty silk long-sleeved top, shoving her feet into flat shoes.

She didn't like to admit that her defences still felt a little battered after yesterday and their intimate supper last night. She'd had disturbing dreams of small boys clinging onto each other as unseen hands forced them apart, and of bright red blood on pristine snow.

When she went down she was surprised to see Julieta up and about, greeting her with a cheery hello. She showed her to a covered part of the terrace at the back of the villa, clearly in deference to the fact that only the faintest trails of dawn could be seen in the sky, like delicate pink ribbons.

Max was drinking coffee. He looked at her and stood to pull out a chair.

Darcy felt exposed, with her freshly scrubbed face and her hair tied back in a ponytail. She valiantly tried to ignore Max and picked at a croissant and some fruit, still feeling fuzzy from sleep.

'You're not going to tell me where we're going, are you?'

Max shook his head cheerfully. 'It's a surprise.'

Darcy was already reacting to the prospect of another day in close proximity to Max... Her body was humming with energy.

She pushed her plate back, having no appetite this

early, and said, 'I suppose now is as good a time as any to tell you I hate surprises?'

She did, too, having learnt long ago that they were usually of the very unwelcome variety—more often than not something promised by one or other of her parents to assuage their guilt or to compensate for their absence at some event or other.

Hence carving out a steady, dependable career for herself, where no surprises would jump out to get her.

Until she'd agreed to this ridiculous charade.

Max stood up and put down his napkin. 'You'll like it—I promise. Ready?'

Darcy looked up and sighed inwardly at the determination stamped on his face. 'I don't have much choice, do I?'

He shook his head. 'Not unless you want me to put you over my shoulder and carry you out.'

Darcy had no doubt that Max wouldn't hesitate to put her over his shoulder—after all, he'd picked her up as if she was a bag of flour yesterday.

She stood up with as much grace as she could muster and said witheringly, 'You don't have to demonstrate your he-man capabilities again. I can walk.'

They drove a relatively short distance to a big flat open field, with several low buildings inside the gates. Max parked the car alongside some other vehicles and got out.

When she met him in front of the car, thoroughly bemused, he handed her something. 'Here, you'll need this—it might be a bit chilly.'

She took the fleece and guessed it must belong to the lady of the villa, because it fitted her perfectly and she'd looked to be about as petite as Darcy—if not smaller. Darcy zipped it up, suddenly glad of the extra layer against Max's far too intense perusal.

He'd put on a fleece too, and now took a basket from the boot of the car. Determined not to give Max the satisfaction of knowing how curious she was, Darcy just followed him around one of the low hangar-like buildings—and then stopped in her tracks and gasped out loud.

As she took in the significance of the scene in front of her she could feel the last of her defences crumble to dust. And, absurdly, tears pricked her eyes.

Max had stopped and was looking at her, the picture of innocence. Darcy curled her hands into fists at her sides and glared at him, willing the emotion to stay down.

In a husky voice she said, 'Of all the low-down, dirty, manipulative things to do, Max Fonseca Roselli...this just proves how cold-hearted you are.'

It was a hot air balloon, on its side, being inflated by a crew.

And it was on her bucket list.

One night, while working late in the office in that first couple of months, Darcy had asked Max idly about what might be on *his* bucket list—because what could someone who had nearly everything possibly want?

He'd given her a typical non-answer, in true evasive Max style. And then he'd asked her what was on hers. She'd replied, with some measure of embarrassment, that she'd always wanted to take a hot air balloon ride.

And now he was giving it to her.

Emotion tightened her chest.

Max just looked amused. 'You don't want to go?'

She glared at him. 'Of *course* I want to go.'

She folded her arms across her chest, hating it that he could make her *feel* so much, wanting to extract some kind of payment.

'But I'm not going anywhere until you tell me what's on *your* bucket list. And I want a proper answer this time.'

Max's expression hardened. 'I don't have a bucket list. This is ridiculous, Darcy. We'll miss the best part of the sunrise if we don't move now.'

She could see the balloon, lifting into the air behind Max. She tapped her foot. Waiting...

He sighed deeply and ran a hand through his hair impatiently. 'Nothing with you comes easy, does it?'

'No.' She smiled sweetly, feeling some measure of satisfaction to be annoying him—especially when he'd hauled her out of bed so early.

'Okay, I'll tell you—but you're not to laugh.'

Darcy shook her head and said seriously, 'I promise I won't.'

Max looked up, as if committing his soul somewhere—or hers, more likely—and then down again, and said in a rush, 'I want to own a football club.'

He'd said it like a young boy, blurting something out before he could lose his nerve, and Darcy's chest squeezed even tighter.

She pushed the emotion down and nodded once. 'Thank you. Now we can go,' she said.

Once she felt on a more even keel with Max she was like a child, with the full excitement of what he'd organised for her—whatever his motive—finally hitting her.

They were helped into the basket alongside the pilot, and then suddenly they were lifting off the ground and into the clear dawn-streaked sky. Darcy wrapped her hands tight around the basket's edge, eyes wide at the way the ground dropped away beneath them.

It was pure terror and exhilaration. Max stood beside her as the pilot edged them higher and higher, but she couldn't look at him, too afraid of what he might see on her face.

Time and time again her father had promised to do

this with her and it had never happened. And now she was here with her husband. Except he wasn't really her husband.

Emotions twisted like a ball in her gut and she took a deep breath.

Max's hand covered hers. 'Okay?'

When she felt more in control she looked at him and smiled. 'Perfect.'

The balloon made lazy progress over the spectacular countryside, with the pilot pointing out Lake Como and the other lakes. Far in the distance they saw the snowy tips of the Alps. Milan was a dark blur in the distance as they passed over fields and agricultural lands.

Darcy was entranced. When the gas wasn't firing, to propel the balloon higher, she thought she'd never experienced such peace and solitude.

When she could, she tore her eyes from the view and looked at Max. 'Is this your first time in a balloon too?'

He nodded and smiled, leaning one elbow on the basket-edge. Darcy had the uncomfortable sensation that he'd been looking at her and not the view. And she hated it that she was relieved he hadn't done this with anyone else.

She teased him now. 'You're not twitching at being so far from communication and Montgomery?'

Max lifted his phone out of his pocket and held it up to show that it had no bars of service, then put it back. 'Nope.'

He sounded inordinately cheerful about the fact, and Darcy marvelled again at this far more relaxed Max.

The view filled her eyes so much that it almost hurt as the sky got lighter and lighter, exploding into shades of vivid pink and red as the sun came up over the Alps in the distance.

She didn't notice that Max had been doing anything until he produced a glass of sparkling wine for her and another for himself. He offered one to the pilot, who smiled but declined.

Max clinked his glass off hers and then the view was blotted out as his mouth came over hers and she fell deep into a spinning vortex that had only a little bit to do with the fact that they were suspended above the earth in a floating balloon.

Only their mouths were touching, but Darcy felt as if his hands were moving over her naked flesh. When Max pulled back she had to grip the edge of the basket tight, afraid she might just float off into the sky altogether. She was telling herself desperately that it had only been for the benefit of the pilot. To keep up appearances.

She took a sip of the wine and the bubbles exploded down her throat and into her belly. She couldn't be more intoxicated right now than if she'd drunk three bottles in quick succession.

They sipped their wine and gazed over the view in companionable silence. Every now and then the pilot pointed something out, or Max asked him a question about the balloon's mechanics.

Darcy hadn't even realised she was shivering lightly until Max came and took her empty glass and moved behind her, wrapping his arms around her, his hands over hers.

She settled into the hard cocoon of his body far too easily. Stripped bare by the experience. His fingers entwined with hers and his head bent and he feathered a hot kiss to her exposed neck. She shivered again, but this time it wasn't because of the cold.

They stood like that for a long time, and then the pilot said something low to Max and she felt him take in a breath behind her. Even though she knew what he was going to say, she didn't want it to end.

'We have to turn back… The air is starting to warm up…'

Darcy was glad he couldn't see her face. Tears stung her eyes but she said lightly, 'Okay.'

The ride back seemed to pass in a flash, and all too soon they were descending and the ground was rushing to meet them. They landed with a soft thud and a small bounce before the crew grabbed the basket and held it upright while they got out.

Max got out first and then lifted Darcy into his arms. For a moment he didn't put her down. Something in his eyes held her captive. And then she realised they had an audience and she blushed and scrambled down.

She went to the pilot and pressed an impetuous kiss to his cheek. 'I know you must be used to it—but, truly, that was magical. Thank you.'

The man looked pleased, but embarrassed, and said gruffly, 'You never get used to it. *Grazie*, Signora Roselli.'

Max took her by the hand, and as they walked to the car Darcy was aware that she'd made a decision. It was as if the balloon ride's unique perspective on the earth had shown her an eagle eye view of just how fragile life looked from above…how silly she was being not to reach out and grab precious moments, no matter how finite they might be.

The thought of continuing to deny herself after what she'd just experienced made her feel panicky—as if something incredibly precious might slip out of her grasp for ever. She didn't care about the consequences.

Max stopped at the car and faced her. He had a look of resolute determination on his face. 'Ready for the next part of the surprise?'

Darcy looked at him. She wouldn't put it past him to have organised something like a trip to Venice for the day... But she shook her head and said clearly, 'No more surprises.'

A range of expressions crossed Max's face: irritation, disappointment, renewed determination...

She took a breath. 'I don't mean what you think I mean. I'm wooed, Max. I don't even really care if that balloon ride was a purely cynical move on your part, I loved it too much and thank you for planning it. And I'm done fighting you. I want you. Take me back to the villa.'

Max wasn't sure how he drove in a straight line back to the villa. He kept Darcy's hand in his and the journey was made in silence, with the mounting anticipation coursing through his body saturating the air between them.

When he glanced at Darcy he could see a similar kind of tension on her small face and it only made his blood flow hotter. *Dio.* He wanted this woman so badly. More than he'd ever wanted anything.

Some kind of warning prickled over his skin at that assertion, but he ignored it.

She'd accused him of being cynical in his decision to organise the hot air balloon ride and he might have been...before. But he'd only thought of it the previous day, when they'd stood on the roof of the Duomo in Milan and she'd been disappointed not to see the Alps.

Max had remembered Dante talking about taking a hot air balloon ride with his family and seeing the Alps, and at the same time Max had recalled Darcy mentioning it some months ago.

In truth, the experience had moved him far more profoundly than he would ever have expected. He'd never seen the earth from above like that when not encased in a plane, with stacks of facts and figures in front of him, hurtling towards yet another meeting to shore up his funds, his reputation. That had all felt dangerously inconsequential when floating soundlessly through the sky.

Max was aware of the fact that this marriage to Darcy was not proceeding at all the way he might have expected when he'd first proposed the idea...the means to his end were veering way off the track. But right now he couldn't care less. All he cared about was Darcy and the fact that she would be *his*.

When they got back to the villa it was early afternoon. Darcy knew she should be feeling hungry because she hadn't had much breakfast, but she was only hungry for one thing: Max. Now that she'd decided to stop fighting him—and herself—the full extent of her desire was unleashed and it was fearsome.

He held her hand as they went into the villa and Julieta greeted them, clearly surprised to see them back early— evidently Max *had* had more plans for the day, but Darcy was too keyed up to care what they might have been.

She heard him say to Julieta that she could take the rest of the weekend off if there were some provisions in the kitchen. The housekeeper only lived in the gate lodge nearby, but still Darcy's face burned with embarrassment, as if it was glaringly obvious what they intended to do.

But the woman took her leave cheerfully, after extracting a promise that they'd ring if they needed anything. Evidently she was used to such instructions.

Once she was gone, and the villa had fallen silent around them, Darcy looked at Max. Within seconds she was in his arms, their mouths fused, desperation clawing up from somewhere...the deepest, hottest part of her.

After long, drugging kisses and shedding outer layers they broke apart, and Max said gutturally, 'I'm not taking you here in the hall.'

Before she could object he'd picked her up in his arms, taken the stairs two at a time and shouldered his way into his bedroom. Sunlight streamed in the window and bathed Max in a golden glow. Never more so than now had he looked so awe-inspiring, and Darcy had to push down the quiver of self-doubt that he really desired her at all.

He put her on her feet and reached behind him to pull his top over his head. His chest was bare and right in front of her face. Wide and muscled. Lean. Dark golden hair dusting the surface.

Darcy wasn't sure if she was breathing—but she was still upright, so she must be. She reached out a tentative hand and touched him, hearing his indrawn breath as her nail scraped a nipple.

He cupped her jaw and tipped her chin up. Dark colour slashed his cheekbones. She could see the question in his eyes and was surprised—she'd have expected him to take ruthless advantage of her acquiescence, giving her no time to change her mind.

To stop the rise of dangerous emotions, and before he could say anything, she put her hand over his mouth. 'I know who you are, I know who I am, and I know what I want—and that's you.'

She felt shaky. That was about as close as she could get to telling Max that she was perfectly aware that he'd move on once he'd had her but she was okay with that. If she didn't want him so badly right now she might hate herself for grinding her self-respect into the dust.

The question faded from Max's eyes and he put his hands to the bottom of her top, lifting it up. She raised her arms and it slipped up and over her head. Next Max pulled free the band holding her hair, so that it feathered down over her shoulders.

His gaze dropped to the swells of her breasts, encased in lace. *'Bella...'* His voice was thick.

Darcy reached around behind her and undid her bra, letting it slip to the floor. She groaned softly when Max reverently cupped her breasts, pushing the voluptuous mounds together, rough thumbs making her nipples spring to attention, tight with need. She'd never felt so grateful for her curves as she did right then.

Her hands were busy on his jeans, undoing the top button. Warm flesh and his hard lower belly contracted against her fingers. It was heady to know she could do this to him.

He'd lowered his head and was exploring her with his hot mouth, his wicked tongue flicking against her breasts, learning the shape of her and the way her flesh quivered and tightened at his touch.

Darcy's hands were clumsy as she ripped free buttons and felt the potent hard bulge of him against her knuckles. Eventually she was able to push down his jeans over lean hips, but then she had to stop because Max had one of her nipples between his teeth, teasing it gently before letting it go to suck the fleeting pain away.

Her legs wouldn't hold her up any more and she fell back onto the bed. Max stood tall, his chest moving rapidly with his breath. He pushed his jeans down the rest of the way, and then his briefs, and Darcy's eyes widened on his impressive erection.

Her mouth watered, and when Max bent over to undo her jeans and pull them down she lifted her hips to help him. She felt only mounting impatience as he looked her over with possessive heat, pulling her panties off to join her jeans on the floor. No teenage crush could have prepared her for this reality. She felt as if she was burning up from the inside out as her hungry gaze roved over Max's perfect form, every muscle hard and honed.

A broad chest tapered down to lean hips, where his masculinity was long and thick, cradled between his strong thighs, long legs. He truly was a warrior from another time.

The ache between her own legs intensified and she widened them in a tacit plea, not even really aware of what she was doing, knowing only that she craved this man deep in her core—*now.*

Max cursed softly and reached into his bedside console for something. Protection. He smoothed it onto his length and then came down over Darcy, an arm under her back, arching her up, mouths fused, tongues duelling. Her breasts were crushed against his chest and she was arching into him, begging…

Max pulled away for a second. 'I need you, Darcy… The first time I can't do slow.'

She felt as if she was caught in the grip of something elemental. 'I don't want slow. I need you too—*now.*'

For an infinitesimal moment everything seemed to be suspended, and then he thrust into her in one smooth move, so deep that Darcy gasped, and her back arched at this invasion of her flesh, ready as she was.

Max stopped. '*Dio*…have I hurt you? You're so small…'

'No,' said Darcy fiercely, wrapping her legs around him as far as they'd go. 'Don't stop…'

The initial sting of pain was fading. She'd never felt so stretched, so full. And as Max moved his big body in and out she felt a deep sense of peace bloom and grow within her even as intense excitement built and built, until all her muscles were shaking with the effort it took to hold on against the rising storm.

Max put a hand between them, unerringly finding her centre and touching her there. 'You first, Darcy... then I'll fall...'

Darcy looked deep into his eyes, locked onto them tight as she finally relinquished her control to this man and fell so hard and so fast that she blacked out for a moment. She only came back to her dulled senses when Max's heavy body slumped over hers, their breathing harsh and ragged in the quiet room.

When the sky was tinged with the dying rays of the sun outside they made love again. Slowly, taking the time to learn everything they hadn't had time to do the first time around. Hands slipped and glided, squeezed and gripped. Max's fingers explored, feeling the telltale slickness between Darcy's legs, needing no more encouragement. He wrapped his hand around the back of Darcy's thigh and lifted it so that he could deepen his thrust into her body. He groaned with sheer pleasure that she held him so snugly.

She smoothed back the hair from his forehead, her hands gripping his shoulders, urging him on. It was a long, slow dance, building and building to a crescendo that broke over them, taking Max by surprise with its intensity.

When he had the strength to move he scooped Darcy against his front, with her knees drawn up so her buttocks were cupped in his lap. Wrapping his arms tight around her, he felt his mind blank of anything but a delicious feeling of satisfaction, and slipped into oblivion.

When Darcy woke it was dark outside. She had no sense of time or space for a disorientating moment, not recognising the room she was in. And then she moved, and winced as muscles—intimate muscles—protested.

Max. His big body thrusting so deep that she'd been unable to hold back a hoarse cry of pleasure... It all rushed back. The desperation of that first coupling, followed by that lengthy, luxurious exploration. Her skin felt sensitive, tenderised.

She sat up now, looking around the moonlit room. No sounds from the bathroom. Moving to the side of the bed, Darcy stood up, wincing slightly again, and reached for the robe left on the end of the bed.

She opened the door and immediately a mouth-watering smell hit her nostrils. She followed it instinctively, realising just how hungry she was as she stumbled to a halt in the doorway of the kitchen.

Max was stirring something in a pot, humming tunelessly, wearing low slung sweat pants and a T-shirt.

'Hey...' Darcy hovered at the door, feeling ridiculously self-conscious.

Max turned around and looked her over, those dark eyes gleaming with something she couldn't read.

'Ciao.'

Darcy came further in. 'What time is it?'

'About three in the morning. You must be starving.'

There was a very wicked gleam in Max's eyes and Darcy fought back an urge to poke her tongue out at that and at his far too smug look. She was ravenous. Not that she'd admit it.

She shrugged a shoulder, feigning nonchalance. 'A little, I guess.'

'Liar,' Max said easily, and came around the kitchen island to scoop her up against him and kiss away any faux nonchalance for good.

He let her go and walked back around to the pot.

Darcy was dizzy. 'What are you cooking?' she managed to get out over her palpitating heart. That kiss had told her that they were nowhere near finished with this mutual...whatever it was...

'Pasta with *funghi porcini* in a creamy white wine sauce.'

Max had dished up the pasta now, into two bowls, and was bringing them over to a rustic table. He brought over some bread, and a bottle of wine and two glasses.

Darcy came over, mouth watering. When she took a bite the *al dente* pasta and its flavours exploded on her tongue. It all felt incredibly decadent—as if this were some kind of illicit midnight feast.

After finishing her pasta, Darcy took a long luxurious sip of wine and asked idly, 'So what was the other part of the surprise that we missed today?'

Max sat back, cradling his own glass of wine, and smirked at her. 'I don't think you deserve to know.'

Darcy dipped her fingers in her water glass and flicked some at him. 'That's *so* unfair.' She mock pouted. 'I put out before you even had to go through with it.'

Max gave her a considering look full of mischief. 'That's true. If I'd known how easy it would be—'

Now Darcy scooped up a much larger handful of water and threw it at him. An incredible lightness infused her as Max put down his glass and smiled devilishly at her. He still managed to look gorgeous, even as water dripped down his face and onto his chest.

He picked up his own glass of water and looked at her explicitly.

She gasped and got up from her chair, inching away from him. 'You wouldn't dare...'

But he would. Of course he would.

Max stood up and advanced on her as Darcy fled behind the kitchen island.

'Max, stop—we're adults, and this isn't our kitchen.'

She was attempting to sound reasonable, but the breathiness in her voice gave her away.

He raised a brow. 'It's only water, Darcy. Now, come here like a good girl. You can't tease me and expect to get away with it.'

Darcy crept around the island as Max followed her and eyed where the door was. When she made her move, feinting left before going towards the door, Max caught her with pathetic ease, grabbing her robe and pulling her into him.

He captured her hands with one of his and pulled her up against him. She caught fire. He was walking her backwards towards the huge table, and illicit excitement leapt in Darcy's blood. She didn't *play* like this. And she suspected Max didn't either. It was heady.

The back of the table hit her buttocks and Max nudged her until she was sitting on it. He still held the full glass of water over her and he said in a rough voice, 'Open your robe.'

A sliver of self-consciousness pricked her. 'Max...' she said weakly.

'Open it, Darcy, or I'll open it for you.'

With far less reluctance than she should have been feeling Darcy undid the tie on her robe and it fell open, exposing her upper body. Max smiled, and it was wicked. His eyes had turned dark and golden.

Darcy felt so hot she feared bursting into flames there and then. It was hard to breathe.

Very slowly and deliberately he tipped the glass over her, until a small stream of icy water trickled down over her chest and breasts. She gasped and tensed, and was almost surprised when the water didn't hiss on contact with her hot skin.

Her nipples pebbled into tight peaks under Max's torturously slow administration, and when she was thoroughly drenched, with water running down over her belly and between her legs to where she was hottest of all, he put down the glass and pushed her robe back further, baring her completely.

He braced himself with his hands either side of her body, holding the robe back, keeping her captive. His gaze devoured her and he bent and dipped his head, his hot tongue a startling contrast to the cold water on her skin as he teased and tormented her breasts, tasting them and sucking each hard tip into his mouth until Darcy cried out and begged him to stop.

He lifted his head and smiled the smile of a master sorceror. 'We haven't even started, *dolcezza*... Lie back on the table.'

Unable to stay upright anyway, Darcy sank back and felt Max's big body push her legs wide, coming between them, baring her to him utterly.

He pressed kisses down her body, over the soft swell of her belly, and his big hands kept her open to him as his mouth descended between her legs and he found the scorching centre of her being. He stroked and licked her with sinful precision, until her hands were clasped in his hair and she was bucking uncontrollably into his mouth...

Later, when they'd made it back to the bedroom, they made love again. And again.

Darcy lifted her head from Max's chest and asked sleepily, 'So, will you tell me now?'

Max huffed a small chuckle. 'I should have known you wouldn't forget.'

Darcy rested her chin on her hand and said, 'Well...?'

Max shifted then, and she could tell he was mildly uncomfortable. But he said, 'I had arranged to take you to Venice... We were going to do a gondola ride and stay the night in a hotel on the Grand Canal.'

He lifted his head then, and looked at her with an endearingly rueful expression—very *un*Max-like.

'It would have been the worst kind of cliché, wouldn't it?'

Darcy's heart twisted painfully. 'Yes,' she whispered, 'but it would have been lovely.'

And then she ducked her head and feigned falling asleep, because she was terrified to admit to herself just how completely Max had seduced her.

CHAPTER NINE

THE FOLLOWING MORNING Darcy woke to an insistent prodding that was becoming more and more intimate as a hand smoothed down over her bare backside and squeezed firmly. She smiled and wriggled, hoping to entice the hand into further exploration, but instead it delivered a short, sharp *thwack*.

She raised her head from the pillow, blinking in the daylight. *Max*. Looking thoroughly gorgeous and disreputable with a growth of stubble. And he was dressed.

'What was that for?'

His hand smoothed where he'd slapped her so playfully. 'That was to get you up and out of bed... I want to take you out on the lake.'

At the word *lake* Darcy went very still. That big body of water that she'd avoided looking at—probably the only person on the planet who didn't enjoy the splendour of Lake Como.

She flipped over and held the sheet to her breasts. Max was already leaning back, tugging it out of her hand, but she held on with a death grip and tried to say, as breezily as possible, 'I'm quite tired, actually... Why don't you go? You can tell me how it was when you get back.'

Max stopped and his gaze narrowed on her. *Damn*.

'Why don't you want to go on the lake, Darcy? I've noticed that you barely look at it.'

She avoided his eye and sat up, feeling at a disadvantage lying down, and plucked at the sheet. 'I have issues with water. I can't swim.'

Carefully, Max said, 'You know, some fishermen can't swim—because they believe that if the sea claims them it's meant to be. It doesn't stop them going out on the water.'

Sensing that Max had no intention of going anywhere until she explained herself, she sighed deeply and said, 'I nearly drowned as a child. We had a pool at our house and my father was teaching me how to swim. My mother appeared and they started having a row. He got out to argue with her, forgetting about me… I don't know what happened… One minute I was okay and the next I couldn't feel the bottom any more and I'd started to drop like a stone. I must have drifted from the shallow end. They were so busy arguing, and I couldn't get their attention. All I could see was their arms gesticulating and then everything went black, there was a pain in my chest—'

Darcy hadn't even realised that she was bordering on hyperventilation until Max put a hand over hers, his fingers twining around hers to make her loosen her grip on the sheet.

'Darcy, it's okay—just breathe…'

She took a deep breath and looked at Max. 'That's why I don't want to go on the lake.'

He looked as if he was considering something, and then he said, 'Do you trust me?'

'Of course not,' she said facetiously.

Max rolled his eyes. 'I mean, would you trust me not to let any harm come to you?'

Physically…yes. Emotionally…no.

Damn. Darcy realised it as the heavy weight of inevitability hit her. She was falling for him. She was a disgrace to womankind. One hot air balloon ride and even hotter sex and she was—

'Okay?'

She blinked at Max, not having heard a word he'd said over the revelation banging around in her head like a warning klaxon going off after the fire had started and the horse had bolted.

'What?'

He said, with extreme patience, 'I want to take you somewhere and I promise you won't have to do anything you don't want to—okay?'

Right now even a lake was preferable to sitting alone with this new knowledge. 'Okay...'

And that was how she found herself, a few hours later, in a swimsuit, shivering with fear by the side of a kiddies' pool at a local adventure centre that Max said was owned by Dante D'Aquanni. A child ran past her and cannonballed into the pool.

Max was standing waist-deep in the water and saying, 'Look, I promise you'll be able to touch the bottom. Come on.'

Not even his body was helping to distract her right now.

'Sit on the edge and come in bit by bit.'

More because she didn't want to look like a total fool in front of Max than anything else, she gingerly sat down on the edge and put her legs in the water. Immediately she started shaking, remembering how the water had sucked her down.

But Max had his hands on her waist and she gripped his arms.

Slowly, and with far more patience than she would have ever credited him with having, Max gently coaxed

Darcy until she was standing in the water. Once she knew she could touch the bottom, he persuaded her to let him pull her along while she kicked her legs.

At one point she saw Max send a glower in the direction of some sniggering kids, but she didn't care.

And then he turned her on her back, which she only agreed to because he kept his arms underneath her. He was talking to her, telling her something, instructing her to kick her feet, and she was just getting comfortable with the feeling of floating when he said, 'Darcy?'

'Hmm?' It was nice, floating like this.

'Look.'

She lifted her head and saw Max with his hands in the air. It took a second for the fact that she was floating unaided to compute, and when it did she started to sink. But just as her head was about to go under she was caught, standing with her feet firmly on the bottom and Max holding her.

She was breathing rapidly and he was making soothing noises.

'I can't…can't be—believe you just let me go.'

'You were totally fine—you'll be swimming in no time.'

Darcy looked up at Max and her heart turned over. The pool was empty now, and she moved closer to him until their bodies were touching.

'I know one way of taking my mind off things…'

She reached up and wrapped her arms around Max's neck, moaning her satisfaction when his mouth came down on hers. Then he was lifting her, and she was wrapping her legs around his waist as he sat her down on the side of the pool and proceeded to do very adult things— until the discreet coughing of a staff member forced them apart like guilty teenagers.

* * *

Much later that night, after Darcy had shown Max her gratitude for helping her to start overcoming her fear of water in a very imaginative way, using her mouth to drive him over the edge of his control, Max couldn't sleep.

His body was still humming with pleasure...but not yet with the full sense of satisfaction that he usually felt after he'd bedded a woman. The sense of satisfaction that led to a feeling of restlessness and usually preceded his moving on.

Okay, so he knew he couldn't move on because he and Darcy were married—whether for real or not, they'd gone way over the boundaries of pretence now. But was that it? *No.* He'd be feeling this way if he and Darcy had started an affair anyway...and that revelation was disturbing.

No woman kept a hold over Max beyond the initial conquest. If he continued a liaison it was usually because it served some purpose not remotely romantic.

But things had escalated with Darcy so fast that his head felt as if it was spinning. She'd made him work for it, but it hadn't really been game-playing. And the final capitulation... It hadn't been sweet—it had been fast and furious and intense.

Even now he knew that if she was to turn to him he'd be ready to take her again and again. And tomorrow all over again.

He cursed softly and got out of bed and went downstairs, raiding Dante's drinks cabinet for some of his fine whisky. He went out to the terrace, where the sound of the lake lapping against the shore should have been calming, but instead Max was remembering the look of stark terror on Darcy's face as he'd had to coax her into the pool.

Inferno. Since when did he mess about in paddling pools, teaching someone to swim? Yet he couldn't deny the sheer pleasure he'd taken from seeing her face lose its dread in the pool.

It had given him a kind of satisfaction that he usually reserved for each pinnacle he conquered on his way to the ultimate acceptance and respect in business. Which he still hadn't attained.

A shiver of something cold crawled up Max's spine—a memory…crying, feeling as though his guts were going to fall out of his body, his legs shaking…his mother gripping him. *'Stop snivelling. I'm taking you with me.'*

He'd told Darcy practically everything. More than he'd ever told anyone else.

He went even colder and realised that he wasn't even sure he recognised himself any more. Who *was* this person who made impromptu wedding proposals? Who chased a woman around a kitchen with a glass of water?

The memory made Max cringe now.

He'd let emotion get in the way once before and had paid the price.

Another more pertinent memory came back: the day he'd seen his old nemesis while he'd been foraging in that bin in Paris. It was one of those moments in life when the fates had literally laughed in his face just to torture him.

One of them had come back and handed Max a five-euro note. Max had taken it and ripped it up, before letting it drop to the ground and spitting on it.

He hadn't needed anyone then, and he didn't need anyone now. He knew better than anybody how life could be as fickle and as random as a pair of dice rolling to a stop, dictating the future.

But he'd changed that. The power to dictate everything lay with *him*.

He'd fought for this control over his destiny and he was damned if he was going to let it slip out of his grasp now just because he was forgetting where his priorities lay. Anger licked through his blood at the knowledge of just how far off course he was in danger of straying.

Darcy was distracting him.

And he was fogetting the most important thing: *She was just a means to an end.*

The following morning, on the plane ride home, Darcy didn't need to be psychic to know that something had changed during the night. Max was back in ruthless boss mode. Brusque. Abrupt.

He'd already been up when she'd woken, dressed and packed.

She'd felt flustered. 'You should have woken me.'

He'd been cool. 'I have some work to catch up on in Dante's study. We'll leave in half an hour.'

She couldn't fault Max for wanting to jump straight back into things—after all Montgomery's party was right around the corner, sealing the deal... But it was almost as if he had just carved out these few days to seduce Darcy and now it was mission accomplished and he was moving on.

She'd expected this. But she hadn't expected it to be quite so brutally obvious.

Was it a dream or had this man gripped her hips so hard last night that she still bore the marks of his fingers on her flesh? Had she imagined that he'd held her ruthlessly still so that he could thrust up into her body over and over again, until she'd been begging for mercy, and only then finally tipped them both over the edge?

No, because she'd seen the marks in the mirror in the bathroom and her muscles still ached pleasurably.

Darcy felt a little shattered—as if the pieces that Max

had rent asunder deep inside her would never come back together again.

Maybe he was regretting the weekend…realising that it had all been a huge mistake. Realising that she hadn't been worth all that effort…the shopping, the hot air balloon… But even if he was, she wasn't going to regret it. She'd made her choice.

'Darcy?'

She looked at Max, who was frowning impatiently. 'I need you to take some notes—we'll be going straight to the office from the airport.'

Ignoring the voices screaming at her to leave it alone, Darcy turned to him and said, 'So that's it, then? Honeymoon over. Back to work.'

Max looked at her and she shivered.

'What did you expect?'

'All that seduction…the hot air balloon…'

Max shrugged. 'You knew I wanted you in my bed—whatever it took.'

Incredible pain lanced her. 'I see.'

For a moment Darcy thought she might be sick, but she forced it down. She had to get away from Max. She hated it that she wasn't strong enough to weather the evidence of his ruthlessness in front of him.

She unbuckled her belt quickly and stood up, muttering something about the bathroom. Once locked inside the small space she saw her face in the mirror, leached of colour.

Stupid, stupid Darcy. How could she have forgotten that this man's two main traits were being ruthless and being more ruthless. He must have been laughing himself silly when Darcy had all but begged him to go to bed after his *piéce de résistance*: the balloon ride. It would be tainted in her head for ever now.

She thought of the pool then, of Max's patience and gentle coaxing, and this time she couldn't stop the contents of her stomach from lurching up.

When she'd composed herself she looked at herself in the mirror again. She had to get a grip. She'd lost herself for a moment and she'd done it willingly—her hands held tightly onto the sink—but it had only been for a moment. A weekend. She was okay. She could put this momentary weakness behind her and get on with things, and as soon as the ink was dry on the deal with Montgomery she'd be gone.

When they returned to Max's apartment after going into the office Max disappeared into his study to do some more work. Darcy took herself out for a long walk around the centre of Rome, coming back with no sense of peace in her head or her heart.

She was feeling increasingly angry with herself for giving in to his smooth seduction, having known what it was likely to do to her.

He was still working when she returned, so she ate alone and went to bed, telling herself that the ache she felt was just her pathetic imagination.

After midnight, just when she was hovering on the edge of sleep, Max came into her room.

'This isn't my room.'

Darcy came up on one elbow, anger rising. 'No, it's *my* room.'

'So why aren't you in my bed?'

'Because,' Darcy said tersely, well and truly awake now, 'I don't care for the hot and cold routine, and you've made it perfectly clear that now we've consummated the relationship you're done with any niceties.'

Max came close to the bed and Darcy hated the way her blood sizzled with anticipation.

'I never said I was *nice*, Darcy,' he pointed out. 'Are you going to come to my bed?'

'No,' Darcy said mutinously.

Max just shrugged and left, and Darcy let out a shaky sigh of...*disappointment*. She lambasted herself. She was pathetic. And then her mouth dropped open when Max walked back in with a bunch of clothes and some toiletries.

She watched, dumbounded, as he proceeded to strip and get into the bed beside her. He leaned on one elbow, unselfconsciously naked in the way that only the most gorgeous people could be, and those tawny eyes glinted with pure devilment.

'The honeymoon is over, but this isn't.'

He reached for her and Darcy had a split second to realise that she could take the moral high ground and resist Max's arrogant pull or, as she asked herself belligerently, why shouldn't she use Max as he was using her? Take her own pleasure from him until *she* was sated?

That was the weak logic she used, anyway, as she hurled herself back into the fire.

When she woke in the morning and all those little voices were ready to rip her to shreds for her weakness she resolutely ignored them and told herself she could do this. Max didn't have the monopoly on being cold and ruthless.

As the days progressed, getting closer to the time they'd be leaving for Scotland, their working hours got longer. And in the nights...the passion between them seemed to burn brighter and fiercer with each coupling. Darcy's anger with herself and Max added something that seemed to hurl her over the edge further and further each time, until she was left spent and shaking.

Some nights Max seemed to forget what part he was playing, and he'd scoop her close and hold her to him with arms like vises around her. It was on those nights that Darcy knew she was fooling herself the most.

This game she was playing with Max *was* costing her. She knew that she wasn't strong enough emotionally to keep it up indefinitely, and that it would have to stop before she got burned in the fire completely.

But just not right now...

The Montgomery estate, north of Inverness

Darcy huffed out a breath and stopped to look at the view. It was spectacular, and it soothed some of the tension inside her. Hills and mountains stretched as far as the eye could see, and small lochs were dotted here and there like black pools. Clouds scudded across the blue sky.

In true Scottish fashion, even though it was summer, it had rained since they'd arrived, a couple of days ago. But now the sun was out and the countryside sparkled.

Darcy was relishing a rare chance to be alone. She'd had enough of Max's tense mood infecting her own.

Wily old Montgomery was playing hard to get right to the end. The party was tonight, and Max still wasn't sure where he stood. To make things even worse, there were several other high-profile financiers invited. Darcy almost felt sorry for Max—but then she thought of the sensual torture he'd put her through the previous night and promptly felt *un*sorry for him.

She sat down on a piece of soft springy ground and sighed, pushing her hair back off her hot cheeks. Here against this timeless and peaceful backdrop she couldn't keep running from her own conscience and her heart.

In spite of everything, she'd fallen for Max. Self-disgust that she should fall for someone so ruthless and single-minded took the edge off the awful tendency she felt to cry. And yet her bruised heart still pathetically wanted to believe that the Max she'd seen that weekend in Como was real...

One thing Darcy *did* know was that Max fooled himself as much as everyone around him. He had feelings, all right, but they were so buried after years of hiding them that it would be like mining for diamonds trying to extract them.

She knew why her instinct had always warned her off deeper commitment if this was the pain it brought.

But she couldn't continue with the status quo. It was a form of self-destruction that Darcy knew she had to stop now—he'd worn her down and broken her apart like the pro he was, and she couldn't let it continue.

Max wasn't going to like it, but he'd get over it. He'd have to, because nothing would compel her to change her mind. Not even his singular seduction.

That night Darcy felt jittery, and Max said beside her, 'Stop fidgeting.'

She sent him a dark look. She had her arm tucked into his, for all the world the happy newly married couple.

Mrs Montgomery had come up to Darcy earlier and said confidentially, 'Why, he's a new man, my dear. He was always so *brooding* before.'

Darcy had smiled weakly and looked to see Max throwing his head back and laughing at something his companion said. Her gut had twisted. *Was* he different?

And then she'd clamped down on that very dangerous line of thought.

She was wearing the royal blue satin dress she'd seen in the window of the boutique that day in Milan. When she'd spotted it hanging in her wardrobe in Max's apartment it had given her a jolt as she'd recalled a much more light-hearted Max.

She hadn't wanted to wear it, but he'd insisted. And the look in his eyes when she'd put it on had been nearly enough to make her skin sizzle.

He'd growled, 'If we weren't already late for dinner I'd lock the door to this room, make you take it off, make love to you and then make you put it on again... But I'd probably only want to take it off again...'

A voice had wheedled in Darcy's head—*What's one more night...?*—and she'd shut it out. She couldn't afford one more night with Max.

The crowd was making a toast now, to Cecil Montgomery, his smiling wife and their four children and assorted grandchildren. Darcy's heart constricted. Happiness was there for some people. The very few.

She felt Max tense beside her. Time for the announcement.

Montgomery started by going into a long-winded account of his career, clearly building up to the big moment. Darcy bit her lip and looked at Max, but his face was expressionless.

'As many of you will know, it's been my life's work to cultivate, protect and grow the famous private equity fund of this family that goes back generations. It's my legacy to my children and grandchildren—not to mention our very important philanthropic work...'

Montgomery cleared his throat and kept going.

'As we all know in these uncertain times, expert advice is necessary to ensure the growth and protection of anything of importance. And this fund is not just my life's work, but my ancestors'. It's been of the utmost importance that I choose someone who has those sensibilities in mind. Who understands the importance of family and legacy...for the benefit of not only my own family but also much larger concerns.'

He paused dramatically and then took a breath.

'There is only one person I would trust with this great responsibility, and I'm pleased to announce that that man is...Maximiliano Fonseca Roselli.'

Darcy could feel the surge of emotion in Max's body. He shook with it. She waited for him to turn and acknowledge her, as much for appearances' sake as anything else, but after a moment he just disengaged her arm from his and strode forward to accept Montgomery's handshake and congratulations.

Darcy could see people looking at her. It was as brutal a sign of where she really stood in his life as a slap in the face, and she realised then that all along she'd been harbouring some kind of pathetic hope that perhaps she was mistaken and he *did* feel *something* for her.

Seeing the crowd lining up to congratulate Max, Darcy took advantage of the moment to slip out of the room and walk blindly through the castle, eyes blurred but refusing to let the tears well and fall.

She would not cry over this man. She would *not*.

Max cursed silently. Where *was* she? He knew Darcy was petite, but he'd realised that somehow he had an uncanny knack of finding her glossy dark brown head in any crowd. He thought of her as she'd stood before him in the bedroom not long ago, the deep blue of the satin dress curving around her body in such a way that it had made him feel animalistic. He'd almost forgotten what the evening was about. *Almost.*

Lingering tendrils of relief and triumph had snaked through him as he'd forged his way through the throng, accepting congratulations and slaps on the back. Funny, he'd expected to bask in this moment for a lot longer, but he was distracted.

Darcy. Where was she?

She'd been standing beside him when Montgomery had called out his name and his first instinct had been to turn to her. She'd done this with him. He wouldn't have done it without her. *He'd wanted to share it with her.*

The surge of alien emotion that had gripped him had caught him right in his throat and at the back of his eyes, making them sting. Horrorstruck, in a nano-second he'd been aware that he was on the verge of tears and about to let Darcy see it. So at the last second he'd pulled away and strode forward. Not wanting her to see the rawness he was feeling. Not ready for the scrutiny of those huge blue eyes that saw too much.

He cursed again. She wasn't here. A quick tour of the surrounding rooms didn't reveal her either, and Max made his way to the bedroom with a growing sense of unease.

When he opened the door to the bedroom the sense of unease coalesced into a black mass in his gut. Darcy barely looked up when he walked in. She'd changed into black trousers and a stripy top. Her hair was pulled back into a ponytail. She looked about sixteen. She was packing her suitcase.

Max folded his arms, as if that might ease the constriction in his chest.

'What are you doing?'

She glanced at him, her face expressionless. 'I'm leaving.'

Seizing on his default mechanism of acerbity, Max drawled, 'I think I could have deduced that much.'

Darcy shrugged as she pulled the top of the suitcase down and started to zip it up. 'Well, then, if it's that obvious why ask?'

Anger started to flicker to life in Max's gut as the full impact of what he was looking at sank in. *She was leaving.* He didn't like the clutch of panic. Panic was not something he ever felt.

'What's going on, Darcy? They've only just made the announcement—dinner hasn't even been served yet.'

Darcy stopped zipping up the bag and looked at him. For a moment he saw something flicker in her eyes but then it was gone.

'I'm done, Max. I've more than paid my dues as your convenient wife. When you can't even acknowledge me in your moment of glory it's pretty obvious that I've become superfluous to your requirements.'

The panic gripped him tighter. He'd messed up. 'Look, Darcy, I know I couldn't have achieved this without you—'

She laughed, short and sharp. 'You had this all along. I think Montgomery just enjoyed watching you jump through hoops… It's not many deals or many men Maximiliano Fonseca Roselli will do that for.'

Darcy picked up the jacket that was laid over the back of a nearby chair and shrugged it on, turning those huge blue eyes on him.

'What did you expect to happen now, Max? Some kind of fake domestic idyll? The deal is done. This is over. There's no more need for the charade.'

Max felt tight all over, in the grip of something dark and hot. He bit out, 'You won't even stay one more night.'

He didn't pose it as a question, already hating himself for saying it.

Darcy shook her head and her glossy ponytail slid over one shoulder. 'No. I've given you enough of my time, Max. More than enough.'

Was it his imagination or had there been a catch in her voice? Max couldn't hear through the dull roaring in his head. He felt himself teetering on the edge of something... Asking her to stay? But, as she'd said, for what? What did he want from her now? And what was this terrifying swooping of emotion, threatening to push him over the edge, spurred on by the panic which made his insides feel as loose as they'd felt tight a moment ago...?

He'd only ever felt like this once before. When he'd stood before another woman—his mother—and let her see the full extent of his vulnerability and pain. He'd tipped over the edge then and his life had never been the same.

He was not going to tip over the edge for anyone else. He had just achieved the pinnacle of his success. What did he need Darcy for? He had everything that he'd ever wanted. He could go on from here and live his life and know that he was untouchable, that he had surpassed every one of his naysayers and doubters. Every one of the bullies.

He and Luca would finally be equals—on his terms.

The realisation that no great sense of satisfaction accompanied that knowledge was not something Max wanted to dwell on. Suddenly he was quite eager to get on with things. Without that incisive bluer than blue gaze tracking his every movement.

The fact that he looked at Darcy even now and felt nothing but hunger was irritating, but he told himself that once she was out of his orbit it would die down... fade away.

He would take a new lover. Start again.

He uncrossed his arms. 'Your bonus will be in your bank by Monday. My solicitor will work out the details of the divorce.'

'Thank you.' Darcy avoided his eye now, picking up her bag.

A knock came to the door and she looked up. 'That'll be the taxi. The housekeeper is sending someone up for my bags when it arrives.'

Max had pushed everything he was feeling down so deep that he was slightly light-headed. Like a robot, he moved over to the bed and took Darcy's suitcase easily in one hand. He took it to the door and opened it, handing it out to the young man on the other side. One of the estate staff.

And then Darcy was in the doorway, close enough for him to smell her scent. It had an immediate effect on him, making his body hard.

Damn her. Right now he was more than ready to see the back of her. That edge was beckoning again, panic flaring.

He stepped back, allowing her to leave the room. He forced himself to be solicitous even as he had a sudden urge to haul her back into the room and slam the door shut, locking them both inside.

And what then? asked a snide voice.

Another one answered: *Chaos.*

'Good luck, Darcy. If you need anything get in touch.'

'I won't.' Her voice was definitely husky now, and she wasn't looking at him. 'But thank you. Goodbye, Max.'

CHAPTER TEN

DARCY WASN'T SURE how she managed it, but she stayed in a state of calm numbness until she was on the train at Inverness Station and it was pulling out in the direction of Edinburgh, followed by London.

As the train picked up speed, though, it was as if its motion was peeling her skin back to expose where her heart lay in tatters, just under her breastbone. It had taken almost every ounce of her strength to stand before Max and maintain that icy, unconcerned front.

She just made it to the toilet in time, where she sat on the closed lid, shuddering and weeping and swaying as the train took her further and further away from the man who had taken all her vulnerabilities and laid them bare for his own ends.

And she couldn't even blame him. She'd handed herself over to his ruthless heartlessness lock, stock and barrel. *She'd* made that choice.

Three months later

Darcy climbed up the steps from the tube and emerged in a quiet road of a leafy suburb in north London. Well, not so leafy now that autumn was here in force, stripping everything bare.

After walking for a few minutes she hitched her bags to one hand as she dug out her key and put it in the front door of her apartment building. A familiar dart of pleasure rushed through her. *Her apartment building*. Which housed her bijou ground-floor two-bedroomed apartment that had French doors leading out to her own private back garden.

The bonus Max had provided had more than covered the cost of the apartment with cash—making the sale fast and efficient. She'd moved in three weeks ago.

Max. He was always on the periphery of her mind, but Darcy shied away from looking at him too directly—like avoiding the glare of the sun for fear of going blind.

For a month after she'd left him in Scotland she'd had to endure seeing him emblazoned over every paper and magazine: the wunderkind of the financial world, accepted into the highest echelons where heads of state and the most powerful people in the world hailed his genius.

The emotion she'd felt thinking that he finally must have found some peace had mocked her.

There'd been pictures of him in gossip columns too, attending glittering events with a different beautiful woman on his arm each time. The pain Darcy had felt had been like a hot dagger skewering her belly, so she'd stopped watching the news or reading the papers.

She put her shopping away with little enthusiasm and thought idly of inviting her neighbour from upstairs for something to eat. John was the first person to make her laugh since she'd left Max.

After a quick trip upstairs, and John's totally overjoyed acceptance of her invitation—*'Sweetie, you are the best! I was about to die of hunger...like literally die!'*—Darcy went back downstairs and prepared some dinner, feeling marginally better.

She could get through this and emerge intact. *She could*, she vowed as she skewered some chicken with a little more force than necessary.

'You know, if you ever want to tell Uncle John about the bastard who done you wrong, I'll get a few boxes of wine and we'll hunker down for the weekend. Make a pity party of it.'

Darcy smiled as she picked up the plates and said wryly, as she hid the dart of inevitable pain, 'Is it that obvious?'

John took a sip of wine, his eyes following Darcy as she went into the kitchen. 'Hate to say it, love, but *yes*. You've got that unmistakable Eeyore droop to your lovely mouth and eyes.'

Darcy laughed just as a knock came to her door. She looked at John and he shrugged. 'Must be another neighbour?'

She went over to open it and swung it wide to reveal a very tall, very beautifully disheveled man with dark blond hair, olive skin and tawny eyes. And a distinctive scar. Dressed all in black.

She could almost hear John's jaw drop behind her. And she was belatedly and bizarrely aware that she was still smiling after his comment.

The smile slid off her face as shock and disbelief set in. 'Max.'

'Darcy.'

Her name on his tongue curled through her like warm honey, oozing over the ice packed around her heart.

'Can I come in?'

It was shock that made her act like an automaton, standing back, opening the door wider so that Max could step in, bringing with him the cool tang of autumn.

Darcy saw him clock John and the way his face tightened and darkened. His jaw was shadowed with stubble, adding to his general air of effortless disrepute.

'I'm interrupting?' He sounded stiff. Not at all like his usual insouciant self. Fazed by nothing.

Darcy tore her eyes off Max, almost afraid that he might disappear, to see that John had somehow picked his jaw back up off the ground and was standing up.

'No, I was just leaving.'

She was glad he'd spoken, because she wasn't sure she could speak.

She felt a quick supportive squeeze of her hand and then her neighbour was gone, closing the door behind him.

Darcy realised how close she was standing to Max and how huge he seemed in her small flat. Had he always been so huge?

She moved away, towards the table that still held the dinner detritus.

'You've lost weight.' Max's tone was almost accusing.

Darcy turned around. Of all the things she'd expected to hear from him it hadn't been that. And for someone who'd spent much of her lifetime lamenting her fuller figure it was ironic that in the past few months she'd managed to drop the guts of a stone without even trying.

She crossed her arms, suddenly angry that Max was here. Invading her space. Invading her mind. Being angry with him was easier than analysing other, far more dangerous emotions.

'You've hardly come all this way to comment on my weight, Max.' Her insides tightened. 'Is it something to do with the divorce?' She hadn't received the papers yet, but had been expecting something soon.

Max shook his head and ran a hand through his hair, mussing it up. The gesture was so familiar that Darcy had to bite her lip for fear of emitting some sound.

'No, it's not about the divorce…it's something else.' Max started to prowl around the flat, as if inspecting it, looking into the kitchen. He turned to face her, frowning. 'Why didn't you buy a bigger place?'

Darcy felt defensive. 'I didn't want a mortgage and I like this—it suits me.'

'I would have given you more money for somewhere bigger.'

She dropped her arms, hands spread out. 'Max…why are you here?'

He looked at her so intently that she began to sweat, becoming self-conscious in her roll-neck top and jeans. It had been 'Casual Friday' at her new job that day. Working as PA to the CEO of a dynamic software company was sufficiently new and different to give her the illusion that she could avoid thinking about Max during the day. That illusion was now well and truly shattered.

'I wanted to make sure you had your place…that you were settled. I owe you that.'

Darcy's insides fluttered. 'I have it, Max. And I wouldn't have had it without you.'

He looked at her. 'You also wouldn't have had the media speculation and the intense scrutiny afforded to our marriage.'

Darcy almost winced. After she'd left him the papers had been consumed by what had happened to her. Luckily she'd been able to return to London and disappear into the crowds, unassuming enough that no one recognised her. They'd been married for such a short amount of time it had really only registered as a story in Italy.

'At least it didn't affect your deal with Montgomery.'

Max's mouth tightened. 'Your assessment of him was right. He'd always intended giving me the fund—he just enjoyed making me work for it.'

Darcy sat down heavily onto the chair behind her. 'So we never had to go through with the wedding?'

Max shook his head.

He came forward and touched the back of the chair next to hers and said, 'Do you mind if I sit?'

Darcy waved a hand vaguely, barely aware of Max's uncharacteristic reticence or solicitude. Or the starkness of his features.

'The man who was just here...he is your boyfriend?'

Darcy came back into the room from imagining what might have happened, or *not* happened, if they hadn't married. She didn't like to admit that she preferred the version where they'd married. In spite of the pain.

Not really thinking, she said, 'No, John's my neighbour. And he's gay.'

Max sucked in a breath and Darcy looked at him sharply. He looked gaunt. The flutters got stronger and she hated it.

Sharply, she said, 'Not that it's any business of yours. You've hardly been wasting any time proving that our marriage was a farce. I've seen those pictures of you with women.'

Max stood up then and shrugged off his jacket, revealing a long-sleeved top that clung almost indecently to his hard torso. For a second Darcy didn't hear what he was saying...she was too hot and distracted.

'...doing everything I could to try and pretend things can go back to normal.'

Darcy blinked. Max was pacing, talking as if to himself. She swivelled in the chair so she could watch him. He was like a glorious caged lion in the confines of her flat.

He turned to her. 'The evening Montgomery announced that he was giving me the fund to manage I was so overcome with emotion that I couldn't bear for you to see it.

In case you'd see that the front I'd put up after Como was just that: a stupid, pathetic front to hide behind.'

'Max, what are you talking about?'

But he wasn't listening to her. He was pacing again, becoming increasingly angry. At himself.

'When I went upstairs and saw you packing I felt panic. *Panic!* I've never panicked in my life—not even when I realised I had no option but to live on the streets.'

Darcy stood up, but Max continued.

'And then you were standing there, so cool and collected, asking me what else I wanted now that I had achieved my goal.'

Max stopped and turned to face her again.

'You were asking me to step out into an abyss and I was too much of a coward to do it. I told myself that I had everything I needed, that I didn't need you. I told myself that the hunger I felt every time I looked at you, which got worse if I wasn't near you, would fade in time. So I let you go, and I went back down to that function, and I told people you'd had to leave for a family emergency. I told myself I was *fine*. That I would be *fine*.'

He shook his head.

'But I wasn't. I'm not. The day my parents split my brother and I up I showed my emotions. I cried because I wanted to stay with my mother.'

His mouth twisted.

'I couldn't believe that she was going to leave me behind with my father... I had no thought for my brother, only myself. But he was the stoic one. I was the one falling apart. And so she took me, and I spent my life paying for it. When you were leaving me I wanted to slam the door shut and lock it to prevent you going. I didn't. Because I was afraid of what might happen if I just let all that emotion out. I was afraid my world would turn on its axis again and I'd lose it all just when I'd finally got it. I was afraid I'd lose myself again.'

Darcy's breathing was erratic. 'What are you saying, Max?'

'I wanted you to be settled, to find the home you wanted so badly. I wanted you to know that you have a choice.'

'A choice for what?'

Max took a deep breath. 'I want you to come back to me. I want you to stay being my wife. But if you don't want that I'll leave you alone.'

Darcy shook her head as if trying to clear it. 'You want me back…because it's convenient? Because—?'

Max held up a hand. *'No.'* And then he sliced into the heart of her with all the precision of a master surgeon. 'I want you to come back because you've broken me in two. I finally have everything I've always wanted—everything I've always *thought* I wanted. But it means nothing any more because you're not with me. I love you, Darcy.'

Darcy blinked. *I love you?* This was a Max she'd never seen before. Humbled. Broken. *Real.* For a second she couldn't believe it, but the depth of pain in his eyes scored at her own heart—because she knew what it felt like.

She whispered through the lump in her throat. 'There's never been a choice, Max. Not since the day we met again.' She waved a hand, indicating the flat. 'I finally have everything I thought I wanted too—a home of my own, a base—but it's meaningless because *you're* my centre.'

Max's face leached of colour. 'What are you saying?'

Darcy's vision blurred with tears and she could feel her heart knitting back together. 'I'm saying I love you too, you big idiot.'

She wasn't sure who moved, but suddenly she was in his arms with hers wrapped around him so tightly she could hardly breathe. They staggered back until Max fell onto the couch, taking Darcy with him so she was sitting on his lap.

She wasn't even aware she was crying until she felt Max's hand moving up and down her back rhythmically, heard him soothing her with words in Italian...*dolcezza mia...amore...*

Darcy finally lifted her head and looked up at Max, who smoothed some hair off her forehead. She manoeuvred herself so that she was straddling his lap and both her hands were on his shoulders. She saw the way his eyes flared and colour came back into his cheeks and moved experimentally, exulting when she could feel the evidence of his arousal.

She moved her hips against him subtly, but pulled back when he tried to kiss her. 'Who were the women?'

His eyes flashed with a hint of the old Max. 'They were my attempt to be *normal* again. And none of them was *you*. Which was *very* annoying.'

He attempted to kiss her again but Darcy arched away, making Max scowl.

'Did you kiss any of them?'

Max's scowl deepened. 'I tried.'

Darcy went still as a hot skewer of jealousy ripped through her.

'But I couldn't do it. For one thing they were too tall, too skinny, too chatty about stupid things. *Not you*.'

Darcy smiled. 'Good.'

'What about Jack, are you sure he's gay?'

Now Max looked as if he wanted to skewer someone with a hot poker.

Darcy rolled her eyes. 'It's *John*. And yes, he's gay, Max. I can practically hear him drooling from here.'

Max looked smug. 'Good.'

Darcy brought her hands up to Max's face, cupping it. And then she bent her head to kiss her husband, showing him with everything in her just how much she loved him. The emotion was almost painful. Max's hands moved all over her, undoing her hair, lifting her top up and off so that she was just in her bra.

She rested her forehead against his, wondering if this was a dream. 'I thought I'd never see you again.'

Max's hands closed tight around her hips. He shook his head. 'I would have come sooner, but I was a coward, and then when I heard you'd bought a place already I thought you were moving on.'

Darcy's heart clenched. She looked into Max's eyes. 'You're not a coward, Max…anything but.'

She ran a finger lightly down over his scar and he caught her hand and pressed a kiss to the centre of her palm. He looked at her. 'The night we met Montgomery for dinner…?'

Darcy nodded.

'I think that on some subconscious level I knew I wanted you badly enough to tie you to me by any means necessary. The thing is, I wouldn't have made that impetuous decision if you had been anyone else… It's because it was *you*, and I had to have you no matter what.'

Max's confession eased some tiny last piece of doubt inside Darcy. She smiled and shifted against him again, putting her hands on the couch behind him, pushing her breasts wantonly towards Max's mouth.

'I think we've said all that needs to be said for now.'

Max smiled at her, long and slow and with a cocksure *Maxness* that told Darcy it wouldn't be long before he was back to his arrogant self again.

'I love you, Signora Fonseca Roselli. These last three

months have been a torture I wouldn't wish on my worst enemy. You're never leaving my side again.'

She brought her hand around to the back of his head, gripping his hair, tugging at it. 'I love *you*, Signor Fonseca Roselli, and I have no intention of ever leaving your side again.'

And then she bent her head and pressed a kiss to the corner of his mouth.

Max growled his frustration, cupping her jaw and angling her head so that within seconds they were kissing so deeply that there was no need for any more words for quite a while.

EPILOGUE

FOR TWO AND a half years Darcy and Max lived an idyllic existence, locked happily in a bubble of love and sensuality. She continued to work for him—but only when he travelled abroad and they didn't want to be separated.

Meanwhile, Darcy set up a business as a freelance business interpreter and frequently travelled all over Europe for different assignments—which Max invariably grumbled about. Darcy ignored him. He liked to use them as an excuse to surprise her, anyway—like the time he'd appeared in Paris when she'd walked out of a meeting and whisked her off on his private jet to the romantic and windswept west coast of Ireland. They'd ended up staying in Dromoland Castle for a week…

They bought a house in Rome's leafy exclusive Monteverde district and together made it a true home, keeping on her place in London as a pied-à-terre. Max still hadn't taken the plunge and bought a football club, but he spent lots of time at matches, investigating various teams.

One of the things Darcy was happiest about, though, was the rebuilding of Max's relationship with his brother Luca. It had been slow at first, but with the help of Luca's wife Serena, whom Darcy now counted as a firm friend, the two men were now in regular contact and needed no encouragement to spend time together. Which suited Darcy and Serena fine, especially when *they* wanted to catch up, without their husbands doing that annoying attention-seeking thing they did.

Max's relationship with his mother stayed strained, but he'd finally come to terms with the way she was and, together with Darcy, had managed to learn how to support her without taking on her addictions as his responsibility.

As for Darcy with her parents, she had learnt to tolerate their various love catastrophes with much more humour and less of a feeling of impending doom.

And then, two and a half years into their marriage, Darcy had walked white-faced into their bedroom one morning, holding a small plastic stick.

Max had looked at her and immediately frowned, concerned. *'Ché cosa?'*

She'd felt a very ominous tightening of her chest at the thought of his reaction and what it might to do them. This was the one thing they'd never really talked about, and when Serena had fallen pregnant Darcy had seen how Max had reacted in private—by shutting it out. So she knew this was a potential minefield for him—for the young boy who had been so hurt by his own parents.

Silently she'd handed him the plastic and watched as comprehension dawned.

He'd gone a little green and looked at her. 'But...*how*?'

She'd shrugged, feeling slightly sick herself at his reaction. 'I don't know. I've never missed a pill... But I had that flu a while back...'

They'd never spoken about Darcy coming off the pill. She'd hoped with time that they would discuss it...but now it was beyond discussion. She was pregnant.

She'd watched Max absorb the news, much in the same way she was, but whereas *she* felt a tiny burgeoning excitement starting to grow, she feared Max might feel the opposite.

After a long moment he'd looked at her resolutely and had come to sit on the end of the bed, the sheets tangled around his naked body. He'd reached for her and pulled her down onto his lap.

Her heart had clenched to see the clear battle going on in the golden depths of those amazing eyes but she'd waited for him to speak, and eventually he'd said gruffly, 'You know that this was never going to be easy for me… but I love you…and I can't imagine not loving any baby of ours even if I am scared to death of hurting it as Luca and I were hurt…'

Overcome with emotion at the extent of his willingness not to run scared from this, which he might have done before, Darcy had felt tears prickle behind her eyes as she'd cupped Max's jaw and pressed her mouth to his, kissing him gently.

'I trust in you, Max. You who overcame adversity time and again and who survived your own parents' woeful lack of care. You aren't capable of giving anything less than one hundred per cent commitment and love to any baby of ours. They'll be the luckiest child in the world to have you as a father.'

He'd looked at her, his eyes suspiciously bright. 'And you as their mother. I wouldn't want to do this with anyone else.'

And now, eight months later the reality that they'd come to terms with was manifest *times two*!

Darcy opened tired but happy eyes to take in the scene in the corner of her private hospital room.

And she would have laughed if she hadn't been afraid of bursting her Caesarean stitches.

Max was sprawled in a chair, shirt open at the neck

haphazardly, jeans low on his hips. His hair was even more mussed than usual, his jaw stubbled. If it hadn't been for the two small bundles carefully balanced, one in the crook of each arm, he might have looked like the reprobate playboy he'd used to be, coming home after a debauched night out.

But he was no playboy. He was a lover and a husband. And now a father. Of twins.

They'd realised that Darcy must have had twins somewhere in her family line too when they'd been informed of the news by their consultant early on in the pregnancy. Much to their stunned shock.

Max was looking at his son and daughter as if they were the most prized jewels in the world. Awed. Domino and Daisy—named after Max's Italian grandfather and Darcy's English grandmother. They'd asked the Montgomerys—who had become good friends—to be godparents to a baby each, and already the older couple had proved to be far more dedicated than *real* grandparents.

Max said now to his son, whose eyes were shut tight, 'Dom, just because you came first it doesn't mean anything. In fact...' He looked at his daughter, whose eyes were open wide, and said, *sotto voce*, 'We'll pretend *you* came first, Daisy, hmm? That way he won't be able to get too big for his boots...and your *mamma* has had a lot of drugs, so maybe we can convince her of this too...?'

He looked up at Darcy then, and smiled goofily at being caught out. Love made her chest swell so much she had to take a breath. She smiled back and love stretched between them, binding them all together for ever.

* * * * *

Prince Reyes paced in a tight circle. 'When did you find out?' he asked.

'I did the tests an hour ago.'

Jasmine held up three pink and white sticks.

Reyes forced himself to move. He took them, examined them. Somehow their presence finally hammered the reality home.

He was going to be a father.

Elation. A strange, undeniable possessiveness.

'Everything has changed.'

Reaching down, he stroked her cheek. He wasn't sure why it hadn't occurred to him before. Jasmine wasn't the perfect candidate, but she was miles better than anyone he knew. There would be no false proclamations of love to confuse issues. They were compatible in bed.

And she was carrying his child…

'I'm calling off next week's wedding. And I'm getting married in three days instead.'

Jasmine felt the blood drain from her head.

'I… Okay. Leave it with me. I'll call Miss Holden and arrange for her to fly over immediately,' she replied through numb lips.

Reyes's brows bunched. 'Why would you be calling her?'

'Because you're marrying her!'

'You misunderstand, Jasmine. The wedding is for you. I intend to marry no one else but *you*.'

Maya Blake's hopes of becoming a writer were born when she picked up her first romance aged thirteen. Little did she know her dream would come true! Does she still pinch herself every now and then, to make sure it's not a dream? Yes, she does!

Feel free to pinch her too, via Twitter, Facebook or Goodreads! Happy reading!

MARR
THE PR
CONVENI

BY
MAYA BLAKE

MILLS
BOON
&

Published in Great Britain 2015
by Mills & Boon, an imprint of Harlequin (UK) Limited,
Eton House, 18-24 Paradise Road, Richmond, Surrey, TW9 1SR

© 2015 Maya Blake

ISBN: 978-0-263-25064-0

Harlequin (UK) Limited's policy is to use papers that are natural,
renewable and recyclable products and made from wood grown in
sustainable forests. The logging and manufacturing processes conform
to the legal environmental regulations of the country of origin.

Printed and bound in Spain
by CPI, Barcelona

MARRIED FOR
THE PRINCE'S
CONVENIENCE

CHAPTER ONE

SHE WAS A THIEF.

A thief...

Jasmine Nichols's heart pounded the indictment through her bloodstream. She hadn't stolen anything yet, but that was beside the point. She'd travelled thousands of miles for the sole purpose of taking something that didn't belong to her.

Telling herself she had no choice didn't matter. If anything, it escalated her helplessness.

By the end of the night, she would wear the damning label as close to her skin as her black designer evening gown clung now.

Because failure wasn't an option.

Fear and shame duelled for supremacy inside her, but it was the deep knowledge that she couldn't turn her back on her family that propelled her reluctant feet up the sweeping crimson carpet towards the awe-inspiring masterpiece that housed the Contemporary Museum of Arts, perched on a cliff-side overlooking Rio de Janeiro. Even the jaw-dropping beauty of her surroundings couldn't detract her from the simple fact.

She'd come here to steal.

The smile she'd plastered on her face since alighting from the air-conditioned limo threatened to crack. To calm her nerves, she mentally recited her *to do* list.

First, she had to locate Crown Prince Reyes Vicente Navarre.

And there was her first problem.

All effective search engines had yielded no pictures of the reclusive prince, save for a grainy image taken at the funeral of his mother four years ago. Since then, no pictures of the royal family of the South American kingdom of Santo Sierra had been released to the public. They guarded their privacy with a rigour that bordered on fanaticism.

As if that weren't bad enough, according to reports, the House of Navarre's Crown Prince had left his kingdom only three times in the last three years, all his time spent caring for his gravely ill father. It was rumoured King Carlos Navarre wasn't expected to live past the summer.

Which meant Jasmine had no means of identifying Prince Reyes Navarre.

How did she get close to a man whose identity she had no idea of, distract him long enough to get her hands on what she'd come for before her mother and, more importantly, her stepfather, Stephen Nichols, the man who'd saved her life, and whose name she'd adopted, found out what she was up to?

Stephen would be heartbroken if he knew she was being blackmailed.

A nerve-destroying shudder rose up from the soles of her feet, making her clench her teeth to stop its death rattle from escaping. She smiled some more, mingled with the insanely wealthy and well heeled, and tried to reassure herself she could do this. By this time tomorrow, she'd be back home.

And most importantly, Stephen would be safe.

If everything went smoothly.

Stop it! Negative thinking was the downfall of many a plan. How many times had Stephen told her this?

She fixed her wilting smile back in place, stepped into the main hall of the museum, but she couldn't summon the enthusiasm to gawp at the stunning paintings and sculptures on display.

A waiter approached bearing a tray of champagne. Accepting the sparkling gold-filled crystal goblet, she smoothed a shaky hand over the pearl choker around her throat, ignored the nervous flutter in her belly, and made her way to the bowl-shaped terrace where the guests were congregating for pre-dinner drinks.

So far the plans set out by Joaquin Esteban—the man threatening her stepfather's life—had gone meticulously. Her name had been on the guest list as promised, alongside those of world leaders and celebrities she'd only seen on TV and in glossy magazines. For a single moment, while she'd waited for Security to check the electronic chip on her invitation, she'd secretly hoped to be caught, turned away. But the man who held her stepfather's fate in his cruel hands had seen to every last detail she needed to pull this off.

Everything except provide her with a picture of the thirty-two-year-old prince.

The first stage of the treaty signing was to take place in half an hour in the Golden Room behind her. And with the occasion coinciding with Prince Mendez of Valderra's birthday, guests had been invited onto the terrace to witness the spectacular sunset and the prince's arrival, before the signing and birthday celebrations began.

Crown Prince Reyes himself was expected at eight o'clock. A quick glance at her watch showed five minutes to the hour. With every interminable second that ticked by, Jasmine's nerves tightened another notch.

What if she was found out? Certainly, she could kiss her job as a broker and mediator goodbye. But even if she succeeded, how could she ever hold her head high again? She'd worked so very hard to put her past behind her, to tend the new leaf she'd turned over. For eight years, she'd succeeded. And now, at twenty-six, she was on the slippery slope again.

Because once a juvie princess, always a juvie princess?

No. She hadn't let that voice of her detention cellmate taunt her for years. She wasn't about to start now.

And yet, she couldn't stop the despair that mingled with anxiety as her gaze drifted over the orange-splashed water towards the stunning silhouette of Sugarloaf Mountain in the distance.

Under normal circumstances, the sights and sounds would have filled her with excitement and awe. For a girl with her past and dire upbringing, sights such as these didn't feature in her *normal*. Except these weren't normal circumstances. And fear was threatening to block out every other emotion.

Which was dangerous. She couldn't afford to fail. Yet success would bring nothing but shame. Would prove that the past really never stayed in the past.

But the reality was her stepfather had gone too far this time, hedged his bets, literally, with the wrong person.

Joaquin, with his soft voice and deadly smile, had calmly given her two choices.

Come to Rio or watch Stephen rot in jail.

Of course, Joaquin had counted on the fact that, aside from his very public humiliation of being thrown out of his Foreign Office position for gambling away government money, Stephen Nichols's devotion to his wife meant he would do anything to save her the distress of watching him suffer. As would Jasmine.

Even when Jasmine was a child, long before Stephen had entered their lives, her mother's fragility had meant she had assumed the role of the caretaker. Her mother wouldn't survive losing Stephen.

So here Jasmine was, about to step into a quagmire she wasn't sure any amount of self-affirmation would wash her clean of.

'He's here!'

She roused herself from her maudlin self-pitying. A quick glance showed it was precisely eight o'clock. Her heart double somersaulted into her throat. When her stomach threatened to follow suit, she took a hasty sip of champagne. Whatever Dutch courage she hoped to gain was sorely lacking as the butterflies in her stomach grew into vicious crows.

Following the direction of excited voices and pointing, she focused on the bottom of the cliff. A sleek speedboat approached, foaming waves billowing behind the fast-moving craft. It gathered speed as it neared the shore. Swerving at the last second, it created a huge arc of water that rushed to the shore in a giant wave before heading away from the jetty.

The pilot executed a series of daredevil manoeuvres that

brought gasps of delight from the crowd and left the other two occupants—bodyguards, judging by their bulging muscles and ill-fitting suits—clinging grim-faced to the sides.

Finally, bringing the vessel alongside the quay, the tuxedoed figure stepped boldly onto the bow of the boat and jumped lithely down onto the jetty. Smiling at the enthusiastic applause, he clasped his hands in front of him and gave a deep bow.

Jasmine released the breath trapped in her lungs. So, this was Prince Reyes Navarre. Considering his near reclusive status, she was surprised he'd chosen such a narcissistic, highly OTT entrance. She wrinkled her nose.

'You're not impressed with His Royal Highness's maritime prowess?' a deep voice enquired from behind her left shoulder.

Jasmine jumped and whirled around. She'd assumed she was alone on the terrace, everyone else having rushed down into the main hall to welcome the prince.

How had this man moved so silently behind her? She hadn't even felt his presence until he'd spoken. Jasmine's gaze raced up, and up, until it collided with dark grey eyes.

Immediately, she wanted to look away, to block the probing gaze. She had no idea why, but the urge was so overwhelming, she took a step back.

A strong hand seized her arm. 'Careful, *pequeña*. It is a long tumble from the terrace and the evening is too beautiful to mar with tragedy.'

Glancing behind her, she realised she'd stepped dangerously close to the low wall bordering the terrace.

'Oh. Thank you.' Her words twisted around her tongue. Her senses dovetailed on the warm hand that held her. She looked down at the elegant fingers on her skin and drew in a sharp breath. His bold touch transmitted an alien sensation through her blood.

As if he felt it too, his fingers tightened imperceptibly. A second later, he let go. 'So, you don't like speedboats?' He nodded over her head at the spectacle below.

She tried to pry her gaze from his face, but she only succeeded in moving her head a fraction, before becoming equally hypnotised by the alluring spectacle of his mouth.

It was just spectacularly…sensual. Like his eyes, the lines of his lips drew equal interest from her stunned senses. Without stopping to assess her reaction, she found herself raising her hand to his face.

A hair's breadth away, she saw his eyes widen. Her heart slammed with horror and embarrassment at what she'd almost done. She snatched her hand back and for a split second contemplated taking that fatal step backwards. Maybe dashing herself over the rocks at the bottom of the cliff would knock some sense into her.

'What makes you say that?' she prevaricated when it became clear he expected an answer to his question.

'You have a very expressive face.' His beautifully deep accented voice was solemn.

'Oh.' She stalled and tried to think fast. What could she say without causing offence? 'They're okay, I guess. I mean, they're not my thing. Too fast. Too…wet.' Not to mention, they reminded her of the times Stephen had taken her out on his boat very soon after she and her mother had gone to live with him. Still in her destructive phase, she'd given him a hard time about those trips. Despite his many reassurances, a part of her had remained untrusting, afraid he'd end up being like all the men her mother had fallen for in the past. Each morning, she'd woken up anxious that that would be the day Stephen tossed them out of his life. He hadn't, of course, but she still couldn't look at a boat without remembering that distressing period. 'But they're nice to look at, I suppose.' She bit her lip to stop further inanity spilling out.

The stranger's grave nod did nothing to distract her stare.

'But exhilarating, some would say. No?'

Light-headedness encroached. Exhilarating. Breath-stealing. Captivating. But all those adjectives had nothing to do with speedboats and everything to do with the man in front of her.

Belatedly, Jasmine realised she hadn't taken a single breath since she'd clapped eyes on him. Sucking in oxygen restored some much-needed brain activity. 'I wouldn't know. I've never been inclined to take a trip on one. Mainly because I get seasick standing on a beach.'

'That's a shame. There is a tranquillity I find on water that I haven't found anywhere else.'

The thought of this man, powerfully built, quietly commanding and confident, craving tranquillity touched a strange place inside her.

'My stepfather loves the water too.' Damn. She needed to watch her tongue.

'But something about it makes you sad?' His voice softened as his eyes grew even more solemn.

Her startled gaze flew to his. 'Why do you say that?'

'You speak with fondness but your eyes darken with unhappiness.'

His intuitiveness disturbed her, made her feel vulnerable. Wrenching her gaze from his, she looked around. The terrace was deserted, but soft lights glowed from exquisite crystal-cut chandeliers and showed the guests slowly filling the large hall.

The hall...

Where she should be. Trying to make contact with Prince Reyes Navarre.

Instead she was alone with this strangely captivating man.

A man she didn't know.

Although she'd talked herself into believing not every stranger meant her harm, she knew better than most which situations to avoid. Being alone with a man twice her size wasn't a good idea.

But rather than fear, a thrum of excitement fizzed through her veins. Her breathing constricted, her heart thumping loud in her ears as she inhaled. Almost drawn by an invisible force, her gaze returned to his face.

His black dinner jacket and crisp white shirt gave his features a vibrancy, helped in no small measure by the golden perfection of his skin. Cast in part shadow by the broad shoulders blocking the light, his taut cheekbones and strong, un-compromising jaw made her fingers tingle with the urge to explore him.

As she stared his mouth hardened into a tight line, as if he held some emotion in. The strong need to touch those lips, experience their firm texture and soothe them softer with her thumb grew. Her eyes flashed back to his to find him regarding her, waiting for a response.

'I have issues with water. Let's just leave it at that.'

He looked as if he would demand more. But he merely nodded. 'Tell me your name.' His authoritative tone demanded nothing but her compliance.

Without questioning why, she answered, 'Jasmine Nichols.'

His solemn expression altered, fleetingly replaced by a small smile that creased his lips. 'You are named after the flower that blooms in the gardens of my home, Jasmine.' His voice caressed her name in a way that made all the hairs on her body strain to life. 'It is a fragile yet sturdy flower that has soothed us with its heady fragrance for thousands of years.'

Overwhelmed by the equally heady blend of emotion swirling through her, she gave a nervous laugh. 'Blimey, I hope I don't look that old!'

'Be assured. You don't.'

His smile disappeared, but she suspected he was still amused by her. The thought created a joyous fizz in her blood. It struck her that this man, whoever he was, hadn't smiled or laughed in a long time. The urgent need to catch another glimpse of that enigmatic smile grew.

'Great. Living to a thousand sounds like fun, but I bet it becomes a nuisance after that. A few more decades will do me just fine, though. I have things to do, people to impress.'

Joy sang in her chest when he rewarded her with another fleeting smile.

'I have no doubt that you will make your mark on the world before you leave it.' His head dipped in a shallow bow. 'Enjoy the rest of your evening, Jasmine.' With graceful, long-limbed strides, he walked away from her.

His abrupt departure stunned her into stillness. She watched four figures detach themselves from the shadowed doorway and fall into step behind him. She didn't need to be told they were bodyguards.

And rightly so. He was far too lethal to walk around without armed escort.

It wasn't until he reached the bottom of the stairs that led into the main hall that she regained the power of speech.

'Holy hotness, Batman,' she muttered under her breath, still more than a little stunned.

Watching him cut a path through the assembled crowd, Jasmine realised she hadn't even asked his name. Without pausing to think, she dashed through the doors after him.

She came to a screeching halt after a few steps.

What was she doing? She hadn't come to Rio to check out its male citizens, or to fall flat on her face for the first enigmatic man who looked at her with deep, hypnotically solemn eyes.

The real reason wrenched her back to reality, making any dream she harboured glaringly impossible. Whoever the mysterious, formidable stranger was, he had nothing to do with her mission here.

A mission that should've been the one and only thing on her mind.

She slid her wrap closer to ward off the sudden chill invading her body.

How could she have lost sight of her objective so quickly? Her stepfather's well-being depended on her. Running after a man who'd made her feel so alive, so special that she would have given up all she held dear to spend another minute in his presence was out of the question.

She clutched her grey silk purse and tried to think clearly, but it was no use. His smell, the feel of his hand on her skin, the intensity of his dark gaze that seemed to see past the outer trappings of civilised conversation to her inner self, remained imprinted on her.

Her breath rushed out shakily. She tried to tell herself what she'd felt didn't matter. That wasn't her purpose here. The only thing that mattered was finding Prince Reyes, getting her hands on the treaty and making it out of here in one piece. By way of grounding herself, she recited the list once more and forced herself to move into the hall as she did so.

The first thing she noticed was that the man she'd been speaking to was now on the other side of the room. Similarly suited men surrounded him, yet he remained curiously aloof, standing out so spectacularly, everyone else faded into insignificance.

Forcing her gaze away, she looked around. In halting Portuguese, she tried to enquire discreetly from her waiter which of the men was Prince Reyes, but her query only drew a blank stare.

Her anxiety returned when she realised most of the conversation going on around her was in Portuguese. Naïvely, she'd assumed since most of the staff at her hotel spoke English, everyone in Rio did too.

But the man who'd spoken to her on the terrace had used perfect English.

So ask him.

Except she couldn't. She'd have to cross the room to get to him, and in the time she'd been dithering his audience had tripled.

Insinuating herself into his crowd would only draw attention to herself. And for what she'd come here to do, anonymity was key. Wishing she'd pressed Joaquin Esteban for more details about the prince, she cast another look around.

A bell sounded nearby, making her jump. Guests started taking their places at the long banquet table. She found her place and had just sat down when a light-haired man joined her.

He looked at her hopefully. 'Please tell me you speak English?'

Jasmine smiled with relief. 'Yes, I do.'

'Thank God! You think your Portuguese is all right until someone asks you a question. Then even the little you know flies straight out of your head. I'm Josh, by the way.'

'Jasmine,' she responded.

'Crazy, isn't it?'

Startled, Jasmine glanced sideways to him. 'Sorry?'

He nodded to the group of men taking their seats at the far end of the long banquet table. 'Unbelievable that between the two of them, those men control nearly half of the steel and precious gems in the world.'

Unwilling to disclose her ignorance, she murmured, 'Right.'

'Shame their trade relations are in a shambles, though. Hopefully once the treaty is signed, there should be some semblance of order, otherwise the chaos will only get worse.' He shook his head. 'Prince Reyes has done an outstanding job of bringing the treaty to fruition, though. Have to commend him on that.' He took a healthy gulp of champagne.

Sneaking in a breath to calm her screeching nerves, she casually asked, 'Which one is Prince Reyes?'

He looked puzzled for a second, then he shrugged. 'I understand how you might be confused. They're descended from the same bloodline, after all.' He nodded to the men. 'Mendez, the shorter one who rocked up in the speedboat, is the birthday boy celebrating the big four-oh. He's in charge of Valderra, the larger of the two kingdoms. The taller one at the head of the table, talking to the prime minster, is Reyes. Don't get me wrong, his might be the smaller of the kingdoms, but Santo Sierra is definitely the big kahuna.'

Jasmine's throat threatened to close up as she absorbed the information. Her fingers clenched around her cutlery as ice drenched her blood.

The lights went up just then and two officious-looking men stepped up to the twin podiums carrying black briefcases. Heart in her throat, she realised what she'd done.

She'd been speaking to Prince Reyes Navarre all along!

And she'd told him her name!

After a short speech, the first stage of the treaty signing was completed. Jasmine watched as the documents were placed back in the briefcases.

Clammy sweat soaked her palms. Carefully, she set down her knife and fork. Every instinct told her to get up. *Run.* Not stop until she was on the next plane back to London.

But how could she? Even if she sold her two-bedroom East London flat and somehow found the balance to pay the half a million pounds owed to Joaquin, the loan shark still possessed enough documentary evidence to bury her stepfather.

Jasmine's heart lurched at the thought. Her family was far from perfect, but Stephen Nichols had single-handedly ensured she and her mother had been given a much-needed second chance. There was no way Jasmine was going to turn her back on him now.

Nervously, she swallowed the moisture in her mouth. 'You mean, Prince Reyes is the tall one...' *with the impossibly broad shoulders, sad eyes and expressive, elegant hands*, she nearly blurted out.

'Looking our way right now,' her table companion muttered, a vein of surprise trailing his voice.

Her head jerked up and slate-grey eyes locked on hers. Even from the length of the banquet table, the stranger from the terrace loomed larger than life, his stare unwavering.

Except he wasn't an intriguing stranger any more.

He was the man she'd come to steal from.

CHAPTER TWO

SHAME SHOULD HAVE been the paramount emotion ruling Jasmine as her gaze remained trapped in Prince Reyes's stare.

Instead, the alien emotion from earlier pulsed through her again, and, impossibly, everything and everyone seemed to fade away. Even the sound of her own breathing slowed until she barely knew whether she breathed in or out.

Alarmed and more than a little unsettled, Jasmine wrenched her gaze away. All through the meal she barely tasted, she forced herself to make light conversation with Josh. But even with her focus firmly turned away from Prince Reyes, she could feel his stare, heavy and speculative, on her.

Now, realising just how precarious a position she'd put herself in, Jasmine was barely able to hold it together. Which was why she didn't hear Josh clear his throat.

Once. Twice.

Her gaze jerked up to find Prince Reyes Navarre standing next to her. Startled, she dropped the knife and cringed as it clattered onto her plate.

'Miss Nichols, was your meal satisfactory?' He glanced pointedly at her half-eaten meal.

Aware of the countless pairs of eyes on her, Jasmine wasn't sure whether to remain seated or stand and curtsy. She opted to remain seated. 'Y-yes, it was, thank you.'

'I am not interrupting, I hope?' A glance at Josh that was at once courteous and incisive.

'No, we're…just two countrymen who find themselves at the same table.' Josh laughed.

'How…fortunate,' Prince Reyes said, his gaze speculative as it rested on the other man.

Vaguely, she saw him gesture. Suddenly, the guests rose

from their places and started to mingle. Sensing some sort of etiquette being observed, Jasmine stood shakily to her feet.

Snagging the edge of her heel on her chair, she stumbled.

Prince Reyes caught her arm. She gasped at the electricity sizzling over her skin. When she straightened, he dropped his arm and just stared at her.

A block of silence fell between them. For the life of her, Jasmine couldn't form any words to ease the sudden tension. Heat crawled over her body and her dress felt suddenly very restrictive.

Josh cleared his throat a third time, glanced from one to the other, then put his glass down. 'I need to find a business acquaintance. Please excuse me, Your Highness.' He bowed quickly, then scurried away before Jasmine could draw breath.

And once again, Jasmine was trapped by a pair of compelling grey eyes.

'Are you here with him?' Prince Reyes asked.

Did she detect a hint of disapproval in his tone? She raised her chin. 'No, I'm here on my own.'

If anything, his disapproval increased.

She scrambled to continue. 'I was told Rio was safe. So far nothing's happened to make me think otherwise.'

A gleam smouldered in his eyes. 'Danger comes in all forms, Miss Nichols. Sometimes in least expected packages. I'd urge you to practise caution.'

Hearing him use her surname instead of her first name as he had on the terrace, made her realise how much she missed hearing it.

'Thank you for the advice…umm…Your Highness.' She didn't add that she wouldn't need it. She didn't plan on being here long enough to get into any more danger than she was putting herself in tonight. In fact, as soon as she'd completed the hateful task, she was heading to the airport to catch the next flight out. 'But it's really not necessary.'

He continued to regard her in that disquieting manner. A

tiny shiver shimmied along her skin; the enormity of her task hit her, sharp and forceful.

Again the instinct to *run* slammed through her and it took everything Jasmine possessed to stand her ground and continue to meet his eyes.

This man possessed her only means to save her stepfather. Instead of dismissing his concern, she should be using it. The shame welling inside her didn't matter. The fear of stepping over the line couldn't be allowed to overtake the most important thing—saving Stephen. Saving her family.

She watched, scrambling to keep her distressing thoughts from showing, as Prince Reyes held out his hand. 'Very well. Far be it from me to cause offence by suggesting one of my bodyguards accompany you to your hotel. It was a pleasure to meet you, Miss Nichols.' He turned away and she noticed said bodyguards take their protective stance behind him. One was carrying the briefcase containing the treaty.

He was leaving! Taking with him the only chance of saving her stepfather.

Gripping her purse, she cleared her throat and quickly back-pedalled. 'Actually, you're right. A strange city isn't a place for a woman to be wandering at night. I'd be grateful for your assistance.'

She heard the indrawn breath of the nearest guests, but ignored it.

Letting Prince Reyes leave was unthinkable. She'd travelled thousands of miles to make sure her stepfather didn't go to jail. Ten minutes was all she needed. Less, if she was really quick. She *had* to get her hands on that treaty. Even if it meant following a predator straight into his den.

He turned. Jasmine's breath stalled as his eyes darkened. He stared at her for what felt like an eternity before his lids descended. She sensed his withdrawal before he spoke.

'I'll arrange for my chauffeur to deliver you to your hotel.' He was already nodding to a dark-clad figure nearby.

Acute anxiety swelled inside her.

She couldn't fail. She just couldn't. Stephen might *just* survive prison but her mother wouldn't make it.

'Or I could come with you. Save your chauffeur making two trips,' she offered, cringing at the breathless tone of her voice.

He held up a hand to stop the bodyguard who stepped forward, his gaze imprisoning hers. Silence pulsed between them. A silence filled with charged signals that made the blood pulse heavily between her thighs. Every sense sprang into superawareness. She could hear every sound, smell every scent on the evening breeze, feel every whisper of air over her heating skin. Her nipples hardened and her cheeks heated at the blatant evidence of her awareness of him.

The thought that she was insanely attracted to a man whom she planned to deceive, albeit temporarily, caused hysterical laughter to bubble up.

She strained not to react. To keep the wrap draped over her arms and not use it to hide the proof of her arousal. She'd never used her feminine wiles to capture a man's attention. Doing so now made her insides clench with disgust. All the same, a small part of her gave a cry of triumph when his eyes dropped to her chest for an infinitesimal moment.

'You want to come with me? Now?' His voice had altered, his eyes narrowing with icy suspicion that warned her to tread carefully.

Jasmine couldn't afford to back away. She had too much to lose.

'Yes. Take me with you. My hotel isn't that far from here. I'll even buy you a drink as a thank you.' The single brain cell that remained shook with astonishment at her boldness. Afraid that her plea had emerged more of a command, and might perhaps cause offence, she hastily added, 'If you don't mind.'

His gaze darkened with a predatory gleam that made Jasmine swallow in trepidation. 'Perhaps it is you who should mind, Miss Nichols. Some would advise you against what you're asking.'

With deliberate slowness, she passed the tip of her tongue

over her lower lip. Stark hunger blazed in his eyes, stealing her breath as the grey depths turned almost black. A warm rush of air whispered over her skin, but even that small change caused her to gasp as if he'd physically laid his hands on her.

'Maybe, but something tells me I can trust you,' she replied, her nerves jangling with terror at the uncharted waters she found herself in. Flirting and sexual games had never been her forte. Not since her one attempt at university had ended in humiliating disaster.

Another step brought Prince Reyes within touching distance. His narrowed eyes, still holding that trace of sadness she'd glimpsed earlier, were now laced with a healthy dose of bitterness.

Jasmine didn't have time to dwell on his expression because his scent engulfed her, fuelling her already frenzied senses. She inhaled, filling her entire being with his essence. As if he sensed it too, his nostrils flared.

'You're playing a dangerous game, Jasmine,' he murmured.

'It…it's just a lift back to my h-hotel,' she croaked.

'Perhaps. Or it is something else. Something neither of us is ready for.' His voice was pitched low, for her ears alone. His gaze slid over her face, its path as forceful and yet as gentle as a silky caress.

'I'll be out of your hair in less than half an hour. Seriously, you have nothing to fear from me.' *Liar.* She tried to curb the accusing voice, thankful when it faded away under the onslaught of the heavy emotion beating in her chest.

His jaw tightened. 'I have everything to fear from you.' Again the bitterness, sharper this time. 'The curse of a beautiful woman has been my ancestors' downfall.'

She forced a laugh. *Beautiful? Her?* Well, if he could flatter, so could she. 'So prove it's not true. Deliver me to my hotel and walk away. Then you'll be free of this…curse.'

He tilted his head to one side, as if weighing her request. His hand rose again, this time to reach down to encircle her wrist.

With a subtle but firm tug, he pulled her to him.

'If walking away resolved centuries-old issues, my kingdom wouldn't be in shambles.'

'I didn't mean—'

He pulled her closer. Jasmine was too mesmerised by this enigmatic man to acknowledge the curious stares of the guests beyond the protective circle of Prince Reyes's bodyguards. And he didn't seem too disturbed by their growing audience.

His stare turned into a frown. 'You intrigue me, Jasmine Nichols.'

'Is that a bad thing?'

He stepped back and he seemed to come to a decision. 'I'm not certain, but I wish to find out. Come.'

Reyes Navarre drew a deep breath.

What in *Dios's* name was he doing? Not since Anaïs had he behaved so rashly. His carefree period of picking up liaisons for a night had come to a jagged halt five years ago when he'd experienced for himself just how duplicitous women could be. His own mother had hammered that lesson home forcefully in the weeks before her death.

Overnight, Reyes had witnessed the family he'd foolishly thought he could bring together disintegrate beyond recognition. He'd watched the will to live slowly extinguish from his father's eyes until only a husk remained.

Reyes's chest tightened painfully with equal parts of remorse and bitterness. Remorse that grew each day because he knew he'd failed to grant his father, King Carlos, his one wish—an heir to the throne while he was still alive. Bitterness because his father had condemned Reyes for choosing to learn from past mistakes. What his father didn't know was the woman Reyes had thought would be his queen had turned out to be just as conniving and as faithless as his own mother.

The double blow had made abstinence a far better prospect. One he'd embraced and pushed to the back of his mind when his father's health had worsened.

But tonight…

He glanced at the woman whose delicate scent filled every corner of the limo.

She hadn't spoken since they'd driven away from the banquet, but Reyes had caught the fleeting glances she sent his way every now and then. Just as he'd glimpsed the little darts of her tongue at the corner of mouth when her gaze fell on him.

She did it again, just then. A different sort of tightening seized his body.

Grinding his teeth, Reyes forced himself to examine why Jasmine Nichols intrigued him. Perhaps it was being away from Santo Sierra for the first time in over a year. Perhaps it was the knowledge that, after months of tough negotiations, Mendez had finally agreed to sign the trade treaty.

Or it could be that he just needed to let himself feel something other than bitterness and recrimination…to experience a moment of oblivion before the relentless pressure of his birthright settled back on his shoulders.

Whatever the reason, he didn't stop himself from pressing the intercom that connected him to the driver.

'Take us to the boat,' he instructed.

Jasmine immediately turned to him. 'You're not taking me to my hotel?' Her voice held a touch of trepidation but no hint of panic.

She knew the score.

As he should.

Except he didn't.

He was acting out of character. Had been from the moment he saw her.

His smile felt strained. 'You owe me a drink, I believe. I'm choosing to take it *before* I have you delivered to your hotel, not after.'

'Just in case I renege? You're not very trusting, are you?'

The twinge in his chest stung deeper, but he refused to acknowledge it. 'No, I'm not.'

Her eyes widened and she looked away. 'Are we really going to your boat?' she asked with a curious note in her voice.

'Yes.'

Reyes remembered she didn't like boats. Was that why he'd brought her to his yacht instead of the royal suite that awaited him at the Four Seasons? Was he hoping she would quail at the sight of the big floating palace and ask to be returned to her hotel?

Or had he brought her here for his own selfish reasons? Because, for some reason, focusing on her made his tumultuous feelings subside just a little?

All through the interminable dinner, he'd watched her, his gaze unable to stray from her for more than a few seconds because every time it had, he'd felt the darkness encroaching.

He watched her now from the corner of his eye, waiting for a reaction. But her hands remained folded in her lap, her gaze on the large vessel they'd pulled up to.

Unfortunately his thoughts and emotions suffered no such languor or calm. They churned in rhythm to the heavy pounding of his heart at what was to come.

Thoughts of sating himself on a woman had been pushed far back into the recesses of his mind, especially in the last year as he'd battled to salvage the trade treaty with Valderra. But his efforts had paid off.

He'd brought Mendez and Valderra to the treaty table, the result of which would mean a much-needed economic boost for his people.

Tomorrow they would complete the signing of the Santo-Valderra treaty. The concessions had been heavy. Mendez had made outrageous demands, like the excessively extravagant banquet held here tonight to honour his birthday. A ceremony Reyes had initially balked at attending, but had eventually given in to, because he suspected Mendez would use any excuse to postpone the final signing of the treaty.

The concessions Santo Sierra had given would be recouped with time. And, most importantly, the trade blockage had been removed.

He still faced an uphill battle in convincing his council

members to accept the changes to come. And there was also his father…

Reyes pushed thoughts of his father and grief aside and reminded himself that his father was alive.

And for one night, *this night*, Reyes intended to turn his mind to more…pleasant matters.

Jasmine sat in silence beside him, a beacon in the gloom that threatened to swallow him whole. But Reyes sensed that she was almost as reluctant as he to test the depths of awareness that zinged between them, just as he was quietly amazed by the depth of his attraction for her.

The memory of her skin when he'd held her on the balcony returned. His hand tightened next to his thigh.

He'd taken one look at Jasmine and the foundations of his self-imposed celibacy had started to shake. All through the banquet he'd been unable to take his eyes off her, a notion that had at once fascinated and irritated him. By the time the banquet was over, he'd known his resistance was severely compromised.

Yet, he'd been determined to walk away. Bitter experience and the heavy burden of duty had taught him to weigh his decisions carefully.

One-night stands weren't his *modus operandi*.

So what in the name of Dios *was he doing?*

He hadn't touched her since that last electrifying contact, and yet a storm unlike anything he'd ever known raged inside him. From the corner of his eye, he watched her fiddle with one earring. The sweet, yet provocative movement fanned the inferno of his lust.

'Are we going to get out?' Her question emerged with that same breathy, husky quality that sent shivers racing through him. Her eyes, blue like the ocean surrounding his kingdom, slid to his and the throb in his groin accelerated.

'Momentarily,' he replied, hoping for some last-minute perspective.

But the only perspective his brain was willing to consider

was the one where this enthralling woman ended up in his bed, her voluptuous body quenching his ferocious need.

She'd shown herself a worthy opponent, and yes, he considered the insane tug and pull of attraction between them a battleground. A battle from which he would emerge the victor and walk away with everything he held dear intact.

During their intriguing exchange not once had her gaze slid from his. In fact, more than once he'd seen a spark of defiance in the blue vividness of her eyes. That spark had ignited something inside him he'd long forgotten.

It had reminded him of a carefree time when life had been less fraught.

He glanced up at the lights of his yacht. He'd deliberately not moored at the same quay as Prince Mendez because he'd wanted to avoid the avid media attention Mendez courted.

Reyes preferred privacy…solitude…silence. His mother had created enough chaos in his life when she was alive.

So what are you doing bringing a total stranger on board?

He faced Jasmine.

Her gaze immediately riveted to his and heat surged through his bloodstream. She gave a nervous smile and pulled her wrap tighter around her. He frowned at the protective gesture. The interior of the car wasn't cold, in fact the night air blowing gently through the half-open windows was sultry. So there could be only one other reason for the telling gesture.

'It's not too late to change your mind.' His statement emerged harsher than he'd intended, partly, he realised, because he didn't want her to leave.

Her eyes widened and she wavered for a second before a curiously resolute look settled over her face. 'No. A deal is a deal. Although I'm not sure how to go about buying you a drink when we're boarding *your* boat.'

Relief made him exhale unsteadily. He signalled to his bodyguard, who opened the door. Reyes handed him the briefcase holding the treaty and held out his hand to Jasmine. 'We'll continue our debate on board.'

She glanced from his hand to his yacht. He held his breath. Slowly, she reached out. His grip tightened on her fingers as he stepped out of the car and helped her out. He'd taken two steps when he felt her tug at his grip.

'Wait. I can't do this.'

Disappointment curled through him. Reyes bit back a sharp retort as he dropped her hand. In the time since his last liaison, the world hadn't changed, then, he mused caustically. Women continued to tease, to engage in sexual games in the hope that playing hard to get would make them seem more attractive to the opposite sex. The bitterness he'd tried to douse welled up again.

'Save the excuses, Miss Nichols. I'm disappointed that women seem to believe creating intrigue involves mind games, but I am not willing to indulge you.' He nodded to his driver, who stepped forward. 'You'll be delivered to your hotel. Enjoy the rest of your stay in Rio.' He couldn't stem the regret that settled gut-deep inside him. Not to mention the uncomfortable arousal that tightened his groin and made thinking straight difficult.

He turned away, wanting to be far away from her, from the temptation of her voluptuous body and seductive scent that insisted on lingering in the air around him.

'Actually, that's not what I want.' She sounded hurt and a little confused. 'I didn't mean that I'd changed my mind about the drink.'

He whirled round. 'Then what did you mean, Jasmine?'

An uneasy look crossed her face. 'I told you, I don't really like boats. But I thought I'd make an exception…just this once…' She shook her head. 'Anyway, I'm not coming aboard wearing these shoes.' She gestured to her feet.

Puzzled, he frowned. 'What?'

'My step—umm, I read somewhere that heels and boats aren't a good combination.' Her shrug drew his attention to the silky curve of her shoulder. 'Of course, I don't know what sort of flooring you have on your yacht, but I don't want to ruin it.'

Laughter replaced Reyes's disappointment. It rumbled through his chest, a sensation he hadn't felt for a while.

'*My floors?* You don't want to ruin the floors on my boat?' His incredulity grew with his words and he barely stopped himself from shaking his head.

'No, I don't. Plus, my feet are seriously killing me. So if you don't mind?' She held out her hand for him to take. 'It'll only take a minute.'

Caught in the surreal moment, Reyes took her hand. He felt the rough ridge of scarred tissue and looked at the thin line crossing her palm. About to ask what had caused it, he was stalled by the sight of one graceful leg, lifted, one ankle strap unbuckled before the process was repeated with the other shoe.

His gaze dropped to her feet. They were small but perfectly formed with pink tips. The sight only aroused him further, tweaked his already dangerously heightened senses.

'Good idea,' he murmured inanely, his voice curiously hoarse.

She nodded and fell into step beside him. 'I think it's only fair to warn you, though, the last time I rode a dinghy, I ended up falling overboard. I hope you'll rescue me if that happens again?'

A smile tugged at his lips. 'As you can see, my boat is slightly bigger than your dinghy. It'll take a lot of effort to accidentally go overboard. But be assured, I'll come to your aid should the worst happen.'

'Well, if you put it that way, then I have nothing to worry about,' she said with a smile.

Reyes smiled, feeling less burdened than he had in a long time. He took her shoes as they approached the gangplank and followed her up the stairs onto the deck and through into the large, open salon. He watched her take in her surroundings, her mouth parting to inhale sharply at the opulence that embraced her.

Reyes had seen different reactions to his yacht, some openly covetous and some hidden behind careful indifference. Jasmine's eyes widened in something close to childlike, uninhibited awe as she took in the polished wood panels, gold ornamentation and monogrammed accessories in royal Santo Sierran blue he'd commissioned for the vessel.

'Wow!' She turned full circle and found him watching her. A faint blush touched her cheeks and she walked over to the large sofa and perched on the edge. 'Sorry, I didn't mean to gush.'

'A genuine reaction is better than artificial indifference.' He walked over to her and placed her shoes next to her.

'Seriously? Who would be indifferent to this?' She waved her hand around the deck.

'People with ulterior motives they prefer to hide?' The last female on this boat had been Anaïs. She'd been in full playing-hard-to-get mode, which had swiftly crumbled when Reyes had threatened to walk away. Of course, she'd had other aces up her sleeve. 'In my experience, people are rarely what they seem at first blush.'

'Oh, right.' Jasmine's eyes darted to his and slid away, and she seemed lost for words. Her tongue darted out to lick the corner of her lip.

Reyes's heart beat just that little bit faster. His fingers tightened as anticipation fizzed faster through his veins.

Her skin, creamy with the barest hint of tan, glowed under the soft lights of his deck. His fingers itched to touch, to caress. But he held back.

There would be time for that later. He had no doubt he was about to indulge in something he'd never indulged in before—a one-night stand; this could be nothing more than that—but he didn't want to rush it.

Morning would come soon enough. The treaty would be signed. He would ensure Santo Sierra's continued economic prosperity. And he would return to his father's bedside to continue his vigil.

But for now... 'I think it's time for that drink, yes?'

* * *

Jasmine swallowed her relief as the heated look in Prince Reyes's eyes abated. For a moment there, he'd looked as if he wanted to devour her where she stood.

And as much as that had sent a bolt of excitement through her, part of her had quailed at the look.

Hastily, she nodded. 'Yes, thank you.'

She watched him walk towards an extensive, gleaming wood-panelled bar. A steward approached, but he waved him away. Opening a chiller, he grabbed a bottle of wine and expertly uncorked it. Rounding the bar, he handed her a glass and indicated a row of low, luxurious sofas.

Taking the seat next to her, he lowered his long body into it, driving the breath straight out of her lungs.

'What shall we drink to?' he asked in a low, deep voice, his stare focused solely on her.

Jasmine's mouth dried. 'Um, how about congratulations on the progress you've made with the treaty so far?' Talking about the treaty helped keep her grounded, reminded her why she was here.

His smile held more than a hint of pride. *'Gracias.'*

'Did you achieve what you set out for?'

Against his usual guarded judgement he found himself sharing with her. 'It was a long, hard battle, but we're almost there. By this time tomorrow, a solid trade agreement will exist between our two kingdoms, something my people have needed for a long time.'

Jasmine's heart thudded loudly in her ears. Her hands started to shake and she hastily put her glass down. Sensing him following the movement, she flexed her fingers and smoothed them over her dress.

'You should be back there, then, at the museum, celebrating. Why did you leave early?'

'I don't like crowds,' he declared. His eyes widened, as if he'd let something slip he hadn't meant to. A moment later, his expression shuttered.

Something inside her softened. 'I don't like crowds, either.'

His head snapped up, his gaze searching hers. At her small smile, his tense jaw relaxed.

'I mean, who does, aside from rock stars and, well, crowd lovers?' she joked. She wasn't making much sense, but at the moment Jasmine would've kept babbling just to keep that smile on his face.

A small, enigmatic smile twitched his lips before he took a sip of his wine. 'So what brings you to Rio alone?' he asked. 'Carnival was last month.'

She forced herself not to tense. For a wild moment Jasmine wondered if he could see through her to the truth of her presence in his life.

Clearing her throat, she shrugged and struck for the half-truth she'd practised in her head. 'I haven't had a holiday in years. An unexpected gap opened up in my schedule, and I took it.'

His eyes slowly narrowed, his fingers stilling around his wine glass. 'And you just happened to gain the most sought-after invitation to the Prince of Valderra's birthday party?' Mild disbelief rang through his voice.

'No. Of course not. My trip isn't all play. The brokerage firm I work for have been following the Santo-Valderra negotiations for some time. When one of my…clients offered me the invitation, I thought it would be good experience to learn more about it.'

'And have you?'

Jasmine shook her head. 'Only what's been released to the press, which is plenty interesting. I mean, from a brokerage point of view, it's mind-blowing what you've achieved—'

Jaw tightening, he set his glass down with a sharp click. 'And you want to know more? To gain first-hand information? Is that why you're here?'

CHAPTER THREE

JASMINE SWALLOWED, TREPIDATION jangling her nerves. 'I am interested, yes. But no, it's not why I'm here.' She spoke through the shame-coated lie.

His gaze dropped to her mouth. Heat rose in her belly, slowly engulfing her chest, her throat.

She fought to breathe as the feral, dangerously hungry look once more stole over his face, permeating the air with thick, saturated lust.

He reached out a hand, caught a lock of hair in his fingers and slowly caressed it. 'Why exactly are you here, Jasmine Nichols? Why did you not demand to be returned to your hotel?'

'I meant what I said. I'm intrigued by the treaty.' That much was true. 'From what I've been able to learn about it—'

He frowned. 'What you've been able to learn? Are you a spy?'

'No!' she replied hurriedly. Hoping she wasn't digging herself into an even deeper hole, she continued. 'The firm I work for brokers deals like these all the time, on a much smaller scale…and I was just wondering if what I'd heard was right.'

'What did you hear?'

'That the treaty heavily favours Valderra…' Her voice drifted away as a dark look blanketed his face.

God, what was she doing?

She wouldn't be surprised if he threw her off the boat for prying.

'Concessions were made prior to my handling of the negotiations that I have no choice but to honour.' He didn't sound happy about it. Just resigned.

She nodded. His fingers grazed her cheek. She only had to

turn her head a fraction and she'd feel more of his touch. Her every sense craved that touch.

He drew closer, slowly, his fingers winding around a lock of her hair; his eyes not leaving hers. 'Why do I get the feeling that you're holding something back from me, Jasmine?' he asked again, softly this time, his breath fanning over her lips. 'Tell me why I'm fighting my instincts when I should be heeding them?'

Her insides quaked with fear...and anticipation. 'I guess I could tell you that you're not the only one feeling that way. There's something about you. Something overpowering, that makes me...'

'Makes you what?'

Shaking her head, she surged to her feet and stumbled to the railing. Frustrated tears stung her eyes as she stared into the dark waters.

She couldn't do this.

She'd come too far, clawed herself back from a destructive, chaotic past. Going through with Joaquin's plan, giving in to the thug's demands would mean stepping back into that dark tunnel.

But walking away meant Stephen's destruction. A broken mother.

She gulped down the sob that threatened.

And jumped when his lips touched the back of her neck. A mere graze. But it pushed back her dark despair, lit her up like a bonfire on a sultry summer's night. As if galvanised by that simple touch, she came alive.

He grabbed her to him, one hand sliding around her shoulder while the other gripped her waist. He kissed the delicate skin below her ear, imprinting himself on her so vividly, every atom in her body screeched in delight.

He spun her in his arms and kissed her.

Jasmine had been kissed before. But not like this. Never like this. The fiery tingle started from her toes, spread through her body like wildfire, stinging her nerve endings. He tasted of wine, of dark, strong coffee, of heady pleasure that made her heart hammer as he drew her even closer.

Her breasts crushed into his chest. The imprint of his muscled torso against hers caused her fingers to tighten on his nape. He growled something under his breath, but the words were crushed between their lips as they both moved to deepen the kiss.

Somewhere deep within, a voice cautioned her against what she was doing. She tried to heed it, tried to pull back. Vaguely she sensed him move towards a doorway in the saloon.

Her good sense kicked in. 'Wait…'

He carried on walking, his lips now straying to the astonishingly sensitive skin just below her ear. She shuddered, a melting deep inside that threatened to drown her.

'Umm…' She paused as she realised she didn't know what to call him. What was the etiquette when you were snogging the face off a South American Crown Prince? 'Your Highness… wait…'

His deep laugh made her blush. 'When we are alone, you may call me Reyes. After all, you can hardly call me Your Highness when I'm deep inside you,' he murmured into her ear. 'Although that does present interesting possibilities…'

Her shocked gasp brought another laugh and Jasmine had to scramble to hang on to her sanity. 'Please…Reyes, put me down,' she pleaded.

Sensing her agitation, he slowly lowered her down before capturing her hands in his. 'What is it, Jasmine?'

For one absurd moment, she wanted to blurt out her guilt, but bit her tongue at the last minute. 'I haven't…I mean, this isn't something I normally do,' she babbled instead.

Raising both her hands, he pressed kisses onto her knuckles, his stunning eyes cooling. 'I understand. This is where you establish ground rules? Where I let you name your price because I'm too lust-hazed to see straight?' he asked cynically.

The ground rocked beneath her. Somewhere along the line, life had dealt this man serious blows. The depths of his sadness, suspicion and cynicism weren't traits he'd picked up by chance. And she should know. Life could be cruel beyond measure. Especially with men like Joaquin calling the shots.

But they only win if you let them...

The rebellious teenager whose antics had landed her in juvenile detention threatened to break through. Reminding herself just what was at stake here, she swallowed. 'Is it too much to believe that I'm nervous and a little bit overwhelmed?'

He lowered her hands. His eyes narrowed, probed and assessed. Jasmine understood how it was that Reyes Navarre had negotiated the sometimes almost insurmountable treaty with Valderra.

'So you don't want anything from me?' he asked.

Only the gritty determination that had seen her stand up to dangerous men twice her size kept her gaze from falling. 'Honestly, I would like to see the treaty. But I won't be sleeping with you because of that...' She realised what she was saying and stopped. A scalding blush suffused her face. 'I mean, nothing happens here that won't be my choice—'

He stopped her with a finger to her mouth.

'Understood. But remember this, too. Whatever happens between us will not go beyond tonight. It cannot,' he stated imperiously. 'My desire for you is finite.'

Hearing the words so starkly drew a cold shiver from her in spite of passion's flames arcing between them. He felt it and immediately captured her shoulders. 'But make no mistake. This desire burns bright and strong and I promise to make the experience—should you *choose* to stay for it—pleasurable for you.'

His accent had thickened, his words burning away the cold as if it had never existed. He lowered his head and brushed his lips over hers.

Jasmine swallowed as his words echoed in her head. A powerful aphrodisiac intent on eroding rational thought.

Walk away. Now!

She groaned and pulled away. 'I can't. I know you probably think I'm a tease, but I promise, I'm not. I'm not in the habit of jumping into bed with a man I just met. I hope you understand?'

Her mind made up, she took another step back and picked up her clutch. She couldn't go through with it. She would find another way to save her stepfather. Whatever the repercussions, Jasmine would find a way to help Stephen and her mother deal with it.

But not this.

Whatever Joaquin needed the copy of the treaty for no longer mattered to her. The man who stood in front of her, who'd battled whatever demons haunted him to achieve this treaty for his kingdom, didn't deserve what she'd planned tonight. *She* would never be able to live with herself if she went through with it; if she took a step back to that dark place she'd sworn never to revisit again.

Her heart lifted, lightened, filled with relief.

She looked up at Reyes and experienced a little thrill at the stark shock and disappointment on his face. She had reduced a powerful, virile man to...what had he called himself before? Lust-crazed?

Slightly heady with the feeling, she took another stumbling step back before she succumbed to temptation.

She was in an exotic country, in the presence of a charismatic man who seemed to set her very soul on fire. Jasmine knew that if she gave in—*and she wouldn't!*—the experience with Reyes would be unique and would remain with her for ever.

After several more moments staring at her, he finally nodded. 'Very well. I'll summon my driver.'

Acute loss scythed through her. 'That would be great, thank you.'

She watched him walk to the intercom next to the bar, holding her breath to keep from blurting for him to stop.

About to press the black button, he paused and looked over

at her. 'It's not every day that I'm surprised, but you've succeeded in pulling the rug from beneath my feet,' he said.

'Umm…thanks. But why are you surprised?'

That reserved smile made another appearance and he
turned. 'You want me, but you're walking away. I may not
know why, but I admire the strong principle behind your decision. Perhaps you deserve a prize after all.'

'Oh?' Renewed excitement fizzed beneath her skin.

He retraced his steps and held out his hand. 'If you still want
to see it, I'll show you the treaty.'

Oh. Jasmine wanted to refuse. Wanted to demand another
prize, one that involved his mouth on hers. But that opportunity had passed. She'd refused Prince Reyes. A man like that
wouldn't place himself in a position to be spurned twice.

But neither could she resist the chance to glimpse a piece
of Santo-Valderran history.

He led her down several flights of stairs into the heart of the
yacht. Images of soft, mellow wood and rich chrome touched
the edge of her consciousness. There seemed to be a lot of
gold—chandeliers, paintings frames, doorknobs—but Jasmine
was too caught up in Reyes Navarre's magnificence and the
electric awareness where his hand held hers for details of the
décor to register.

She finally regained her senses when he released her upon
entering his study. The space was masculine, the furniture
rich antique. Expensive books on diplomacy, economics and
culture lined one wall. First-edition literary works lined the
other. Behind his desk, a Renaissance painting that would've
had museum curators salivating graced the wall.

He smiled at her and skirted his desk. He pressed a lever
beneath the painting and it swung back to reveal a safe. He entered a code and pressed his thumb against a digital scanner.

Jasmine held her breath as he slid out an expensive leather
folder and came to stand beside her. Very conscious of the
breadth of his shoulders and the heat emanating from his whip-
cord body, she struggled to focus on the treaty.

When the terms finally registered, she frowned. 'Why would you agree to this?'

'The terms aren't up for discussion. I need to make the best of this situation.'

Puzzled, she stared at him. His gaze captured hers before dropping to her mouth. Awareness crackled through the air. Sucking in a breath, she refocused on reading the final pages. She noticed that various preliminary terms had been agreed every year for the past three years, the first signed by his father. Prince Mendez had played a cunning game, increasing his demands with each passing year.

She started to turn the last page. Reyes put his hand over hers. 'The remaining terms are confidential.'

The effect of his hand on hers again made her pulse jump. 'And what? You don't trust me?' she joked, hoping to inject a little lightness to ease the thick tension filling the room.

His hand trailed up her arm to slide around her nape. Tilting her head, he looked deep into her eyes. 'Trust doesn't come easy to me, but I've trusted you with more tonight than I have anyone in a long time, Jasmine.'

Her breath squeezed through the lump clogging her throat. 'Why?'

He shrugged. 'Perhaps I'm learning to trust my instincts again. Perhaps because you're the only one who didn't enjoy Mendez's antics earlier.' He smiled again.

Despite his attempt at a joke, Jasmine remained fiercely glad of her decision not to give in to Joaquin's threat; she blinked back hot tears and smiled. 'You have no idea how much that means to me.'

The lightness evaporated. He stepped closer, an almost desperate hunger screaming from his body. 'I still want you, Jasmine. Very badly.'

Throwing caution to the wind shouldn't have come so easily, shouldn't have felt so freeing. Because she'd learned very early that everything came at a cost.

But she replied, 'Take me,' before she registered the enormity of the plunge she was taking.

The sensation of luxurious covers beneath her back was the first inkling that they'd left his study. The equally luxurious feel of him as he lowered himself on top of her confirmed that thought.

Crushed by his delicious weight, she couldn't mistake the imprint of his impressive arousal pushing against her. Hot sensation pierced her, settling low in her belly as he deepened the kiss. His tongue delved into her mouth, commencing a bold exploration that left her reeling and struggling to hold on to the last of her sanity.

His hands slid down her sides, creating a path of heat wherever he touched. Locating her side zip, he eased it down.

At the touch of fingers on her skin, Jasmine gasped.

He raised his head, his dark grey eyes spiking into hers. 'Your skin is so soft, so silky,' he murmured huskily.

'Thank you,' she responded, then cringed, feeling suddenly gauche and awkward. The first time she'd done this, it had ended badly. *Beyond badly.* The second time had been worse. What if third time *wasn't* lucky…?

She lost her train of thought as he gripped her hip. His heat penetrated the silk material to her skin, fanning the flame already building inside her. Wanting to experience even more of his warmth, she raised her head and traced his mouth with her tongue.

Her action drew a gasp from him, his eyes darkening even further as heat scoured over his taut cheekbones. 'I hope you'll forgive me,' he murmured distractedly as he nuzzled her jaw, planting feverish kisses that caused her heart to pound harder.

'What for?' she managed to squeeze out.

He settled firmer against her. 'It's been a while for me. I will want to take my time.'

A wave of heat engulfed her face. 'Oh. Yes…well, it's been a while for me, too.'

A look crossed his face, almost of relief. Jasmine's heart

swelled, her hand finally unclasping itself from his neck to caress his cheek. He planted an open-mouthed kiss in her palm. That intimate caress drew another gasp from her. Pleased by her reaction, he traced his mouth over her wrist, down her arm to the curve of her elbow, and licked the pulse.

Fire erupted in her pelvis so fierce and sweet, she moaned.

Galvanised by her response, he levered himself off her and stood beside the bed.

Jasmine had never imagined watching a man undress would trigger anything but embarrassment. But watching Reyes shed his clothes became another heady experience. Enthralled, she watched him ease his tuxedo jacket off his broad shoulders before releasing the studs of his shirt. Her mouth watered as his deeply bronzed chest was revealed. Her fingers itched to touch, to explore. Curling them into the covers, she held still and adored his beauty with her eyes.

'The look in your eyes threatens to unman me, *querida*,' he rasped. His fingers went to the button on his trousers.

Embarrassed that she'd done something wrong, Jasmine started to look away.

'No. Don't look away,' he commanded.

Her eyes flew to his. 'But you said—'

'*Sí*, I know, but I hate the thought of being deprived of your attention.' With an impatient shove, he kicked the rest of his clothes away and stood before her, gloriously, powerfully naked.

Jasmine silently thanked him for giving her permission to look. Because she couldn't have looked away now if her life depended on it.

He was spectacular! He stepped closer and she watched, fascinated, as the clearly delineated muscles moved beneath his skin.

Her stomach clenched with renewed arousal when he reclined next to her. 'I want you naked.'

She wanted to find fault with his imperious tone, but Jasmine would've been a hypocrite if she didn't acknowledge that every word that fell from his lips only further increased her excitement. Lending action to his words, he brushed aside her hair, slid one hand under her dress's thin strap and eased it off her shoulder.

He feasted his eyes on her, scouring every inch of her breasts as if committing them to memory. With a firm tug on her bra, he bared one nipple, a guttural groan rumbling from his chest as he lowered his head and sucked her flesh into his mouth. He teased, he tormented. His fingers traced, paused over a scar on her shoulder, a remnant from her shady past.

She held her breath, her fingers convulsed in his hair, holding him to his task even as she tensed in anticipation of a query. His touch moved on. When he turned his attention to her other breast, Jasmine whimpered in delight and relief.

Dazed, she felt him tug her dress off. Her panties and bra followed, discarded by urgent hands that caressed her skin with masterful strokes.

Wet heat pooled between her legs, a fact Reyes's exploratory fingers didn't miss when one possessive hand cupped her feminine core.

Raising his head from her tight, wet nipple, he speared her with a fiery gaze. 'Maybe I won't go slow after all. I have to have you now,' he rasped.

The next few seconds whizzed by in a blur, the sound of the condom wrapper tearing open barely impinging on her heated senses. He gathered her to him before she could draw breath. Placing himself between her thighs, he speared his hands in her hair and angled her face to his.

Eyes the colour of gunmetal held her prisoner.

He thrust inside her fast, hard, then immediately set a blistering pace that stripped her of every thought.

Their coupling was furious. Heady in ways she'd never dreamed sex could be. She screamed as the first, fierce climax hit her. He kissed away her shocked cries, almost greedy in his possession of her mouth, then slowed his pace just long enough for her spasms to ease.

Then he surged to his knees, placed her in front of him and entered her from behind. Guttural, indecipherable Spanish words spilled from him as he thrust over and over inside her, one strong arm clamped around her waist. Her throat clogged with emotion, her heart pounding wildly in her chest as tears gathered in her eyes at the magic she hadn't come looking for, but had miraculously found.

Reaching up behind her, she clasped his nape, turned her head and met his lips with hers. They stayed like that, their sweat-slicked bodies rocking back and forth until he tensed, a harsh groan rumbling through his chest, followed by convulsions that triggered her second, deeper orgasm.

His arm remained locked around her as he eased them back onto the bed, their harsh breaths gentling. He brushed away the damp hair from her face before placing a gentle kiss on her temple.

'This wasn't how I foresaw my evening ending when I arrived at the museum tonight.'

Jasmine tensed, the thought that he could be regretting what happened sending a vein of ice through her chest. Some otherworldly, more experienced woman would've found a sophisticated answer to his comment. But no such words rose to her mind, so she clamped her eyes shut and held her breath.

'Nor mine,' she murmured.

'You were amazing,' he muttered, his tone hushed.

The breath whooshed from her lungs, joy making her lips curve in a smile that seemed to emerge from her very heart. 'You weren't so bad, yourself.'

He laughed, a low, husky sound she'd begun to seriously like. With a kiss on her shoulder, he eased himself from her body and stood up.

'Come.' Again his tone was more command than request.

Again, Jasmine found she didn't mind. 'Where are we going?'

'I have a sudden need to see your body slick with water.'

He tugged her off the bed and led her into a luxurious

shower room. After adjusting various dials and testing the water with his fingers, he turned.

He dropped a kiss at the juncture between her neck and shoulder. With swift, efficient motions he secured her hair on top of her head.

Grasping her shoulders, he walked her into the misty cubicle and proceeded to wring every last ounce of pleasure from her body.

Afterwards, wrapped in a warm, fluffy towel, Jasmine watched Reyes, his lean, masculine body stealing her breath once again.

'I'm glad I met you tonight.' The words spilled out before she could stop them.

Their eyes connected, held. 'I feel the same,' he said simply. They both looked away at the same time.

In silence he led her back to his bed. And this time, their lovemaking was slow, languid, an unhurried union that brought an alien tightness to her chest and tears to her eyes. Before their heartbeats had slowed, Reyes had fallen asleep.

The low buzz of her phone woke her. Squinting in the dark, she saw the light from her smartphone illuminate the inside of her small clutch purse. The call could only be from England. And since her boss knew she was on holiday and was unlikely to disturb her, it could only be her parents...or Joaquin.

Her heart jumped into her throat.

Reyes had eased his tight hold of her during the night and now lay on his stomach, his head turned away from her.

Quickly, she slid out of bed and retrieved the phone. Seeing the name displayed on the screen, her heart plummeted. 'Hello.'

'Jasmine!' Her mother's frantic voice rang in her ears. 'Where are you? They took him. Oh, God, they broke his arm...and then they took him away!'

Walking on tiptoe to the door, Jasmine slipped out and hurried down the hallway to Reyes's study. 'Mum, take a deep breath and tell me what happened,' Jasmine said, even though deep down she suspected the answer.

'Some men broke into the house and they took Stephen!'

'*What?* When?'

'About an hour ago. They wouldn't say where they were going. But they hurt him, Jasmine. What if they…they kill him?' Her voice broke in a strangled sob.

Ice slithered down Jasmine's spine. She clutched the phone to her ear to stem the shaking in her hand. 'It's okay, Mum. I'm sure they won't. Did they…what did they say?' She tried to steady her voice so her mother's panic didn't escalate.

'They left a number…asked me to give it to you to call. Jasmine, I don't know what I'll do if anything happens to Stephen— *Oh, God!*'

Knowing how adversity had affected her mother before Stephen came into their lives, Jasmine clutched the phone harder, unwilling to contemplate the worst. Her earlier bravado began to wither before her eyes.

She took a deep breath. 'Well, stop worrying.' Jasmine tried to infuse as much optimism into her voice as she could. 'Text me the number. I'll sort this out, I promise.'

Her mother's teary, panic-laced goodbye wrenched at Jasmine's heart. Hands shaking, she started to dial the number her mother had sent through when her phone buzzed with another incoming text.

Jasmine read it. Once. Twice. Her fingers went numb.

The message itself was innocuous enough. But the meaning hit her square in the chest.

One hour. Rio Hilton. Room 419. A simple exchange. Good luck.

She returned to the bedroom on leaden feet and froze as Reyes shifted in the bed, exhaled heavily before settling back into deep sleep. Moonlight filtering through the open windows silhouetted him in soft light, his glorious body bare from the

waist up. Momentarily, she stared, recalling the way he'd unleashed all that potent power on her, his generosity in showering her with pleasure.

Her insides quivered as harsh reality hit her in the face.

She had no choice.

She'd been willing to abort her despicable mission even if
it meant exposing her stepfather's misdeeds and possible incarceration to the authorities.

But she couldn't stand by and do nothing while Stephen
was being physically harmed. Or worse. She would never be
able to live with herself.

As for Reyes…

She bit her lip and forced her gaze from the man lying on
the bed.

Numbness invading every atom of her being, Jasmine
stealthily pulled her clothes on and went back into the study.
Reyes hadn't had the chance to place the treaty back in the safe.

Insides clenched in shame, she walked to the desk, opened
the folder and lifted the heavily embossed papers.

Her hands shook as she lifted the treaty and held it in her
hands.

*'I am merely a concerned citizen of Santo Sierra, wishing
to reassure myself my crown prince's actions are altruistic,
Miss Nichols. That is all…'*

Joaquin's words reverberated in her head and she clenched
her teeth. She might only have known him for a few hours,
but Jasmine didn't doubt that Crown Prince Reyes Navarre
cared deeply about his people and held only their best inter-
ests at heart.

It was Joaquin's motives that were highly suspect.

Whatever happened, Jasmine didn't have any intention of
letting the document out of her sight.

Taking a deep breath, she folded the treaty, slipped into the
hallway and made her way to the deck to retrieve her shoes.
Clutching them to her chest, she made her way down the steps
towards the gangplank.

The bodyguard materialised in front of her, large and threatening. His searching eyes stalled her breath.

With every last ounce of strength, she straightened and lifted her chin, all at once ashamed and thankful that her old skills were coming to the fore.

Never show fear, never show fear. 'Can I get a taxi, please?' she asked, praying he spoke enough English to understand her request.

For several seconds, he didn't respond. Finally, he nodded and indicated the exit.

Despite the pre-dawn hour, people and cars rushed past on the road beyond the quay, the post-Carnival Rio nightlife as vibrant as it had been during the festival a month ago. Another set of bodyguards guarded the gangplank and exchanged words with her escort, who shrugged and said something that made the others chuckle. Jasmine tried to remain calm, regulate her breathing as she walked beside him.

Twenty minutes later, she stumbled into the foyer of the Rio Hilton. The night receptionist directed her to the bank of lifts without batting an eyelash.

When she reached the room, Joaquin Esteban's burly sidekick held the door open for her. She entered. The diminutive man rose from a cream-coloured sofa, his hands outstretched in false greeting. Jasmine sidestepped him, her fists clenched.

'What did you do with my stepfather?' she demanded.

Joaquin paused, his hard eyes glittering before his sleazy smile slid back into place. 'Why, nothing, Miss Nichols. He's fine and currently enjoying the best hospitality at my home in London until our business is concluded.'

'You broke his arm!'

'Ah, that was rather unfortunate. My men merely wanted to make sure everyone understood what moves needed to be made. But he got a little...excited.'

Rage built inside her. 'So you broke his arm? God, you're nothing but a thug!'

'I would caution against name-calling. You were on the

prince's yacht for over five hours. And from the looks of it you weren't there against your will.'

Her skin crawled. 'You were having me watched?'

'I'm very vested in our deal. It's imperative that you understand that.' His eyes slid from her face to her handbag, the question in them undeniable.

For a wild second, Jasmine wanted to tell him she'd failed.

She wanted to turn back the clock; to return the treaty, return to the bed and the magnificent, captivating man she'd left in it. A man whose haunted eyes made her yearn to comfort him.

Even now she craved one more look, one more touch...

But it was too late. Defying Joaquin would be condemning her stepfather to a horrific fate.

And yet, she couldn't just hand the document over.

'You're not merely a concerned citizen of Santo Sierra, are you?'

Joaquin shrugged. 'No. Valderra is my home.'

Her mouth dropped open in shock. What on earth had she got herself into? 'Why are you doing this?' she whispered. Just then another possibility dawned, cold and unwelcoming. 'Do you work for Prince Mendez?'

'Enough questions. The document, please,' Joaquin said coldly.

'No.' Jasmine shook her head and eyed the door. 'I won't give it to you.'

She whirled about and was confronted with the thick wall of muscle in the shape of the bodyguard. His beady eyes narrowed before he snatched the clutch out of her frozen grasp and removed the treaty from it.

Jasmine had been in enough fights to know which ones she stood a chance in and which ones were hopeless.

Joaquin's eyes glittered as he perused the sheets, before rolling up the document.

'Thank you, Miss Nichols. I think this concludes our business together.' He started to turn away.

Sick with self-loathing, she stepped forward. 'Wait! Please tell me you'll return the treaty to Prince Reyes before tomorrow?'

'You don't need to trouble yourself about that,' Joaquin answered. 'I'll make sure it reaches the right hands.'

Sweat coated her palms. 'But if the document isn't returned tonight, Rey…the prince will know I stole it.'

'And what does that matter? It's highly unlikely you and the prince will ever cross paths again, is it not? Besides, going on past experience, I wouldn't have imagined you would be bothered by something as trivial as your reputation,' he scoffed.

'I'm not that person any more. I've turned my life around.'

'So you say. But once a thief, always a thief. You reverted to type quite easily.'

Pain frayed the outer edges of her heart. Holding her head high, she stood her ground. 'I don't need to prove myself to you.' Anxiety churned through her stomach. 'What about Stephen?'

'He'll be home for breakfast. Goodbye, Miss Nichols.' He walked out of the room.

Jasmine wanted to chase after him, rip the document from his hands.

As if guessing her intentions, the bodyguard cleared his throat.

Jasmine didn't flinch. She'd dealt with brutes like him before, taken down one or two, even. But she knew she wouldn't win this battle. She'd been damned from the very start.

Nevertheless, the enormity of what she'd done settled like a heavy mantle on her shoulders. Ice flowed through her veins as she clenched her fists.

'Taxi?' the bodyguard snarled.

'No, thank you. I'll find my own way.'

The first rays of dawn slashed across the sky as Jasmine returned to her hotel. With disjointed movements, she wheeled her suitcase out of the closet and stuffed her belongings into it. Forcing herself not to think, not to feel, she undressed and entered the shower.

But tears, scalding hotter than the scouring spray, coursed down her cheeks as she desperately scrubbed her skin.

Tonight she'd sunk to a despicable low. She'd lied. She'd stolen.

She'd let herself down spectacularly.

And in the blink of an eye, stripped back the years and reverted to her old self.

CHAPTER FOUR

One month later

APRIL HAD BROUGHT an abrupt end to the cold snap and incessant rain that had engulfed London and most of the country for months.

Jasmine stepped out of Temple tube station into brilliant sunshine and stumbled past a group of tourists debating which attraction to visit. Their excited conversation barely touched her consciousness. Arms folded around her middle, she struck a path through the crowd towards the building that housed her office, clinging to the near fugue state she'd inhabited since returning from Rio. A blank mind meant she didn't have to think. Didn't have to feel.

Didn't have to remember Reyes.

Or what she'd done.

Most of all, she didn't have to acknowledge the fact that the past she'd thought she'd left behind was still with her, buried underneath her skin, ready to rear its ugly head and reveal itself in all its glory.

Naïve. She'd been so naïve. To imagine that she could escape unharmed.

A lance of pain shot through her chest. By now Reyes Navarre would know her for what she was. And despise her for it.

Despite the thousands of miles separating them, Jasmine could almost feel the weight of his disappointment.

'I've trusted you with more tonight than I have anyone in a long time.'

A moan rose in her throat. With a shake of her head, she ruthlessly suppressed it, sucking in a deep breath as she neared her office building.

Her boss had been sending her anxious looks over the past few days. Twice this week, she'd forgotten it was her turn to get the coffee and muffins.

Yesterday she'd returned from a hurried trip to the coffee shop with a serious case of nausea. One she hadn't been able to shake since.

Numbness and absent-mindedness when she was alone was fine…welcome in fact. But she couldn't afford to let it affect her work—

Her thoughts scattered as a body slammed into her.

Jasmine grasped the nearest solid thing to break her fall, but it was too late. She slid sideways, taking with her half of the contents of the small newsstand as she stumbled.

'For goodness' sake, miss, watch where you were going! Now look what you've done!'

Glaring at the retreating back of the man who'd barrelled into her, Jasmine regained her feet and started gathering the magazines. 'I'm so sorry,' she muttered.

'It'll take me ages to sort out the newspapers,' the kiosk owner grumbled.

'It's fine. I'll pay for—' Jasmine's words dried in her throat.

From the numbed state she'd lived in for the past four weeks, the fiery bolt of electricity that smashed through her body made her reel. Her heart thundered, sending a rush of blood roaring through her veins so she didn't hear the concerned voices around her as she grabbed the newspaper, her gaze riveted on the picture on the front page.

Reyes!

Her fingers shook, wildly fluttering the paper as she stared. Reyes…the reclusive crown prince…on the front page of an English newspaper. The why slammed into her brain a split second before her eyes sought the headlines.

Santo-Valderra Trade Treaty In Chaos… Economy Threatened!

An anguished moan scoured her throat, her heart lurching so painfully she had visions of it stopping altogether.

'Miss, are you all right?' the kiosk owner's voice finally impinged.

Trembling, she dug into her bag and paid for the newspaper, mumbling at the seller to keep the change to pay for the damage she'd caused.

Clutching the paper, she darted through the crowd, breaking into a full run as fevered urgency flooded her bloodstream.

In her office, she sank into her seat, her shaking fingers spreading open the newspaper.

She blinked eyes that stung, forced back her panic and focused on the words of the story.

The Santo-Valderra talks had broken down after Prince Reyes Navarre had been unable to produce his part of the treaty. Prince Mendez of Valderra had agreed to continue treaty talks on condition his further demands were met.

Mendez had walked away from the negotiation table when his demands had been refused. Now both kingdoms were at an economic stand-off.

Acid churned through her gut as she turned over the pages to find the rest of the story. But things only got worse.

Unable to keep the bile down, Jasmine stumbled from her desk and barely made the toilet before she emptied the meagre contents of her stomach.

Oh, God, this was all her fault!

Shakily, she returned to her desk, read the story one more time, and fished out her phone. The small part of her brain that could function sent a small prayer of thanks that her boss had left last night for an overseas assignment.

After sending a quick email taking the day off, she entered a search into her computer. Locating Santo Sierra's embassy in London, she jotted down the address, slipped it into her bag and left her office.

By the time the taxi delivered her outside the embassy in Kensington, her shaking had abated. Her insides still trembled, but outwardly she projected the picture of calm she'd strived so hard to achieve over the last few years.

Striding into the opulent reception, she made a beeline for the receptionist. Jasmine wasn't sure exactly what her game plan was, but she had to do *something*.

Maybe she could speak to the ambassador, convince someone to let her try to fix the chaos she'd created...

God, she was grasping at straws. But she couldn't cower away—

'Can I help you?'

She focused on the receptionist. 'Yes.' She stopped and cleared her throat. 'Can I see the ambassador, please?'

The receptionist's eyebrows rose. 'Do you have an appointment?'

'No...but I...this is important...' Jasmine ventured, her voice trailing off when the neatly dressed woman shook her head.

'Perhaps you'd like to leave your name and the reason for your visit and I'll arrange an appointment...?'

Jasmine smothered a grimace. 'My name is Jasmine Nichols. And it's about the Santo-Valderra treaty.'

The other woman's eyes narrowed suspiciously. 'What about it?'

'I just read in the paper about it breaking down. I wanted to offer my help in any way I can...?'

The receptionist stared at her in silence, her scepticism turning to downright incredulity as the seconds ticked by. The phone rang. She picked it up. The conversation in rapid Spanish flew over Jasmine's head.

She focused when the receptionist gasped. *'Sí. Sí. Su Alteza.'*

Her eyes widened as she replaced the handset. 'Please take a seat, Miss Nichols. Someone will be with you shortly.'

The flood of relief that surged through Jasmine nearly crippled her. Reaching out, she gripped the edge of the desk. 'Oh, thank you. I know he's busy, but I really appreciate it.' She started to walk towards the plush seats, then froze when her stomach heaved.

Swallowing, she turned. 'Can I use your bathroom?' she asked, alarm rising when her stomach roiled harder.

The receptionist was still staring at her as if she'd grown extra limbs, but Jasmine was too desperate not to heave onto the polished floor to decipher why. Eyes wide, the other woman pointed down a small hallway. 'Through those doors.'

Nodding, she rushed into the bathroom and locked the stall. Five minutes of wretched heaving later, she stared at her reflection in the mirror and groaned.

How did she expect anyone to take her seriously when she looked like an electrified corpse? She dampened another roll of hand tissues and pressed them to her cheeks. Whatever was ailing her would have to be investigated later.

Drying her hands, she pinned a confident smile on her face, exited the bathroom. And came face to face with Prince Reyes Navarre.

The pounding in Reyes's head when he'd learned that Jasmine Nichols was in his embassy had subsided to a dull throb.

For a single moment his rage had been total. All-encompassing. The feeling had been followed closely by shock at her sheer audacity.

It'd been several moments before he'd realised the ambassador was about to turn her away. His countermand had raised several eyebrows around the conference table where he'd been conducting his meeting. He hadn't explained his reason.

He didn't need to.

His plan for retribution where Jasmine Nichols's betrayal was concerned was no one's business but his.

He watched with satisfaction as she paled. That prim little smile on her face disappeared and her eyes rounded.

'Reye—Prince Navarre!'

Was that a tremble of fear? Good.

'You will address the prince as Your Highness.' His ambassador spoke sharply from beside him.

Jasmine's gaze swung from him to the short, fatherly figure, and back to him. Noting for the first time that they had an audience, she blinked. Reyes noted her drawn features.

If she had a conscience, he hoped it was eating away at her. But he knew women like her possessed no conscience. They seduced and betrayed with no thought for anyone else but themselves.

His jaw tightened as her lashes swept down in a false gesture of apology.

'Of course. My apologies, Your Highness. I wasn't... expecting you here.' Her hand shook as she clutched her handbag. When she bit her lip, Reyes smothered the memories threatening to awaken.

Turning to where his bodyguards hovered, he waved one forward. 'I have confidential business with Miss Nichols. Take her down to the basement. Until I say so, she's not allowed to contact anyone or leave the premises under any circumstances.'

'*What?* You can't do that!' She'd paled further and her breaths jerked out in shallow pants.

Reyes smiled. 'You're on Santo Sierran soil. I can do whatever I please with you.'

'But I came here to help. *Please*, Reyes—Your Highness!' she screeched as Reyes stepped back. Her fear was very real.

Reyes steeled himself against it and walked away. Never again.

He'd failed his people because of this woman.

Remembering brought a burn of pure white rage that obliterated any lingering mercy.

Even before he'd come fully awake the next morning on the yacht, he'd known something was wrong. The silence had been deafening. Complete. Where he should have heard the soft breathing and felt the warm, supple body of the lover he'd taken to his bed, there'd been a cold, empty space.

His instinct hadn't failed him. Even faced with the discovery of the theft, he'd hoped he was hallucinating. For endless minutes, he hadn't believed what he'd let happen. How much he'd let his guard down.

How spectacularly he'd failed in his duty to protect his people. That was what made the burn sting that much deeper. The full realisation that he'd taken a stranger to bed, a stranger who'd turned out to be a thief, had pointed to a singular lack of judgement, preyed on his mind like acid on metal for the last four weeks.

In the time since then Reyes could've hired a team of investigators to find and bring her to justice. But that would've served no purpose besides granting him personal satisfaction. Seeking personal vengeance, although tempting, had been relegated very low on his list. Rescuing the trade talks with Valderra had been paramount.

Of course, Mendez, handed the perfect opportunity to sink his hands deeper into the Santo Sierran coffers, had sought to do exactly that.

Relentless greed had threatened to destabilise the economy. Jasmine Nichols's actions had accelerated the process as surely as if she'd lit a fuse to a bomb.

Reyes breathed in and out, forced himself to focus through the rage and bitterness eating at him. There was no time for recriminations. For the sake of his father, for the sake of his people, he had to put personal feelings aside.

First, he would salvage the economy.

Then he would deal with Jasmine Nichols.

Jasmine pushed away the tray of tea and sandwiches. The thought of eating or even taking the smallest sip of tea made her stomach churn. She took a deep breath, folded her hands in her lap and silently prayed for strength.

The room she'd been brought to was comfortable enough. Sumptuous sofas were grouped in one corner, centred round a low antique coffee table. A conference table took up a larger space and, mounted on the far end of the wall, a large screen TV and a camera.

The red light blinked, telling her she was being observed. The memory of Reyes's cold rage slammed into her mind. Unable to sit, she jumped up. She'd been shown into this room two hours ago. Luckily, her nausea had abated but her shock and anxiety had risen in direct proportion as the realisation of what she'd walked into ate at her.

She paced, twisting her hands together. Reyes was angry and disappointed with her. No doubt about that.

She'd foolishly thought she, a junior mediator in a small-sized firm, could help rectify the situation she'd caused. Make amends for what she'd done...

Jasmine's heart lurched, a feeling of helplessness sliding over her. Reyes was probably laughing his head off at her audacity. And for all she knew, he could've already left London. The newspaper article had mentioned he was visiting several European countries to garner economic support for Santo Sierra.

If he'd truly left her to be dealt with to the fullest extent of the law, she would probably be prosecuted for treason and thrown in a Santo Sierran jail.

Her legs threatened to give way, but she forced herself to walk towards the camera. Swallowing, she looked up at the black globe.

'Can I speak to His Highness, please? I won't take up much of his time, I promise. I just... I need five minutes. Please...'

The light blinked at her.

Feeling foolish, she whirled about and paced some more. Another hour passed. Then another.

Jasmine was ready to climb the walls when the door swung open. Breath stalling, she rushed towards it. Only to stop when confronted by yet another bodyguard bearing a tray.

It held several tapas dishes, fragrant rice and a tall carafe of pomegranate juice.

'Your lunch,' the guard said in heavily accented English.

As violent as the nausea had been, the hunger cloying through her now, when the appetising smells hit her nostrils, was equally vicious. But she forced herself to shake her head. 'No. I won't eat until I speak to His Highness.'

The thickset guard blinked. Pressing home her advantage just in case she was being watched on camera, she pushed the tray away, sat on the far end of the sofa, and crossed her legs.

The door shut behind the guard. Hearing the lock turn, her insides congealed. Another half an hour passed in excruciating slowness before the handle turned again.

Reyes stood in the doorway.

The shock of seeing him again slammed into her. But she took advantage of the wider distance between them to observe him.

His face had grown haggard since Rio; perhaps it was the short designer beard he sported, his hair a little longer, shaggier. But his body was just as masculine and breathtaking as before, or even more so with the added angle of danger thrown in.

Or she could be going out of her mind, dwelling on superficial things when there was so much at stake.

'You wanted to see me.' He stepped into the room and the door shut behind him.

Now that he was here, Jasmine wasn't sure where to start. *I'm sorry* seemed so very inadequate.

So she nodded, struggling to hide the guilt eating her up inside. 'Yes. I think I can help with your…situation.'

He sucked in a sharp breath. His fingers opened and closed in a gesture of restrained control. '*Help!* You don't think you've helped enough?' he snarled.

'Please, I'm trying to make things right any way I can. Please tell me what I can do and I'll do it, Reyes—'

His eyes turned to dark pools of ice. 'You will address me as Your Highness. Addressing me by my first name was a one-time privilege. One you abused with the coarsest atrocity. And Miss Nichols?'

'Yes?'

'I suggest you eat. You won't be enjoying luxuries such as three-course meals for very much longer.'

CHAPTER FIVE

JASMINE'S BREATH SNAGGED in her throat. 'What do you mean by that?'

'I mean your situation is precarious. Once I apprise the ambassador and my council members of your crimes, your destiny will be sealed.'

'But you haven't done it yet. And you...you said earlier that the matter between us was personal.'

'I only meant I have more important matters to attend to.' His mouth compressed in a grim smile. 'You will get what's coming to you. My intention was to deal with you at a later date. I didn't think you would be foolish enough to cross my radar of your own accord just yet. So perhaps I'll watch you suffer for a long time.' His gaze went to the tray of cold food and his jaw clenched. 'You'll be brought another tray. Eat.'

He stepped towards the door.

'Wait. Please.'

'What?'

She cleared her throat. 'Will you join me for lunch? That is, if you haven't eaten yet? I can tell you why I came here while you eat? Please.'

The icy incredulity in his eyes didn't recede as he shook his head. 'You're brazen and audacious, I'll give you that. But your offer is declined, Miss Nichols,' he replied sarcastically. 'Was there anything else?'

She squeezed her eyes shut for a second. 'Please tell me what I can do to make things right. I'll do anything.'

He raised an eyebrow at her. 'I don't trust a single word out of your mouth. So I suggest you save your breath.'

She licked her lower lip and tried anyway. 'You can't leave me here for ever.'

'Can't I?' The smile that curved his lips could not in any way be described as affectionate, warm, or even cordial. The starkness of it struck pure terror in Jasmine's heart.

'I…I guess you can. But, please don't.' Her nausea was rising again. She didn't think she could stand being cooped up in here for another minute, let alone hours on end.

His shark-like smile widened, the growth of beard emphasising the feral whiteness of his teeth. A dark shiver swept over her.

'Never fear, *querida*, your sins will be addressed in due course. This subject is closed. For now.'

She'd been dismissed. Just like that. Jasmine wasn't sure which emotion—despair or trepidation—churned greater in her stomach as she watched Reyes leave. She couldn't force him to listen to the apology she'd practised for a month now. From his blatant hatred of her, she'd have to abandon any hope of asking for his forgiveness.

For now she had no recourse but to stay a prisoner.

Despair cloying through her, she paced for another hour before exhaustion deadened her limbs.

Kicking off her shoes, she sank onto the sofa. Despite the creature comforts, there were no windows in the basement. The remote for the TV had been removed. She had no idea exactly how much time had passed because her bag and phone had been taken away. The second tray Reyes had ordered delivered had also gone cold, its arrival coinciding with another case of severe nausea.

That, coupled with the exhaustion, convinced Jasmine she'd definitely picked up a bug of some sort.

Stretching out, she shivered and tried to tuck her skirt down to cover her legs as much as possible. Then, closing her eyes, she succumbed to the darkness tugging at her consciousness.

'Jasmine, wake up!'

'Mnnnh.' Her tongue felt too thick to convey the *no* she'd been attempting. She tried to burrow into the blanket some-

one had draped on her, but a sharp shake of her shoulder stopped her.

'Wake up!'

She groaned at the effort it took to pry her eyes open. 'What?'

A man, presumably a doctor from the stethoscope clinging to his neck, hovered above her. She squirmed and started to raise her hand as he shone a light in her eyes.

Sharp pain shot up her arm. 'Ouch.'

'Lie still. You have an intravenous needle in your arm.'

Reyes's deep voice was unmistakeable. Her attention swung to him as he barked at whoever else was in the room. When the volley of Spanish ceased, he was holding out a glass of water with a straw to her lips, and someone was pressing a soft pillow beneath her head.

Questions swirled in her fuzzy brain. 'Reyes…what…?'

'Don't try and speak,' he said, his eyes narrowed on her face as he addressed the doctor in Spanish.

The doctor nodded repeatedly and patted Jasmine's shoulder.

'What's he saying? What happened to me? And why do I have a needle in my arm?'

Reyes glared at her, but she saw shadows lurking in his eyes. 'You fell asleep but you didn't respond when I tried to wake you.'

The doctor spoke to Reyes. Reyes turned to her. 'Are you on any medication?'

Frowning, she shook her head. Then noticed her new surroundings for the first time. 'Where am I?'

'You're in my suite in the guest wing of the ambassador's residence.'

About to ask why she'd been relocated, she paused as the doctor addressed Reyes again. After a few minutes, the thin man bowed and left the room.

'Should I be worried that the doctor didn't want to speak to me, his patient?'

'You don't speak Spanish. And you're not a patient. You're a prisoner.'

Jasmine's temper twitched despite the knowledge that she deserved his caustic tone. She glanced at the pole next to the bed holding the IV bag. 'I know. But I'd still like to know what's wrong with me, if it's not too much trouble?' she muttered.

Reyes's mouth firmed. 'You're severely dehydrated and a touch malnourished. The fluids should do the trick. And I've ordered more food to be prepared for you. When was the last time you had a healthy meal?' he asked with a dark frown.

Her eyelids dragged heavily as she blinked. 'You mean the last time before I was incarcerated in your basement?'

'Answer the question, Jasmine.'

Her heart shouldn't have jumped at the sound of her name on his lips. But it did. 'I don't know. Yesterday afternoon, I think. I haven't had much of an appetite lately.'

Her eyes met his. Stayed. A piercing awareness lanced between them.

Reyes lunged to his feet and uttered a sharp command in Spanish. A bodyguard entered, glanced her way and nodded. She didn't need a translator to know she was the subject of the discussion. Feelings of vulnerability rose along with the hairs on her nape. 'What's going on now?'

Reyes didn't answer. He merely turned on his heel and walked through a door to a connecting room.

'His Highness requires me to attend your home...bring you a few things before we leave,' the bodyguard delivered in halting English.

Surprise froze Jasmine for all of ten seconds before her head swivelled towards the door Reyes had just walked out of. 'Leave? I'm not going anywhere.'

'You misunderstand. This is not a request from His Highness. It is a summons.'

'*A what?*' she asked dumbly, unable to immediately compute the words.

'You are required to pack a bag, *señorita*. We leave tomorrow.'

'You have your orders, I understand. But perhaps I can talk about it with *His Highness* when he has a minute?' Her words were delivered loud in the hope that Reyes would hear her from wherever he'd disappeared to. She didn't want to create any more waves, but neither could she let Reyes take over her life.

Silence descended in the room, the bodyguard eyeing her as if she'd gone insane.

Reyes re-entered the room. With a nod, he dismissed the security detail, waiting until they'd shut the door behind them before addressing her.

'I think during your exchange with my men something may have become lost in translation. My *request* was actually a command. There was nothing of a suggestion about it. When I leave here in the morning, you're coming with me.'

Despite her hammering pulse and the exhaustion sapping at her, she found the strength to speak. 'I understand that I'm your prisoner, but even prisoners get advance warning of their fate,' she implored.

One dark eyebrow rose. 'You forget you have no rights here. I hold all the cards. You go where I wish you to go.'

Jasmine's mouth dried up. The back of her hand itched and she yearned to rip the needle out, grab her shoes and handbag and run as fast as her legs could carry her. But she knew, even if her conscience allowed her, she wouldn't make it to the door.

Desperation made her blurt out, 'I have a life, a job to return to.'

'You will resign tomorrow.'

A death knell sounded somewhere in her head. 'Please, don't do this, Reyes.'

His eyes narrowed. 'Resign. Or I'll take pleasure in informing your superiors of the true depths of your character. *After* I hand you over to the authorities.'

'Are you saying that if I resign you won't tell them I'm—' She stopped, unable to speak the hated word that sealed her guilt. But he already knew she was guilty. His eyes narrowed scornfully.

'Afraid to say it out loud? *A thief,* Jasmine Nichols, that's what you are,' he condemned through clenched teeth. 'You not only stole from me, you stole from my people. You single-handedly set back years of trade negotiations.' His eyes blazed at her, grey fire that stripped her to the bone.

Her heart lurched as her sins were laid bare in front of her. The heat of shame burned through her, from the soles of her feet up through her body until the acrid taste of it flooded her mouth.

'Rey—I'm sorry. What happened wasn't supposed to happen.'

His laughter mocked her. 'You mean the sex was supposed to addle my brain so much I'd suspect someone else of the theft?' he snarled.

'No. I mean I shouldn't have taken the treaty in the first place.' Jasmine couldn't contain the sob that rose in her throat. Tears flooded her eyes. To hide it, she turned away and plugged a fist to her mouth.

But he heard it. Of course he heard it. 'Tears, Miss Nichols?' he taunted. 'How original. Almost as original as your pick-up line in Rio.'

Her sob emerged, thick and broken. Desperately, she tried to gulp it down.

His scorn reached her from across the room. 'Spare me the histrionics. You cry as if your heart is breaking. Which cannot be because you don't have a heart.'

Her head whipped round at the cruel assertion. He stood against the window, his hands shoved deep into his pockets. She deserved every accusation he threw at her, but she needed him to see she wasn't all bad.

'What I did was wrong, I know that. And I have a heart, or I wouldn't be here, trying to make amends.'

A cruel smile curved his lips. 'Well, that's a shame and a curse for you. Because I aim to make you pay for your betrayal.

And by the time I'm finished with you, you'll feel that heart you claim to possess ripped from your chest!'

Reyes watched her eyes widen. The same eyes had gazed adoringly up at him that night on his yacht, then darkened as passion had gripped them both. Eyes he'd drowned in as he'd sunk deep inside her.

Deceptive, duplicitous eyes that had taken his lust and turned it against him. Played him as a virtuoso plucked at willing strings. Deep down in a place he rarely liked to visit, it still burned him that he'd never seen it coming. That he'd been so completely and utterly duped for the second time in his life.

Duped by a woman who'd proclaimed to be one thing and turned out to be another.

And this time, the consequences threatened to be worse.

Anaïs had ruined one life, devastated one family. Jasmine's actions threatened thousands.

He'd been willing to bide his time. But he'd never been one to miss an opportunity. And while he hadn't expected the opportunity to arise so soon, he was perfectly willing to take his revenge now.

Jasmine Nichols had walked into his life, brazen and unrepentant. He had every intention of making her pay for her sins. Seeing the tears on her face only strengthened his resolve.

Reyes didn't doubt they were genuine, but he knew they were born of self-preservation rather than a show of repentance. He'd witnessed it many times before. From Anaïs. From his mother.

One hand came up and scrubbed at her face. In the blink of an eye her tears were wiped clean. As if they'd never been there. Just like in Rio. She'd charmed her way into his bed for long enough to get her hands on what she'd wanted. Then she'd vanished like a spent tornado, leaving devastation behind.

His jaw tightened. 'Who hired you to steal the treaty?' He hadn't meant to question her here, like this. But the need to know burned fiercely inside him. 'Was it Mendez?'

'No. I didn't…no one hired me.'

'So it was merely an opportunistic theft? The moment presented itself and you thought, *why not*? To what end, though? Blackmail?'

He caught her wince and felt a sliver of satisfaction. At least it showed she wasn't as unfeeling as he'd thought. Or maybe she didn't like her flaws pointed out to her. Tough. Before he was done, her every flaw would be exposed to the light of day.

She lifted a hand, as if to beseech him. 'No… Yes, it was blackmail, but you don't understand—'

He snorted. 'Theft is theft, Miss Nichols. It can't be explained away.'

The knock on the door made her jump. Reyes barked out an order and a member of staff walked in with a tray.

He took it and walked to the bed. Waiting until Jasmine sat up against the pillows, he set it down across her lap.

'I will force-feed you if necessary, but you will eat this meal, understood?' He didn't want to look at her, see how pale she was. Or remember his gut-churning anxiety when he'd been unable to wake her earlier.

Her head bowed as she looked down at the tray. 'No force-feeding necessary. I seem to have my appetite back.' Her stomach rumbled and one corner of her lush mouth lifted.

Reyes looked away and stepped back.

'Your things are being collected from your home. My plane will be ready to leave in the morning. Make sure you're packed and ready to leave.'

He headed for the door before he was tempted to do something idiotic. Like watch her eat.

CHAPTER SIX

'Is THERE REALLY no other way for me to make amends?'

Reyes took the empty tray and handed it to the member of staff hovering nearby.

'No.'

He glimpsed a touch of rebellion in her eyes and something fizzed through his blood, almost an anticipation of his battle with her. Which was curious. And ridiculous. All he was interested in was making her pay for her actions. 'You'll come with me—'

'Or you'll report me to the authorities? Have me thrown in jail?' Her fingers twisted in her lap. 'I know. Maybe that's a better option than...'

'Facing my brand of justice? You know, I think that's the first sensible decision you've made since we met. But seriously, do you want to take your chances locked in the basement again? You didn't last half a day. The bureaucracy before you're brought to trial alone would take months, if not years. On the other hand, a Santo Sierran prison is so much better. We deliver justice swiftly. If nothing else, you'll have wall-to-wall sunshine all year round; you can acquire a permanent tan during your lifelong incarceration.'

Fear clenched her heart. 'Is that where we—you're going?'

'Eventually. You have until morning to decide. Then I abandon you to the ambassador's mercy.'

She paled further. 'I've suffered worse, I'm sure. But I really don't think it needs to come to that.'

Surprise sparked through Reyes at her reply, then he berated himself for his reaction. Obviously his wasn't the first threat of punishment Jasmine Nichols had received in her life. Curious, he regarded her. How many other men had she tricked with her body, then stolen from? How many others had fallen for her sensual beauty? Been duped by the promise of her *bed-me* eyes and silken skin?

Anger rose inside him.

The need to deliver his own brand of justice grew stronger. Needing to turn up the heat, he stalked closer. 'You mentioned your family,' he started conversationally. 'Do they know you're a thief?'

Her colour receded a little more, her full lips firming just a tiny fraction. Satisfaction coursed through him.

'Will they be prepared to lose everything they have in order to make reparations to the Santo Sierran people?'

She drew in a sharp breath. 'This has *nothing* to do with my family.'

'That's where you're wrong, Jasmine. You wronged *my people*, my *family*. It is only right that you *and* your family make the appropriate amends.'

'No! Please—'

'A simple phone call is all it would take to round them all up. Santo Sierra has extradition treaties with the United Kingdom—'

'No. I meant what I said. It doesn't have to come to that.'

'So you would prefer me to leave your family out of this?'

Her lips worked for several tense seconds, which stretched to a full minute. Then a sigh of defeat escaped her parted lips. 'Is it worth me saying anything else but that I would like you to leave my family alone?'

He took a deep breath. And smiled. 'No.'

'Then I'll…come with you…wherever you want me to.'

He turned and walked out of the room. Jasmine set her cutlery down and tried to think through the roller-coaster speed of her thoughts. In the end, she could only hope she'd made the right decision.

Sunset bathed the hills in orange and red as their car climbed the roads leading to Reyes's Spanish hacienda. Jasmine had long given up any hope of trying to memorise her where-abouts. All she knew was that they were somewhere deep in Northern Spain.

They'd long left behind the tourist traps and sandy beaches of Barcelona. Here the houses were few and far between, with occasional villages flashing past before she could take meaningful note of where she was.

Reyes sat beside her but he might as well have been thousands of miles away. A pair of designer sunglasses shielded his eyes from her and the phone he'd commandeered since boarding his plane remained glued to one ear.

From the snatches of conversation she'd heard, he was planning several more meetings with government ministers and his own council here in Spain.

Looking carefully, she could see the signs of strain around his mouth and the skin pulled taut over his cheekbones, but he was very much a man in command.

Sensing her scrutiny, he swivelled his head in her direction. A second later, he ended his call.

'Where exactly are we going?' she enquired.

'To my estate in Zaragoza,' he replied in a clipped tone.

'And…how long will we be staying there?'

'As long as it takes. If you have any aspirations of escape, kill them now.'

She clasped her hand in her lap, refusing to rise to his baiting. 'My family will be worried if I don't let them know how long I'll be away,' she tried to reason with him.

Her mother had been confused when she'd called to say she was taking a holiday and had no idea when she would be returning. Stephen had been even more difficult to convince. Jasmine had been avoiding him since her return from Rio, but she knew her stepfather suspected she'd had something to do with him being suddenly free of debt and the prospect of jail.

'And you always strive to maintain the appearance of a dutiful daughter, do you?' Scorn poured from Reyes, the naked

censure in his voice stinging her skin. 'Obviously, you've succeeded in pulling the wool over their eyes all these years.'

Jasmine bit back her retort to the contrary. It *was* because of
her past that her mother worried when she didn't hear from her
daughter. The past she'd tried so hard to escape from but had
stepped firmly back into with her one wrong decision in Rio.

Finding no adequate words to defend herself, she kept silent. With an impatient movement, Reyes ripped the glasses
from his eyes and caught her chin in his hand. Jasmine found
herself locked into his intense gaze.

'Are you going to speak or do you intend to play mute?'
he asked.

'I don't really have anything to say to you.'

He folded the glasses and slipped them into his shirt pocket.
'Your father, Stephen Nichols, works for the British government, does he not?'

His announcement startled her. His eyes held rigid ice that
threatened to stop the blood flow in her veins. 'He's my stepfather, but how…what does that have to do with anything?'
Her instinct warned she wouldn't like the path this conversation was taking.

'I'm merely trying to form a picture in my head. And your
mother…what does she do?'

Jasmine licked dry lips, her thoughts churning as she debated the wisdom of evading his questions. In the end, she
decided withholding the information would serve no useful
purpose. 'She's his PA.'

'So to all intents and purposes, they're both upstanding citizens?' he asked, one dark eyebrow raised.

Her pulse increased as her gaze followed the graceful arch
of his brow. Even when her eyes dropped to encounter his frozen regard, her pulse still thundered. Because deep inside, Jasmine knew his questions weren't as innocuous as he'd couched
them.

She tried not to let him see how much he riled her. 'If you
have a point, please state it.'

'I'm just wondering how come you've strayed so far from the righteous path.'

She flinched. 'I beg your pardon?'

His teeth bared in a semblance of a smile, but all it did was send a wave of dread over her. 'I'm trying to understand you, *querida*. How a woman such as you, with a seemingly stable background and upbringing, ends up being a thief.'

'You know nothing about me, except for an impression you think you got from us spending a few hours together. I can understand how what I did would colour your judgement, but that's far from the whole picture.'

His face hardened. 'I *know* you were instrumental in demolishing my country's trade treaty. You don't think that's enough?' he finished on a snarl.

Remembering how she'd felt when she saw the headline announcing the breakdown of talks, Jasmine slid her gaze from his. 'I'm sorry. But technically, Mendez is also responsible—'

'And since all evidence points to you working for Mendez, isn't the conclusion the same?' he sneered.

Her head snapped round to his. '*No!* You're wrong. I don't work for Mendez. I've never even met the man!'

'Really? You work as a broker and a mediator, do you not?'

Puzzled, she nodded.

'And over the past three years, your specialty has been in brokering agreements in Latin American companies?'

Her frown deepened in direct proportion to the escalation of her dread. 'How do you know all this?'

He continued as if she hadn't spoken. 'When we met you told me you'd been watching the Santo-Valderran talks *with interest*.'

Jasmine found his reasoning difficult to comprehend. 'And you think by interest I meant to sabotage it? For what purpose?'

'What other purpose could there be aside from financial?'

'Feel free to search my finances. You'd be surprised to find I'm not as flush as you think I am.'

'You're too intelligent to display the fruits of your duplicity. Are you so confident that I won't find the evidence I need if I cast my net a little wider, like, say, your parents?'

Jasmine felt the blood drain from her face. Despite her bravado, the last thing she wanted was for Reyes to start digging into Stephen's affairs. The evidence of his gambling, misappropriation and connection to people like Joaquin Esteban would become public knowledge if Reyes took that route.

Her stepfather had been visibly shaken by his ordeal at the hands of Joaquin's men, enough to induce an angina attack that had laid him up in hospital for a week.

Unfortunately, it had taken that experience to wake him up to his dangerous addiction. He had just started a programme to help overcome his gambling problem; the last thing she wanted was for his life to be thrown into turmoil by Reyes.

Watching him struggle to overcome his weakness, she'd been reminded of what Stephen himself had said to her years earlier.

Nobody was perfect.

She'd reminded herself of that over and over again in the last four weeks. Except she was sure, when it came to Prince Reyes Navarre, that belief wouldn't hold water.

She tried to remain calm as Reyes, sensing her turmoil, tilted her face up to his.

'I see I've stumbled onto something. Who were the beneficiaries if not your parents?' His fingers tightened. 'Your lover?'

With excruciating effort, she wrenched herself free. 'What does it matter? I did it,' she admitted, not seeing the point in prolonging the agony.

Beside her, he tensed. Her fingers clenched in her lap, the rush of memories threatening to eat her alive. Desperately, she tried to push them away, but they pushed back. Hard.

I did it. This wasn't the first time she'd said those words. But she'd hoped back then it would be the last. How wrong she'd been.

Squeezing her eyes shut for a single heartbeat, she took a deep breath, opened them and tried to plead with Reyes.

'I did it. I'm willing to take the consequences. Just tell me what I need to do.' Because the earlier she could make reparations, the earlier she could put him behind her.

CHAPTER SEVEN

REYES FOUND HIMSELF riveted by the frank admission, unable to look away from the open candour in Jasmine's face as she looked back at him. For the first time in his life, he found himself speechless.

I did it.

In all the imagined scenarios when he'd dreamed of exacting his revenge, not once had he entertained the notion that she would admit her guilt so readily.

He wondered why he was surprised. Weren't her audacity, her sheer bolshiness what had attracted him a month ago in Rio? Yet even now, Reyes could see that her reaction, while mostly convincing, was just a front. But a front that hid what? What was Jasmine Nichols keeping from him?

He continued to stare at her. She stared back, her gaze unflinching. Against his will, he felt his blood firing up, his heartbeat quicken. Shifting in his seat, he sat back, took a deep breath.

Jasmine had made things easy for him. He now didn't need to bother with interrogating her. She'd admitted her guilt and he had her confession. Her punishment would wait until he'd dealt with more important matters.

'*Gracias,*' he murmured, breaking eye contact. The strange sense of loss he felt was immediately pushed aside.

'What are you thanking me for?' she asked.

'Saving me the time and energy of interrogating you. Who did you give the treaty to?'

She shook her head. 'I can't tell you that.'

'You're wrong. When the time is right you'll give me a name. Every person responsible for this chaos will be brought to justice.'

Despite the fire in her eyes, she swallowed and looked away.

His car swung into the last stretch of road leading to his estate and a sense of satisfaction stole over him. In London, he'd felt at a slight loss; that control wasn't totally within his grasp. Within touching distance of the place he called his second home, his control returned.

San Estrela was his mother's birthplace and where she had married his father. Reyes had maybe one or two fairly happy holidays here as a child...until everything had turned sour. He wouldn't be creating any more happy memories by bringing his prisoner here, but he had no choice.

As much as it burned him to admit it, he couldn't yet return to Santo Sierra. He needed to rally economic support in order to get the talks with Valderra back on track. Plus, at present, he wasn't entirely sure whom he could trust in his own council.

His insides clenched as he thought of his father. Ruthlessly, he pushed the feeling aside. If he was to achieve what he was aiming for, he needed to clear his mind of his grief; of making things right with the father he'd lost for so long. Ironically, it was his own downfall with Jasmine Nichols that had made Reyes see his father in a different light. To not judge the old man so harshly for his own mistakes.

He would return to his father's bedside soon enough. Make amends. Hopefully before it was too late.

He alighted from the car and automatically held out his hand. Jasmine took it and straightened beside him a second later. He dropped her hand, not wanting to acknowledge how her skin felt against his.

A frown crossed her face before she masked it.

Reyes didn't know what to do with that look. On the one hand, she remained stoic in the face of her guilt, yet on the other she looked at him with contrition. The enigma unsettled and irritated him.

Pushing aside the feeling, he mounted the stairs as the door swung open to reveal his major-domo, Armando. The man wore the same anxious look he'd seen on so many Santo Sierran faces.

Reminded that his people were living in a state of constant worry made Reyes's chest tighten.

Knowing the cause of all this turmoil stood two steps behind him made his blood simmer as he greeted Armando.

'This is Miss Jasmine Nichols. She'll be my guest for the duration of my stay. She is, however, not permitted to leave the house or grounds under any circumstances. If she attempts to leave, use all means necessary to prevent her,' he instructed.

'You don't need to do that. I know why I'm here. You have my word that I won't run away.'

'You'll forgive me if I don't find your *word* reassuring?'

She inhaled sharply. 'I suppose I deserve that,' she murmured.

Reyes frowned at the hurt in her voice.

Armando, his usual capable, unruffled self, barely blinked at the exchange. 'I will put her in the Valencia Suite, Your Highness.'

'No, the Leon Suite next to mine will suffice.'

'Very well, Your Highness.'

Reyes turned down the hall towards his study and had barely taken half a dozen steps when he heard the click of heels racing after him.

He stopped. 'Did you want something?'

She looked pale, her face creased in concern as her eyes fell. When she began to visibly tremble, Reyes frowned. She hadn't been well yesterday, but she'd reassured the doctor this morning that she was fine.

'What do you mean by any means necessary?' she asked.

'Stay in the house and within the grounds and you'll never have to find out. Understood?'

A tinge of relief brought colour to her cheeks. Reyes didn't realise how disconcerting her paleness was until she regained her composure.

She shook her head. 'I can't just do nothing. I'll go out of my mind.'

'That's your punishment for now. Do otherwise and I'll have to revise my decision.'

She sighed. 'Rey—I mean, Your Highness.' Her hand lifted, as if to touch him. 'Can I have my phone back? Please, I need to let my parents know where I am. My mother will send the cavalry out in full force if I don't, and, trust me, you don't want that.' A small, wistful smile touched her lips.

The idea of her delusional mother, sitting snug in her home, worrying about her perfect daughter, made his teeth clench. No doubt Jasmine had succeeded in pulling the wool over her parents' eyes the way she'd done with him. And yet the thought of the perfect family picture all that *togetherness* presented sent a dart of something very close to jealousy through him.

He'd never had a parent worry over him like that. His mother had been too caught up in trying to turn his father's existence into a living hell to worry about the two children who'd needed her attention. And his father had been too busy turning himself inside out for a faithless woman. Reyes had been a young boy when he'd realised there wouldn't be any scrap of attention from either of his parents.

It was the reason boarding school had been a relief. It was the reason he'd chosen not to form attachments to any woman. Sex for the sake of it had been his mantra.

Until Anaïs. Until his mother's death.

After that even sex hadn't mattered.

Nothing had mattered. Nothing but duty.

Feeling the bitterness encroach, Reyes whirled and stalked towards his study. 'See Armando. He'll show you where the phone is. But one call is all you get. Make it count.'

Jasmine ended the call to her mother and put the phone down in the seriously gorgeous solarium Armando had shown her into. She took a calming breath and looked around her. Outside, a carpet of rich green grass rolled away towards a stand of cypress trees at the bottom of the valley they'd climbed out of. To the right, a more cultivated garden, hedged with roses, bougainvillea and hyacinths grew beyond a sun-washed terrace. She stood for a moment, letting the sun and stunning surroundings wash over her.

As prisons went, this one wasn't so bad, she mused. Although if she had to compare jailors, she would've preferred one who didn't make her pulse jump, who didn't make her wish her path to this place had been different.

In the car earlier, she'd refused to give Joaquin's name, partly because of what it would mean for her stepfather. But she'd also shied away from the conversation because she'd been afraid Reyes would find out about her past. That he'd discover that the woman he'd taken to bed had grown up in a council estate and been nearly initiated into a drug-dealing gang. That she had a juvenile record she'd never be able to erase.

He might detest her now, but that was far better than his repulsion, his scorn.

The chirp of a bird steered her from another unwanted trip down memory lane. She'd been taking those trips far too often these last weeks. Ever since that night in Rio, in fact. She needed to snap out of it. Put it behind her.

She would face whatever punishment Reyes chose to dole out on her, but the past belonged in the past.

A sound from behind her made her turn.

Armando entered, pushing a trolley laden with food. 'I do not know the *señorita's* preference, so I have brought a selection.'

She'd missed breakfast again because she hadn't been able to stomach any of the food the embassy had laid out for them this morning. Lately, any thought of food made her stomach roil. So she approached the trolley cautiously. And breathed easier once she could look at the mouthwatering selection of *tapas* without turning green.

Perhaps telling the doctor she was fine this morning had been a mistake...

Thanking Armando, she heaped her plate with bread, ham, and a green salad and took a seat at the dining area near the window. She polished off the food in record time and went back for seconds, adding plump olives marinated in chilli oil.

She was about to pick up her cutlery when Reyes strolled in. Without a word, he selected his own food, then pulled up a chair opposite her.

In low tones, he dismissed Armando and shook out his napkin.

'So,' he started conversationally, 'you told your mother I was your boyfriend.' It wasn't a question. It was an observation, marred with thick layers of distaste.

Jasmine's appetite fled. Her cutlery dropped noisily onto the table. 'How did you know that?'

One sleek brow arched. 'Did I not mention it? All incoming and outgoing calls from San Estrela are monitored. And yes, I have a zero-trust policy where you're concerned.'

Despite the heat engulfing her face at the pointed remark, she met his gaze head-on. 'If you were listening then you would've heard that my mother *assumed* you were my boyfriend. I didn't—'

'Correct that assumption. You've been caught in yet another lie, Miss Nichols. It's quite astonishing how they trip so easily from your lips.' His gaze dropped to her lips and she felt a guilty tingle as if he'd branded her mouth with just that one look.

'I could hardly tell her I was being held prisoner somewhere in Northern Spain!'

He ripped a piece of bread in half, dipped it in his olive oil and took a healthy bite. 'Maybe you should have. For her own good, she needs to know she doesn't have the perfect daughter she seems to think she does.'

'You don't know me and you don't know my mother, so don't presume to judge us. Besides, what makes you think she believes I'm perfect?'

'She must do. She seemed to eat up all the lies you fed her without question.'

Jasmine was tempted to tell Reyes of her mother's one fatal flaw—she refused to see the bad in anyone. Her blindly trusting nature had seen her duped out of her money over and over by ruthless men. It was that nature that had landed them where Jasmine had been forced down a path of near permanent ruin.

It was a place Jasmine didn't like to remind her mother of, or ever revisit herself, if she could help it.

'It's easier for my mother to take things at face value.' Her words emerged with much more bitter introspection than she'd intended. Aware of just how much she'd let slip, Jasmine clamped her jaw shut and tried not to even breathe. But it was too late.

Reyes's head cocked to the side in the now oh-so-familiar way. 'Interesting. She knows and she accepts you just the way you are?' The way he said it, almost wistfully, drew her gaze to him.

He was staring at her and yet she got the feeling his mind was somewhere else altogether. Somewhere he didn't want to relive, but couldn't seem to help.

She picked up her fork and speared an olive. A quick whiff of it had her setting it down again. She tried a piece of ham and chewed that instead. After swallowing, she answered, 'Yes, she does. She likes to think that people change. So do I, incidentally.'

As if snapping out of whatever place he'd been, he sharpened his gaze. 'No, they don't. They like to pretend they do. Some do their best to present a different face to the world, but people inherently remain the same underneath.'

'I don't believe that.'

'Why, because *you've* changed? You've somehow seen some mystic light and repented all your sins?'

She swallowed. 'Yes.'

'We both know that's not true, don't we, Jasmine? Otherwise you wouldn't have stolen from me.'

'I had no choice.'

His jaw tightened. 'You had a choice. You made the wrong one.'

After a moment, she nodded. 'Yes, maybe you're right.'

Her answer silenced him for several moments, his speculative gaze on her face. 'And how many times have you made the wrong choice in the past?'

'My past is none of your business.' And not a place she chose to willingly visit. The stigma of being judged was one she'd learned from when her college boyfriend had treated her like a pariah when she'd confessed her past. 'I'm more concerned about the future. If you're going to hand me over to the authorities, I'd prefer it to be sooner rather than later.'

His face slowly hardened into the mask she detested, but had unfortunately become very familiar with. 'Don't push me, Jasmine. If you didn't steal from me for yourself, tell me who you did it for.'

Her heart lurched. 'I can't. Punish me, if you need to, but leave anyone else out of it.'

'Why?'

'Because the person I did it for is important to me.'

'How important?' he flung back.

'He...saved me. He didn't have to, but he did. I'm sorry, Re—Your Highness, but I won't let him pay for my mistakes.'

'So this person saved you, but decided it was okay to set you back on a destructive path to suit his purposes?

'No, it wasn't like that.'

His hand slammed down. 'That was exactly what it was, Jasmine. To trap me so you could steal from me. From my people. To throw years of hard work into utter chaos and endanger the livelihood of millions, all for the sake of one person.'

'Yes, I know it seems irrational but that's what happened. Believe me, I'll do anything to make things right.'

He relaxed in his seat with the grace of a born predator, his long, rangy frame seeming to go on for ever. His smile held no mirth, only cynicism. 'How bravely you embrace your sins. It's almost admirable.'

She set her fork down. 'Stop toying with me and just get this over and done with.'

His smile widened, his teeth stark against the darkness of his beard. For some reason, the sight made her belly flip over. Whether it was from fear or another emotion, Jasmine didn't want to examine too closely.

'You're not in a position to dictate terms to me, Miss Nichols. Remember, you're *my* prisoner. *I* will choose the time of your trial. And the terms of your punishment. Push me and you'll like the consequences of either even less.'

Over the next four days she barely saw Reyes. She caught glimpses of him—as he paced the terrace just before the midday sun hit full blast, or as Armando took a tray into his study. Once she looked down from her window early in the morning and saw him swimming, his powerful strokes carrying him from one end of the enormous pool to the other.

Voyeuristically, she watched him, unable to look away from his magnificent, streamlined body. When he heaved himself out of the pool and scrubbed a towel through his wet hair, desire settled low and heavy in her belly.

As she lay in bed now, remembering how that body had felt up close against hers in Rio drenched her whole body in sensation. Ashamed, she flipped over, punched her frustration into a pillow and pulled the covers over herself as if her actions would block out the feelings.

But being in bed only reminded her of another bed, where their bodies had writhed, strained into each other as they'd ridden the storm of passion breaking over them.

Unnerved by the sheer depth of her riotous feelings, Jasmine threw back the covers and jumped out of bed.

Too late, she remembered that, lately, her mornings were best approached gingerly. Rushing to the bathroom, she vomited until her eyes stung.

Afterwards, clutching the sink, her fingers dug into the cold porcelain as she calculated dates and tried not to panic. She'd had her period two weeks ago, albeit a lighter than usual one.

And Reyes had used condoms in Rio. Hadn't he?

No, it was all in her head. Being cooped up in San Estrela was making her stir-crazy!

Today she was going to offer Reyes whatever input she thought would help with salvaging the treaty. Failing that, she'd ask him what he intended to do with her. This suspended limbo was sending her imagination into overdrive.

Why else would she think she could be pregnant with Reyes's baby? The very thought made her tremble.

Quickly showering, she dressed in a light blue sleeveless linen dress with a tan belt and slipped her feet into tan heels. Brushing her hair and tying it loosely at her nape, she massaged a small amount of sun protection into her skin and face and left her suite.

Carmelita, the housekeeper, was carrying a large bale of towels towards the guest suites in the west wing when Jasmine reached the top of the stairs. About to ask the whereabouts of Reyes, Jasmine paused at the sound of male voices in the hallway.

Reyes strolled into view, accompanied by four men. The first thing she noticed was that his beard was gone. A tiny, completely unprepared and shocking part of her mourned that she'd never got to experience the rasp of his facial hair against her skin.

The second thing she noticed was that all the men wore suits. And that she was the sole focus of their attention as she stood, poised, at the top of the stairs.

A block of silence passed.

Reyes turned to the men, his voice low. Without glancing her way, he led them to his study and shut the door with a firm click.

Jasmine stood rooted to the step, unable to move. She wasn't sure why she was so hurt that she'd been dismissed like a piece of trash.

What did she expect?

She was a prisoner here. Barely worth the food or accommodation she took up. Did she really expect Reyes to introduce her as his guest?

With leaden feet, she came down the stairs and went onto the terrace, where she usually breakfasted.

Carmelita brought her fresh coffee. She helped herself to a slice of toast and a plump orange, but her mind churned. When Carmelita emerged again to clear away the dishes, Jasmine's curiosity got the better of her.

'Who are those men with His Highness?' she asked casually.

The housekeeper looked uncomfortable for a moment, then she replied, 'One is the Santo Sierra *embajador* to France. Other men are from Santo Sierra.'

'How long have they been here?'

'They came late last night.' She bustled about, hurriedly gathering the used tableware.

Unwilling to question her any further, Jasmine left her in peace. Clearly, her meeting with Reyes would have to take a backseat to his meeting with his ambassador and council. But she needed something, *anything* to stop her thinking of what her past week's morning sickness meant.

Because if her suspicions were true…then…oh, God!

Going back to fetch her sunglasses, Jasmine came downstairs and let herself out through the solarium.

She bypassed the gardens and headed for the trees. In a distant past, she'd harboured a secret wish to be a gardener. That was before another one of her mother's liaisons had run off with her savings and they'd ended up in a tower block, where the only green in sight had been from the bile-coloured paint on the walls.

Jasmine had been only six at the time, but she'd vowed never to let her emotions blind her the way her mother did. In fact she'd killed off all her emotions…until Stephen had forced her to face them. To choose a better life than the one she'd been contemplating at seventeen.

She trailed her fingers over the expertly pruned foliage and imagined herself tending the plants and trees all year round.

Spotting a greenhouse at the end of a row of hedges, Jasmine veered towards it.

Before she could turn the handle, heavy footsteps pounded the ground behind her. In a heartbeat, Armando and two of Reyes's bodyguards had surrounded her. One bodyguard took her by the arm and marched her towards the villa.

'What are you doing? Let go of me!'

He didn't respond. Back indoors, she managed to rip herself from the guard's grasp as the door to the study flew open.

Jasmine stared at a fuming Reyes, refusing to cower under his oppressive stare.

'I thought we had an agreement.' His grey eyes flashed with barely suppressed anger.

She massaged her stinging elbow. 'The agreement still holds. I haven't run away, have I?'

'You left the house without permission.'

'To go to the garden! I'm going insane cooped up in your gilded prison. How did you know I'd left the house anyway?'

'Every time a door is opened in the house, an alarm goes off in the security suite. My men alerted me.' His gaze dropped to where she was nursing her elbow. His face grew darker. 'Why are you rubbing your elbow? Are you hurt?'

'Do you care?'

He glared at her for several seconds. Then, turning to his bodyguard, he murmured a few words.

Jasmine's heart twisted, then thundered in outrage when she saw what was being handed to Reyes.

'No! If you dare come near me with that thing, I'll—'

'You'll what? Scream? Go ahead. Give it your best shot.' He stepped closer, the handcuffs gleaming in his hands.

Memories, the worst kind of memories, crowded her mind,

pushing fear up through her belly into her chest. Her breath shortened. 'No, Reyes— No, don't. Please!'

Hyperventilating, she tried to step back. Her feet wouldn't move. The blood drained out of her head as she fought to breathe. Her head grew woozy with fog. She started to sway.

'If you insist on disobeying me, this is your only—Jasmine?'

His voice wove in and out. She blinked, fighting the light-headedness. Damn, either she really was unwell, or she was turning into a pathetic shadow of herself around this man.

Either way, it had to stop!

CHAPTER EIGHT

'JASMINE!'

Reyes caught her by the arms and watched her pull herself together. She'd gone deathly pale at the sight of the handcuffs and for a moment he'd thought she would pass out.

She continued to stare at the restraints as if they were poisonous serpents ready to strike at her.

She willingly admitted to being a criminal yet the sight of handcuffs terrified her. Surely she was used to them by now?

Puzzled, he slipped the cuffs into his back pocket and dismissed his bodyguard. Her trembling had increased and even though she tried to hide it, he caught the haunted look in her eyes.

Dios, something had happened to her.

'Jasmine.'

She didn't move. Didn't react. It was almost as if she hadn't heard him. Stepping closer, he gripped her tighter. Felt her tremble. An unwelcome emotion shifted through his chest.

'You will respond when I address you.'

Her reaction was immediate. She wrenched herself from him, almost violently. Eyes wide, she glared at him, but he was sure her consciousness was elsewhere.

'No! I won't let you use those things on me!'

'It's fine. It's okay,' he murmured, brushing her soft, silky cheek. He realised what he was doing and removed his hand, puzzled and annoyed with himself for offering comfort where he should be doling out punishment.

She stared at the hand suspended between them. Then she searched for the handcuffs before her wide, frightened eyes darted back to his face.

'Do you want to tell me what just happened?' he asked.

She sucked in a shaky breath and gathered herself with that strength of will he couldn't help but admire. 'I have no idea what you're talking about.'

A cold hand clamped around Reyes's neck. How many times had he heard his mother utter those same words? When he'd demanded to know what she was doing in the papers being photographed in the arms of a man other than his father...when Reyes had confronted her about the alcohol on her breath or the hazy look in her eyes, she'd always uttered those words.

I have no idea what you're talking about, Reyes. Don't be so fanciful, Reyes.

'So you deny that the sight of the restraints disturbed you? Then you won't mind if I use—'

She tried to snatch her hands away. 'No. Don't use it. I promise...I won't leave the villa.'

He was dying to know what had happened to her. But not so badly that he wanted to be lied to. He might have tried to fool himself into believing that it didn't matter, but Jasmine's untruths somehow managed to get under his skin. Sting that little harder.

'Your promises are worthless to me—surely you know that by now? So I'm afraid you'll have to do more than that.'

She swallowed. 'What do you mean?'

Reyes stepped back and indicated the door to his study. 'You'll stay where I can keep an eye on you.'

'So I guess a request for a trip into town is out of the question?'

Reyes let his cool stare speak for him.

She rolled her eyes before her gaze dropped to his pockets, where the cuffs were hidden out of sight. 'Fine. I'll go and find a book to read.'

For some reason, Reyes couldn't suppress a smile as she firmed her lips and sent him a glance of pure loathing.

He stopped her as she stepped past him. 'Wait.'

Surprised, she looked up. Then frowned. 'What now?'

Reyes grasped her elbow and examined where she'd rubbed

it before. Faint marks marred her skin. A touch of fury flared within him. He would be having words with his bodyguard later. 'You didn't tell me whether you were hurt or not?' he repeated his earlier question. *Why was that so important to him?* He stemmed the mocking voice and waited for her answer.

'It's nothing I haven't endured before.' As if realising her slip, she bit her lip.

The memory of doing the same to those lips, and much more, slammed into him. His groin stirred to life. Smashing it down, he concentrated on her words.

'You've been manhandled before?' The very thought made something tug hard in his chest.

'Not without fighting back, I can assure you.' The blaze of defiance and determination flared higher in her eyes.

He wasn't reassured. Intrigued, he stared at her for a long time before he could form the words. 'You will not be treated like that under my roof. Be assured of that.'

'So what do you call using those handcuffs tucked away in your pocket? An early Christmas present?'

His mouth twisted. 'Perhaps I should rephrase that. No one but I will be allowed to touch you while you're under my roof.'

'Well, that makes me feel heaps better.' Despite the bravado in her voice, a dart of apprehension crossed her eyes.

About to reassure her again that she would come to no harm, he stopped himself. Reminded himself of what this woman had done. To him. To his country.

Right at this moment, he had members of Santo Sierra's council in his study, trying to find a way out of their current predicament. So far they seemed to be agreed on only one course of action. One that Reyes was determined not to give in to.

Meanwhile, here he was trying to placate the woman responsible for causing the turbulence in his kingdom.

Twisting on his heel, he barked, 'Come.'

'You want me at your meeting?'

'I want you where I can keep an eye on you.'

He heard her footsteps behind him as he entered his study. Two of his advisors gaped at his guest. The third, most senior of them, frowned as Reyes shut the door and directed Jasmine into the seat in the corner of the room.

His senior advisor shifted in his seat. 'Your Highness, what we're discussing is highly confidential. I hardly think it appropriate to have a stranger—'

'Miss Nichols is here as my guest. She won't divulge anything we say in this room.' He looked at her. She read the clear warning and nodded.

He sat down but not before his gaze caught her bare legs as she crossed them. Again heat lanced his groin. Those legs had curled around his waist, urged him on as he'd thrust inside her.

Inside her duplicitous body...

He cleared his throat and shifted in his seat. 'You said you know how many people were thinking of backing the new treaty?' he addressed his senior advisor.

Costanzo Alvarez nodded. 'It is currently seven to nine, Your Highness. With each day that passes, the older members are being swayed to the idea of the original treaty your father agreed to sign.'

Reyes's hackles rose. 'Those terms are no longer on the table. The new treaty will create at least another five thousand jobs.'

Alvarez shook his head. 'Mendez won't sign the new treaty, and Santo Sierra needs economic stability sooner rather than later. Any delay in providing that stability is a delay we can't afford.'

His second advisor leaned forward. 'As Costanzo said, stability is what will steer the people into calmer waters. I think Santo Sierrans are more afraid than anything else of what the future holds—'

'Make your point,' Reyes cut across him.

'Should you marry and produce an heir quickly, it'll restore the people's faith in—'

'Are you seriously suggesting that the only way to please

the people is to marry? I'm supposed to be garnering economic support for Santo Sierra, not hunting Europe for a bride.'

'Santo Sierra has always thrived in direct proportion to how well its monarchy is thriving. With your father's health in rapid decline, the people are worried about their future, yes, but they're also worried about you.'

Reyes frowned. 'So I'm to conjure up a bride out of thin air, marry her and produce an heir instead of pursuing our economic growth?'

Alvarez tented his fingers. 'No reason why you can't do both. But we suggest you do it more…visibly. You've always been a private person, Your Highness. Even when you're in Santo Sierra you're hardly seen. Besides the council, most people believe you've been at the King's bedside for the past few weeks. Only a handful of people know differently.'

Reyes shook his head. 'Even if I agree to this plan, even if I calm my people for a while, we still need to bring Mendez to the table to sign another treaty.'

He heard a muffled sound and glanced at Jasmine. Her eyes met his and he read the bleak apology in them.

He wanted to believe her. Wanted to believe she was anywhere near sorry for the wrongs she'd done. But he'd let himself be fooled in the past. Let his guard down enough to believe his mother's lies.

Each time, she'd stabbed him with savage lies and callous indifference. She'd done the same to his father. Reyes and his sister had watched their father, the King of Santo Sierra, wither with each deception, each act of adultery.

And yet, if Jasmine was to believed, she'd done it not for personal gain, but to save someone she cared about. She'd sacrificed her safety, her reputation for the sake of another…

The curious tug at his chest made him tense. There was no redemption in what Jasmine had done. He was a fool to look for any.

* * *

Jasmine bit her lip as Reyes turned away. His whole body bristled in rejection of her silent apology.

She looked down at the file she'd picked up as the men talked. She refused to acknowledge that dart of discomfort that had lodged itself in her heart when the idea of Reyes marrying had been brought up.

It had nothing to do with her. She had no claim on him. She never would. She was only in this room because Reyes didn't trust her to wander his house without making a run for it.

Once he'd decided what her punishment was to be, she would serve it and be done. The fate of his country was his to deal with as he saw fit.

And yet…

Reyes…married to a princess befitting his station. An equal who would complement his heritage, who would have his babies and be gifted the privilege of waking up next to him for the rest of her life.

Her throat tightened. This time the bile that rose had nothing to do with nausea and everything to do with blind, raging jealousy.

Gripping the file, she forced herself to read the copy of the trade treaty that she'd handed to Joaquin.

Each kingdom had agreed to supply resources to one another. On execution, the two kingdoms would have combined power equivalent to the United Arab Emirates' control of the world's oil and steel. Despite Santo Sierra being the smaller kingdom, it held the richer resource. No wonder Mendez had his greedy eyes set on it.

Jasmine finished reading and closed the file.

This was what she'd wrecked.

The trade agreement would have created thousands of jobs, made countless lives better. She'd jeopardised all those lives to save one.

Caught between the fresh vice of guilt and the loyalty that

wouldn't be snuffed out, she wrapped her arms around herself. Then, unable to sit still, she jumped up.

'Let me help. Please…'

Four sets of eyes slashed to her. Condemnation. Bitterness. Curiosity. Contemptuous dismissal. All expressions she'd seen before displayed through varied gazes when she was growing up.

Seeing most of those in Reyes's eyes, she felt a lance of hurt pierce her heart.

What had she expected? That he would simply forget that she was the reason he was here, now, instead of back in his kingdom?

She cleared her throat as their gazes continued to sear her. 'I've assisted in a few international brokerage deals that—'

'Excuse me, Miss…?' Costanzo Alvarez glared at her.

She bit back a retort and breathed deep. 'Jasmine Nichols,' she replied.

He gave a curt nod. He looked at the youngest advisor at the table. The man gave a subtle nod and started tapping the tablet keyboard in front of him.

'What we're dealing with here isn't a petty squabble between two fashion houses. Or a divorce settlement where you decide who gets to keep the prized goldfish. We're dealing with—'

'I know what you're dealing with,' she retorted.

'Then perhaps you should sit down and—'

'Let her speak.' A low, terse command from Reyes.

Jasmine looked at him. His eyes were narrowed, displeasure weaving through the grey depths. But he wasn't displeased enough to instruct her to be quiet, which was a small blessing. Or perhaps he was waiting for her to make a fool of herself so he could mock her some more?

She licked her lips.

His gaze followed the movement. Electricity zapped her spine as she recalled how the potency of his kisses, the expert way he'd ravaged her, made her yearn for more.

'Have you changed your mind? Or do you wish for a dictionary to find the right words?'

She snapped herself free of the mesmerising, surely overblown, memory and struggled to focus. If she managed to prove her worth, maybe redeem herself a little in this room, she could begin to right the wrong she'd done.

'The previous treaty was skewed in favour of Valderra, we all know that. And yet Mendez never went through with it.'

'He didn't go through with it because the only copy of the Santo Sierran version, which had been witnessed by the King and legalised by each member of the council, went missing. To this day we do not know what happened to it.'

Jasmine's gaze snapped to Reyes.

The clear warning in his eyes stilled any words she'd been thinking of speaking. Fighting to keep her composure, she faced the council as Alvarez continued. 'And also because he's propelled by greed, but at the moment he holds all the cards.'

Jasmine shook her head. 'He holds all the cards because you choose to hide away in the dark.'

'Excuse me?' Reyes rasped.

An icy shiver raced across her skin but she persevered.

'Why don't you just call his bluff?'

'I won't gamble my kingdom's economic future on a bluff, Jasmine. If the choice were mine to make, I'd cut him off at the knees. But I can't do that. Not yet.'

The sound of her name on his lips produced another shiver. One that stalled her breath and made her lose her train of thought.

Jasmine frowned. 'So…what's the alternative?'

Silence descended on the table. The hairs on her nape stood up and Jasmine had a sense of foreboding so strong, she stumbled back and sank into her chair.

Reyes locked eyes with each member of his council before linking his fingers together. Poised, regal, his profile was so captivating, she couldn't have looked away if she'd tried. But she still knew she didn't want to hear what he was about to say.

'Unless another solution is forthcoming, or a new treaty is negotiated in the next few weeks, it seems my solution is to buy time by finding myself a bride.'

CHAPTER NINE

'BUT...THERE HAS to be another way!'

Reyes stared at Jasmine. Her lips were pressed together after her outburst.

'Miss Nichols—'

Reyes held up his hand to stop his second advisor. 'Go on,' he said to Jasmine. His curiosity was getting the better of him by the minute. If what she was proposing was better than the idea of marrying a faceless stranger in order to maintain peace, he was all for it.

His one attempt to marry had left harrowing scars that he would never forget. Until his sister, Isabella, had dissolved her engagement recently, Reyes had accepted that he would rule Santo Sierra in his lifetime, then let his sister's heirs inherit the throne.

But once again, the mantle was firmly on his shoulders.

'What if we can prove that he was behind the treaty going missing?'

Reyes surged to his feet, knocking the chair over. 'Gentlemen, give me the room.'

His men continued to stare at Jasmine with varying degrees of astonishment and suspicion. He slammed his hand on the table. 'Now!'

They scrambled up and hurried out.

'What the hell do you think you're doing?'

She jumped back at his bellow. 'I'm trying to help.'

He speared a hand through his hair. 'By putting yourself in the crosshairs of a dangerous man?' he demanded.

'But this is your council...'

'Some of whom are set in their ways and don't welcome

the sort of changes I hope to implement when I ascend to the throne.'

She frowned. 'And you think if they know...?' She stopped and gulped.

'Until I know who I can trust, I'm not prepared to take that risk with your life.' The knowledge that she'd almost given herself away greatly agitated him. He paced in front of her, trying to decipher why protecting her meant so much to him.

From the corner of his eye, he watched her reach out.

'Reyes—'

'No, don't defy me on this, Jasmine. I won't change my mind. I can't have another destroyed life on my conscience.' The words tumbled out.

They both froze. He saw the shock rocking through him reflected on her face.

'What...what do you mean?' Her voice was whisper-thin, puzzled.

He chopped off her question with a flick of his hand. 'It doesn't matter.' He took a deep breath to regain the balance he seemed to lose so easily around her. 'I'm calling the council back. You'll refrain from mentioning what happened in Rio. Am I clear?'

For the first time since he'd known her, she nodded readily.

He strode to the door, shock still rocking his system. His men came back. They tossed ideas around half-heartedly, until he clenched his fist.

'Gentlemen, we need to discuss the subject of my bride.'

Jasmine made a rough noise of disagreement. He ignored her. Looking at her would remind him of what he'd let slip. Remind him how easily she got under his skin.

'Well, in a way your current trade visits are a good way of introducing any prospective brides to the people. But...' Alvarez cleared his throat '...you need to be a little less closed off, Your Highness.'

'Excuse me?'

'I think any further visits should be less clandestine. The

people need to see their prince embracing life a little. Remind them that you're flesh and blood, and not a fairy-tale figure locked away in an ivory tower.'

Reyes pinched the bridge of his nose. 'Are you saying my discretion is a flaw?'

'I'm saying the people don't really know you. You brought Santo Sierra right up to the treaty table after your father fell ill, but the fact remains that the finish line was never crossed. And Santo Sierrans aren't quite sure how to take that. You don't want to estrange yourself from the people.'

Fury bubbled beneath his skin. Beside him, Jasmine's tension slammed into him. Her face was clouded with a mixture of displeasure and misery. When her eyes met his, he glimpsed regret in them.

'So you're saying whatever I do, the people won't be satisfied until they have me pressing the flesh, kissing babies with a promise of a royal wedding and an heir to swoon over?' Reyes couldn't suppress his sneer. The thought of putting himself out there, to be prodded and gawped over by the media, turned his stomach.

Alvarez knew Reyes's personal history and how he felt about the media. But his councillor nodded warily. 'That would be one way to reassure the people, yes.'

Gathering his fraying control, he turned back to his men. 'And there's no chance of presenting them with a royal wedding via Isabella?' He tried for one last ounce of a reprieve. 'Perhaps we can still rescue the situation with her ex-betrothed if we move fast enough…'

He stopped when Costanzo shook his head. 'Her fiancé declared he didn't want anything to do with Her Highness any longer after she broke things off. We had to pay his family reparations for the cancelled engagement. They won't reconsider Her Highness as a suitor.'

'Dios!' He looked at Jasmine, his blood boiling.

That look was still on her face—worry, regret. He looked

past that. To the luscious mouth that was parted slightly as her chest rose and fell in shallow breaths.

He wanted to forget that she was responsible for all this. Forget that the more he spoke to her, the more he doubted that her character was as black as he'd first thought. Reyes just wanted to forget. And in that moment, he wanted to use the most elemental way possible to achieve oblivion.

Her.

That stirring grew until his whole body thrummed with a carnal demand he couldn't deny.

What was wrong with him?

His youngest advisor cleared his throat. 'If Your Highness prefers, we can pursue this as a short-term union. Only until the economic situation in the kingdom stabilises.' He tapped a few keys on his tablet.

Reyes drummed his fingers on the table as he waited.

Finally, the advisor looked up. 'And I think Miss Nichols may be right. She's suitably placed to help.'

'She hasn't brought up any new solutions to Santo Sierra's problems that we haven't already considered.'

'No, but she could be the right person to broker a temporary marriage for you.'

'Excuse me?'

Reyes's eyes narrowed at her outraged tone.

His advisor glanced at her, then back at his tablet. 'According to the information I have here, you brokered the marriage between a US senator and his mistress once you arranged a discreet divorce from his wife of thirty years.'

Jasmine's mouth dropped open. 'That's supposed to be confidential.'

A douse of cold water cooled Reyes's raging temperature. 'Seems there's no end to your dubious talent,' he murmured.

Her face flushed. 'I wasn't responsible for him leaving his wife, nor was I responsible for finding the mistress, if that's what you're implying. I only assisted with the financial arrangements and ensured each party walked away happy.'

Her gaze swung to the men at the end of the table. How was it possible that one look from her commanded their silence? Reyes watched, intrigued, as she crossed her arms and narrowed her eyes for emphasis.

'That's not what you're asking me to do, surely? For what you need for Re…His Highness, you require an elite professional matchmaker. That's not what I specialise in. When I said I'd help I meant with the *economic* issues facing the kingdom.'

'This is an issue facing the kingdom. And one that has to be addressed sooner rather than later. With Isabella's marriage off the table, we need to give the people something to sustain their faith,' Alvarez said.

Pressure built at Reyes's temple. He wanted to deny what his council were saying. But deep down he couldn't dismiss that his people needed a healthy dose of bolstering news. Reyes had dashed their hopes of a royal wedding once before, five years ago, when he'd thrown Anaïs out of his life.

With his mother's subsequent death four years ago behind the wheel of her lover's car, and his father's illness soon afterwards, the only good news the Santo Sierran people had been given was the signing of the treaty and Isabella's wedding.

Both had failed to materialise. In the meantime, Mendez was pushing his greedy fingers into Santo Sierran affairs. It needed to end.

But marriage…

The only template he'd witnessed had been one mired in deception, misery and acrimony. It wasn't something he wanted to reproduce. If he was to take this road, it needed to be permanent. With both sides clear in their role and with no room for misunderstanding.

He looked down the table. Clenching his jaw, he nodded. 'The marriage will be a permanent one, not a short-term try-it-and-see-what-happens. My life isn't a scripted reality show to peddle to the people.'

Costanzo beamed with pleasure. 'Of course, Your Highness. That's a very wise decision. We'll set the ball rolling straight away—'

Reyes held up his hand. 'No, we'll reconvene in three days.'

The smile turned into a frown. 'But, Your Highness—'

'Arrange for the royal press secretary to include an addendum to my Paris itinerary. They can sell it as an investment-stroke-leisure trip.' He turned to Jasmine, noting that she'd gone pale again. 'Miss Nichols will be responsible for finding me five suitable candidates. Fly them to Paris for interviews after my investment meetings.'

'You're going ahead with it?' Her face was deliberately blank, but her eyes were pools of shock.

Somehow that bothered him. He shook himself out of the curious feeling. 'For my people's sake, yes.'

She drew in a shaky breath and looked down at her linked hands.

He surged to his feet, not liking the feeling that he'd been judged and found guilty. Nor did he like the sensation of a noose closing around his neck.

'Three days, gentlemen.'

'Yes, Your Highness.

In that moment, Reyes hated his title. Hated the responsibility weighing down on his shoulders. But despite the mixed emotions, there was one solemn vow he couldn't deny. He owed his people a better life than they'd enjoyed so far. And he intended to do whatever it took to make right his mistakes.

'You know you could've been done with me much quicker if you'd told them.' Questions had been swirling in her mind since Reyes's councilmen had left hours ago. But the one she'd wanted to ask wouldn't form, so she was trying a different route.

Reyes turned from the view to stare at her. 'Told them what?'

'What my role was in…'

'The treaty's disappearance?'

Jasmine jerked her head, still surprised he'd joined her for dinner and even more so that he'd stayed after they'd shared a delicious Spanish tapas meal on the terrace. Although the meal had gone by in near total silence, she couldn't help but feel a little less apprehensive of her fate.

She cradled the as yet untouched glass of red wine in her hands, watching the sun set on the horizon. Trying not to stare at Reyes Navarre's stunning profile as he leaned against the large pillar, facing the garden.

'Because if I had you'd be on your way to a maximum security prison in Santo Sierra. Your crime would be condemned as treason in my kingdom.'

Her heart stopped and her palms grew clammy. 'Aren't I headed there anyway? Something about getting a permanent tan?'

'Perhaps. But you might want to do something about delaying your arrival there. Before I came to Rio, I was in the process of enforcing a law that prohibited male and female prisoners being housed in the same penitentiary. That law hasn't passed yet.'

She inhaled sharply. 'You mean men and women are kept in the same prison?'

He shrugged. 'The old council deemed all criminals to be worthless regardless of their gender.'

Ice cascaded down her spine. 'But...that's barbaric!'

'They didn't care that they were potentially turning criminals who could be rehabilitated into irredeemable monsters. So do you regret my silence on your behalf?'

She slowly shook her head. 'No, I don't.' Her eyes met his. Whatever he saw in hers made him lift an eyebrow. Jasmine looked away quickly. 'I... Thank you.'

His mouth compressed. 'I neither want nor accept your gratitude. Retribution is still coming your way, one way or the other.'

The warning sent further chills dancing over her skin. While a part of her wanted him to spell out her fate and get her punishment over and done with, another part of her wanted to plead with him for mercy. She'd wronged him. Wronged his country. And he'd still saved her, albeit temporarily, from whatever the consequences were for her acts.

Reminding herself that this was the man who was contemplating marrying to please his people, she took a fortifying breath.

'My stepfather was kidnapped.'

His head whipped towards her. 'Excuse me?'

'First he was blackmailed through me, then kidnapped. He has…or had a gambling problem. He's been battling with it for almost twenty years. He embezzled government funds. And I'm not talking pennies. It was serious money. Getting caught would've meant a long prison sentence for him. So he borrowed money from a loan shark.'

'Who then turned the tables on him and demanded even more?'

She nodded. 'He said unless I brought him the treaty, he would harm my stepfather.'

Chilled grey eyes narrowed. 'Who was the loan shark?'

'His name was Joaquin Esteban. I don't know whether that's his real name or not—'

'Don't worry, I'll find him. So he took your stepfather?' he asked.

She nodded. 'In the middle of the night, right in front of my mother. They roughed him up. Broke his arm.' She shivered and he straightened from the wall.

'Did they hurt you?' His was voice was grave, intense.

'No. It happened when I was…with you, on your boat.'

His eyes narrowed. 'I don't recall you receiving a call.'

'You were asleep. My mother called. She was beside herself. I didn't want to do it, Reyes, please believe me, but I couldn't leave him in the hands of those men.'

If she'd expected sympathy, she was to be sorely disappointed. But for a heartbeat, his expression altered. Softened a touch.

'So where is this moralistic gambler of a stepfather, then? Still in his comfy government position?'

Irritation snapped along her nerves. 'Yes. But he's seeking help.'

'How noble of him.'

'He doesn't know what I did. He suspects but I don't want him to know. He'll be devastated. We can't all be perfect role models. Some of us try to put unfortunate deeds behind us and seek better lives.'

'And some of you fail miserably at it.'

Turning sideways, she set her glass down on the table. 'You have a right to condemn me. Believe me, I've condemned my-self countless times. But I wanted you to understand why I did what I did. Obviously I was wasting my breath.'

Reyes twirled his wine glass, one broad shoulder still lean-ing against the white pillar. Dressed in a white shirt and casual trousers, he looked sinfully breathtaking. Until she glimpsed the shadows in his eyes.

Her heart lurched as his words once again swirled in her mind. *I can't have another destroyed life on my conscience.*

Her eyes rose back to his face. He was watching her with that incisive look that seemed to see right into her soul. He took a slow sip, savouring the wine before swallowing.

'Contain your righteous indignation. You'll have to fall on your sword a hell of a lot more times before you breach the surface of my mercy. But I have a few minutes to spare, so please...carry on.'

She sighed. 'I'm sorry. I never intended for you to...for any-one to suffer for what I did.' Her gaze dropped to his midriff. His mouth tightened. 'If you could find it in your heart—'

His mocking laughter stopped her painful pleas. 'My *heart*?'

She gripped the edge of the table. 'I don't see the funny side to what I just said.'

'My heart is the last organ you should be attempting to appease.'

'I don't... I'm afraid you've lost me.'

His smile held that hint of sadness she'd glimpsed at their first meeting in Rio. 'You'd be wasting your time trying to appeal to something that doesn't exist.'

CHAPTER TEN

JASMINE STARED AT HIM, trying to work out if he was mocking her or not. He wasn't. That bleak look was deepening and his breathing was growing shallow and choppy as if he was caught in a distressing memory.

Before she could stop herself, she reached out and touched his arm.

He flinched. Brows clamped together, he stared down at her. 'What are you doing?'

'You seem a little...lost.'

One corner of his mouth lifted. 'And you thought you'd rescue me?' he bit out.

'Yes. Obviously, I was wrong to do so.' She turned away, unable to stomach the wildly volatile moods she experienced around this man. One minute she wanted to hurt him for his mockery, the next she wanted to ease whatever emotional pain haunted him.

And it was clear he was suffering. As for his reference to his non-existent heart, the lengths he was willing to go to for his people proved otherwise.

'You were talking about your stepfather?'

She frowned. 'I'm not sure that I want to any more.'

'Because I'm not whimpering with sympathy?'

'Because you pretend you're devoid of empathy, but I know that's not true.'

'Your dubious powers of deduction at work again?'

She perched on the edge of the table and folded her arms before the temptation to touch him spiralled out of control. Far from being cold as he tried to portray, Reyes was warm, passionate.

Any woman would be lucky to have him as her husband...

Her thoughts screeched to a halt. The stone that had lodged itself in her belly since his announcement in his study grew larger.

Which was ludicrous. All they'd shared was a one-night stand. An incredible one for her, but a brief, meaningless one nonetheless.

She had no right to experience this ongoing bewildering pain in her heart when she thought of what he planned to do. And the idea that he wasn't looking to marry for the short term, but for ever, shouldn't make her world darken with despair.

She had no claim on Reyes…

Jasmine started when he lifted his glass and abruptly drained his wine. She jerked upright when he lifted an imperious hand and summoned a guard, who'd been somewhere tucked out of her sight.

'What are you doing?'

'Since you're unwilling to carry on even the semblance of conversation, I'm having you escorted to your suite. We'll meet at noon tomorrow and you'll present me with a list of suitable candidates.'

Her fingers curled around the edge of the table at the thought of the task she'd been set. She wanted to refuse; wanted to tell him she'd rather rot in jail than help him find the next woman to warm his bed.

But how could she go back on her word to do whatever was needed to right her wrong?

One of his bodyguards approached. He wasn't the one who'd accosted her in the gardens this morning. In fact, from being a constant shadow, that other guard seemed to have disappeared.

This guard nodded at whatever Reyes was saying to him.

'Wait!'

Reyes lifted a bored brow at her.

'It's still early.' At his continued indolent look, she pursed her lips. 'Fine, I'll talk. My stepfather is perfect in every sense, except when it comes to his gambling.'

She looked from Reyes to the bodyguard. After several

heartbeats, Reyes dismissed the guard with a sharp nod. Walking past where she remained perched, he grabbed the half-finished bottle of wine, frowned at her untouched glass and refilled his own. He sat down, crossing his legs, so his thighs were dangerously close to her knee.

Jasmine pulled stronger on her runaway composure. 'He's a kind, gentle man and he cares deeply for my mother.'

A look passed through his eyes, but was gone before she could work out what it meant.

'Where does your biological father fit into this scenario?'

His voice lacked mockery, a fact for which she was thankful. 'He left when I was barely out of nappies. And he was the first in a long line of "fathers",' she quoted, 'who came and went before I was a teenager.'

Reyes sipped his wine. Said nothing.

'I know what you're thinking,' she ventured when the silence stretched.

His eyes gleamed. 'I sincerely doubt that.'

She shrugged. 'Well, whether you're thinking it or not, my past shaped me. I was angry with the world and with a mother who couldn't see how hopeless the men she dated were. By the time my stepfather came along, I was…in a bad way.'

'How bad?'

Jasmine didn't want to tell him. Didn't want to see the contempt in his eyes, or relive the bleakest point in her life. She'd been there, done that, and wore the shame underneath her skin and physical scars on her body.

She didn't want to go there, but Reyes's steady gaze demanded an answer.

'A spell in juvenile detention when I was sixteen,' she found herself confessing.

He froze. *'Dios…'* he murmured.

Thick mortification crept over her. Struggling to cover it, she laughed. 'Now you know my deepest, darkest secret. I'm guessing you'll be holding this over my head, too—'

'Stop talking, Jasmine.'

She clamped her mouth shut. He watched her with a curious expression, his gaze intensely assessing.

'How long were you in detention?'

Strangely she couldn't read any judgement in his tone. She reminded herself that as a prince he was skilled in hiding his true emotion. But then, he hadn't held back so far—

'Answer me,' he bit out roughly.

'Nine months.'

'What for?'

She grimaced. 'I *accidentally* set fire to a drug dealer's warehouse.'

'Is that experience why you found the handcuffs distressing?'

'You mean there are people who love being handcuffed?' she threw back.

One brow spiked.

Heat stained her cheeks. 'Yes, well, I didn't like it at the time. Still don't. Those days were the most traumatic of my life. Please don't force me to relive them.'

He put his glass down and leaned forward, elbows on his knees. His intensity increased a thousandfold. As did the intoxicating scent of his aftershave and warm skin. Jasmine clenched her thighs to keep from moving closer.

'What happened after you were released?'

'My stepfather. And yes, it may sound like a fairy tale, but he saved us. And even with his flaws, he turned out to be better than any man out there, even the man whose blood runs through my veins.'

Grey eyes snagged hers. Still no condemnation in them, just a stark curiosity.

'But the gambling became a problem, obviously,' he said.

She nodded. 'He was married before, but his wife died. That's when the problem escalated for him. He stopped for a while when he and my mother were dating, but after they married he started again. No matter how much we tried, we couldn't convince him to give it up. It made me sad. I know it worried him, too, that he couldn't beat it. But I couldn't condemn him. No matter what, he was the best father I knew. When Joaquin sank his claws into him, I had no choice. I couldn't let Stephen suffer.'

'Where was your mother in all of this?' The question was framed so tersely, with a bitter underlay that grazed sharply over her senses.

She looked at him. Whatever emotion he was holding had triggered tension in his body, like a predator ready to unleash its base nature should its prey fall within his grasp. Despite her nape tingling in warning, she wanted to move closer, experience that overwhelming danger.

Clearing her throat, she answered, 'My mother is what a psychologist would term wilfully blind. She means the world to me, but doesn't see what's right in front of her. Or she chooses to ignore it in favour of burying her head in the sand.'

The misery that her mother's attitude to life had brought her before Stephen had fallen in love with her had been a stark warning for Jasmine not to travel down the same path. She understood her mother better now, but it didn't make the pain of her late teens go away.

She glanced at Reyes and saw grudging understanding. But the look was wiped clean a moment later.

'Understanding the motive doesn't negate the crime.'

The unexpected surge of tears shocked Jasmine.

What was wrong with her? He'd told her he didn't have a heart. If she chose to disbelieve him, any hurt she felt was her own fault.

Blinking rapidly, she started to rise. 'No, but a little forgiveness goes a long way.'

He clamped a hand on her thigh.

Her heart took a dive, then picked itself up and banged hard against her ribs.

Reyes questioned his sanity. Except the voice was quickly smothered beneath the headier emotions swimming in his head.

His hand was halfway down her thigh, the soft cotton of her sundress crushing beneath his fingers. He moved his hand lower.

She gasped as they connected, skin to skin. Hers was soft, smooth like the fur of his sister's pet cat. And as with Sheba's pelt, he wanted to keep on stroking her.

He watched her struggle, knew the emotions she fought were the same as the ones he battled with. The chemistry that had gripped them the first time he'd set eyes on her flared high, spiking through his blood until he didn't bother to deny its existence any longer.

'You dislike me for stating the truth?'

'I dislike the brutality of it. And the complete absence of sympathy.'

Knowing he'd done a good job of hiding his feelings should've pleased Reyes. If his feelings weren't apparent, they couldn't be manipulated, used against him. So why did the thought that he'd succeeded send a pulse of discontentment through him? Why did he want to wipe that hurt look from her face? 'I warned you not to search for feelings that don't exist—'

'And I told you I don't believe that emotion doesn't exist inside you.'

He surged to his feet. 'I've never met anyone like you,' he said, not sure whether his agitation stemmed from the Tempranillo he'd consumed or the fact that she challenged him at every turn where no else dared to.

She sucked in a breath and her eyes stayed on his. Daring. Searching. Apprehensive. 'Nor I you. So this should be fun.'

A reluctant smile tugged at his lips. *Fun*...

Another word he'd associated with her that first time. A word he hadn't let into his life for a very long time.

He started to draw back from the brink of whatever fever gripped him.

She stepped closer. Her hands slid around his waist, holding him in place.

Again her daring floored him...excited him. The women

he'd dated in his distant past had been either too overawed with his status to show much spine, or had been so eager to prove they were worthy of his time, they'd overreached. Either way, he'd tended to lose interest long before they were done in the bedroom.

Jasmine Nichols made his senses jump without uttering a word. And when she did speak, he found himself held rapt.

In the last hour, the woman she'd revealed herself to be intrigued him even more. She'd experienced adversity of the worst kind, and come through it.

And with her hand on him and her parted lips so close, all he could see, smell, *anticipate*, was her.

Drawn into a web he couldn't shake, he angled his head. 'I don't do fun, Jasmine.'

Her back arched, bringing her closer. Her mouth brushed his. He jerked at the zap of electricity. Her hands tightened around him. 'Sure you do. You just don't like to admit it.'

The sound that rumbled from inside him emerged harsh and bewildered. *'Dios...'*

He spiked his hand through her hair and kissed her. Hard. Roughly.

He palmed her breasts, gloried in their fullness, and swallowed her jagged gasp of pleasure when his thumb grazed her nipple. The sight and taste of them flashed through his mind. He squeezed the bud. Harder. She made a rougher sound. More demanding. More receptive.

His blood thrummed faster.

Capturing her waist, he pulled her into his body. Her hands drifted up from his torso, up to his shoulders. Every nerve yearned for closer contact. The ultimate contact.

He was fast reaching the point where he would be unable to deny the need to take, the need to reprise the headiness of their encounter in Rio.

Her mouth parted wider, her tongue caressing his. Reyes drove in, tasting her with deep, hungry kisses that robbed them both of breath.

His erection throbbed. Demanded satisfaction.

Dios, this was crazy. Making the same mistake twice was unconscionable. He needed to pull back.

But he couldn't. His thumb angled her jaw and he claimed another kiss. He didn't realise he'd bent her backwards until her elbows propped on the table to support herself.

Needing to breathe, he took a beat. Looked at her, spread before him like a banquet.

A tempting, *forbidden* banquet. He'd given in once and the resulting chaos still echoed through his life. Perhaps he understood her motivations a little now. Perhaps he would even contemplate forgiveness at some distant point in the future.

But he couldn't revisit the eye of the storm.

Sucking in a deep breath, he stepped back, smashing down on his body's insistence that he finish what he'd started.

He denied his body, denied his mind. It would've been easy to take what he wanted; what he craved. But he knew it would come at a price. A price he couldn't afford to pay.

CHAPTER ELEVEN

'So, JUST SO we're clear, you want me to enquire whether she's a good kisser, or should I go the whole hog and ask her if she's dynamite in bed, too?' Jasmine folded her arms and drummed her fingers against her elbows.

She knew her foul mood stemmed from the tossing and turning she'd done last night. And her triple vomiting session this morning. She knew *why* she'd tossed and turned. Just as she feared her suspicions on why she was throwing up would be confirmed, as soon as she found a way to visit a chemist. She wasn't afraid to admit she was terrified of what the results of a pregnancy test would show. And not just for herself. She'd already thrown Reyes's world into chaos once. How would he react *if* it turned out she was carrying his child?

She'd debated through the night whether to tell him of her suspicions, and had elected to wait. There was no point stirring the hornet's nest even harder until she had concrete proof.

Feeling weak and more than a little apprehensive of what fate held in store for her, she'd have given her right arm not to perform the task of finding Reyes Navarre a bride.

He leaned back in his chair, his gaze coolly assessing. 'The latter qualities I will discover for myself long before our wedding night. Once you've tackled the more important characteristics of loyalty, trust and dependability, of course.'

'I'd never consider anyone who didn't possess those qualities. But how on earth am I supposed to know whether she's a good kisser or not?'

His eyebrow quirked and she had a feeling he was toying with her. 'Aren't you supposed to be good at your job?'

'Brokering deals and calming anxious parties before multinational mergers, yes. Judging whether a woman is a good kisser based on her pedigree, not so much.'

'So you're admitting failure before you've even started?' he asked.

She looked away, afraid he'd see the depth of the anguish she couldn't will away, no matter how much she tried. 'I'm not afraid to admit I'm not the right person for this job. We slept together, Reyes—' she saw him tense, but she forced herself to continue '—and despite everything that happened afterwards, it wasn't a casual thing for me. I can't just brush it off...' She stopped before she dug herself into a hole she'd never be able to emerge from.

'Are you saying you can't stay objective in this task?'

She forced herself to meet his gaze. 'I'm saying I have feelings. I'll do it if you want me to but I don't have to like it.'

A look crossed his face, but his expression shuttered before she could read it. 'Understood.'

Jasmine forced herself to glance down at the shortlist she'd compiled at four a.m. when she'd finally conceded sleep was a pipe dream. She rattled off the names, watching his face for a reaction. His features remained blank.

'I'm going to call their representatives. Arrange for us to meet them in Paris next week. Shall I arrange to send your private jet for them or do you want them to fly commercial?'

'I don't micromanage. Liaise with my head of security on modes of transport. And we're not flying to Paris next week. We're leaving tomorrow, and then on to Santo Sierra at the end of the week.' He slid his chair closer to his desk and opened a file.

'What?' Her heart thumped harder with a mixture of desolation and anxiety. 'I'm good at my job, but I can't find you a bride in twenty-four hours, *Your Highness*.' Pressure built in her head with the knowledge that she needed to find out once and for all whether she carried his child.

'Have you seen the news today?' he enquired.

'No. Should I have?'

His fists tightened on the desk for a moment before he relaxed. 'There was a riot in San Domenica last night.'

'Santo Sierra's capital?'

He nodded. 'Several people were hurt, including women and children, in the main square. Thankfully, no one was killed. My people are growing restless. Their anxiety is being fuelled, no doubt by Mendez's people. I have to return soon or things will get worse.'

The throb of worry in his voice was unmistakeable. For the first time she accepted that his councillors were right. Santo Sierra needed a good news story to bolster the people's confidence in its monarchy.

Caught in the quandary of having her feelings ravaged in the process of finding Reyes a wife, while suspecting she was carrying his child, and doing what she could to fix the damage she'd caused, Jasmine took a deep breath and gathered her composure.

'I'll make sure the candidates are in Paris for when we arrive.' She picked up her tablet and headed for the door.

'Jasmine?'

Her heart stuttered at the use of her first name.

'Yes?' Her answer emerged shakier than she would've wished.

'Cross Petra Nikolova off your list. We dated briefly once. She's been known to take certain banned substances on occasion. The last thing I intend to foist on my subjects is a drug-dabbling queen. And you can also delete Sienna Hamilton.'

Every single good intention fled out of her head. Her anxiety ramped up, along with a buzzing in her head and a sick feeling in her stomach she shockingly diagnosed as writhing jealousy. Coupled with the suspected extra hormones raging through her body, Jasmine had to lock her knees and count to ten before she could speak.

'What's wrong with Miss Hamilton?' Her voice trembled in a way she detested.

When his eyes locked on hers, his expression was far from mocking. 'She's a serial cheater. She's discreet about it, but I prefer not to wonder in who else's bed my wife has been when I return home at night.'

She stared at him, dying to ask why pain clouded his eyes when he talked about adultery. But, unwilling to drive the knife that seemed to be wedged in her chest further, she wiped the question from her mind. Realising she hadn't taken a breath since Reyes mentioned kissing other women, Jasmine forced herself to breathe.

'You realise that leaves me with just three candidates?' she said around the knot in her throat. It was three more than she wanted to deal with, but she couldn't see any way around this harrowing task.

He cracked a hard, sad smile. 'Then you need to make doubly sure they are right for the job.' His tone said she was dismissed.

Which was good because Jasmine couldn't get out of there fast enough. Except she couldn't leave just yet.

Reyes raised his head when she retraced her steps to his desk. 'Can I help you with something else?'

'I need to go into town this morning.'

He frowned. 'Why?'

Because I need to know whether my life is about to change for ever.

'I need stuff.'

He looked down his nose at her. Waited.

A blush warmed her cheeks. 'Women's stuff.'

Her tiny hope for him to feel a little bit of her embarrassment died a quick death when he returned his attention to his papers.

'Reyes? Can I get one of your men to drive me into town?'

'No,' he replied.

'Come on—'

'I'll drive you myself. We'll go after lunch.'

No, no, no!

* * *

Entering the solarium, she sank into the nearest lounger, clenched her fingers around the tablet to stop them shaking.

She tried to reason with herself. The likelihood that a crown prince would be caught shopping for feminine products in a chemist was very minimal.

But then so had the likelihood of her ending up in his bed in Rio. The odds that she could be pregnant with Reyes's child were one in a million, but she knew to her cost that fate was vested in singling her out for her parlour tricks.

She could be worrying over nothing. The tenderness in her breasts could be the result of her imagination. Or the residual effect of Reyes caressing them last night…

She forced herself to look at the list of candidates she needed to contact…and flung the tablet away. Covering her face with her hands, she caught a low moan before it escaped.

What was wrong with her? One night of sex and one heavy-kissing session with Reyes Navarre and she couldn't handle the idea of him with another woman? No, she couldn't deny that her feelings were more to do with the fact that she might be carrying his baby. And the growing sense that she couldn't stand the thought of him being married to someone else whether his child was growing inside her or not.

Would Reyes go ahead with marrying someone else if she was carrying his child, or would he consider another option? Like her…

Hope rose up inside her. She pushed it away.

She was going crazy…

He would never consider her in a million years. Her heart lurched. Shaking her head, she focused on the names.

One young duchess. One daughter of a media mogul. One self-made millionaire with an extensive philanthropic background.

On paper any one of the remaining three could be crown princess material and would no doubt do whatever it took to secure the attention, if not the heart, of a man like Reyes Navarre.

So get a move on...

The quicker she got this over with, the quicker she could return to her life. Forget all about Reyes and the feel of his mouth on hers, his strong arms around her.

By the time Reyes strode into the solarium, Jasmine had secured the enthusiastic agreement of all three and had arranged for their travel to Paris.

'Something's come up. I can't take you into town. Make a list of what you need. I'll have Carmelita get them for you.'

Her stomach lurched in a queasy roll. Having Reyes find out what she suspected before she knew for sure was out of the question. 'Umm...I'd rather get them myself. If you're busy, it can wait till we get to Paris.'

He frowned, but nodded and walked away.

Jasmine wasn't proud of taking the coward's way out, buying herself some more time before she had to face whatever fate had in store for her. So when the tears stung her eyes, she raced up the stairs to her room and let them fall.

'You'll be dining with the duchess at the Paris Ultime this evening at eight. I've reserved a private dining room for you and once you review the menu I can provide it to the private chef who'll be catering for you. The duchess is allergic to shellfish. Oh, and she doesn't eat carbs after six, so she requests that a bread basket not be served. She can't resist the temptation, apparently.' Jasmine made her voice crisp, businesslike, so the pain of the vice tightening around her heart wouldn't bleed through her voice.

Reyes raised an eyebrow at her as their limo left the private airport and drove towards the French capital.

'You think it's a good sign that the woman who's to bring hope to my people can't resist a simple bread basket?'

Jasmine shrugged. 'We all have our faults. If hers is a simple carbs issue, then you're all set.' She tried to keep her voice light, but the stone wedged in her belly made even thought difficult.

The last thing she wanted to discuss was the eating habits of Reyes's future queen.

'Do you resist bread baskets after six, Jasmine?'

God, why couldn't she stop her heart from flipping over each time he said her name like that? 'Nope. Bread is a vice I happily embrace.'

The moment the words were out of her mouth, she regretted it. A chill permeated the atmosphere. Reyes stared at her, tight jawed. Jasmine wondered whether to apologise, but then dismissed it. She'd apologised enough. She was here, making amends. Even if it involved doing a job every fibre of her being rejected.

After several minutes, she cleared her throat. 'Liliana Simpson will have lunch with you tomorrow, and I've scheduled Berenice Holden for an early dinner. Once you make your decision, I'll liaise with your royal press secretary about making an announcement. I've also arranged for a few photographers to take some pictures…' She stopped when his jaw clenched harder. 'What?'

'One camera, one photograph, one photographer.' His tone was acid.

'But I thought you wanted the world to see that you're alive and dating? You can't hide away for ever. You need to get in front of the people. Show them that you care about them. That you're excited to lead them. And that you're also not a eunuch.'

'Excuse me?'

She attempted a shrug that fell short of the mark. 'One photograph isn't going to do the job.'

'You forget there was a riot in my kingdom less than twenty-four hours ago. I can't be seen living it up in Paris, proving my manhood, while my people are suffering. The article will stress heavily that I'm on my way home, possibly with a potential bride in tow. The intention is to take their minds off their anxiety without making it seem like I've forgotten about them, is it not?'

'Yes, of course. I'll take care of it.'

As she made unnecessary notes in her tablet her mind raced. She could feel the waves of tension coming off his body, and knew Reyes would rather be in Santo Sierra, seeing to his people, than here in Paris vetting potential brides.

While the thought perplexingly lifted her heart, she couldn't help but be concerned for him.

'Have you thought about what you'll do about Mendez?' she asked.

His mouth compressed. Wedging his elbow on the armrest, he glanced at her. 'Once the wedding is done and I've elected a new council, I'll make him a take-it-or-leave-it offer. The time for pandering to his whim is over.'

She nodded. When he turned to look out of the window, she stared at his profile. The question she'd been avoiding hovered on the tip of her tongue.

'Can I ask you a question?' she blurted.

Grey eyes narrowed on her. 'Go ahead.'

'Why are there no pictures of you taken since your mother died?'

A chilled look entered his eyes. 'Because I don't court publicity. Not like…' He stopped and exhaled harshly.

Her heart clenched at the bleakness in his eyes. 'Like your mother? I know she liked to…that she was a media darling.'

'Less of a darling, more of a whore,' he countered mercilessly.

Jasmine flinched. 'I'm sorry.'

'Why? We finally have something in common. Mothers who would've been better off remaining childless.'

'I wouldn't go as far as that. After all, if that had happened, neither you or I would be here.'

His gaze raked her face, as if he were trying to burrow under her skin, see inside her soul again. 'And our night in Rio would never have happened,' he murmured.

Her breath stalled. 'No…I guess not.'

'Do you regret that, Jasmine?' he rasped.

'I like it when you call me Jasmine. Miss Nichols makes me sound like a kindergarten teacher.'

A low, deep laugh broke from his lips, but he continued to stare at her. Then he lifted his hand and traced a finger down her cheek. 'You haven't answered my question, Jasmine.'

'Do I regret Rio?' The truth wasn't difficult to admit. But she feared the can of worms she would be opening by admitting it, even to herself. She licked her dry bottom lip. 'The first part, not at all. It was the most memorable night of my life.'

His eyes darkened and his nostrils flared. 'And the second part?' he demanded.

'The second part...very, very much. I would do anything to take it back.'

He said nothing, but he nodded after several seconds. And she dared to hope that he believed her.

CHAPTER TWELVE

THE DINNER JACKET he wore felt tight, restrictive. And someone had turned up the temperature in the private dining room. Or had it been turned down?

Dios...

Reyes passed a finger underneath his collar and moved the food around on his plate.

'I would need to fly to Europe at least twice a month. I have a standing appointment for full works at my favourite spa in Switzerland.' Carefully styled blond hair curtained to one side as the duchess tilted her head. 'That won't be a problem, will it?'

The bread basket. Suddenly, Reyes needed it more than he needed to breathe.

'Reyes…you don't mind me calling you Reyes, do you? Or do you prefer Rey?' She smiled.

Perfect teeth. Perfect hair. Perfect manicure.

No character-forming scars on her body. As Jasmine had across her palm. Or that thin two-inch scar on her shoulder.

He growled under his breath. He was sitting opposite a beautiful, poised woman who was warm enough for his people to fall in love with. Visually, the duchess was the antithesis of his mother and Anaïs, and that alone would sway his people, who'd hated Queen Isolde Navarre, towards her.

And yet he couldn't stop thinking about the reluctant thief with the body that called to his like a siren to a sailor.

He forced himself to focus on his dinner companion. After another minute, he threw down his napkin, stood and smiled down at the duchess.

'We won't need to worry about what you'll call me. After tonight we'll most likely never meet again.'

He entered his suite twenty minutes later. It was barely nine o'clock so he knew Jasmine would still be up. He told himself he was searching for her to give her a piece of his mind about how appallingly his evening had gone.

He had a right to, after all.

When the living room proved empty, he contemplated leaving the dressing-down till morning. Going to the bar, he poured himself a cognac and walked out onto the penthouse terrace.

He heard the splash of her swimming before he rounded the corner to where the private pool was located.

Despite warning himself that he needed to stay away, he couldn't stop his feet propelling him forward until he was standing on the edge of the aqua-tiled pool, staring at her stunning figure as she swam underwater.

Her arms and legs kicked in a graceful flow, the sight of her scantily clad figure robbing him of breath and sanity. That feeling of skating on the edge of his control escalated to the point where he was in a foul mood by the time she broke the surface.

'You failed.' His snarl was deep and ruthless enough to make him inwardly grimace.

Nevertheless, he felt a measure of cheap satisfaction when she whirled to face him. 'Actually, I was winning. Twenty laps without stopping is an achievement for me.'

'I don't mean your swim. I mean you failed with the duchess.'

A single frown line marred her perfect skin. 'Okay. I guess that's why you're back early? What happened?'

Her legs continued to swirl lazily underwater as she stared up at him. Reyes's groin pounded hard as he followed the sexy movement.

When she raised her eyebrows, he dragged his gaze away, tried to find words to enumerate the duchess's faults. None came to mind. 'She lacked the qualities I need.'

Jasmine's eyes shadowed. She glanced away, then back at him. 'You did the kissing test?' An odd note in her voice made something jerk in his chest. He didn't have time to examine it because she kicked away from the edge. Her breasts bounced, and he nearly swallowed his tongue as flames spiked into his groin.

'I didn't need to. I knew she would fail.'

'Wow, you're psychic now?' Her tone had returned to normal. She swam towards the steps.

He followed, mesmerised by the curve of her spine and the roundness of her behind. He watched her rise from the pool and pluck a towel from the chair. His fingers tightened around his glass when she patted the towel over her body.

Focus! 'Perhaps you need to be reminded of my earlier statement. You *failed*.'

'You have two more candidates. Maybe you'll strike it lucky second time round. If not, three times will be the charm.'

The restlessness that prowled through him intensified. 'You'll come with me tomorrow.'

She froze and stared at him with wide, wounded eyes. 'I'd rather not, Reyes. I'm not the one marrying these women!'

He exhaled harshly. Ploughing a hand through his hair, he glared at her. 'I…need you.'

Her eyes widened further. He kicked himself for uttering words he had no business saying. 'No, you don't. I've done my bit. It's time to do yours.'

'*Dios!* Have you always been this infuriating?'

Her face fell. 'You think I'm infuriating?'

Reyes was overcome with a desire to placate her. Take that look off her face. Replace it with one of those stunning smiles that lit up his insides.

He pondered the feeling, adding extreme puzzlement to the many emotions he felt around this woman.

This woman should be in jail somewhere dark and harrowing, not enjoying the luxury of a Parisian emperor suite, wearing a sexy bikini, and swimming in his pool.

'Yes. You're infuriating. And you're also supposed to be good at your job. So far you're doing a pathetically poor attempt. Were you in my permanent employ I'd have fired you a long time ago.'

She looked down at the floor for several seconds, before she glanced back up. 'Wow, you don't hold back when you really get going, do you?'

He dragged a hand through his hair. 'I had a call on my way back. My father had a better health day today than the doctors have seen in the last six months. I missed it, Jasmine. I missed it because I'm attending dinners and vetting potential brides just so my people's faith in me can be restored. You think I should go easy on you for that?'

She'd grown paler as he spoke, and tears filled her eyes by the time he finished.

Reyes felt like a toad for upsetting her. He cursed silently when her mouth trembled.

'I wasn't going to apologise again. I think saying sorry loses its power after the first dozen times. But once again, please know that I never wished for this to happen to you, Reyes. I was protecting those I love and misjudged the consequences. But what's happening with your father is good news. You weren't there to witness it but that doesn't take away from the fact that he's better.'

About to denounce her for her unwanted optimism, he paused in surprise when she leaned in close and kissed his cheek.

His breath punched out as her alluring scent engulfed him. Too soon, she stepped back and he fought down a keen sense of loss.

Rocking back on his heels, Reyes eyed her. 'Why did you do that?' He was shocked enough for his voice to emerge flat. At every turn this woman threw him for a loop.

'You looked like you needed it. You'll be back home soon enough and in control of things. And Santo Sierra will get better with you in charge. I'm certain of it.'

She secured the towel around her, grabbed another one and

proceeded to dry her hair. He found himself transfixed, unable to take his eyes off her.

When she sat cross-legged on the lounger, Reyes fought to avert his gaze from her bare thighs. Seeing another scar on her knee, he frowned. From what he knew about her, he was aware her childhood hadn't been a bed of roses. But the physical marks caused him to wonder exactly what had happened to her.

'Did this happen to you in juvie?' he asked tersely as he sat opposite her.

She followed his gaze and shook her head. 'No. It was yet another product of my misspent youth.'

His fist clenched. 'That's not an answer, Jasmine.'

Her throat moved in a small swallow. 'I was pinned between two gangs during a turf war on the council estate where I lived. This is the result of flying glass from a shattered window.'

He forced himself to release his hold on the glass before it broke in his fist. 'Shattered glass from…?'

'Bullets.'

Icy fury washed over him. 'Your mother let you live in such a dangerous place?' His voice sounded gruff and almost alien in his ears.

'We had nowhere else to go.' No self-pity, just a statement of fact. And yet he knew that the situation must have been gruelling. Why else would she have fought to never return to a place like that again?

Overwhelmed by the protective instinct that continued to build inside him, Reyes looked at her knee. He barely resisted the urge to run his hand over the jagged scar. Just as he fought to ask whether there were more signs of her traumatic childhood on her body.

It wasn't his business. She was a transient presence in his life. He wasn't even interested in punishing her for the theft of his treaty any more. Her life had been a difficult one. She'd made choices she wasn't proud of, but she'd made those choices out of loyalty, a need to survive.

As much as he wanted to damn her for the turmoil she'd

left behind, deep down he knew that, faced with the same choice, he would choose the same path. How many times had he shielded his own father from his mother's misdeeds? Lied to protect his father's feelings? Even knowing what his mother had been doing the day she died, he'd tried to keep the truth from his father for as long as possible.

Except Reyes didn't want to let Jasmine go...not just yet.

What he wanted was to assuage the alarming, visceral need to flatten her on the nearest surface and rediscover the heady pleasures of her body.

His eyes rose to her face.

Awareness throbbed between them. Then she glanced away to the view of Paris at night.

'I was about to order room service. Do you want some food?' Her voice was husky, warm and sexy in that way that reminded him of their encounter in the darkened bedroom on his yacht.

He forced his gaze from her sensual mouth, and nodded. '*Sí*. I'm starving. Make sure you order an extra-large bread basket.'

She picked up the phone to make the call to his chef. Reyes traced the seductive line of her neck, and resisted the urge to jump into the pool to cool down his out-of-control libido.

Reyes dismissed the second candidate after a mere twenty minutes.

'What was wrong with her?' Jasmine asked, despite the heady pool of relief building inside her. Taking pains not to examine the feeling too closely, she hurried after him as he strode away from the restaurant on the Champs-Élysées.

'Your notes said she had nothing to do with her father's media business. That turned out not to be true.' He rounded on her once they were in the car and driving away. 'In case I haven't made it quite clear, I detest the media. They made my and my sister's lives a living hell when we were growing up, thanks to their insatiable interest in my mother and her infidelities.' His mouth was pinched and the lines around it deep and pale.

'I didn't know that about your mother. I'm sorry.'

He inhaled deeply and loosened the blue-striped tie he'd worn with a pristine white shirt and a dark grey suit. A muscle twitched in his jaw as he exhaled. '*Gracias*. Perhaps I did you a disservice by not giving you enough time to prepare for this.'

It was the closest he'd come to an apology for the unreasonable demands he'd made for her assignment. But even though she nodded her acceptance, Jasmine couldn't shift from his statement about his mother.

'Did your subjects know…about your mother?' she asked.

He wrenched at his top buttons and pulled his tie free. 'Yes, they knew. They thought my father weak for not divorcing her and by the time she died in her lover's car, she was very much a hated figure.'

'So by definition…'

'*Sí*, the whole House of Navarre hasn't endeared itself to the people.'

The question she'd been trying to avoid asking ricocheted through her head.

Ask. This is your chance.

'Back in Spain you said something about not wanting another destroyed life on your conscience. Did something else happen with your mother?'

His features froze and he remained silent for so long, she was certain he wouldn't answer.

'Five years ago, I almost got engaged.'

It was the last response she'd expected. Her mind blanked for a second. 'What?'

His laugh was bitter. 'You wanted to know why marrying wasn't my first choice, so…' He stopped and his face contorted with bitter recollection. Jasmine wanted to tell him to stop, wanted to wipe whatever wretched memory was causing the distress on his face. He spoke before she could form the appropriate words.

'Anaïs Perdot and I met the last time I was here in Paris. It was my first diplomatic tour. Her father was doing a lot of business in Santo Sierra and Anaïs and I grew…close.'

Jasmine didn't want to guess what memory was making his jaw clench. She held her breath as he continued. 'Her parents were eager for a match. I suppose on paper we were an ideal couple. She was young and exciting. For a while she made me forget that I was the son of a queen who didn't feel any remorse about dragging the family name through the mud with her infidelities. Hell, she even helped me to forge an easier relationship with the father I detested because I thought him weak for not stopping my mother's behaviour.' His chest heaved on a deep exhale.

'For a while?' she ventured.

His lips firmed. 'Her parents thought Anaïs should live in Santo Sierra for a while before we announced our engagement. Within weeks, my mother got her claws into her.'

'How?'

He shrugged. 'It started off as lunches and shopping sprees while I was busy with matters of state. Then they turned into late-night parties when she wouldn't return to the palace until the early hours, and then not at all.'

Jasmine frowned. 'Behaviour not exactly befitting a future queen, but European royalty have been known to indulge in much worse antics.'

His eyes turned arctic. 'Really? How many female members of your royal family have been photographed having sex with another man the week before their engagement was announced?'

Her hand flew to her mouth. 'Oh, my God! What did you do?'

Reyes stared at her for several more seconds before he shook his head. 'I handed over an obscene amount of money to the camera-wielding blackmailer to prevent the pictures hitting the papers. And I set back my relationship with my father by having our biggest fight yet when he refused to lift a finger against my mother for her part in Anaïs's behaviour.'

'I'm so sorry, Reyes.' She laid a hand on his arm and felt his palpable tension.

'That wasn't the worst of it. The day I told Anaïs it was over, she went to my mother. My mother convinced her that I was merely throwing a tantrum; that I would get over it. And then she talked Anaïs into partying one more night. On their way back from the club, they were involved in a hit-and-run accident. Anaïs claimed my mother was driving. My mother claimed the opposite. The result was that a teenager was left paralysed for life, his plans to become a doctor shattered.'

'And still your father did nothing?'

Reyes pinched the bridge of his nose. 'After I threw Anaïs and her family out of my life, she decided to share her version of her time in Santo Sierra with the media. My father finally tried to do some damage control, but it was too late. We were vilified in the media. My mother's behaviour spiralled out of control. A few months later, she was dead. That's when the first ramblings of unrest began.'

'And your father's illness just compounded the problems.'

That sadness she'd glimpsed on his face that first night in Rio appeared again. 'I never really got a chance to tell him that I regretted our fight. Last night would've been a good opportunity, had I been home.'

'You'll be home in a matter of days. You'll get your chance.'

He fell silent for a stretch of time, then he sent her an intense glance. The imperious ruler of one of the world's richest kingdoms was back. And despite the determined look on his face now, Jasmine couldn't help but feel desperate heartache for what he'd suffered. She realised her hand was still on his arm and lowered it to her lap.

'You understand now why finding the right candidate is imperative?' he asked.

Despite her heart taking a cliff-dive, she nodded. 'Yes, I do.'

Again her heart wrenched at the thought that weeks from

now he would be a married man. It would be a marriage of convenience, of course, but one he intended to commit to for a lifetime.

He would be out of reach for ever.

Last night, sharing a relaxing dinner with him, she'd wondered what it would've been like if they'd met under different circumstances. Then she'd kicked herself for the absurd thought.

Their backgrounds were too diverse for that to have happened in any lifetime. As she'd thought in Rio, they were two ships passing in the night, never to meet again.

But they'd met once…and again. Right at this moment, they could share a lifetime connection.

Because of Reyes's tight schedule and his edict that she wasn't allowed anywhere on her own, she hadn't been able to get her hands on the pregnancy test yet.

Instead she'd ordered it online and was expecting it to be delivered to the hotel today.

Until it arrived and she was forced to confront whatever consequences it brought, she would concentrate on carrying on as normal. Reality would come soon enough. Certainly before Reyes left for Santo Sierra.

And if her suspicions were right and she really was pregnant…

Reyes's door opened, and the driver bowed. 'Your Highness.'

Her heart lurched as she watched him struggle to suppress painful memories behind a bland façade. Again, the need to comfort him grew until she gripped her handbag to stop herself reaching for him.

Jasmine prayed the last candidate would be what Reyes wanted, while studiously ignoring the spear of pain that lanced her heart.

CHAPTER THIRTEEN

'WELL, I THINK we've discussed everything that needs to be discussed. I hope I've proven that I can be trusted and that I will be discreet, especially in matters of media liaisons.' Berenice Holden smiled at Reyes.

'You're comfortable with this arrangement being permanent? Or at the very least a long-term proposition?' Reyes asked.

'Of course. I like to think I'm bringing a lot to the table, but I'm aware I have much more to gain by ensuring any union between us works.'

Jasmine tried to keep her composure as the cold-blooded negotiations flew between Reyes and Berenice. They'd been hammering out terms for the last hour. And Jasmine had felt her heart wither each time they'd reached a compatible agreement.

She watched Reyes cross off the last item on his list, set his pen down and reach for his cutlery.

'Excuse me.' She rose and stumbled from the table. From the corner of her eye, she saw Reyes jerk to his feet, but she didn't stop until she slammed and locked the toilet door behind her. Shaking, she collapsed onto the closed lid.

Breathe...

This would be over soon. The test kits had arrived. Her attempt to take the test had been thwarted when Reyes had summoned her to grill her about Berenice before his meeting with her, and then insisted Jasmine accompany him.

Breathe...

In just over an hour she would know. Among other things, she didn't think it was healthy, if she was pregnant, to reside in this perpetual state of anxiety.

Her fingers trembled as the thought took root. She... pregnant...with Reyes's baby.

She closed her eyes and forced herself to breathe through her anxiety. Waiting until it was impolite to linger any longer, she returned to the table, sat through the last course. Tried to stop herself from trembling each time Berenice looked at Reyes.

Vaguely she noticed Reyes stand. 'Jasmine?'

She raised her head, met his probing glance. 'Yes?'

'Are you okay?' he asked.

Her head hurt when she nodded. He touched her arm to get her attention. All of a sudden, each of her senses zinged to life.

She looked round. Berenice had left. Jasmine was alone with Reyes again.

'Are you ready to leave? Or would you like dessert since you hardly touched your food?' He frowned down at her plate.

'I'm fine. I wasn't that hungry.' She rose and followed him out to the waiting limo. Heart in her throat, she slid in beside him. Silence throbbed in the car for several minutes, until she couldn't take it any more.

'So, you think she's the one?' Jasmine realised she'd stopped breathing as she waited for him to answer.

After a few moments, he shrugged. '*Sí*, she ticks all the boxes. I'll call a meeting of the council when we get back to Santo Sierra tomorrow. Tell them to start planning my wedding.'

She was pregnant.

Three sticks had confirmed it. Several online translations of the word *enceinte* along with three thick blue lines had sealed her fate.

Setting the tablet down on the bedcovers, Jasmine lay back on the bed and spread shaky fingers over her stomach.

Several emotions eddied through her, but gradually the fear, the anxiety, the complete and utter paralyzing notion that she was in no way equipped to be a mother, fell away to be replaced by one paramount sensation.

Joy.

She had a child growing inside her. Not just any child. Reyes's baby. The situation was completely messed up, but if fate had requested in a normal world that she choose the father of her child, Reyes Navarre would've been her first, her only choice.

Reyes...

She closed her eyes and inhaled deeply. She had to tell him. No question about that. The pain of never having known her father was one she'd smothered away during her childhood and teenage years. And although Stephen had filled the desolate hole left by her father's rejection, the dull ache remained.

She would never dream of subjecting her child to the same fate by choice. But then this wasn't just any child...

The enormity of what this pregnancy entailed burned through her joy.

God, she was pregnant with the future heir of the Santo Sierran throne. And its father was getting married to someone else in a matter of weeks.

Jasmine rolled to her side and hugged a pillow to her chest. Her eyes stung. She blinked rapidly. When her vision continued to blur, she dashed her fingers across her eyes, cursing the hormones running riot through her veins.

Think! She'd faced the worst dilemmas, protected herself and her mother from the most vicious thugs. She'd even faced bullies in juvie and emerged victorious. Stronger for it.

But did she possess the right skills to be a mother to a future king or queen? She squeezed her eyes shut and tried to ignore the tears. She wasn't a crier. Never had been...

She just needed a minute to absorb the life-changing news before—

'Jasmine!'

She started and opened her eyes to see Reyes crossing the vast suite towards her bed.

Sitting up, she eyed the tablet, breathing a sigh of relief to notice it'd gone dark. The actual pregnancy tests were safely tucked beneath her pillow.

'Have you heard of knocking?' she demanded. Her heart slammed into her ribs with its usual state of excitement at the sight of Reyes. But this time there was an added urgency. He was the father of her child. Which meant, one way or the other, they would be connected to each other for ever.

'I knocked. Several times. I entered because I was concerned. Are you okay?' He frowned down at her, those hawkish grey eyes tracking her face.

Too late, Jasmine remembered she'd been crying and probably had dried marks on her face. She dashed her hand across her cheeks.

'I'm…fine. Just a little tired.'

His frown didn't dissipate. Mouth dry, she slid her legs to the side of the bed and stood up. 'Did you want something?'

'You were supposed to supply my press secretary with Miss Holden's details. He hasn't received them yet.' His eyes narrowed further. 'Are you sure you're okay? You look pale.' He started to move forward, one hand raised to touch her.

She jerked out of reach, propelled solely by self-preservation. Her emotions were on enough of a roller coaster for her to risk disturbing them further by letting Reyes touch her. She needed to formulate her thoughts rationally before she broke the news to him. And Reyes touching her had never triggered rational thinking.

She risked a glance at him. His jaw was tense and his hand suspended mid-air. A look of hurt passed over his face before it was quickly veiled. She sucked in another breath. 'I'm fine. Really. I'll send the details now.'

He nodded tersely. Expecting him to leave, she gasped when he stepped closer and cupped her cheeks. 'You've been crying. Tell me what's wrong.'

'Reyes—'

'Don't tell me it's nothing. *Something* is wrong with you.

You've been jumpy lately. The chef tells me you hardly touched your breakfast and I know you didn't eat more than two mouthfuls at lunch. If you insist you're not sick, then it must be something else. Are you worried about what will happen to you when we get to Santo Sierra?'

'Should I be?' Honestly, she'd been too preoccupied with whether she was carrying his child to worry about whether Reyes would throw the book at her once they arrived at his homeland.

'I don't condone what you did, but I understand the motives behind it.'

She searched his gaze, and only saw steady reassurance. 'You do?'

He nodded. 'You were boxed into a corner, trying to save what was precious to you. It felt wrong when I chose to pay the blackmailers for those compromising photos of Anaïs instead of turning the whole thing over to the police but—'

'You were trying to protect your father from the pain of finding out.'

'*Sí*. And also myself to some extent.' His thumbs brushed her cheeks, traced the corner of her mouth. She locked her knees to keep them from giving way. 'You did what you had to do to protect your family. I can't condemn you for that.'

She swallowed hard as a lump rose in her throat. 'Thank you.'

His gaze drifted from her eyes to her mouth. In that moment, Jasmine didn't think she'd craved anything as she craved a kiss from him.

Her gaze caressed his mouth, and every nerve in her body screeched with delight. Then reality crashed. She couldn't kiss him. Would never be able to touch him again. He was marrying someone else.

Resolutely, she stepped back. 'I need to send the email. So if there's nothing else…?'

He tensed. Then, without a word, he left her room.

Jasmine collapsed on the bed, her hands fisted at her sides.

Ten minutes passed as she stared into space. Reyes had forgiven her for what she did in Rio. Which meant, she could leave once she'd finalised the task he'd set her. And once she'd told him about the baby.

She had to leave. The longer she stayed around him, the more she yearned for things she had no business yearning for. As for the baby, parents hashed out living arrangements every day. She was sure they could come up with an arrangement that suited them both.

So why the hell were her eyes brimming again at the thought of returning to London on her own?

Shaking her head, she forced her thoughts aside and dealt with the email to Reyes's royal press secretary. Once it was done, she went to the bathroom, washed her face and brushed her hair. Taking a little bit of pride in her appearance bolstered her confidence. And for what she was about to do, she needed all the armour she could muster.

Her knock on his suite next door received a deep-voiced response to enter. She'd never seen the inside of Reyes's suite and stopped a few steps after entering.

Decorated in bold swathes of black and white, the luxurious space was dominated by a king-sized bed with four solid posts made of cast iron.

The carpet was stark white and contrasted stunningly with the black velvet curtains. The design was bold, masculine and oozed quiet sophistication.

'Did you come to admire the décor?' Reyes said from where he stood at the window, gazing at the Parisian skyline.

Once her eyes fell on him, she couldn't look away. Dear God, she was like a crazed moth, obsessed with this particular flame. A flame that didn't belong to her.

She cleared her throat. 'There's something I…need to tell you.' Her voice was little above a whisper.

He tensed. Then slowly turned and strode to where she'd stopped in the room. His hands remained in his pockets as his gaze raked her from head to toe. 'So speak.' His tone was rough, terse.

'I don't know how else to say this so I'm just going to spill it,' she said.

He stared at her. Silence stretched. He quirked an eyebrow.

Heart hammering, Jasmine closed her eyes for a split second and gathered her courage. 'I…we…'

'Jasmine?' he snapped.

'Yes?'

'Take a breath and find the words.'

'I'm pregnant.'

He was a crown prince. He was allowed a gamut of emotions. Courage under fire. Pride. Anger. Even bewilderment at times.

But Reyes was certain that somewhere in his kingdom's constitution, there was a clause that said he couldn't feel blind panic.

And yet that was the emotion that clawed through him once he convinced himself he hadn't misheard her. Panic and intense, debilitating jealousy.

Stop, he admonished himself. *Think for a moment.*

But he couldn't think beyond the naked fact that she'd slept with someone else, was pregnant with another man's child. That in the very near future she would no longer be in his life. She would belong to someone else.

He turned abruptly and headed for the living room adjoining his bedroom. 'Come with me.'

She followed. When they reached the set of sofas, he jerked his chin at the nearest one.

'Sit down.'

'I don't need to—'

'Sit down, Jasmine. Please.'

She sat, crossed her ankles, and folded her hands in her lap. He tried not to stare at the silky fall of her hair. The perfection of her face.

She belonged to someone else.

A piercing pain lanced his chest. He paced to the window, as if the different view would provide cold perspective.

'Obviously this changes things. You wish me to release you from your obligations?' The words felt thick and unnatural. Not at all what he wanted to be asking her.

When she remained silent, he turned. Her mouth was parted in surprise. And shock?

'Umm, eventually, yes. But I'm not doing anything that would risk the baby's health, so I can see this task through.' She stopped and bit her lip. 'If you want me to, that is.'

Did he want a woman he'd made love to, who was now carrying another man's child, completing her task of seeing him wed another woman?

Dios. When had his life turned into a three-ring circus?

'Who is he?' he bit out before the words had fully formed in his mind.

Realising the panic had been totally annihilated by jealousy didn't please him. Nor did he welcome her confusion.

'Who is who?'

'The father of your baby.' Why did the words burn his throat so badly?

Her eyes widened. 'The father? You mean you think…' She shook her head. 'It's you, Reyes. You're the father of my baby.'

He willed the cymbals crashing through his head to stop. *'What did you say?'*

'I said this baby is yours. Ours.'

Panic. Bewilderment. Panic. Pride.

Elation. Pride. Anger.

'Mine. Do you take me for a fool?' he rasped.

'No, of course not. Reyes—'

'Or did you think you'd wait until I'd forgiven you before you sprang this *happy surprise* on me?'

'I really don't know what you're talking about,' she replied. Her bafflement was almost convincing.

'You know exactly what I'm talking about. Was that the

plan all along? To innocently run into me at the embassy in London and plot your way to a higher payday?'

She shook her head. 'Plans and plots? Next you'll be accusing me of mind-controlling you into forgetting to use a condom in the shower back in Rio.'

The bolt of shock rocked him backwards. Frantically, he searched his memory.

The shower...no condom...Madre di Dios...

He stared at her, rooting for the truth. 'The child is mine?' he croaked.

Her eyes met his. Bold and fierce. 'Yes. I know my credibility isn't worth much to you, but believe me when I say that I'd never stoop to such deplorable deception. No matter what.'

He nodded, still reeling. He believed her. But the inherent need to seek the absolute truth pounded through him. The past still had a stranglehold on him he couldn't easily let go of. 'You weren't on the pill?'

'No. I didn't need to be.'

He paced in a tight circle. 'When did you find out?' he asked.

'I did the tests an hour ago.'

She pulled three pink-and-white sticks from her jeans pocket and held them up.

Reyes forced himself to move. He took them, examined them. And slid them into his own pocket.

Somehow their presence finally hammered reality home.

He was going to be a father.

Jasmine wasn't carrying another man's child. She was carrying *his*.

Elation. A strange, undeniable possessiveness.

'I'll arrange for the doctor to see you. We need to address that poor appetite of yours.'

Jasmine licked her lips. 'There's no hurry. It can wait—'

'No, it cannot wait. Nothing can wait. Not any more.'

'What does that mean?' she enquired.

'It means everything has changed.' Reaching down, he

stroked her cheek. He wasn't sure why it hadn't occurred to him before. Jasmine wasn't the perfect candidate but she was miles better than anyone he knew. There would be no false proclamations of love to confuse issues. They were compatible in bed.

And she was carrying his child...

Her silky skin made his pulse jump. Or was it his own senses jumping from the situation presented so perfectly before him? So perfect, he wanted to kiss her!

Walking away before he was tempted to give in to the hunger churning through him, Reyes strode to the polished teak desk.

'Reyes, you're not making much sense.'

They both stopped at the knock on the door. 'Yes?'

His young aide entered. 'The council is here. I've put them in the conference room, as you requested.'

Reyes nodded. '*Gracias*, Antonio. I'll be there shortly.'

Antonio retreated and Reyes rounded the desk. There was so much he wanted to say, and yet he couldn't find the right words to say it. In the end, he crouched in front of Jasmine and took both her hands in his.

'This was as much my responsibility as yours. I failed in my duty to protect you, and for that I apologise. I got carried away...but I can assure you I don't have any adverse health issues you should worry about.'

'Neither have I,' she blurted.

He nodded. 'Good. I hope you're agreeable to what needs to happen next, too.'

She frowned. 'I'm not sure I follow.'

'It means I'm calling off next week's wedding. And I'm getting married in three days instead.'

Jasmine felt the blood drain from her head. It was a good thing he was holding on to her because she was sure she would've collapsed in an agonising, pathetic heap.

'I... Okay. Leave it with me. I'll call Miss Holden and arrange for her to fly to Santo Sierra,' she replied through numb lips. Her whole body was going numb and she really needed to sit down before she fell.

Reyes's brows bunched. 'Why would you be calling her?'

'Because you're marrying her?'

'You misunderstand, Jasmine. The wedding is for you. *I intend to marry no one else but you.*'

As proposals went, it wasn't the most romantic she'd heard. But even through the shock engulfing her, she realised there would be nothing resembling romance, or love, in whatever Reyes planned for them.

CHAPTER FOURTEEN

THE PICTURES JASMINE had seen of Santo Sierra didn't do it justice even in the slightest.

As the royal jet circled majestic green mountains and turquoise waters in preparation for landing, she could barely contain her awe.

'Now I get a reaction from you. I thought I'd have to surgically remove you from that tablet.'

She turned sharply from her avid landscape gazing. 'I'm sorry?'

'You've hardly spoken a word since we took off.' He frowned. 'In fact, you seem to have lost the ability to speak the last twenty-four hours.' His gaze raked her face. 'Are you feeling unwell?'

She struggled to keep her features composed and not show how much turmoil she'd been in since he'd announced *she* was his choice of bride.

Her bewildered 'Why?' had been met with incredulity.

'Are you serious?'

'Of course, I'm serious. You have your perfect candidate already picked out.'

'And you are carrying my baby. My heir.' His brows had clamped together. *'What did you think was going to happen when you told me?'* he'd asked with a heavy dose of astonishment.

And there their discussion had ended.

The council had been waiting. He'd summoned Antonio to call the doctor, who'd arrived just as the council meeting had ended.

Reyes had peppered him with questions and he'd listened with an intensity that had terrified Jasmine. Even before the poor doctor had been dismissed, she'd known Reyes was heavily vested in his baby's welfare. And that she wouldn't be returning to London to raise her child as a single parent.

She was going to Santo Sierra to marry Prince Reyes Navarre.

She, a juvenile delinquent with a chequered past, was going to be crowned Princess in just over forty-eight hours.

And if that weren't terrifying enough, the realisation of what she was trying desperately to deny had finally hit her in the face this morning. She was developing potentially heart-risking feelings for Reyes. Ironically, her mother had called this morning just as she was busy denying her feelings.

Jasmine would never have thought in a million years that she would adopt her mother's head-in-the-sand approach to life one day.

'Jasmine?'

God, the Latin intonation to the way he said her name...

'No, I'm just a little nervous.'

He waved her nerves away. 'Don't be. The palace staff will cater to your every need. And my sister, Isabella, will also be on hand should you need a female perspective on any concerns.' He smiled.

Her breath caught.

Scared he'd read any unwanted emotion on her face, she looked out of the window again, towards the mountain she'd learned was called Montana Navarre. Set on the highest peak, it was where the Royal House of Navarre had been born and where Reyes's ancestors had ruled Santo Sierra for several centuries. Airplanes were restricted from flying directly over the palace, but the aerial view she'd seen of it had taken her breath away.

With supreme effort, she looked at him. 'Are you sure we're not rushing this? I'm sure there must be special protocols to royal weddings that I need to learn first?'

His eyelids descended and his nostrils flared slightly before he pierced her with that incisive grey gaze once more. 'You're carrying my child, Jasmine. Everything else ceases to matter in light of that reality.'

She couldn't read anything into that thick emotion in his voice. It was just shock.

Recalling how his councilmen had beamed at her when they'd emerged from their meeting, Jasmine added another reason as to why Reyes was pleased about the turn of events.

Next to a royal wedding, a royal baby was the most joyous celebration for any country. Reyes was returning home not just with his future bride, but with his future heir, although the formal announcement of her pregnancy wouldn't be made for another few weeks.

Coupled with his economic plans for Santo Sierra, those two events would surely regain him his people's love and devotion.

A part of her felt relieved and thankful that her actions wouldn't leave permanent damage on Santo Sierra. The other, selfish part of her couldn't hide the pain of feeling like collateral damage.

'You're still troubled,' Reyes observed.

She'd forgotten how well he could read her. Clearing her throat, she passed restless fingers through her hair. 'It's my problem. I'll deal with it.'

His face darkened. 'You're no longer an individual, fighting against the masses on your own. And I prefer not to start our marriage with secrets between us.'

She shook her head. 'Trust me, Reyes, you don't really want to know what's going on in my head right now. I'm hormonal and perhaps conveniently irrational.'

Firm, sensual lips pursed. 'I want to hear it, Jasmine.'

The voice of caution probed, and was promptly ignored. 'Fine, if you insist. I was right in front of you, Reyes. And yet you never considered me as a bride. So excuse me if I'm feeling a pauper's sloppy seconds.'

* * *

Oh, God. Why on earth did I say that?

Jasmine was still reeling hours after they'd landed and she'd been delivered to her suite in the palace.

Despite her opulent surroundings and the rich history etched into every arched wall, mosaic-tiled floor, and ancestral painting, she couldn't see, couldn't think beyond the stark, soul-baring words she'd uttered moments before the plane had touched down.

How utterly pathetic she'd sounded.

The shock on Reyes's face alone had convinced her she'd stepped way over the line. No wonder he'd beat a hasty retreat the moment they'd reached the palace.

She rose from the beautifully carved brocade love seat by the window in her vast bedroom and entered the bathroom.

The marble-lined tub had already been filled with scented water and huge fluffy towels laid within arm's length by the palace staff assigned to cater to her needs.

She'd been lost for words when she'd walked into a closet filled with designer clothes and accessories. And even more stunned when the member of staff had told her they'd been provided for her.

Shrugging off the silk robe, she sank into the enveloping warmth. She'd been summoned to dine with Reyes and his sister this evening, no doubt to be checked out by her future sister-in-law.

Jasmine looked out of the wide tub-to-ceiling trellised bathroom window and her breath caught all over again. With nothing to mar the mountaintop view she could see the kingdom for miles.

The bustling, vibrant capital of San Domenica was spread below her. Whitewashed churches vied with modern architecture, green parks and historical buildings.

As they'd driven through it on the way to the palace she'd glimpsed the look of pride and worry in Reyes's eyes. They'd also driven past the square and his fingers had tightened on the armrest when he'd seen a woman crying next to a broken statue.

Her insides had clenched for him. But he'd relaxed against the seat, his face averted from her as they'd climbed up the highway leading to the palace.

The moment they'd been escorted inside, he'd made his excuses and strode off.

And she'd been left grappling with her mangled feelings. Feelings she still hadn't been able to resolve by the time she dressed in a long sweeping gown in emerald green with a coloured-stone-embroidered bodice that had made her gasp when she'd spied herself in the mirror.

Sweeping her hair up into a bun, she secured it with several hairpins and slipped her feet into black slingbacks.

Fernanda, the staff member appointed to shepherd her to the dining room, left her with a smile and walked away after delivering Jasmine to the high-ceilinged room displaying ancient Mediterranean frescos.

Jasmine was busy admiring it when she heard voices outside the dining room.

Going to the door, she followed the sound down a long hallway, hurrying closer to where the raised voices came from. Rounding the corner, she came upon Reyes and a tall, slim woman in the middle of a heated argument.

He wore a thunderous look as he glared down at the stunning woman. A stunning woman who was giving as good as she got, her voice rising higher as she gestured wildly and responded in Spanish.

Jasmine thought of retreating. But they both turned as they sensed her presence.

For a moment, Reyes appeared frozen at the sight of her. His hooded eyes raked her from head to toe. Then he exhaled, his massive chest drawing her eyes to his impressively broad shoulders. His black shirt moulded his lean torso and washboard stomach before disappearing into dark grey tailored trousers that caressed his powerful thighs. His hair looked damp from a recent shower. He slicked it back now as he spiked his fingers through it.

Jasmine forced herself not to remember how those strands felt beneath her fingers.

'Hi,' she ventured. The breathlessness in her voice made her cringe.

Reyes's mouth compressed before he turned to the woman. 'Isabella, meet Jasmine Nichols, my future wife. Jasmine, this is my sister, Princess Isabella. She'll escort you to the terrace for drinks. I'll join you shortly.' Without waiting for a response, he stalked off down the opposite end of the hallway.

Isabella watched him leave, her expression hurt and angry. She looked spectacular in a cream gown laced with gold and black thread. The satin material fitted her svelte figure and complemented her golden, flawless skin.

Turning to Jasmine, she shook her head in frustration. 'Apparently, I was wrong to call off a wedding to a man I did not love.'

Jasmine's insides clenched. 'Duty is very important to your brother.' She tried a diplomatic approach.

Isabella threw up her hands in despair. 'Well, duty doesn't keep you warm. From the examples we've both had, you'd think he'd know that marriage is hard enough without going into it with a cold heart. I told him if I had to wait a thousand years for a man who makes me happy, I would.'

A spurt of laughter erupted from Jasmine's throat. 'Bet he didn't take that lightly.'

Isabella smiled. 'As you saw, storming off was his reaction.' She released an exasperated breath, then eyed Jasmine. 'Or maybe it was something else?' One perfectly shaped eyebrow rose.

'I'm not sure what you mean,' Jasmine replied.

'You'll find out soon enough how difficult it is to keep a secret in this place. You are not the woman my brother's press office was gearing up to announce as his bride two days ago.

Which makes me wonder if whatever's irking him has nothing to do with me and everything to do with you?'

Jasmine licked her lips, uncomfortable about having this conversation with Isabella when she was unsure what her role entailed in this marriage of convenience. She'd have to pick it up with Reyes. Once he could have a conversation with her again without that look of consternation.

'Please, can we drop the subject?'

The other woman wrapped her hand around Jasmine's arm. 'Of course, I didn't mean to upset you. *Dios*, I can't seem to breathe for causing upset today.'

'No, please. Think nothing of it.' She flashed a smile.

Isabella's shrewd gaze rested on her for a moment before she nodded. 'Fine. Come, we'll enjoy some cocktails before dinner. If Reyes gets over his tantrum, he can join us. Otherwise it's his loss.'

Jasmine followed her down the hallway to a large, skylit room with wide doors that led onto a wide terrace. Soft lights glinted through the space dotted with large, potted ficus trees. In the centre an extensive bar had been built, manned by two servants.

One came forward with a tray holding an array of gaily coloured drinks. Isabella pointed to the iced green one.

'Try that one. It's made with guava and a local fruit called *santosanda.*'

'It's not alcoholic, is it?' Seeing the instant speculation in Isabella's eyes, she hurriedly added, 'I'll never get over the jet lag if I add alcohol to the mix.'

Isabella shook her head. 'It doesn't contain any alcohol.'

Jasmine picked up the drink and took a sip. Different textures exploded on her tongue, the dominant one a tangy sweetness that sent a delicious chill down her spine. 'Wow.'

Isabella smiled and sipped her own peach-tinged drink. She drifted out onto the terrace, and she stood staring at the horizon.

Lights came on as darkness fell and her thoughtful gaze

rested over the view of San Domenica. 'In case you're wondering, I'm really pleased about your wedding to my brother. The council is right. We need a boost of good news. We've lived with doom and gloom since Mamá died.' She shook her head. 'I know I followed my heart in not marrying Alessandro, but I had been wondering lately if I took the selfish route.'

Jasmine shook her head. 'You would've caused each other too much pain in the end. Once the rose shades come off, relationships are an uphill struggle of hard work.' *Especially without love.*

'Are you speaking from experience?'

Despite her subtle probing, Jasmine warmed to Isabella. The princess had an open, honest face that went with her take-no-prisoners attitude.

'I watched my mother turn herself inside out for men who didn't deserve her love.'

Isabella's mouth pursed. 'My mother had all the love a man could give a woman, yet she went searching for more. Over and over, and in the wrong places. My father has never overcome the knowledge that he wasn't enough for her.'

'One-sided love is just as hard to keep up as no love at all.' Her heart lurched as she said the words, but Jasmine refused to examine why too deeply. She was too scared to find out. She went to take another sip and realised she'd finished the cocktail. The servant stepped forward with another. She smiled her thanks, took it, and turned back to the view.

'How is your father?'

Isabella looked towards the south wing of the palace, and sadness cloaked her face. 'He's hanging in there. I don't mean to sound callous and it'll break my heart when it happens, but I just wish he'd let go. I want him to find peace—'

'Isabella!'

She jumped at the admonishing voice.

Reyes stood behind them, his face more thunderous than it had been before.

'I'm...sorry, *mi hermano*, but you know I'm right.'

Reyes's fists bunched. 'If those are the sorts of views you choose to share with Jasmine, then perhaps you should consider eating dinner on your own.'

Eyes widening, Isabella gulped. Then her face closed with rebellion. 'Fine. I think I will.'

Before Jasmine could draw breath, the princess had stormed off.

Her gaze collided with Reyes's. 'Upsetting women seems to be your speciality. Are you sure you don't want to relocate to a faraway monastery and live the rest of your life as a monk?'

His expression lightened a touch. Grey eyes surveyed her from top to toe before they lingered at the drink in her hand. 'The silence I can probably handle. The chastity would unfortunately be a deal-breaker. How many of those have you had?' He nodded to her drink.

'This is my second one. Isabella recommended it. That local fruit...*santosanda*? It's delicious.'

'It is, but did she mention that, once fermented, it's also a powerful aphrodisiac?' he asked silkily.

CHAPTER FIFTEEN

REYES WATCHED HER eyes widen in shock, before a flush of awareness reddened her cheeks. She glanced at the drink, then back to him.

'No, she didn't!' Her voice had grown huskier. She blinked slowly as she passed her tongue over her plump lower lip.

Dios, had she even noticed the effects taking hold of her?

She'd been languidly caressing the lip of her glass for the last several minutes. And her nipples were hard and clearly outlined beneath her dress.

Reyes swallowed. 'I think you've had enough,' he rasped. He took the half-empty glass and handed it to the hovering waiter. Picking up two glasses of water, he thrust one into her hand.

'Umm…thanks.'

He nodded tersely.

Walking onto the terrace, he'd been hit between the eyes again by her stunning beauty. So much so, he'd stood frozen while her conversation with Isabella had unravelled.

It wasn't until his sister's utterance that he'd shaken off the red haze of lust that seemed to enclose him when he was around Jasmine.

Watching her now, he recalled what she'd said to him before they'd landed in Santo Sierra.

And the resulting tailspin his emotions had been flung in. Once he'd been able to draw breath, he'd tried to analyse his reaction. Yes, the knowledge of Jasmine's pregnancy had been the catalyst that had driven everything forward. But he could just as easily have maintained the initial date of his wedding. He was a modern enough man to admit the distance between his wedding day and his heir's birthday didn't bother him. And he was sure it didn't bother Jasmine.

So why had he been intent on rushing her to the altar?

He'd tried and failed to convince himself it was because of his need to make his people happy. A week's difference wouldn't have mattered. Neither did it matter that Jasmine's past would be an issue once it became public knowledge. Unlike his mother's behaviour, Jasmine's reasons for her unfortunate past were a result of trying to survive her horrific circumstances. He was sure his people would forgive once they knew.

Just as he'd forgiven her? Just as he suspected his reasons for marrying were more selfish than he wanted to admit to himself?

Reyes thrust his balled fists into his pocket, willed the confusing emotions away, but they returned stronger. More demanding.

He didn't do feelings. Hadn't let any in, except maybe for his father, since he'd thrown Anaïs out of his life, and then stood at his mother's graveside mere months later.

But Jasmine was making him feel. Making him want... no, *need*. As for the thought that his child was growing in her belly...it pounded him with terrifyingly powerful emotions every time it blazed across his mind.

Would the mistakes that he'd made with his own father affect his child? Was failure emblazoned in his blood for ever?

More and more he'd found himself wanting to take Jasmine's example. She had found a way out of the barren wasteland of not having anyone to lean on, anyone to trust. But she'd let herself trust, allowed her faith in the goodness of humanity to be restored. Despite the harrowing experience of juvenile detention and a mother who clearly wasn't equipped for the job, she'd found herself back on a road Reyes himself was struggling to find.

He couldn't deny it. She compelled him to be a better

man. Would raising their child together make him a better father, too?

Swallowing his blind panic, he glanced at her.

Her eyes were on him, her fingers curled around the glass. 'I feel funny.'

Unaccustomed laughter rumbled out of his chest. 'You need fresh air. Dinner won't be for another hour. Come, I'll show you the grounds.'

She peered down at her feet. 'I don't think these shoes will go well with walking the grounds. They're already pinching something fierce.'

'You won't need to walk further than the bottom of these steps.' Golf buggies were housed at various points around the palace for ease of movement around the extensive grounds.

He guided her down and waited till she was seated on the buggy. Reyes wasn't at all surprised when she kicked off her shoes and sighed with relief.

The sight of her dainty feet gripped his attention. Mesmerised, he watched her rub her big toe along her other instep. Heat flared through his gut and pooled in his groin. Pulling himself out of the daze, he reversed the buggy and stepped on the accelerator.

Floodlights illuminated their path as he drove towards the northernmost point of the palace. Beside him, Jasmine oohed and aahed at the elaborate fountain his great-grandfather had built for his children to splash in, the huge lake containing white majestic swans gliding serenely in the rising moonlight, and ruins of an amphitheatre set into a cliff.

Jasmine pointed to the spotlights strung along the outer edge of the theatre. 'Do you still use it?'

He nodded. 'Isabella holds a children's Christmas concert every year.'

'That's so cool. Everything about Santo Sierra is so cool,' she amended with a husky chuckle. Then she glanced at him. 'But snapping at Isabella like that? Not cool.'

Reyes's fingers tightened around the wheel, but his reaction was more to do with her laugh and less to do with his sister.

He brought the buggy to a stop on the grassy landscape and helped her out. She started to put on her shoes.

'Leave them. You won't need them where we're going.'

With a happy smile, she dropped them.

Hiking up her dress to keep the hem off the grass, she stepped out.

Reyes tried not to stare at her feet. 'We have a temperamental relationship, Bella and I. She'll have calmed down by now.'

Jasmine frowned. 'But you won't apologise? I think you should.'

'*Sí*, I will apologise. In the morning, when I'm convinced she won't bite my head off.'

She laughed.

He stopped in his tracks as the intoxicating sound transfixed him.

When she realised he'd stopped moving, she froze. 'What?'

He cleared his throat to dislodge the uncomfortable knot. 'You should laugh more. It's an entrancing sound.'

She blushed as her eyes rounded, then her expression turned gloomy. 'I haven't had much to laugh about. Not since…' She stopped and bit her lip.

He held his breath. 'Since?'

'Since Rio,' she muttered. 'And especially since I found out what my actions caused.'

The sincerity in her voice shook the foundation of his armour. He searched her face. Her eyes met his with frank appraisal and in that moment he was sure she'd never been more sincere.

He held out his hand, his breath lodged in his chest.

She hesitated, and his hand wavered. Looking down, she indicated her dress. 'I don't want to let go in case I get grass stains on it.'

His breath punched out. 'It's just a dress, Jasmine. I'll buy you a hundred more. Let go.'

She made a face. 'Yes, Your Bossiness.' She released her grip on the dress and slid her hand into his. Warm. Firm. Almost trusting…

A simple gesture. And yet he couldn't stop thinking about it as he walked her twenty yards up the small hill.

'Where are we going?' she asked breathlessly.

He realised he'd been marching and slowed his pace. 'Up there.' He pointed.

She stopped and gazed at the stone monument planted in the earth. 'What is it?'

'You need to get closer to see it.'

She followed him. When she tried to free their linked fingers, he held on, unwilling to let her go. Smiling at him over her shoulder, she stepped closer to the stone and ran her fingers over the ancient markings set into the rough surface.

Still clinging to her fingers, Reyes walked her round the stone, then led her to the jagged crevice.

'Oh, my God,' she whispered. Reyes watched the wonder on her face as she peered into the black three-foot-wide crack scorched into the earth. 'How deep is it?'

Stepping behind, he let go of her hand and wrapped his arms around her waist. 'No one knows. All past rulers of Santo Sierra have forbidden the site from being explored.'

She leaned back in his arms and stared up at him. 'But how did it get here?'

He bent his head, and his lips brushed the top of her ear. 'Legend has it that the original Crown Prince of Santo Sierra ran off with the betrothed of the Prince of Valderra the day before they were to be married. The jilted prince hunted them down and caught up with the lovers at this spot. They fought to the death and both lost their lives. The day after they were buried, the subjects woke up to find the fissure here. The two kingdoms have been separated ever since.'

Her arms folded over his and she rested her head on his shoulder. She rocked slowly from side to side in a silent dance.

'That's tragic, but I bet it can all be resolved with a good mediation.'

He laughed, found himself moving along with her, swaying to her inner music. 'You believe you can succeed where countless others have failed?'

'Mediation is about breaking things down to the basest level and routing out what each party needs the most. Once it's clear, most people will settle for their innermost desires instead of what their greed dictates they need.' Her voice had softened to an introspective murmur.

Reyes stared down at her sweet face, her perfect nose and gorgeous mouth. Something moved within him. Not his libido, even though it was awake and alert to any imminent action.

His innermost desire included kissing her, making her his. Permanently…

He realised she was growing drowsy from the drink and visibly forced his gaze away from temptation. 'What are your innermost desires, Jasmine?' he asked before he could stop himself.

'World peace. Or barring that a magical carriage to whisk me back down this hill so I don't have to walk.' She giggled, and a smile cracked across his face again.

Dios, he was in danger of slipping deeper into her web. Maybe this trip hadn't been such a good idea.

Or maybe he just needed to take a leaf out of his sister's book and follow his heart rather than his head for once. He and Jasmine might have arrived at this arrangement unconventionally, but fate had gifted them a compatibility that he would be foolish to ignore.

Tomorrow morning, there would be a vote to elect a new council, after which he'd be named Prince Regent. The palace press had already announced his impending wedding. His father's doctors had assured him that the King's health was holding for the moment and he'd seen a slight improvement in his father's condition when he'd visited him today.

As for Mendez, the Valderran prince knew something was

up. He'd been putting out feelers as to Santo Sierra's position on the old treaty. Reyes had ignored him so far. Let him stew for a while.

For now, Reyes intended to enjoy an evening free of guilt and anxiety. With the woman who would become his in less than forty-eight hours.

The woman who was carrying his child.

He paused as a bolt of satisfaction lanced through him. Reyes realised having Jasmine and their child in his life was a prospect that didn't terrify him as much as it had this time yesterday. Yesterday, he'd convinced himself it was duty driving him.

Today, his feelings were more of...elation.

Bending, he swung Jasmine into his arms. She gave another giggle and curled her arms around his neck. Her nose brushed his jaw and his belly tightened.

Sí, a worry-free few hours were just what he needed.

'We don't have a carriage, but I have something in mind that might please you.' He strode to the top of the hill, turned ninety degrees and nudged her with his chin. 'There,' he murmured in her ear.

Jasmine pried her gaze from Reyes's breath-stoppingly gorgeous face and jawline and glanced where he'd indicated.

She was aware her mouth had dropped open. Again.

Could she help it when Santo Sierra had so far delivered one stunning surprise after another?

'It looks like a giant, gorgeous wedding cake,' she whispered.

'Because it was designed as a present for a bride's wedding day. But it's actually a summer house.'

'Set into the hillside so it looks like layers. It's perfect.'

The smile that had flashed on and off for the last half hour curved back into sight. Again her heart beat wildly, sending her blood roaring in her ears.

Although she was thankful he wasn't growling at her or

walking away from her as if she didn't exist, she was terrified at seeing this new, relaxed side of Reyes. This Reyes was too much for her senses. Too breathtaking. Too charming. Too... close.

But not too much that she wanted to get away. Or return to her lonely palace suite. She tightened her arms when he started towards the utterly splendid structure.

If she'd truly believed in fairy tales, this would've been her dream house. But she didn't, so it was just as well that the effects of the punch had worn off enough for her to realise this was nothing but a short interlude in time for both of them.

He climbed the stairs to the surprisingly large square structure and the wooden shuttered doors slid back. Jasmine's gaze slid from the love seat on the porch to the interior.

Bypassing the simple, lamplit living room furnished with more love seats and twin sofas festooned with cushions, Reyes walked her into the bathroom and set her down on a pedestal next to a wide porcelain sink.

He stepped back and turned on the tap in the extra-wide bath.

'Umm...is one of us taking a bath?'

His mouth tilted. 'I thought you might want to wash your feet since you've been walking in the grass.'

Jasmine looked down at her feet. 'Oh, I guess that's a good idea, what with the wall-to-wall white carpeting.'

She started to step down from her perch. He stayed her with a hand on her waist and leaned over to add bath salts to the warm water.

This close, his scent assailed her, claimed her senses. When he breathed his body moved against hers.

This was getting out of hand...

Despite the thought trailing through her head, she stayed where she was.

Once the water reached a quarter way, he turned to her. 'Lift up your dress.'

She tugged the material up her hips. He picked her up and

sat her on the edge of the tub. Expecting him to leave her to it, she gave a small gasp when he dropped to his knees beside her.

Grabbing a washcloth, Reyes dipped it in the scented water and started to clean her feet.

The punch of feeling through her chest made her jerk. He looked up, took her arm and slid it around his shoulders. 'Hold on to me if you think you're slipping.'

Nodding dumbly, she held on. Traced her fingers over the strands of hair at his nape. Her fingers brushed his skin. A rough sound escaped his throat. The soothing cloth cleansed her feet.

Jasmine looked from Reyes's arresting profile to what he was doing. She, Jasmine Nichols, originally from one of the roughest neighbourhoods in London, had a bona fide prince washing her feet.

The moment couldn't get more surreal than this. And yet she didn't want it to end.

'You have the most perfect feet,' Reyes murmured.

'Thank you.' Her voice emerged as shaky as she felt inside.

He raised his head and pierced her with eyes wild with raw, predatory hunger. 'The most perfect legs.' His wet hands cupped her ankles, drifted up over her calves.

Jasmine forgot to breathe. Her hand gripped his nape, her only stability in a world careening out of control.

'The most perfect thighs.'

'Reyes…'

His gaze dropped to her lips. Her heartbeat spiked a second before his mouth claimed hers.

Groaning, she fell into the kiss, wrapped both arms around his neck when he lifted her out of the tub and out of the bathroom. He returned to the living room and lowered her in front of the fireplace.

Lowering his body on top of hers, he deepened the kiss, ravaged her mouth with an appetite that grew sharper, rougher by the minute. His hand trailed up her leg, her thigh, to close over her bottom.

They both groaned when he squeezed her flesh. '*Dios*, you're perfect,' he breathed into the side of her neck when he let her up for air.

But she didn't want breathing room, didn't want even the slightest doubt to mar this incredible moment.

Catching his jaw between her hands, she raised her mouth to his. 'Kiss me, Reyes. Please.'

He swore again, the sound ragged. Scooping her against his chest, he rolled them over. Firm hands lowered her zip and tugged down her dress and flung it away. Then he reversed their position again. 'Now I can kiss you properly. Everywhere.'

He devoured her lips, her throat, the tops of her breasts.

Her moans grew louder as he rolled her nipple in his mouth before sucking in a hot pull. Jasmine's back arched, her fingers digging into his hair to keep him there, pleasuring her, torturing her. A sharp cry erupted from her lips when his teeth nipped her skin just above her panties. Rising up on her elbows, she stared down at him, drunk on the sight of what he was doing to her.

'Reyes…'

He glanced up. The look on his face threatened to send her over the edge.

'Do you want this, *querida*?' he enquired thickly.

'More than anything,' she whispered.

She smothered the voice that cautioned her as to what she was doing. Her first time with this man had ended in disaster. Granted, it'd been one of her own making. But now she knew it was more than her body involved. Her heart was at risk, too.

She was in danger of falling in love with a man who would never love her.

'I can hear you thinking.' He paused in the line of kisses he was dotting along her pantyline. 'Tell me what's on your mind.'

'I don't want anything we do here today to…confuse issues.'

His eyes narrowed. 'Shouldn't that be my line?'

Unwilling to help herself, she cupped his shadowed cheek.

'You may be a crown prince, but I believe in equal opportunities when it comes to the bedroom.'

He turned his head, kissed her palm and raised both her hands above her head. 'Well, this is my opportunity. You get your turn later.'

He took her mouth in a hard kiss, then raised his head. 'In answer to your question, there is no issue to confuse. We already know we're compatible in bed. Whether we say our vows tomorrow or the next day, we both want this, now. *Sì?*' His eyes probed hers.

Her heart lurched. 'Yes.'

CHAPTER SIXTEEN

REYES WATCHED HER expression turn from hesitant to erotically pleased as he cupped her breast and teased the hard nub.

The voice that told him he wasn't giving her room to change her mind was ruthlessly squashed. His hunger for her had flamed higher than every other need. And just as he'd taken her in Rio, he intended to let nothing stand in the way of his claiming her tonight.

He resumed his exploration of her body. Much to his very male satisfaction she arched her back and purred. And grew increasingly, pleasingly demanding.

She grabbed at his clothes and he hurriedly undressed. He yanked away her panties and positioned himself between her legs.

'Yes. Please…now,' she cried hoarsely.

Reyes surged inside her with a guttural roar. Sensation exploded all over his body at her wetness, her tight heat. She embraced him, rolled her hips in helpless abandon as pleasure overtook her.

He established a passionate rhythm she matched with enthusiasm. Much too soon, he was following her into bliss, shouting his ecstasy as he emptied himself inside her.

He watched her as they caught their breaths. Her face glowed with the flushed aftermath of sex. Reyes had never seen a more beautiful woman. His groin stirred. Her eyes slowly widened.

Smiling, he pressed a kiss against her heated cheek. 'You have that effect on me.' He pulled out of her. They both groaned at the sizzle of electricity.

Tucking her against his side, he caught her free hand in his, kissed her soft palm. Almost inevitably, his hand slid over her flat stomach. He heard her breath catch and searched her face.

A look of wonder, much like what he was experiencing at that very moment at the thought of his child growing inside her, passed over her face. For several heartbeats, he held her gaze. Then she blinked.

'Reyes?'

'*Sí?*'

'I know you're a prince and all, but please tell me you're as terrified as I am at the thought of getting it wrong with this baby.'

'I will not discuss my silent mental breakdown with you, except to mention that it's very acute. And very unsexy.'

She laughed. The sound filled his chest with pleasure so strong, he forgot to breathe for a minute.

When he had it under control he moved his hand, explored some more. When he grazed a scar, he glanced down at her.

'Tell me what happened here.'

She tensed and he pressed his mouth against her palm again. 'Everything, Jasmine. I want to know everything. Before and after Stephen.'

Indecision blazed in her eyes for several seconds before she exhaled.

'Have you heard the saying that some people are just born bad?'

She shook her head at his frown and continued. 'For a long time I believed I was one of them. You know how my mother handled our situation. I just kept rebelling whenever I could. I think I wanted my mother to *see* me, deal with me. When she pretended like I didn't exist, I turned truant at a young age. Fell in with the wrong crowd.'

'What happened?'

'I just…spiralled out of control for a long time.'

'You were trying to get yourself heard the best way you could.'

'That's no excuse. I was a brat with a mother who didn't care whether she lived or died and I lashed out.'

'That's not the end of your story though, obviously.' He trailed his mouth over her palm again.

'No.' She shivered in his arms. He reached for a cashmere throw next to the fireplace and settled it over them. She snuggled into him and that alien feeling in his chest expanded wider. 'You remember that turf war I told you about?'

Reyes nodded.

'*I* was the turf they were fighting over. It happened a few months after I came out of juvie. Each side wanted me to join their gang. I seriously considered it. But I knew I would be burying my pain with destruction. So I refused, and all hell broke loose.'

He reared up and stared down at her. '*Dios*. How did you get out of that?'

'I let myself be arrested again. I reckoned the police station was a safer place than the street. It was where I met Stephen. He was an MP then, touring the police station and I…' She stopped and grimaced.

'You what?'

A dull flush crept up her cheeks. 'I may have tripped him up when he walked past me.'

He couldn't help his smile. She answered with one of her own. Unable to resist, Reyes kissed her. When he lifted his head, she was breathless and her delicious mouth was swollen. 'I presume that got his attention?'

She nodded. 'He could've filed charges against me for assault. Instead bailed me out and he took me out for a coffee. We talked for hours. He delivered me home and met my mother. Then he started visiting us every week. A few months later I started taking on the gangs myself. But instead of knives and guns, I used words. I managed to mediate a truce between them and even extracted a promise from the leaders not to recruit children to run drugs for them.'

'That's where you got your passion for mediation from?' he asked.

'Yes. I returned to school, made good grades and got my

first job at twenty-one. Stephen married my mother, and I guess the rest is history.' Her eyes met his and shifted away. 'Until Rio, that is. I'm so sorry about that, Reyes.'

Catching her chin with his finger, he tilted her face. 'I know you are. I forgive you. I judged you harshly before I knew the truth behind your actions. You tried to protect your family the only way you knew how.'

'But I ended up making things worse for you and your people.'

'You're here now, helping to fix it. That matters to me. With a new council in place, Mendez will no longer be able to play his games. The route may have been unfortunate, but perhaps it achieved something positive in the end. So from now on, we'll consider Rio another lesson we'll both learn from. Agreed?'

'Agreed,' she replied tremulously.

He brushed away the tears forming in her eyes. His head swimming with sensations he could barely grapple with, Reyes slanted his mouth over hers. When he was kissing her like this, he didn't have to think. Didn't have to wonder why he craved her even more with each kiss, each heartbeat.

He didn't have to wonder why he wished they were already married and this were their honeymoon.

A stomach growled. He raised his head. 'I believe that was you.'

She grimaced. 'Jet lag kept me asleep through lunch, and I think we missed dinner.'

Reyes reached for his discarded trousers and took out his phone. He sent his chef the appropriate instructions and hung up.

'Dinner is coming to us?' A smile that seemed to grow more breathtaking each time curved her lips.

'*Sí.* The perks of being a prince. You will command equal power once you're my princess.'

A shadow passed over her face. He wanted to demand to know the reason behind it. Something stopped him.

Her fingers drifted over his brow and down to his cheek. 'What will we do after we eat?'

'I will bathe you and you will let me explore the rest of your scars.'

Jasmine woke in the middle of night. Although the bedroom in the wedding-cake house where they'd relocated to boasted a fire, Reyes hadn't lit it when he'd carried her in. They'd had more urgent things in mind.

Now the room had cooled and she shivered. Glancing down, she realised why. The covers had slipped to the floor and the only things keeping her warm were Reyes's muscular thigh and arm. Which left the rest of her body chilled.

Carefully sliding away, she picked up the nearest sheet and walked into the bathroom.

After using it, she came back to the bed.

Reyes was snoring softly, his face even more relaxed in sleep than it'd been this evening. A lock of hair had fallen over his brow and she itched to smooth it away but stopped herself.

Over and over tonight, her heart had filled to bursting when he'd made love to her. Somewhere around midnight, she'd finally admitted that she'd fallen in love with the Crown Prince of Santo Sierra.

She loved a man who had had his heart broken, not just by one woman, but by two. And while Anaïs's betrayal had been short-term, his mother's had gone on for years.

Her heart stuttered and tears prickled her eyes. He stirred in his sleep.

She turned away and walked quickly out of the bedroom before he woke. She couldn't risk him seeing her expression. He'd been too adept at reading her moods lately. She couldn't afford to let him see that, while she was certain he'd love their baby, she could foresee herself yearning for a love he could never give her.

Going to the window, she gazed out at the twinkling lights

of San Domenica. This place was now her home, for better or worse.

She intended to do everything in her power to make sure it was the better.

She was going from delinquent to princess. Was she being selfish in asking for the icing on the cake?

Yes! She wanted it all.

Tears slipped down her cheeks before she could stop them.

'You're crying. Tell me why.'

She whirled around.

Reyes stood a few feet away, dressed in only his boxers, intense eyes scouring her face.

'I wasn't crying.'

One eyebrow was raised at her wet cheeks. 'Unless it's raining in here and I'm not aware of it, I beg to differ.'

'I never cry. Tears are for the weak.'

His eyes narrowed. 'Who told you that?'

'A gang leader years ago.' She shook her head. 'I'm sorry. That whole trip down memory lane has dredged up things I'd rather forget.'

He stepped closer, cupped her cheeks. 'And that's what woke you?'

About to nod and let that assumption hold, she hesitated. And spoke the words that scrapped up from her shredding heart. 'Are you sure you're making the right choice, Reyes? Not for your people, but for you?'

His eyes grew wary. 'Why the sudden introspection?'

'I know we're only doing this primarily for the baby, and for your people. But we'll be in this marriage, too.'

Jaw clenching, he paced in tight circles in front of her. 'What are you saying?'

'That you need to be sure before we take a step we can't retrace.'

He froze. His nostrils flared as he jerked his fingers through his hair. 'What's going on, Jasmine? Why are you crying? Are you having second thoughts?'

She swiped at her cheeks and grappled with what to say. Settling on a half truth, she met his gaze. Slowly, she nodded. 'Yes, and I think deep down you probably are, too.'

His brows clamped together. 'Don't put words in my mouth.'

Jasmine would've given anything not to utter the words. 'Then tell me in your own words.'

He stared at her for a long time. Then shook his head. 'I don't have the luxury of being whimsical about this situation. It is what it is.'

The vice tightened around her heart. 'What about love, Reyes? Surely you have a view on whether you want love in your life or not?'

His hand slashed through the air. 'My father married for love. Look where that got him.'

'Are you saying if you fell in love and were loved back, it wouldn't be enough for you?'

'I'm saying love is never equal, no matter what anyone says. Someone always loves more, and that person has the most to lose.' Shadows flickered in his eyes before he turned to pace the room again.

Her beautiful eyes clouded. 'You really believe that, don't you?'

Striding to her, he grabbed her arms. 'I don't believe in fairy tales. And my reality speaks for itself.'

She pushed out of his arms and padded to the window. Tugging the sheet closer, she wrapped her arms around herself.

Reyes watched her, the action both angering and disturbing him. 'Jasmine?'

After a moment, she turned. 'How is your father?'

He frowned, struggling to keep up with everything she was throwing at him.

Waking up to find her gone, he'd had a chilling sense of déjà vu, before he'd remembered he was back home, in a place where Jasmine wouldn't be able to escape him easily. Except she was trying now. The woman he'd gone to sleep certain of spending the rest of his life with was having second thoughts.

And probing subjects he didn't want to discuss. Yet he found himself answering. 'As well as he can be considering his heart and organs are days away from failing.' The throb of pain the thought brought made his breath catch. His father had had a good day today. Straight after his council meeting, Reyes had gone to see him. They'd talked for a full hour, during which Reyes had stumbled over himself in his plea for his father's forgiveness for treating him so harshly.

His father had merely smiled and said, 'Finally, you love,' before he'd fallen asleep.

'Can he speak?' Jasmine asked.

He shoved a hand through his hair. 'A few words when the medication isn't strong enough to make him sleepy.'

She nodded. 'Can you do me a favour? The next time you see him, ask him if he'd do it all over again. Love your mother with unconditional love.'

His insides clenched and he exhaled. 'I don't need to ask him. I know he would.'

'Do you think that's foolish? Those brief moments of happiness to balance the pain and the betrayal?'

'Jasmine—'

'Just humour me. You have no idea how many times I wished for my mother to just tell me she loved me, or for her to remember it was my birthday without the shopkeeper down the road having to remind her. Was it always that bad between your parents?'

Reyes thought back to birthdays, skiing holidays, family gatherings. His mother had made an effort on those rare occasions. Those were the happiest he'd seen his father. But as with all things, the happy moments were fleeting, the painful moments lingering the longest.

He shook his head. 'It wasn't, no. But it was a life...so-called *love*...without trust and respect. And to me that's no life at all. Do you not agree?'

Her shoulders slumped. A flare of panic lit his insides.

'It doesn't really matter what I think, does it? You've made up your mind. We have a wedding to plan and a baby to look forward to.'

She was staying. The panic should've abated, yet it escalated. 'We can make this work, Jasmine.'

Her dejection grew even more palpable. 'Reyes—'

He cupped her shoulders. 'We *will* make it work. That is my edict.'

Her chin rose and although her eyes filled with more tears, they didn't spill. But they spiked her lashes and clung like tiny diamonds.

'I know you're the Crown Prince, possibly soon to be King, but I'm really tired of you ordering me around like I'm some type of minion. Get over yourself already.'

She flung away from him, trailed the sheet to the bedroom and then reversed her trajectory back to the living room to snatch up her gown.

Watching her try to manoeuvre the dress on while keeping hold of the sheet tugged a reluctant smile from his lips, despite his churning feelings.

She saw it and glared at him. 'You think this is funny?'

'Firstly, I don't think I've ever been told to get over myself before. Secondly, I suggest you stop hopping around like that before you fall over and break a bone. Or worse.'

'*Firstly*, I think it's high time someone told you to get over yourself. Secondly—' She yanked the dress up, dropped the sheet, and tripped over her feet. He lunged forward, all mirth gone from the situation, and caught her in his arms.

'You can let me go now. I'm done putting my dress on.'

His chest tightened again, harder than before. 'And where do you propose going at three in the morning?'

'Back to the palace, of course.'

'No. If you're upset we'll talk about it now.'

That look of inevitable acceptance of defeat crossed her face again. *Dios*, what was going on? 'You can't will something into place that doesn't exist, Reyes.'

'What are you talking about?'

'We're only marrying because of the baby. I think we should focus on that and not fool ourselves into thinking this can ever be something more, okay?'

Something more. A part of him wanted that. The part that wanted to say *to hell with everything* and jump in blind. But he couldn't afford to do that. This time the stakes were much too high. 'Jasmine, I can't give you what—'

She held up her hand and shook her head. 'I know. I'm not what you wanted. You don't need to spell it out.' She turned away. 'I'd really like to return to the palace now, please.'

He dressed. Made sure she was warm enough in the predawn air as he settled her into the buggy. All the while feeling terrified that he had lost the most important battle of his life.

CHAPTER SEVENTEEN

THEY WERE MARRIED two days later in the largest cathedral in Santo Sierra. Church bells tolled at the strike of midday and white doves were released in commemoration of the historic event. Quite how the palace staff had managed to gather and accommodate world leaders and royalty in such a short space of time would've blown Jasmine's mind, had she not been in a continued state of numb shock.

Stephen and her mother had flown in this morning on Reyes's jet, and, although Jasmine had had a hard time managing her mother's questions and tearful exclamations of how beautiful Jasmine looked, she was thankful for their presence. They were literally two familiar faces in a multitude of strangers.

Her mother was riding in the second car with Isabella, while Jasmine rode to the cathedral in the back of a Rolls-Royce Phantom. Beside her, Stephen enumerated the many luxuries of the car. Jasmine nodded absently, too preoccupied with not throwing up over her astonishingly beautiful gown to answer.

All too soon, they arrived at the church. A dozen ten-year-old pageboys lined either side of the royal-blue carpet that led to the aisle, each one holding up a jewelled-hilted sword that signified the twelve generations since Reyes's ancestors had ruled Santo Sierra.

Jasmine gripped Stephen's arm as her stepfather led her down the aisle. She tried to pin a smile on her face as the sea of faces on either side of the aisle gawped at her with unbridled curiosity.

The surprise wedding and unconfirmed reports of a possible pregnancy had sent the world's media wild. The press office's *no comment* on the subject had been taken as tacit confirmation.

'Almost there, my darling,' Stephen murmured. His reassurance calmed her nerves, helping her to focus on her destination.

The top of the aisle, where Reyes waited. She couldn't see his face clearly through her lace veil, but his imposing figure was hard to miss. Dressed in formal military regalia complete with shoulder tassels, sash and sword, he looked more dashing than any man had the right to look.

The butterflies in her stomach multiplied.

Since their night at the wedding-cake house, she'd seen him for less than a handful of minutes. Each time, he'd been reserved to the point of being curt. At their last meeting, he'd presented her with an engagement ring belonging to his grandmother. The stunning baguette diamond ring she now wore on her right hand, according to protocol, was flanked by two further teardrop diamonds and completed in a platinum band.

Reyes had stopped only to ask whether she liked it before, after her startled nod, he'd walked away.

She couldn't help but think that her probing questions about love had twigged him to her feelings for him. Feelings he didn't welcome.

All through the many fittings and wedding protocol, she hadn't been able to dismiss the knowledge that Reyes would never love her, no matter how much she tried. Again and again she recalled the look on his face when she'd blurted out that damning statement on the plane. A statement he hadn't so far denied.

Stephen eased her hand from his arm, and she realised they'd reached the steps of the altar. Eyes damp, her stepfather gazed down at her. 'I'm so proud of, my dear. So very proud,' he murmured. 'You're the daughter I wished for, and I hope you'll forgive me for not always being the father I could've been.'

She knew he was referring to the business with Joaquin.

Her throat clogged and she blinked back her own tears. 'There's nothing to forgive. Absolutely nothing,' she whispered back.

His own eyes brimming with tears, Stephen placed her hand on the gloved hand Reyes held out.

She searched Reyes's face, and her heart dropped. Nothing in his demeanour showed he was happy to be here. He flinched when a muted roar sounded from outside where the crowd was watching the ceremony on giant screens.

Intent on discovering a hint of emotion that would abate the fear beating beneath her breast, she stepped closer to him.

A discreet cough sounded half a step behind her. She turned to find a teenage usher holding out a polished silver tray. Flustered, Jasmine placed her bouquet on it, and tried to ignore the hushed murmuring behind her.

Reyes squeezed her hand. Heart lifting, she glanced at him. But he was staring straight ahead, his chiselled profile holding no signs of tenderness.

They exchanged vows in Spanish and English, with the sermon and following register signing also conducted in both languages.

When the priest urged Reyes to kiss his bride, his lips barely warmed hers for a moment before he stepped back.

Through it all, Jasmine smiled, and felt her heart break into tiny pieces. She'd fallen in love with a man who she had a soul-deep suspicion would never love her back.

A cheer from the thousands of subjects lining the streets roused Jasmine from her dazed state. Her hand tightened on Reyes's arm as he helped her into the gilt-framed glass carriage.

'Smile, *querida*. Anyone would think you were attending a funeral, not your own wedding.'

Plastering a smile on her face, she waved to the crowd. 'I haven't seen anything of you in the past two days,' she muttered from the side of her lips.

Reyes lifted his hand in acknowledgement of the crowd.

'And neither will you be seeing me for the coming weeks. I'm going to be very busy. I assume you saw Mendez among the guests?'

The heart that had squeezed painfully at his first words lurched in anxiety at the reference to Mendez. 'Yes, I did.'

'I sent the opening salvo yesterday. He's desperate to re-commence talks.'

She continued to wave as she'd been instructed and glanced at Reyes from the corner of her eye. 'What about the new council? Will they back you?'

'Yes, I have people in place I trust. I don't intend to stop until a new treaty is signed.'

She nodded, feeling miserable inside. Trust was important. Would he ever trust her enough to let himself feel more for her?

Not likely.

Her hand drooped. Thankfully, they were going through a long archway that connected San Domenica to the palace, where the wedding banquet was being held.

'Are you all right?'

Her breath huffed out before she could stop it. 'I'm an ex-juvenile delinquent who's just been crowned Princess of one of the most influential kingdoms in the world. I'm very, very far from all right.'

She startled as he picked up her free hand and placed it on his thigh. 'You've overcome the adversities thrust at you many times before. You'll rise to the challenge this time, too.'

Her limbs weakened and, against her better judgement, hope sprang in her chest. It bloomed when he picked up her hand and kissed the back of it.

The roar vibrated against the glass, and she became pain-fully aware of the reason for the gesture. Pain slammed into her. She couldn't pull away, not without thousands of eyes wit-nessing the withdrawal.

She kept the smile on her face until she feared her jaw would crack. 'So the honeymoon is over even before the ink has dried on the marriage certificate?' she demanded waspishly.

His eyes gleamed. 'I'm sure you'll agree that ours hasn't been a straightforward route to the altar.'

If it hadn't been for the baby, they wouldn't have found themselves in front of an altar at all. 'No. I guess not.'

His lips pursed, an infinitesimal motion no one else would've caught. But she saw it.

'Can I suggest, however, that we make the best of it?'

When his gaze dropped to her stomach, and an intense emotion passed over his face, Jasmine's world greyed further.

'Of course.'

She tried to breathe, but there was little room in her wedding dress for such frivolities. The lace-and-satin gown cupped her breast and torso and dropped to flare in a long dress and train. Isabella had called every fashion house in Europe and had started a bidding war on who would design the Crown Princess's wedding gown. The two-day deadline hadn't daunted even one of them.

Jasmine had finally settled on a Milanese couturier who'd worked magic with fabric right before her eyes. The material was heavy without being oppressive and the lace provided her with means of keeping cool in the hot Santo Sierran sun.

Now her crown was a different story. It weighed a ton, decorated as it was with ninety-nine diamonds, rubies and emeralds.

She touched it, felt the sharp bumps of precious gems beneath her fingers, and hysterical laughter bubbled from her throat. 'Is it true the crown designer stopped at ninety-nine because the palace decreed at the time that a hundred was too ostentatious?'

One corner of his mouth lifted. 'You've been learning Santo Sierra history.'

'I thought I should, seeing as I have no choice now.'

His smile dimmed. '*Sí*, we all have our crosses to bear.'

* * *

The wedding banquet carried on much like the wedding. Except where several priests muttered homilies, Jasmine had to sit through several speeches from well-wishers from around the world.

Numerous toasts were also raised in honour of the absent king, whom she'd met for the first time that morning.

So very like his son in stature, but with a defeated look in his eyes that made him seem...*less*. He'd haltingly given them their blessing before his medication had kicked in again.

She'd watched Reyes kiss his father's forehead with tears trapped in her throat. The love between father and son had been palpable, and Jasmine could just imagine what the turbulent period had done to them.

The clear love in his eyes when he gazed down at his father had given her a little more hope. Hope that was very quickly dwindling as the distance between them grew with each hour.

She smiled for a solid hour. Then smiled some more. Finally, she couldn't stand it any more. They'd finished with the formalities and those guests who wished it were getting into the dancing session of the evening.

Jasmine rose.

'I'm going to bed.'

Reyes glanced up from where he'd been in deep conversation with one of his advisors. Rising, too, he tucked her arm through his.

'I'll escort you.'

She shook her head. 'You don't need to—'

'*Sí*, I do.' The implacable dominance behind the words shut her up.

As they mounted the stairs her heart began to flutter.

Everything had gone at such a fast and furious pace, she hadn't thought to the wedding night.

Liar.

She'd thought of nothing *but* the wedding night since she

woke this morning, and terrified herself with different scenarios, most of which had ended with her going to bed alone.

Now, as she walked beside Reyes…her *husband*…she allowed herself to believe everything would be all right.

They reached their door and he raised her hand to his mouth, kissed the back of it. 'I've arranged for two of the servants to help you with your gown. Sleep well, *querida*.'

CHAPTER EIGHTEEN

One month later...

JASMINE WAS EXHAUSTED. Her feet ached and a headache throbbed behind her left ear. Relaxing in the air-conditioned car that was taking her back to the palace, she massaged her nape.

The four hours she'd been scheduled to teach her mediation class at Santo Sierra's municipal college had stretched to six. Not because her students were dying to learn everything she could teach them about mediation.

No. She'd been delayed because her young students had been fascinated about what it was like to be Queen.

Hysteria rose in her chest. She'd been Crown Princess for a pathetically short time before the King's sudden decline in health and subsequent death had propelled Reyes onto the throne and her into being Queen.

Beyond that, nothing had changed in her world. Jasmine had wanted to rip the rose-coloured glasses from her students' eyes. Tell them to find and settle for unconditional love and nothing else.

They wouldn't have believed her, though, even if she'd managed to utter the words. They all believed she'd captured the world's most eligible man and brought him to his knees after a whirlwind romance. Just as she, Reyes and his councillors had planned in San Estrela what felt like a lifetime ago.

What they didn't know was that she hadn't seen her husband for two weeks and she hadn't shared his bed since the night they'd spent at the wedding-cake house.

He'd spent the days leading up to his father's death in a vigil by King Carlos's bed with Isabella. Jasmine had berated herself for feeling left out.

Then, after the King's passing, they'd had to deal with the arduous protocol of the coronation. Reyes had accepted his duties as King with gravity and pride, but the result had been an even greater distance between them as he'd dived headlong into securing economic ties he'd fought so hard for.

Jasmine understood the duties that being King demanded. And yet she couldn't help but think her husband was using them as a perfect excuse to stay away from her.

She had woken up one night two weeks ago to find him in bed with her, his hand spread over her flat belly. Choking back tears, she'd placed her hand over his and gone back to sleep, her heart lifting with the hope that maybe they'd turned a corner.

She'd awakened hours later to an empty, cold half of the bed.

Jasmine hadn't thought a heart could shatter into tinier pieces until that moment.

The limo turned onto the mile-long drive leading to the palace.

Unable to face the palace and her lonely suite, she pressed the intercom on the armrest that connected to the driver. 'Can you take me round to the other house, please?'

Her driver glanced sharply at her. 'But, Your Majesty, it's Thursday today, not Friday.'

Jasmine nodded. 'I know, Raul. Take me there anyway.'

'Of course. As you wish, Your Majesty,' he replied deferentially.

She'd started going to the small house every Friday and staying the night. If she'd had a choice, Jasmine would've moved into the adorable little house. But considering she needed an armed escort wherever she went, she couldn't subject her guards to nightly patrols in the cold. So she'd restricted her visits to once a week. But this week, she might make it two nights…

Reyes was off hammering out the last terms of the new trade treaty, and Isabella had left for Milan this morning to consult over her autumn/winter wardrobe.

She'd urged Jasmine to go along with her, but she hadn't

been in the mood. Besides, by the time winter rolled around she would be in the late stages of pregnancy.

Leaning her head back, she rubbed her hand over her belly. The morning sickness had finally waned and, according to the team of doctors tending her, both she and the baby were healthy.

In a way, she understood how anyone on the outside would believe her world was rosy. She had everything her heart could wish for...

Except a husband who loved her even a fraction as hopelessly as she loved him.

They arrived at the house. Her door opened and Raul helped her out. She smiled and stepped out. 'Don't worry about informing the palace. I'll let them know when I get inside.'

'Yes, Your Majesty.'

She wanted to ask him to call her Jasmine. But protocol was protocol. She could go inside her little house, pretend she was at her flat in London for a while, but the palace, the Santo Sierran people who'd welcomed her wholeheartedly, and her absentee husband would still be her reality when she stepped out again.

Jasmine climbed the steps into the house and shut the door behind her. Ten minutes later, clutching a bowl of warm popcorn and a bottle of water, she plopped herself down in front of the TV and activated the chess game she'd started last week.

She was in the middle of checkmating *GrandChessMaster231* when the door burst open.

Her heart somersaulted, then banged against her ribs. 'Reyes!'

'Do you know how long the staff have been looking for you?' he burst out.

She rose on shaky feet, the unexpected sight of him rendering her senses stupid. 'But I...Raul knew where I was. I told him...' She stopped and grimaced.

'You told him what?' he demanded.

'I told him not to bother telling the palace staff where I was because I would ring them. I forgot.'

He kicked the door shut and clawed both hands through his hair. 'Raul discovered a slow puncture after he dropped you off so he went straight to the garage without stopping at the palace. The staff have been searching for you for the past four hours, Jasmine.'

'I'm sorry, I didn't think… I just wanted to be on my own for a little while.'

He dropped his hands, took a good look around the room, before he zeroed in on her again. This time, his gaze travelled from her head to her toes and back again. His hands slowly curled and uncurled at his sides.

'I've been told you spend a lot of time in here.'

She shrugged and considered sitting back down before her weak knees gave way. But sitting down would make Reyes's presence more overwhelming. So she settled for propping herself on the armrest.

'When did you get back?'

'This afternoon.'

They stared at each other a full minute before she managed to tear her gaze away. 'How was your trip?'

He scowled. 'I don't want to talk about my trip. Why have you not been sleeping in our bed?'

The bitter laugh escaped before she could stop it. 'It's not *our* bed, Reyes. I sleep in it alone, even when you're in Santo Sierra…even when we're under the same roof, I sleep alone. I'm sorry I worried the staff but you know where I am now, so you can go back to…wherever you came from.'

He looked stunned at her outburst. Jasmine wanted to laugh again, but she couldn't trust that it wouldn't emerge a sob.

She plopped herself down on the sofa and released the pause button.

After several minutes, he sat down beside her. Awareness of him crawled all over her body. But she didn't dare look at him or she was afraid she'd beg him to stay. Beg him to love her. While she wasn't afraid of begging, she was terrified of the rejection.

Was it her imagination or had he moved closer?

'Jasmine, we need to talk.'

Her hands shook. 'So talk.'

He shifted his gaze from her face to the screen. Or so she thought until his breath caressed her ear. 'Can I make a wager, *por favor*?' he asked, his tone rough.

'Can I stop you?'

'Ditch *GrandChessMaster231*. Play me. For every game I win, you stop and listen to me for three minutes.'

Her pulse tripped over itself. Her head started to turn, but she snapped her gaze back to the screen. 'Okay.'

He beat her at the first game in less than five minutes.

'What did you—'

His lips took hers. It was thorough, hungry, incandescent. Even as her mind reeled Jasmine's lips clung to his, already desperate for the pleasure only he could provide. The pleasure she'd missed more than breathing. Her nerveless fingers let go when he tugged the control from her grasp and dropped it on the floor, all without taking his mouth from hers.

He pulled away from her, his breathing ragged. 'I have two minutes remaining. Why do you not sleep in our bed, *mi corazón*?' he rasped.

'Because…because you're not in it,' she choked out. 'It's cold and lonely without you, and I can't stand it.'

He nodded solemnly, then captured her lips in another scorching kiss. Freeing her when his time was up, he picked up the control and handed it back to her.

He won the next game, too. Another bone-melting kiss, followed by a long look into her eyes. 'If I told you I missed you every day I was away from you, would you believe me?' His voice was low, deep. Almost prayerful.

'No.'

The hand in her hair trembled. 'I deserve that. I know I've behaved badly, have approached things the wrong way—'

'Your time's up.' She handed him his control.

She had burning questions of her own, so Jasmine put all her effort into winning the next level.

Her control fell from her fingers. 'You scheduled sex with your other candidates. But you left me, your wife—'

'My queen,' he growled.

'Your queen, to sleep in our marriage bed alone. Why? Am I so unlovable?'

He squeezed his eyes shut for a split second. 'You are far from unlovable, *querida*. It was me. I was afraid.'

She looked at him, stunned. 'Afraid of what?'

'The last time we were in this house together, you tried to get out of marrying me. I was afraid you'd change your mind about staying with me. We didn't have to get married in three days. I rushed it because I didn't want to let you go. I couldn't see past the fact that you'd woken up in the middle of the night determined to leave me. I'd already jumped on the pregnancy to make you my bride—'

She gasped. 'You wanted to marry me before you knew I was pregnant?'

'I dismissed perfectly good candidates because they were not you. I didn't want to admit it to myself, but I couldn't see any of them as my wife. None of them touched me the way you did. When the pregnancy presented itself as an option for me keeping you, I took it.'

The timer on the screen beeped. They both ignored it.

Tears filled her eyes. He brushed them away with his fingers.

'I thought you were only with me because of the baby.'

He looked down at her belly, then back at her. 'I love our child more than I can adequately put into words. I was overwhelmed with terror that you'd wake up in the middle of the night and ask for your freedom.'

Her mouth wobbled before she pursed her lips. 'And the night you came to me?'

'I came to tell you that Joaquin Esteban had been arrested.'

She gasped. 'What?'

'Mendez handed him over as part of our agreement. If I have anything to do with it, Esteban won't see the light of day again.'

Tears threatened. She blinked them away. 'So you came to tell me…and?'

'You looked so beautiful. I couldn't stay away. I missed you so much I couldn't breathe, never mind sleep. I planned to leave a note and be gone before you realised I was there. Leaving you ripped me apart. After that I didn't want to put myself through it again…so I used my duties as an excuse to stay away.'

A deep tremble shook her. 'Oh, Reyes.'

The timer beeped again.

She asked the question burning its way through her heart. 'Why are you here now, Reyes?'

'Because staying away from you is killing me. I need to be with you. With our baby. Loving you, protecting you both.' He started to reach for her.

She pulled back. 'Loving me?'

He closed his eyes. '*Dios.* This wasn't how I intended it to go—'

'Stop trying to wrap everything perfectly and just tell me how you feel!'

'I love you.' He exhaled, then struggled to catch his breath again. 'You blew me away that first night in Rio. I went to sleep thinking I could have found the one, even though I wasn't looking for you or even dreaming that the overwhelming feelings I felt for you existed. I let how I felt about my mother and Anaïs cloud my judgement so I could hate you for what you did. Even after I understood your motivation I was too scared to let you in.

'But you wormed your way in anyway. I admire your courage, your intelligence. My people love you already and it's been mere weeks since you entered their lives.'

Jasmine smiled. 'I love Santo Sierra. I've loved your home and its people since I stepped off the plane, Reyes. And I adore its king. When he's not breaking my heart by staying away from me for weeks on end.'

He caught her to him and smothered her with long, breath-stealing kisses. 'Your king is back. He will never leave your side again.' He spread his hand over her belly again the way he'd done, painfully briefly, weeks ago. 'He will never leave either of you. Ever again.'

With a flick of his finger, he turned the screen off. When he pulled his shirt over his head, she could barely keep from crying with joy. 'Reyes…'

'I'm here, *querida*,' he rasped.

Strong hands reached for her, lifting her up and carrying her into the bedroom. About to kiss him back, she paused. 'Did you bring any guards with you?'

A look, almost of regret, passed over his face. '*Sí*, it's protocol. But they know not to disturb us, even when you scream with passion. Now, where was I?'

The look in his eyes set off spirals of excitement through her. Feeling almost wanton, she slowly licked her tongue over her upper lip. 'Somewhere here, I think.'

She expected his customary growl, a sound she'd become accustomed to when he was fully aroused. Not this time. His eyes fixed on hers, he slowly inhaled, taking in her scent, imprinting her on his senses.

Jasmine found that even more enthralling than his growl and she watched, fascinated, as his chest expanded on his breath. Slowly he breathed out. 'I don't know what it is about you, Jasmine Navarre, but you captivate me. I might even go as far as to say I'm completely obsessed by you.'

Her breath stalled in her throat. 'Stay that way, and we won't have a problem at all.'

'I love you, my queen.'

'I love you, Reyes.'

His eyes misted. Then he cleared his throat. 'No more talking.'

His kiss was hard, possessive, sucking out every last ounce

of sanity from her as he unleashed the raw power of his arousal. He broke from her mouth to let her inhale a mere breath before he was back again, demanding. And receiving the unfettered response she couldn't hide.

Jasmine touched. Stroked. Nearly wept with delight at the sheer pleasure touching Reyes brought her. And everywhere she touched his skin seemed to react, to heat, bunch and flex, as if his every nerve ending was attuned to her.

That thought only served to increase her bliss. He pulled away for a moment. 'I know you'll berate me if I ruin your precious shirt, so I'll let you take it off.'

She wanted to tell him she didn't care if he ripped her shirt to shreds! But no way would she be able to articulate those words, not when her brain was too busy devouring the solid, sculpted lines of his naked torso. With shaking fingers, she divested herself of her shirt, letting it fall to the ground unheeded.

She arched her back, reached for her bra.

He growled low in his throat.

'I love that sound.'

'I growl only for you, *mi amor*. Always and for ever.'

* * * * *

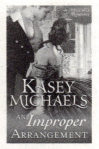
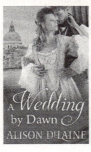

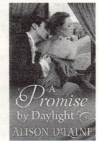

MILLS & BOON®

The Thirty List

At thirty, Rachel has slid down every ladder she has
ever climbed. Jobless, broke and ditched by her
husband, she has to move in with grumpy
Patrick and his four-year-old son.

Patrick is also getting divorced, so to cheer themselves up the two decide to draw up bucket lists.
Soon they are learning to tango, abseiling, trying
stand-up comedy and more. But, as she gets
closer to Patrick, Rachel wonders if their
relationship is too good to be true…

Order yours today at
www.millsandboon.co.uk/Thethirtylist

MILLS & BOON®

The Chatsfield Collection!

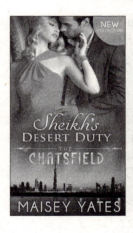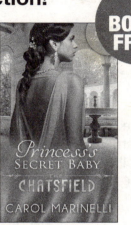

2 BOOKS FREE!

Style, spectacle, scandal…!

With the eight Chatsfield siblings happily married and settling down, it's time for a new generation of Chatsfields to shine, in this brand-new 8-book collection! The prospect of a merger with the Harrington family's boutique hotels will shape the future forever. But who will come out on top?

Find out at
www.millsandboon.co.uk/TheChatsfield2

0615/01